I0822091

TORN HEART

ALSO BY EMMA HAMM

The Otherworld

Heart of the Fae

Veins of Magic

The Faceless Woman

The Raven's Ballad

Bride of the Sea

Curse of the Troll

Of Goblin Kings

Of Goblins and Gold

Of Shadows and Elves

Of Pixies and Spells

Of Werewolves and Curses

Of Fairytales and Magic

Once Upon a Monster

Bleeding Hearts

Binding Moon

Ragged Lungs

and many more...

TORN
HEART

Visit author online at www.emmahamm.com

Cover Design by Trif Book Designs

For you.

You know who you are.

Hall of He
Lu
Dracomaquia
Castle of the Lost
Umbral Ki
The Gloamin
Solis Occasum

Kingdom of Umbra
MALIS
Stygian Peaks
Field of Somber
City of Tenebrous

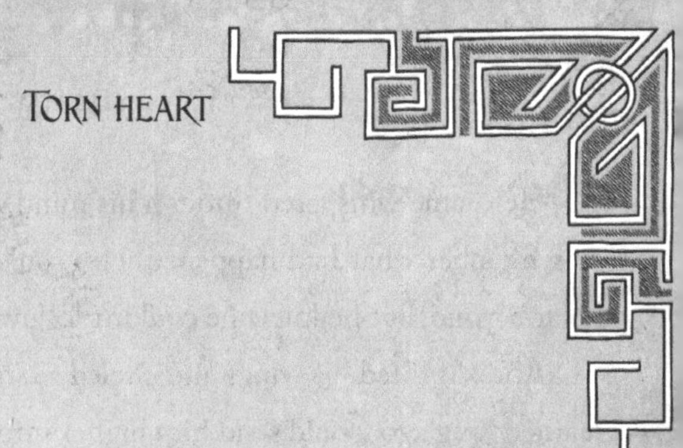

CHAPTER 1

Abraxas had flown over these seas before. Long ago, when he was but a child, his mother had told him they needed to seek a new land. Though his memory was hazy of that time. It felt like another lifetime when he could remember his mother's face, the sound of her voice, the silk of her hair. But he'd never forgotten her fear as they flew over the rolling seas. How she'd watched for storms that would ground them, and sought shelter on a tiny island where she had been pleased to find enough food for them to hunt.

That was where he took his children.

The island was a long flight from Umbra, and it was made even harder by carrying two baby dragons the size of horses in metal cages that added even more weight to their forms. And perhaps it was harder because his heart broke into a thousand pieces with every beat of his wings.

Lore.

Her name whispered through his mind, even though he didn't want to remember what had happened. Her soul called out to him from the great beyond, but he knew he couldn't follow her. Not yet, at least. Soon.

Abraxas tilted his wings and circled a large, nebulous cloud that he'd learned long ago would send him higher into the air than he wished. He rode the wind as a captain rode the seas, and he knew the air was a fickle beast. It required his attention, and so he pushed thoughts of her out of his mind.

His fracturing mind, that was. He'd known the mate bond when he felt it. Lore had wiggled her way underneath his guard and that meant she was so much more to him than just a woman he loved. His soul needed hers to ground him.

What was it that his mother had said? Crimson dragons required more help than other dragons. Their mates were more important because they were the ones who held the key to their massive amount of strength and deadly abilities. She'd told him that right before she lost her own mind. He still remembered her wild screams and how three other dragons had been required to pin her down. They'd gotten her back, but not for much longer.

Abraxas had been alone for such a long time, and now he wasn't. He had children to care for. He'd promised Lore that he would care for them.

But then his mind splintered and he could almost feel her on his back. Her thighs holding on so tight and her hands gripping onto his spines. Great heights terrified her, and though she loved to ride through the clouds, he knew he couldn't bank as hard as he had or she'd scream. Although, sometimes he enjoyed hearing her scream.

He shifted his wings, spreading them wider, so it was easier for her to hold on. He'd have to be more careful, so she didn't slip, although perhaps they could figure out a saddle-like system for her. It would perhaps be a little demeaning, but he'd endure. For her. He'd do anything for her.

The two young dragons in his grasp let out little sounds of terror and the thoughts of her drifted away. He wasn't flying with Lore on his back. He wasn't flying anywhere with her at all.

She was gone. And he had to continue onward.

The island appeared on the horizon. It was a scraggly beast with steep sides so no one could get onto the island without climbing gear or wings. But the top was mostly forested, some of the trees looking rather worn, but the small area had once been host to a herd of animals similar to deer. They'd grown on their own, diverting their population from the rest of the deer he'd seen in Umbra. Perhaps they were more similar to the creatures in Dracomaquia. He couldn't quite remember.

Circling the island, he searched for a safe spot to land and set his prized children on the ground. A small clearing was in the center of the island with a pool of water that he remembered tasting rather salty. Safe to drink, but not as fresh as it looked.

Yes, they'd landed here. His mother and his kin. They had found shelter from a storm; he thought. Maybe. The memory was so hazy suddenly.

He beat his wings against the air, slowing them down so that they could all land safely. One cage, then the other, he placed into the moss until he could land much harder a few paces away from them. Abraxas let his wings droop onto the ground, the membranes feeling thin and pulsing with each of his heartbeats. He'd catch his breath eventually, he knew, but it had been a long time since he'd flown so far.

"Father?" Nyx asked, peering between two of the bars. "Are you all right?"

The contraptions they were in had been made by human hands, he realized belatedly. He couldn't rip them open and release his children. They still couldn't fly the remaining distance to Dracomaquia. He needed to carry them again, in a day or two, so he would have to change back into his mortal form to release them.

Damn those mortals. Damn them all for taking what had been his and for making this journey even more difficult.

Abraxas let the change roll through him and every joint in his body ached. The pain that came with flying such a far distance was only made worse by compressing into this smaller form. But he still staggered all the way to their cages, desperately holding onto the bars to keep himself upright. With massive effort, he threw open the cage door for Nyx and then made his way over to Hyperion.

"Father," Nyx said again, this time her tone a little more hard. "You need rest."

"I need you two to get some fresh air outside of a cage," he grumbled.

"We can manage on our own."

"I know you can." But the words were a lie. He didn't know if they could manage on their own. Dragons grew faster than most. His children would be full grown in half a year of their lives, but that didn't mean they knew how to hunt. How to protect themselves. Nor even how to fly. Not yet, at least.

He had to teach them all of those things before he could trust them to be on their own without worry running through him like poison. Someday he knew he'd be able to let them go. He'd have to. The madness already clung to his mind like a spiderweb that he couldn't brush off.

Hyperion moved past him, his body already growing long and lean as the green dragons of old. "We will bring you food. Rest."

"There is no rest in a place like this. We need to be on our guard."

But his daughter loomed over him, her shadow blotting out the heat of the sun. "There is nothing to guard from. This isle is too tall for any mortals to climb, and there are no more dragons. Sit down, Father, and let us take care of you."

The idea was so tempting. He wanted to let them care for him as children should, but what if something happened? What if he broke his promise to Lore?

Nyx bumped him with her nose, the dark sapphire color glinting in the sun. "It's going to be okay. I know you miss her. We miss her too."

And if that didn't almost break him down. He needed to... He should... Abraxas looked from left and right so she wouldn't see the tears in his eyes, but hiding such a thing was impossible from a dragon. She'd smell his emotions in the air, even with the pool of water making the air a little salty.

She nudged him one last time before turning toward Hyperion and gesturing for him to follow her. They were getting older already, his children. He'd known they would grow too quickly for his liking, but he had thought that he had more time.

Perhaps letting them grow up felt a bit like letting go of her memory as well. She'd loved them so much as dragon babes, and he hadn't seen that love on her face enough.

Scrubbing his hands down his face, he sighed. "Get a hold of yourself," he muttered. "They can't see you like this."

He wandered toward the pool and splashed the icy water onto his face. It helped to ease the burn of his cheeks, though it made his eyes sting even worse. And, as he stared into the reflection, he saw her.

He'd never forget the beauty of her face. The way her nose and chin were slightly pointed, or how the tips of her ears were like little daggers. She was beautiful in an untouchable way, as though her entire being wasn't meant for this realm.

The reflection saw him looking at her and made a face. She always hated catching him with "moon eyes", as she called them. Said his expression made her sick, but he saw the way her cheeks burned after she caught him. Lore always snuck a few extra glances after, making sure he was still looking at her that way. He knew she secretly liked it.

The crystal clear waters turned silver, and then all he saw was his own reflection staring back at him. Alone, again.

He shook his head to clear the image from his mind. He was hallucinating. Likely a rather deadly combination of exhaustion, not eating or drinking anything for days, and losing his mind to the mate bond. He knew that this wasn't real. She hadn't come to haunt him, even if that's what they both would have wanted.

Abraxas would take a ghost of her than nothing at all. At least then he could see her and not fear that her memory would drift away from his mind as easily as his mother's had.

He stood and turned his attention to the trees beyond. Their dusky color wasn't the emerald of Umbra. Lore might have had some knowledge about why they looked so dark. Perhaps the salt made the trees into something else. Or perhaps they were a different species that he did not know.

Shadows warped along the silver trunks. A form shifted and moved with the breeze that fluttered the leaves. Her lithe figure stepped out from behind one tree and he swore the wind toyed with the ends of her hair. If he closed his eyes, he could believe she was there. Right there. He could walk over to her if he wanted and touch her. She'd be warm and real and alive beneath his hands.

More alive than she really was. His mind knew that she was gone.

But even her skirts twisted in the wind, dark as they were. Everything about her reacted to the environment and for a moment, just a brief moment, he let himself believe she was there.

"Lore," he said, his voice quiet and low. "I know you aren't here right now, but I miss you."

Her figure blurred as a strong breeze blew through her, and then she reformed. He took a step closer, almost afraid that she'd disappear if he got too close. But she stayed right where she was until he walked up to her. He lifted a hand toward her face, then froze.

"You were supposed to be here," he whispered. "You should see them grow. Soon, they'll be able to fly and you won't see the wind catch underneath their wings for the first time."

The thought gutted him. She should be with them at all times, as a mother should. Lore had wanted to see all those moments. She'd wanted to be with them for every single one.

He spread his fingers as though cupping her cheek, not quite touching the mirage in front of him. Not yet. "You are the better half of my soul, my beloved. I do not know how to do this without you, but I promised I would keep them safe. I fear the best I can offer you is getting them to my homeland where no one will ever hunt them or find them again. After that, I do not know how long I can keep this madness at bay."

He wished it were easier. He wished he could be the strong dragon mate she needed. If he were more like the legends of old, then he would fight the madness for years to come. He would take the terror of the crimson dragon back to Umbra and lay waste to all who had harmed her. Many would learn what it meant to anger a crimson dragon, and then they would watch as he feasted upon the flesh of thousands.

Except she wouldn't want that. Lore only wanted him to be happy, and he wouldn't be happy as the mad beast of destruction.

His face crumpled with emotion as he tried not to cry. "You should be here," he said, his voice thick with emotion. "You were meant to be here."

And then, because he couldn't stop himself, Abraxas let his hand touch her face.

For a moment, his fingers touched cool air, and he thought... was she here? Did she feel him too?

But then the wind shifted and blew right through her. The soft smile on her face never wavered or changed. She disappeared as quickly as she'd come. His hand fell through the visage of her beautiful form and his heart shattered all over again.

"No," he whispered as he fell to his knees. "You can't go. Not again."

His shoulders slumped forward and all the grief, guilt, and loss surged forward from where he'd buried it. He hadn't been there when she'd died. He had fought on the other side of the battlefield and she had been alone, completely, when her soul fled her body.

There was nothing left of her to bury.

Not a hint of who Lore had once been remained, and he only had a dagger to remember her by. A weapon. She was worth so much more than a weapon.

Resting his hands on his knees, he took a deep breath and tried to still the rioting emotions in his heart. He couldn't fall apart now, not when they had so far to go. He needed to pull himself together for their children. Lore had given him a task. And a crimson dragon was nothing if they could not complete the easiest of tasks.

So he staggered to his feet, forcing himself upright, and dragged himself to the pool. First, he would get clean. Then, he would clear a more comfortable spot for them all to rest. And then, only then, would he let his mind return to darker, more tragic thoughts.

Until that moment, he had work to do.

CHAPTER 2

Time had... slowed.

No, that wasn't quite right. Lore didn't know how to describe what was happening to her. She floated, but without buoyancy. She drifted, but there was no water to guide her. Her mind, though, was at perfect peace. She had never felt such an ease in her soul.

Throughout her entire life, she had struggled. Every step of every day was a battle against a hundred different obstacles. Guilt. The desire to remain alive. Margaret. The King. Even the little things, like what was she going to eat that day and how would she avoid the guards? Those moments weighed her down so much more than she had thought.

She remembered good times too, but they were so hard to see through the fog of her exhaustion. Every inch of her body and soul wanted to rest. She'd earned this quiet.

But then she heard it.

The whisper started so low that her ears almost didn't pick up the sound. It was a quiet hum in the back of her mind. A repeated request that was as annoying as it was intriguing. Someone called out to her, likely far more often than she had realized.

Perhaps they were far away. Her mind could understand that strangeness. They were too far away for her to hear, and that meant she could ignore them. Lore sank deeper into that void of her mind that promised a deep, dreamless sleep. Just as she was about to drift away, she heard the sound again.

Like an annoying bug that refused to go away, that whispering noise wriggled underneath the comfort of her sleep. It forced her to stay awake. It pulled her away from the relaxation, the ease, the rest that she had so well deserved.

Eventually, she couldn't stand it anymore. Why wouldn't they leave her alone? Hadn't she earned this? Others had manipulated her entire life and now they wanted to dig into her very sleep?

The anger fueled her. Rest would not come to someone as enraged as she was. She pushed and clawed and scraped her way out of this pool of relaxation, growing more and more angry with every movement until suddenly, her hands hit dirt.

Jagged rocks cut into her nails and sliced through her palm. The anger only grew. How dare there be a barrier between her and the person who was still humming? No, not humming. There were words to it. She could understand those words now, although she only caught a few snippets.

"Umbra... Needs... Castle... Lore... Dragon."

She didn't care about hearing her own name. That didn't matter. She was Lore, and she wasn't. There were a hundred different versions of her in her own head and Lore was only one of them. She was many and few. All she had to do was decide which one she wanted to be.

But the last word, that one rocked through her form like someone had punched her in the belly. Dragon. There had been a dragon. A man. No, a beast. The memories were all jumbled in her head, but they all came together as she focused on that word.

Dragon.

Abraxas.

Gasping now for air, she clawed through the roots and stones that prevented her from seeing the light. And all the while, she felt that anger and power growing ever stronger inside her. She remembered him. Her dragon. The only person who actually mattered.

He should be here. Maybe it was him who was humming, although she knew that wasn't his voice. An electric shock trailed between her shoulder blades as she remembered the depth of his voice, the guttural sound of it as he whispered her name. No, moaned it.

They had been more than friends, her and that dragon. They were more than just mates as well.

He was the other half of her soul. The part of her which saw reason and logic in a world that had none. Without him, she was nothing. With him, she was a goddess reborn.

The earth gave above her head and she knew there was fresh air on the other side of it. Rather than dig with her hands, Lore made a small space around herself inside the hole she'd dug and pressed her back against the earth. With one last, hard shove, she lifted the sod and ground up and burst out into the fresh air.

Power surged through her, from her, out of her fingers and chest as she emptied all the rage inside her. It burst out of her in a glittering wave that, once it touched the ground, spread a thousand moonbeam flowers all across the field. The glistening silver petals were full of magic. Someone would gather them someday to use in a spell, but those flowers would die the moment they were picked. Her magic would return to the earth, as it should. No elven magic should be used for the benefit of anyone but the elves.

Sighing, she tilted her head back and let the wind play on her face. She'd missed this, she realized. How? She hadn't been gone that long, or couldn't remember how long she'd been gone at least.

Her heart and soul, however, knew when to miss something as wonderful as the wind. It cooled her overheated face and helped the sweat on her brow gather to drip down her temples. The sun heated her soul, which felt as though ice dripped from her. The heat cracked through the cold and she felt… happy.

It was strange, though. She didn't feel like the sun was as warm as she remembered. It was all a rather dull experience that wasn't the same as before.

She remembered the heat of the sun bothering her. She certainly remembered long, cold nights where she would lie awake shivering in the dusk. Blankets hadn't warmed her. Nothing had warmed her other than the heat of a fire and that could be too much.

What had changed?

Her body felt... different. Not quite the same as it had been the last time she remembered being awake. Lore lifted her hand and stared down at it, the palm streaked with blood and dirt. She opened and closed her fingers. They seemed to work the same as before. But they didn't feel the same. It was like she didn't quite fit.

"Lore?"

The word ripped through her silent reverie. She turned toward the sound and saw a young woman on her knees before her. The lovely round face with those beautiful golden curls was in her memory, somewhere. She had a hard time yanking it forward, as though her mind still wanted to drift back to that resting place.

Now was not the time for rest, however. It was time for her to focus.

"Beauty," she said, acknowledging the young woman who had been her friend for such a long time. "What are you doing on your knees?"

Beauty knelt in a bed of flowers, along with other trinkets. There were gold coins, necklaces, scrolls that were withered from the sun and rain. All of them seemed to connect in a giant circle around where Lore stood. Had she accidentally stepped on someone's grave? But she hadn't seen people leave offerings like this at graves before.

Even Beauty clutched something in her hands that suspiciously looked like a locket a priest might give the grieving.

Beauty's eyes were so large in her head as she stared at Lore. "Is it... Is it really you?"

Lore frowned. "It's unlikely to be anyone else. I'm standing right in front of you, Beauty."

"But you... This isn't possible. I'm hallucinating you, aren't I?" Beauty stood, though, and lifted a shaking hand toward her. "You can't be real."

Her patience had thinned even further. Lore didn't want to hear that she couldn't be real. She was, obviously. She was standing here, her hands opening and closing, her skin feeling so damned tight, but she was here.

Humans. They rarely made any sense. She shouldn't be so surprised that Beauty spoke nonsense, and that Lore needed to find someone of her own kind to explain to her what was going on. Elves weren't easy to find though, she remembered, her memory still filtering through in small spurts.

Abraxas. She'd find him. He would know what was going on and he'd be able to guide her through this strange fog in her mind.

Why wasn't he here already? She knew that he rarely left her side for fear of... something.

Damn it, her mind. A headache bloomed in her temples on both sides as though someone had grabbed her head in a vise. She needed her weapons, her dragon, and for everyone to leave her alone.

She stepped out of the circle of brick-a-brack and then paused. Abraxas had knelt here, she remembered. He'd screamed as though someone had died, a great loss that tore through his very soul and threatened to rip him asunder. She hadn't been here, though, not for that torment that had plagued him. Where had she been?

Lore didn't think she'd traveled recently. Her body didn't feel as though it were tired, albeit a little dirty. What had happened to Abraxas?

A spike of anxiety flushed through her body like a heat wave. She needed... No, had to find him. There was no other option.

"Lore!" Beauty called out, staggering toward her like the wights they had fought together. "Stop, wait. You need to rest. You shouldn't—"

Lore lifted a hand to silence her. "Don't tell me what I need, Beauty. I've rested long enough."

Massive tears filled the lovely girl's eyes, rolled down her cheeks, and dripped from her chin in heavy plops. "Is that where you've been? You've been resting?"

The question made her pause. Lore didn't remember leaving at all, although she supposed it made sense. She hadn't been here, even if her mind didn't remember where she had gone or why she'd gone there. She barely remembered what had happened before. None of it lined up as memories came back to her, but never in the right order. It was all wrong, but it would come back to her. In time.

"Resting," she muttered, rolling the word around her tongue as though she might find answers if she tasted it a little longer. "I don't know. There was an air of rest to it, but I remember being tugged toward a deeper darkness. A peace that I have searched for my entire life."

Beauty's face crumpled, and a sob escaped her lips before she pressed her hands against them. Finally, she garbled, "Then why did you come back?"

Now that was an easier question to answer. With a crooked grin, she touched her finger underneath Beauty's chin and lifted her head to look at her. "Because someone wouldn't let me rest."

Beauty gulped. "My prayers?"

"In part." She thought that was the only reason, but maybe she simply had enough of rest. Lore turned her attention toward the line of trees and narrowed her gaze. "I could hear you, even there. Your voice wouldn't let me rest, but there was more to it than that."

They'd fought a battle here. She could sense the screams of the fallen, and the blood that had soaked the ground.

The King? Yes, she'd fought him. She didn't remember that battle between them, but she knew he had been here. That they all had feared the man full of darkness who should have been dead.

Death. Was that it? Had she died?

She shook the thought free from herself. She hadn't died, obviously, otherwise she wouldn't be standing here.

"Lore," Beauty whispered. "Your hands."

She lifted them and saw they were clear as glass. Tilting her head, she held them up to the light and watched the sun filtering through them. The longer she looked, the more they solidified until it was just her skin again.

"Strange," she said. "They didn't do that before."

Some part of her mind whispered that she should be uncomfortable with the change. Her hands had disappeared, turned into a spectral glass-like form and she didn't have any response other than "that's strange". Lore knew that wasn't normal. She should at least feel some nerves about what had happened to her body but... Nothing. All she felt was an odd detachment.

"That's not the only thing," Beauty whispered. "Your eyes, Lore."

"What about them?" She again found no anxiety in the question, only a strange curiosity that things had warped in her form while she'd been gone.

"You have two different colored eyes." Beauty pointed to her right eye. "It's silver now, almost... milky."

Was that why she could see into the past? Lore hadn't ever known what had happened in an area without actually being there. The memories were there now, though. She could see Abraxas's sorrow and she could hear the sounds of the battle. None of that seemed in the right order, though. She'd rather thought she was gone before it happened. But then she couldn't remember why she would be gone.

Then, all the memories flooded back at the same time. In the right order. She remembered the battle and the choice she'd had to make. She remembered that Abraxas was so far away on the battlefield that they hadn't been able to say their goodbyes.

Lore had gone against his orders. She'd saved them all, and in doing so, she'd sacrificed herself. Exactly what she promised she wouldn't do.

"We have to go," she said. And for the first time since returning, a glob of anxiety stuck in her throat.

"Go?" Beauty asked, staggering after her. "Where are we going?"

"To the castle."

To him. Abraxas must be so worried about her. Lore knew how losing him would tear her apart and she couldn't guess the pain that he was in right now. He didn't deserve to suffer when she was fine. See? Her hands were only a little different, and maybe she'd lost an eye, but that didn't mean she wasn't the same person. She was fine.

And her babies.

Lore saw Beauty had arrived on a horse and she leapt up onto the back of it with ease. She held out her hand for Beauty to take, who let out a little squeak as Lore easily hauled her up.

"You're stronger," Beauty whispered against her back as Lore urged the horse to move forward.

Maybe she was.

Maybe a lot of things had changed, and she didn't remember them, but Lore would not dwell on that. Not right now. Not when he was waiting for her and she had been waiting for him. They needed each other. The sooner she was in his arms, the sooner she would know everything was all right.

They rode for the better part of the day and into the night. The trees of the Gloaming didn't stop them as they thundered through the dark elves' forest. And when Lore thundered into the castle, she pulled up on the reins a little too hard. The horse reared, though both its riders remained on its back.

Everyone in the castle courtyard froze. They stared at her as though they had seen a ghost, but they'd always done that. Lore slid off the horse and didn't wait for Beauty to catch up to her.

Her friend, true as always, raced after her. "Lore! Lore, wait. I have to tell you—"

She didn't have time to listen. She walked right up the castle steps and slammed the doors open. Her companions would be there, she was certain of it.

In a strange, new way, she could sense them. Lore marched to the Great Hall with Beauty trailing behind her. Draven was there, and the look on his face when he saw her made her grin. Her wild expression must have looked mad on her face.

"Draven," she called out, "Where is—"

He fell to his knees. Draven pressed his forehead to the ground in complete silence. The only sound in the room was his ragged breaths that fogged against the polished stone floor.

What was he doing?

Perhaps she'd entered a little too excitedly. He must fear what her plans were or why she wanted to see him? Though she'd never been all that much of a threat to him.

"Where is Abraxas?" she asked.

He finally looked up at her through watery eyes. "Not here."

"Hmm," she intoned. "Fine. I'll wait for him in my rooms. I'll talk with the both of you tomorrow."

Beauty grabbed onto her arm, forcing her to stop and remain in place. "Lore, there's so much we need to tell you. Don't you have questions? Or want to say anything to us?"

Why did they both seem to hang on her every word? It was unnerving.

Lore shook herself free from Beauty's grip. "No. I want a bath. And my dragon."

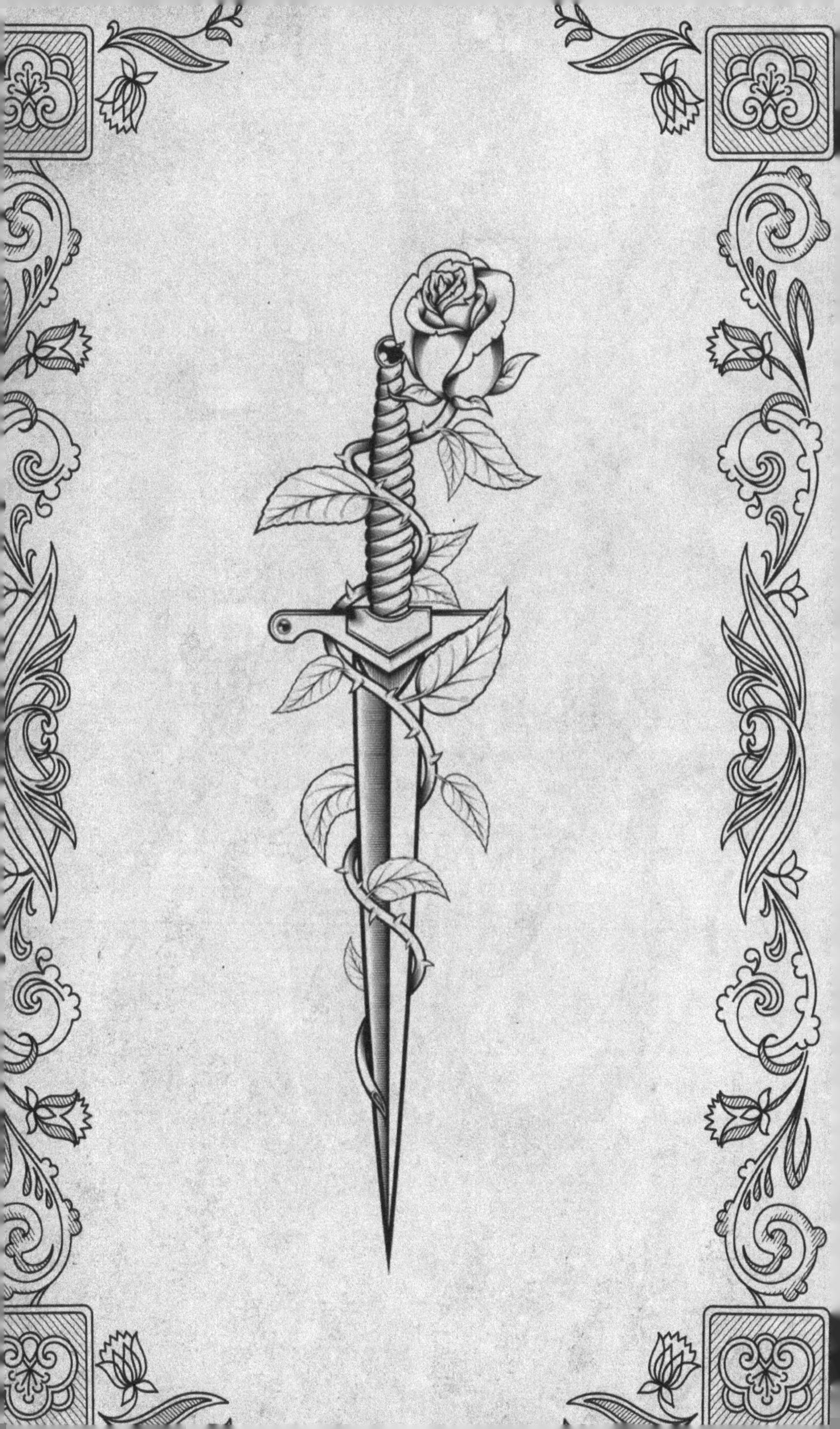

CHAPTER 3

Wings aching, he finally saw the land he'd been looking for. Dracomaquia spread out in front of him, unveiling like the lovely edges of a gown that continued for hundreds of miles. The continent was filled with all the pleasures he and his children would enjoy.

Together. For the first time in hundreds of years.

The cages swayed in his grip; the wind tilting them from side to side. He wouldn't drop them, though. The doom of their demise, if he did, was never far from his mind. They couldn't unlock their cages, and their weight would sink them to the bottom of the sea. He'd never be able to swim fast enough to catch them, especially not both of them.

Abraxas adjusted his grip, holding the handles on top of the cages a little tighter. Just in case.

The sands were ones he remembered. Suddenly, a rush of those memories accosted him. They weren't his own, or at least, he didn't think they were. But somehow he remembered the warm feeling of that sand between his claws and how the icy chill of the waves that would cool his long tail after a flight. He knew where to land. How to find it. He knew this island like it was his home.

And it was. Finally, after all these years, he was home.

Abraxas set the twin cages down and then landed beside them. He took the tops in his mouth and unceremoniously ripped them open. His dragon children spilled out onto the warm sands. They flattened themselves into it, spreading their wings wide while nuzzling their heads into the grains.

Their slow stretching like cats amused him, and Abraxas realized he had no reason to hold himself back either. They were unapologetically dragons, and he should be a dragon as well.

Though his heart and soul ached with pain and anguish—neither of those ever truly went away—he allowed himself a respite. With his children, dragons now the size of massive draft horses, he stretched in the sand and dug his claws in.

The warmth spread through his entire body. The hot sand eased the aches in his wings. He swished his tail through the waves behind them and splattered both Nyx and Hyperion with the next swell. They shrieked in delight and then scooted over the sands, as though trying to get away from him.

He chuckled, the sound rusty in his throat. It wasn't that he was really happy, as the sound might suggest. But there was a little hope in it. Hope that they might all find some happiness on these shores. More than they could have found by remaining in Umbra.

Except one large part of their family was missing. And they all felt that loss at the same moment. His children stopped their rolling and laid on their backs, staring up at the clouds wandering by. Nyx let out a long, unhappy sigh and Hyperion draped his wings over his eyes.

Abraxas knew what they were thinking. He could feel it, too.

"She would have loved this," he said quietly. It was the first time he'd talked about her since... Well. They didn't talk about that.

Nyx nodded, her tail lashing in the sand. "She once described it to me, even though I don't think she had any idea what it would look like. But she said the cliffs would loom over my head, and my wings would grow tired before I could see all of it. She was right."

He liked that Lore had talked to them about his homeland. Those were the stories he'd told her, after all. They had spoken at great lengths about Dracomaquia and what his homeland would look like. Though he didn't really know himself, Abraxas had felt as though a part of his soul never left this isle.

Now he knew why he felt that way. He knew that all dragons returned here, even after their deaths. Their souls were tied to this place.

"She was excited to come here," he said quietly, returning his gaze to the sky. "She wanted to see more of our kind here. She hoped we would find more eggs of many colors. That we would bring about a new age of dragons."

"We will," Hyperion said, his voice confident. "We'll do it for her."

The love he felt for these children took his breath away. And then he looked back at them to realize they weren't children anymore. Lore would have argued with him, of course. They were only a year old at this point. They were children in every sense of the word. And maybe Hyperion still was, compared to his sister, but neither of them acted their age.

They were not human. They were not even elves. Dragons had to grow up quickly so they could survive all the elements and dangers that would be thrown at them.

They'd turned into little adults underneath his nose and he hadn't noticed until this moment. He wanted to tell them to stop. To slow down. Children should enjoy their early years without rushing. But after all they'd been through, he also realized that he had no right to tell them any of that.

"We will do exactly that," he replied with his heart in his throat. "I think she'd be pleased with us."

All the dragons remained on the sands by the sea for a long while. Abraxas didn't think his children were tired. They had done none of the hard work, but perhaps they were waiting for him to feel better. He'd carried them much farther than he'd thought he could, and their respect meant a lot.

Besides, his memories didn't go so far as to tell him what awaited them on this island. There could be beasts to hunt, or beasts that hunted dragons.

They should get up and start exploring. He needed to find them shelter for the night, and that would take more time than he expected. After all, there were three different types of dragons here.

He could sense there were places for them. Nyx needed to go to the pools of fresh water waiting for her to lounge in. Hyperion would seek the forests with their emerald leaves and long blades of grass that easily hid his kind. And Abraxas? His gaze tilted up to the high cliffs where he could see everything that approached from the sea.

They would not find their places tonight, however. They would remain together, as they always had. He was certain their safety lay in numbers.

"It's been a long time since anyone was here," he mumbled, but his voice echoed over the sands. "I don't know what lies in wait for us."

"Nothing," Nyx replied. "It is a tomb."

"This isle has been abandoned by many for centuries. No dragons, no people. There has to be some creature that has risen to the top of the food chain, and I want to make sure that creature is not larger than all of us." Now that he'd caught his breath, he knew it was time to explore. He couldn't rest until he knew they were all safe, and that required movement.

His ancient body didn't want to move. His muscles protested at having to give up the warmth and comfort of the sand. But he'd promised Lore that he would take care of their children. He'd promised.

"Come on," he said. "We've got to explore."

Unlike him, his children were more than ready to move. They leapt up with bubbling laughter. Hyperion tried to bite Nyx's tail, likely to get his sister moving faster. She spun with a hiss, but tripped over one of her wings and rolled to the edge of the sand. Thankfully, she came up hard against a few trees, and their leaves rained down over their heads.

Abraxas glanced up, perplexed. The trees were still bright green, but he'd thought it would be autumn by the time they arrived here. Had he really flown that fast?

But then he was distracted for another reason. Hyperion, the boy who always wanted to play and couldn't stop wriggling for a single moment, remained still as he looked up at these trees. A low hum started in his throat, and Abraxas closed his eyes to listen to the sound he hadn't thought to hear again.

Forest dragons sang, he remembered now. Their long, lithe bodies twisted through the trees above the others and they sang a deep, echoing song that made the tree roots grow deeper. They were the heart of the forest, and apparently his son remembered.

Hyperion's eyes were glassy as he stepped foot into the trees that so many dragons of his ilk had lived in for centuries before.

"What is this place?" Hyperion asked as he weaved through the trunks.

"It is the Forest of Many Colors," he replied, though Abraxas wasn't sure where the memory had come from. "Your people have lived here for thousands of years. Every tree was planted by a dragon and then helped flourish throughout the centuries. We care for them. We help them grow and keep the undergrowth clear so that the trees are the only part of this forest that is nourished."

"It's more than that. The trees are full of... memories." Hyperion tilted his head up and closed his eyes as the wind played through the budding tendrils of his mustache and beard. "I can almost hear them if I listen hard enough. The trees talk, Father."

He'd never have guessed that was how the forest dragons kept their memories, but he supposed it made sense. Or his son was feeling the centuries of dragons like him who had walked the same path. Either way, it didn't matter. Clearly, Hyperion knew this was his home.

Swallowing hard, he was loath to drag his son away from the trees. But this was not the safest place for them. Only a single path had been left for a dragon to walk through, but that meant that anyone could find them without difficulty. They had to keep moving.

He nudged Hyperion forward. "Come on, my son. We need to keep moving."

Together, they trudged through the rest of the forest and came out to a field of sapphire pools. They stretched as far as the eye could see, dotting the horizon with beautiful colors and still waters. Not even the wind touched the pools here.

Nyx sucked in a deep breath. "I remember this place."

"Remember?" he frowned, but then watched as his daughter slipped into one of the nearest pools. She hardly made even the slightest of ripples as she disappeared into the water and then surfaced again.

Long tendrils of green grass hung on her back and shoulders. They tangled on the small spines that would eventually grow down her back. The greenery hid her inside the pool if she lowered herself deeper. Nyx's eyes closed in happiness.

"How do you remember?" he pressed.

"The crystals," she replied with a little laugh. "I found them in Umbra and they showed me the memories of the sapphire dragons. We've forgotten so much, but I remember this. This pool was one of theirs. She liked it best because it was always warmer than the others. There's a warm spot near my right foot! The water entering the pool is warm, Father. It's not cold at all!"

Her excitement overshadowed the words she'd said. Crystals?

Warning bells went off in his mind, but he couldn't push aside his own memories to understand why. Why was the thought of those crystals so devastating to him?

It was like something snapped that he couldn't catch, didn't want to catch. No wait, yes he did. He wanted to catch it because he didn't want to remember those red crystals in that cave when he was a child. How his mother had loomed over him and told him that no matter what happened, he'd always be her child. He didn't have to give up foolish, childish things if he didn't want to. But the crystals had taken that away.

They'd taken it away from his daughter, as well.

Swallowing hard, he watched as she lolled in the pool. Nyx had fared better than him. She'd absorbed the memories stored in those crystals as a separate part of herself.

Abraxas had become the memories. He'd honed them into a weapon of his mind and he had taken to the older crimson dragon's memory all too well. Now, he struggled to know just how many of the memories were his and how many were another's. How old was he? How long had it been since he'd actually seen his mother? The time was all warped in his mind. It was wrong.

He'd thought bringing them here would make it easier for them to be children. But now, he wondered if it had been a mistake.

Movement caught his eye on the rocky outcroppings above them. Belatedly, he turned his head and stared up at the nearest rise that led toward the cliffs.

An elf stood there. The silhouette was dark against the sun, and the breeze caught on the flimsy clothing that covered the figure. Long hair blew in the breeze, and he knew that she was watching over them.

A deep sound echoed in his chest as he stared up at Lore. She must have known this would happen without her. She must have seen how much they needed her, how hard it was going to be without their mother. Did she think that he'd failed them? That, by bringing them here, he'd ripped away their childhood in a way they could never get back? He wouldn't blame her if she did.

He hadn't known, of course, but he'd still brought them here where they would never be children again.

Sighing, he glanced over at the two dragon children who meant the world to him. How was he supposed to tell them he saw their mother's spirit following them? They'd either be terrified or laugh at the thought of a ghost that never left him alone. And she didn't. Lore would never leave his side, even in death.

But the two dragons were also staring up at the cliffs. Nyx had flattened herself further into the water, her eyes wide and wings spread as though she were preparing to run. Hyperion's lips already drew back in a wicked snarl that made him look almost terrifying.

Did they... Did they see the elf, too?

Eyes narrowed in anger, he turned and placed his body in front of the young dragons. Hissing, he drew himself up to all his great heights and let out a roar that shook the ground around them. If there really was an elf there, and he still wasn't certain there was, then they would know the true meaning of fear.

Except the elf on the rise didn't quake or shiver. It raised its hand in greeting and waved.

Confused, Abraxas held his wings even wider and tried not to waver in his terrifying stature. The elf clearly meant no harm if he was showing them where he was, but what if this was all a trick? Maybe the elves were trying to hold his attention while something more deadly crept up behind them.

He was about ready to make a wide circle of flames around them, but then the elf did something equally confusing.

The man cupped his hands around his mouth and shouted, "Welcome, dragons! We've been waiting for you!"

CHAPTER 4

"What do you mean, he's gone?" Lore pressed her steepled fingers to her lips and eyed her two companions in front of her. She'd assumed that Beauty and Zephyr would be the most likely to tell her the truth. Clearly, she'd been wrong.

Beauty had barely said a word since they made their way into the room. She sat down in front of Lore's desk and stared at her hands. Zephyr tried his best to be brave, but he was not quite suited for such a situation. He took a deep breath, blew it out, looked at Lore, then looked at the ground. Really anywhere other than her, so he didn't have to explain what he'd just said.

Abraxas is gone.

Gone could mean a lot of things. The two of them needed to clarify that quickly or they would realize she'd come back with very little patience. Lore didn't care where Abraxas had gone off to, or even if they hadn't tried to stop him. They were humans. What were they going to do to stop a dragon from doing what he wanted?

But they had better explain, or she would snap this table in half.

Beauty cleared her throat and finally spoke. "We tried to stop him. I tried more than anyone else. But he wouldn't see reason, Lore. You were dead. We all thought you were dead, and I'm still not all that certain how you aren't still. He said he couldn't stand to be here without you, and that he owed nothing to the rebellion."

"He doesn't," she agreed.

"Yes, well, I said he owed something to his friends. We were all grieving the loss of you. Of Goliath—" Her throat seemed to close up as she choked on his name. "He just left us and we needed him to stay. But I suppose that's bound to happen when a dragon is involved."

It wasn't. Abraxas had always been very caring. Sure, he ordered the humans around with a little more gruffness than necessary, but he'd only done it because he wanted to make sure they all stayed alive. He did what he must to look after his family. He was a good man, her Abraxas, and if he had left, then he only had done so intending to keep everyone else safe.

Frowning, she narrowed her gaze at Beauty. "What else did he say?"

"Nothing. Just that he didn't owe us if you were gone, and that he was leaving."

Her cheeks turned a bright shade of pink. She'd always been a terrible liar.

Lore shifted behind her desk. She didn't know how to intimidate this young woman who had been her dear friend for a while. And Lore knew that they were all suffering for a long time without three of their companions. The war had taken its toll.

Lore hadn't even dealt with the loss of Goliath. The thought of his name made her head feel like someone had bashed the back of it with a sledgehammer. He had been her brother. The only family she had left and a good man who had never let her down. Not once. All of them seemed to forget that Goliath had died in her arms.

But if she could juggle those emotions while also keeping everything in check around this place, then they should be able to talk to her about Abraxas.

The hard press of magic lifted into her chest. It wasn't just magic anymore, but raw power that made her anger seem even more hot. It burned the back of her throat and she curled her hands into fists as she ground out, "Tell me what else he said, Beauty."

At least the human had the brains to gulp. "It was a load of nonsense, Lore. He was just giving us excuses to leave, so we didn't feel bad that he chose the dragon babies over us. And he should have!" she rushed to add. "Those children deserve his full attention and he can't give them that here."

"I didn't ask for your opinion on what he said, Beauty. I asked for you to tell me everything."

Why couldn't she think straight anymore? That anger pressed against her like a physical weight between her shoulder blades. A fist, no, a mace. Like the one that had killed Goliath.

Slowly inhaling through her nose, she let the air out in a long glide of exhalation that was supposed to ease her emotions, but did nothing to slow the fury in her heart. "What did he say?" she asked one last time.

"Lore," Zephyr interjected, his words slow and precise. "Your hands are gone."

She looked down at the fists she could feel and realized they weren't there again. "Yes, they seem to do that."

"Are you..." He swallowed and then looked her in her mismatched eyes. "Are you going to disappear again?"

She didn't know. There was no way to tell, unfortunately. It appeared her entire being wanted to disappear, but she didn't think she'd go back to the same place as before.

She'd been gone for six months and to her, it felt like a matter of seconds.

Shaking her head, Lore let out the breath she'd been holding. "No, I will not disappear again, Zephyr. I simply want to know what was said while I was not here."

"Then can you..." He gestured to her hands. "You know. Come back?"

"If I knew how to do that, then yes. Unfortunately, I am not yet adept at controlling this power. So if you would just tell me what I want to know, then you can leave this room and free yourselves from the discomfort of looking at my current state."

Beauty leapt into the conversation, much more likely to speak on this topic, it seemed. "It's not that we're uncomfortable looking at you, Lore! We're worried about you. It isn't often that someone comes back from the dead."

Grinding the words between her teeth, she bit out, "I only want to hear one thing from you, Beauty, and those are the words you seem uninterested in telling me."

Beauty dropped her head and sighed. "He said something about how dragons mate for life, and that if one dies, so does the other. It didn't sound like he would wither away, but he said his mind would stretch thin and he wouldn't be able to tell what was real and what wasn't. The loss of you would eventually drive him mad, and he wasn't willing to threaten all of our lives with a dragon like that on the loose."

"That fool," she muttered.

Of course, he would pull something like this. Abraxas had always wanted to be the hero of the story, and he would never let himself turn into the villain. If that meant flying all the way to his homeland where the dragon babes would actually be safe, then he would do so. Though it must have been difficult for him to leave the rest of his family here, he had made the only choice he thought possible.

Leaning back in her hair, she tilted her head back to stare at the ceiling. "Why would he leave? He had to know that you would all take care of him. That whatever madness lingered in his mind could be dulled by having those he also loves around him. What a mess."

Her office door creaked open, and she knew who stood there without having to look. The two elves would enter whether or not she invited them.

"You're supposed to be dead," Margaret said, her voice cracking through the room like a whip.

"Sorry to disappoint." Lore let her eyes drift open and met Margaret's angry stare. "I have bigger problems to deal with than the strangeness of my return."

And honestly, she didn't want to deal with the what ifs and hows. She was here. That was enough for her at the moment.

Draven trailed Margaret into the room with an apologetic look on his face. Clearly, he had been the one to tell Margaret that Lore had returned. Her fanatical follower, who had deemed her a goddess, wanted others to see.

The last person she wanted to talk with right now was Margaret.

That woman was a menace, although she'd honorably fought alongside her people. Still, Lore didn't trust her with a pen from her desk, let alone with the rest of this kingdom.

Margaret stood behind Zephyr, while Draven moved to stand behind Beauty. They looked very much as though they were keeping the humans captive in front of her. Why was that?

Lore let her mind drift away from the dark thoughts of the past and zeroed in on the now. "Why are you here?"

"I thought it would be prudent to speak with you directly rather than wait for others to fill you in on what has happened in your absence. Much has changed about the castle, and there is a lot for us to go over." Margaret's eyes narrowed, like that of an eagle who had sighted its prey. "You have returned in a strangely opportunistic time. Are you sure you didn't come back after you'd heard something?"

Ah, yes. Because Lore would want to come back and ruin Margaret's plans when she had been so restful and asleep. Margaret always had a talent for making things about her, as though everyone in this realm wanted to hunt her down.

Lore let her lips split into a feral grin and she felt her hands reappear again. "I only heard prayers while I was asleep, Margaret. Did you come and pray at my gravesite with the rest of them?"

The elven woman stiffened. "I did not."

"Then perhaps I heard them pray to get rid of you."

The tension in the room was palpable, and thankfully Draven stepped in when he saw his opportunity. "We have released all the prisoners throughout Umbra that are magical. Most of the creatures came here, initially, but we've cleaned out the dark magic from Solis Occasum. Though it was once a place to house the King and all his dark magic, it has now become a sanctuary for people like us."

And she was supposed to care... why?

Lore had done everything they'd asked. Not only had she won the war for them, killed the King, and provided them the victory that led them to right now, she'd died.

Died for this cause.

Were they expecting more from her?

Glancing between the two elves standing in front of her, Lore realized they absolutely were. These two had plans for Lore yet again and she'd be damned if she fell into the same trap.

"Get out of my office," she said. "Both of you."

Beauty and Zephyr stood immediately.

"Not you two." Lore pinched the bridge of her nose and sighed. "I'm not finished talking with the two of you yet. Margaret and Draven, you will wait to speak to me until I have called upon you."

"Lorelei," Margaret said, as if using her full name would make her see reason. "Yet again, you find yourself in a position where you are more than just an elf."

"I am myself more than I have ever been." The anger in her bubbled to the surface. "Now leave."

The other elves hesitated. They didn't even move an inch, other than to look at each other, and she couldn't stand it anymore. She couldn't be this person who was constantly ordered around as though she didn't get a damned say in her own fucking life!

Power thundered out of her and burst through the room. The beams of light roped around Margaret and Draven before tossing them into the hall. She had the mind to at least throw the door open before they struck through the very wood. Both of them hit the wall on the outside, terror in their eyes, before the door to her office slammed shut again and shook the walls of the castle.

All the castle was shaking, she realized. The power inside her had rocked the entire building to the foundation and back again.

Both Beauty and Zephyr sat back down hard, staring at her with wide eyes that were filled with terror. No one knew what had happened to Lore while she was gone. No one knew what she had returned as, not even Lore.

That was a question for another day, she resolved. Her life had taught her many tricks, and putting aside that which scared her was one of them. She would try to understand these changes someday. But that day would not be soon, and no one was going to change her mind about that. The powers would remain, or they would get worse. She'd maybe fade out of existence a couple of times. She knew how to return now, though, and she wouldn't get sucked back into that dreaming realm.

Leaning back in her chair again, she eyed the two humans in front of her. "So Abraxas left because he thought he would become a danger to you all."

They blinked at her.

Right, she hadn't addressed the fact that she had somehow made an entire castle shake with her anger.

Lore waved a hand in the air. "I'll figure that out later. Right now, I want to know what happened to the love of my life and the other half of my soul. I should think that's not unusual to you, especially after traveling with us for so long."

Beauty swallowed hard, then nodded. "He said he was taking them to Dracomaquia. He had us create cages for the little ones so he could fly with them, rather than have to wait to teach them to fly."

"How big were they?" Her curiosity got the better of her.

"Larger than the wolfhounds when I last saw them." Beauty tried a tremulous smile. "They're probably much larger now. It was almost six months ago that he left, Lore."

She hummed low in her throat. "Of course. They must be nearly full grown if he's fed them enough."

Had he? Traveling across the ocean wouldn't leave them a lot of options. He'd need to find them food and rest, all while struggling to maintain his own health. And what if he wasn't? What if he had lost her and then didn't care about how he arrived on Dracomaquia?

Her Abraxas had always been too giving, even at the cost of his own health. If he wasn't careful, he might plummet from the sky and die before ever reaching those shores.

"Right," she said with a sharp nod. "I have to go after him."

"You can't," Zephyr quickly replied. "We need you here. There is so much we haven't told you yet, Lore. The entire world seems to have changed in your absence, but we need you to listen to us. Something is horribly wrong."

She waved her hand in the air, dismissing his words. "And you will take care of it, Zephyr. You're the brother of the King. Shouldn't this castle be your responsibility now?"

He blinked at her. "That is the problem, Lore. Margaret is taking the throne for herself."

CHAPTER 5

Abraxas was hesitant to trust this new elf who had hopped down the cliff and approached them without an ounce of fear. Even when Abraxas had reared up on his back legs, wings beating at the air and a snarl that should have melted the skin from the elf's face, the man had merely smiled and held up his hands.

"We didn't think you'd get here so quickly," he said. "Of course, Tanis always thought you would travel quite fast, but that doesn't mean that I believed her. Dragons still confuse me with your strength. After all these years, you'd think I would learn how to not be surprised. But alas! You still surprise me."

And with that, the man never stopped chattering.

He introduced himself as Rowan. The man was the oldest elf that Abraxas had ever seen. His skin even showed signs of that age, with slight wrinkles around his eyes and a mottled texture to the back of his hands that usually only happened to humans. His hair was nearly completely gray as well, although the top of his head still had a stripe of dark color. His eyes, though, his eyes were sharp.

Rowan had been here since before the dragons of Dracomaquia had fallen. He remained here with his mate when all the dragons had died. They stayed because they knew someday there would come a time when the dragons would return. Eventually, one of them would come home.

"There was only me," he snarled. "And three eggs that were left behind in Umbra."

Nyx stilled at those words. He'd forgotten that he never told his children they'd had another sibling. Although some part of their soul must have sensed that they were lacking. The other dragon had not made it, murdered by the King and his blade. They didn't need to know the suffering that Abraxas had gone through as he berated himself for allowing such a terrible thing to happen.

Unfortunately, now they knew.

Rowan softened at his words and inclined his head. "And we always knew that it would be a hard journey for you. A difficult time to get here, yes, but you are safe now."

He didn't know the meaning of safe. This elf had been here, harbored in his own haven on the forgotten island while surrounded by ghosts. Abraxas had fought tooth and nail his entire life to see that his kind didn't die out and become the stuff of legends. What had this elf been doing?

Eyeing the man's clothing, he could only assume that he'd been putting his elven skills to good work. The weaving of his tunic was dyed a lovely blue, and the edges were intertwined with what looked like vines dyed a brilliant green. That would take effort and time to learn, even if the elf was nearly a thousand years old.

"Come," Rowan said, gesturing with his hand that they should follow him. "Tanis will want to meet you."

He shouldn't trust a stranger who had appeared out of the mist on an island that should be deserted. And Abraxas didn't. But if there was another person here, then he wanted to know who they were. What their threat was. And if he had to kill them before he could sleep at night. He was tired of sleeping with his eyes open.

At his nod, they all started forward. Rowan led them through the remains of a village which appeared to be little more than rubble. He could make out tiny houses that had been built out of stone once, although their roofs had long caved in and the walls of their structures were toppling over.

Deep underneath the scent of clean air and loam, there was the faintest hint of ash and burned wood. As though a fire had gone through this village and wiped out everything.

"What happened here?" he asked.

Rowan's shoulders curved in. "This was where the last battle took place. It was a nightmare. All the dragon tenders and their dragons, murdered in cold blood because rumors had spread on the mainlands. This was a place where all people of magical bloodlines could live in safety and harmony with the dragons who protected them. It is a shame it came to such a tragic end."

Turning a critical eye to the mounds of earth and stone, he tried to pick out anything in the history that would call out to his memory. He couldn't. If he'd absorbed any memories from crystals that knew this place, they were long lost to the line of crimson dragons.

Humming low in his throat, he nodded and moved on.

"Where are the bodies?" he asked. "If there were so many dragons murdered here, there should be bones."

Again, Rowan's face crumpled for a few moments before he wiped away the expression. "Tanis took care of them. She called it her penance, and I asked no more questions of her."

This Tanis must be strong, then. Stronger than her companion, who, though whip smart and clearly quite charming, was still just an elf. He didn't know many creatures who could move a dragon skeleton without needing spells.

Was that what she was? His thoughts turned toward witchcraft and his hackles rose. He knew that this was the perfect place for a coven to brew. With all the ingredients of a dragon carcass, there would be so much magic they could create.

He might be leading his children into their worst nightmare.

Lingering away from the elf, he muttered low and deep, "Keep your guard up."

"He's an elf, father." Hyperion leaned his head around Abraxas's shoulder to watch as Rowan continued tromping forward, still talking as if the dragons were listening. "He's like mother."

"That doesn't mean he's trustworthy."

"Who is this Tanis he speaks of?" Nyx asked. "We should seek her out before we cast any judgment upon them."

His daughter was wise, but perhaps a little too lenient. She was curious to find out the truth about who the man in front of them was, but she didn't see the potential for danger in that. He'd have to teach her before she learned through experience.

Sighing, he turned and caught up to Rowan. The elf's strides hadn't carried him far from them, although he didn't seem to have noticed.

"Ah, there you are," Rowan said. "Now I should warn you that meeting Tanis might be a little surprising. She's lovely, if a bit abrasive upon first encounter, but I need you to understand that she wasn't expecting you today either. I've been walking those cliffs every day now for months because she had a gut feeling. We'd almost given up on you! But here you are, and now we move forward in the way she'd planned. And that planning has been hundreds of years in the making, so I expect you to listen to her."

He continued on, but Abraxas was no longer listening to him.

There was a scent on the wind. A smell he hadn't thought to catch here, even though some small part of him had maybe hoped he might. It wasn't the bitter scent of witchcraft, nor was it the strangely spicy smell of warlock. It wasn't the earthy scent of elf, either.

The heat that blasted him in the face could only be that of a dragon, and a powerful, full grown dragon at that. He hadn't... He didn't...

Glancing over his shoulder, he realized his children had stopped moving as well. Nyx's eyes were wide in shock and Hyperion had stood with his wings spread out to balance him.

There was another dragon here, he realized in shock. He wasn't making it up or hallucinating that scent.

After all these years, he hadn't been alone after all.

Rowan set his hands on his hips and stared up at the dragons, who he must have seen were agitated. "Ah, well, that ruins the surprise, I suppose. Go on, then. She's in the meadow ahead of us."

"Stay here," Abraxas snarled at his children.

"Father," Nyx replied, stepping closer with worry in her eyes. "Should we not join you? What if we've unwittingly stepped into her territory?"

"The time for battles over land is over," he replied. "Besides, there are none larger than me."

He knew that, deep in his soul. This Tanis could not win a battle with a full grown crimson dragon. He did not know if he was the largest, or even if he met one of his own kind, if they would have thought him small or underdeveloped. He was large enough to make things difficult, and a female dragon could not fight against him for very long. Abraxas had learned his skills through hardship. What had she battled here?

Catching Hyperion's eye, he nodded toward Nyx. The boy knew to stay close to his sister. She had already grown larger than him, and her knowledge from those crystals would keep them both safe.

They'd run if they had to. He trusted them to know when or if that was necessary.

He moved forward down the path toward what the elf had claimed would be a meadow. Some part of him remained on its guard, waiting for all of this to come crashing down upon him. Would they send rocks to rumble from the cliffs above in an attempt to crush him? Perhaps they would rain down acid balls that even now had left scars on his wings.

None of those attacks came. And though he was expecting to find a massive dragon in the meadow, curled around itself and waiting to strike like a cobra, all that waited for him was a woman standing in a field of flowers. Her long hair swept to her hips and swayed with her movements. The smooth length was white as snow, a testament to her age. Her hands were delicate and gentle as she reached for a plant.

She turned at his approach, her arms full of some herb he couldn't name. All of that greenery tumbled from her grip the moment she saw him. Purple eyes widened as she looked at him, perhaps trying to see as much of the red dragon as she could.

All the breath rushed out of her lungs. He heard the great wheeze and took an extra step forward in fear, a part of him not wanting to see another dragon die in front of him.

He'd seen so many dragons die.

"Abraxas?" she asked, somehow knowing his name.

"How do you know me?"

"I don't." She smoothed her hands down her homespun dress, a white muslin that looked as though perhaps it was made of deerskin. "I knew your mother, and I have seen your memories through the crystals. It was always you that I hoped to find us, and now I am afraid I do not know what to say as you stand before me."

She looked up at him and he stared down at her. Abraxas didn't know what to say either. He was alone for such a long time, and anger bubbled in his chest that after all those years of heartache and terror, she'd been right here. He could have flown to his homeland at any time and found her.

Instead, he had suffered. Though that had been his own choice and was no fault of her own, he found he wanted to blame her for it. She should have told him she was here. She should have found him.

He was just a child for so many of those years. Terrified in the dark and she had let him suffer.

Tanis took another step toward him, then another. Then she lifted her hands as though to touch his nose. He reared his head out of her reach, but something in her eyes told him to drop his head again. For her touch. For her to hold on to him as she so clearly wished.

He lowered his head so she could place her hands against his nose and feel the steady breaths that bellowed in and out.

"I have never thought in the many hundreds of years since our decline that I would see another like me." She smoothed her hands along his ruby scales, watching her fingers as they trailed over the grooves and chips from his many battles. "I knew many crimson dragons while they roamed these lands. I have always found your people to be honorable and true, no matter how gruff or terrifying they could be."

He knew that was the truth as well. Abraxas couldn't change who he was any more than they could have. But it still warmed his chest to hear her say such a thing. "And you?"

"You likely haven't heard of me. There weren't many of me to begin with." She smiled, her eyes still on her hands. "I am an amethyst dragon. Purple, perhaps you would call me. In my days, you were a ruby dragon. I keep track of the history of our people through crystals that are dotted throughout all the lands. I can see the messages and memories placed within, and I remember the past. I preserve those memories in the crystals, ensuring that they never disappear and we never forget."

An honorable job, to be true. However, he could not imagine that she had been alone for this long and not suffered as he had. "And Rowan?"

"A dragon tender who turned into something much more. He is the other half of my soul, as many elves were in the olden days."

So he wasn't as strange as he thought. Perhaps the legends were true then that dragons were often drawn to the elves. Perhaps because they shared the same longevity. Or perhaps because there was something more between their kinds that he had yet to understand.

Tanis let out a long breath. "It seems you already know the bond of which I speak."

He nodded. "My other half passed away into the realm beyond before we left Umbra."

The sorrow in her eyes nearly flattened him. It was the first time someone had looked at him after saying that with understanding. Of course, those of his friends in Umbra had been saddened to know of Lore's death. They grieved for her in a similar way that he had, but none of them understood the dangers her loss brought him. Or that he would soon follow her to that early grave.

This woman knew. The words were all she needed to hear to know that his end would be swift and sooner than any of them would wish.

She nodded and drew her hands from him. Then she tucked those hands behind her back like a war general. "After all you have done for our kind, I have no right to ask you of anything, Abraxas. You have brought so much to these shores just in the forms of those children that somehow you protected and then hatched, against all odds. Against everything we know to be possible."

He sighed, already knowing where this was going. "But?"

"But," she repeated with another nod. "If that is the case and you are not to be with us for very long, then I will need your help."

"I cannot stop what has already been put in motion." And he would not feel guilty for following Lore wherever she went.

"I would never dream of asking you to do so. There is another way for us to continue to be safe, for living without a crimson dragon is a sore loss indeed." She gazed up at him with hope in her eyes, and he thought for a moment that he could deny her nothing. "Would you help me, Abraxas? Will you help me bring about another crimson dragon?"

CHAPTER 6

Darkness turned the castle into a hundred rooms full of silver light and threads of dust that were only disturbed by a single person who wandered through them. Lore took her time, making sure no one would hear her as she left.

Margaret had made it very clear that she wanted Lore to remain here. Beauty and Zephyr had claimed they feared their world would turn on its axis if she disappeared again. Rather than the magical creatures in chains, it would be the humans. Everyone wanted something from her, and she'd given enough.

After all this time, Lore would not do what they wanted. She brushed aside the guilt of leaving them to their own devices and reminded herself that she deserved to do what she wanted. There was no more blackmail. Nothing to hold over her head.

If they tried, she would rip this castle down and leave it in shambles.

Sighing, she pressed her back against the wall and waited for the candlelight to move past her. The guards weren't very good at their jobs. They never saw her, nor did they attempt to seek her out. Instead, they just blearily walked the halls and then moved out onto the ramparts as they stumbled about in exhaustion.

Margaret should know that, if she was worthy of being queen.

The thought nearly made her snort and give up her location. An elf queen of Umbra, as if anyone would accept that.

The guard walked by her, stumbled over the lip that led out to the ramparts, cursed, and then opened the door. That was all the opportunity Lore needed. She followed close behind him and put her foot between the door and the wall. When he let it close behind him, it caught on her foot and stayed open. She waited to see if he'd return to close it but.... nothing.

The guards here, she thought wryly. They were useless.

Rolling her eyes, she slipped out onto the walls of the castle. This was the dangerous part of her plan. Where it was easy to hide in the shadows within the castle, outside was much harder. The full moon could give her away, and that would mean she would have to thrust herself back into the room where they were keeping her. Of course, there would be other nights to sneak out, but tonight was preferable.

She didn't want to travel in the winter, and it would take time for her to get to the docks. Besides, there were fewer captains who sailed during the cold. This could very well be her last chance for the year before Margaret figured out a better way to bind her.

The guard continued his march ahead of her, pausing now and then to peer out onto the plains that surrounded the castle. He clearly didn't intend to look behind him, and that worked out well for her.

Dropping into a crouch beside a box that was meant to hold arrows, and instead was rather empty, she pulled the bundle off her back. She'd made sure she had everything necessary for the journey. Rolls of comfortable sheepskin, a few hides that would cover the ground and prevent bugs from getting underneath her clothing, food, water, and weapons. That would keep her going.

She had no need of a tent, although she hesitated when she decided not to pack it. The forest was her home. She'd figure out a way to keep safe without wasting more precious space.

Dangling the bag from her fingers, she let it drop over the side of the ramparts and into the courtyard below. She might have once kept it on and leapt into the unknown, but she'd be honest with herself. Lore was tired.

Even though she'd rested for a ridiculous amount of time and thought herself strong enough to do this, her body hurt. The power inside her made it feel as though her innards were bruised. She even had a hard time breathing some days, and that made her a little worried about pushing too much. She had a lot of questions to answer, and giving herself a little time wouldn't hurt anyone.

The bag hit a small wagon full of hay with a soft sound and then tumbled onto the stone ground. She winced at the heavy thump with a slight hint of metallic hum, but the guards didn't notice.

Placing her hand on the edge of the stone, she vaulted over it and plummeted toward the hay herself. She'd feared the cart might break the moment her weight hit it, giving away her location. But, miraculously, the entire thing held.

Hay poked into her back and stuck through her hair, but no one had noticed that the goddess who'd returned had left her rooms and snuck out.

Good enough.

Grabbing her bag, she rolled off the crate and crept toward the stables. This was the next part of her plan that would take a bit of risk. Some horses were more inclined to make noise when they spotted a stranger, and she needed them to keep their horse mouths shut. Hopefully, they wouldn't mind if she walked in like she owned the place. Sneaking would only make a horse more nervous.

She entered the stables like she'd done it a million times. Lore put her things next to the door and stopped trying to be quiet. Even if the guards heard someone in here, her hope was that they'd assume it was a stable boy doing his job. Or someone else that was allowed to be in here. Still, she didn't light any of the lanterns hanging from each stall. No need to get everyone up in arms just yet.

The horses let out little noises of disgruntled unhappiness. They didn't appreciate being woken up at such an early hour, and she wouldn't have liked it either if she were them. But at least none of them made a noise loud enough to bring the guards.

"Thank you," she muttered as she walked by a couple of horses who gave her wide-eyed stares. "Just keep quiet for the rest of this and we'll be best of friends."

Her plan was ironclad if everything worked out. Lore knew the exact horse she wanted to steal and that it would be a rather easy one to do so. The black stallion had met her before, after all. She'd seen him when she had first come here to meet the King and knew no one else would want him. He was too big. Too wild. Perfect for what she planned to do with him after she made it to her destination.

His was the last stall. They'd put him in the back because no one knew how to control him. From what she'd heard, the stable hands had tried their best to tame him, but he wouldn't let anyone close enough without trying to stomp on them.

He'd let her close. She knew he would.

"Easy," she said, walking into his stall with her hands raised. Already her skin glowed like sparkling moonlight, and the beast watched her with the whites of his eyes showing. "I won't hurt you."

He didn't know that, but then something inside her reached out. A tendril of magic echoed from her chest and she could almost see it floating through the air toward the stallion. It settled over his heart and then sank underneath his twitching hide. Then, suddenly, he fell silent. He watched her with a patience that he had not felt for any other who had tried to ride him.

Apparently, her magic was a little more useful than she'd thought.

She didn't know how to use it, though. And if it only came out in great emotion, then she had no control over whether it would tame a wild horse or if it would shake an entire castle from its foundation. She needed to be able to control that, and soon. But she hoped that would come a little more naturally once she had Abraxas beside her again.

He'd always helped her find calm, even when she was so angry that she couldn't see straight.

"You're going to take me far from here," she murmured as she stroked her hands along the giant horse's neck. "And that will make up for all you did during the war."

"I don't think the horse cares about making amends." The voice interrupted her and with no small amount of unwelcome disdain.

"Draven," she sighed. "I should have known you'd follow me."

She should have felt his eyes upon her as well. But he was a master at sneaking and she supposed getting angry at herself for not noticing would only prolong the inevitable. He'd followed her many times before, so it made sense that he would follow her now.

"You're supposed to be in your room," he said.

"I am not supposed to be anywhere." She turned to look at him and crossed her arms over her chest. "I'm dead, remember?"

He leaned against a post beside him, his shoulders wide in the darkness and his grin apparent even with the meager moonlight. He wore leather clothing that befitted a man going on a trip, and she already knew the argument he had before he said it.

"You're not coming with me," she hissed.

"Actually, I am. Beauty and Zephyr planned to remain behind. The kingdom needs him in case Margaret ever loosens her grip. I'm the only one that can go with you on this mad journey to find a dragon in the middle of nowhere."

"I didn't ask for anyone to come with me. I don't need anyone to come with me." She noted he had her pack at his feet, along with his own. "You should go back to your bed and in the morning, tell Margaret you saw nothing."

"I'll tell her exactly what your plan is and where you intend on going. That's the right thing to do, after all." He inclined his head at the horse. "Especially since you're stealing something of value. She'll want to know where that horse got off to. And then she'll know that you likely went after Abraxas, and we all know that means you went to the docks."

"If it's so obvious, then she'll know where I went with or without you telling her." Lore's hands fisted at her sides. She didn't want to hurt him, but if he continued to stand in her way, she would.

"Or you could let me go with you while Beauty and Zephyr cover for us." He shrugged. "Your call. They already plan to tell Miss Margaret that you and I went off to look at the battlefield to see if there's any correlation between your death and your return. That will buy us a couple of days, and that should be enough time to be on a ship by the time Margaret contacts her spies. Does that sound about right?"

It was a solid plan, but not one without holes. "And if she sends her ravens rather than physical messengers to the docks? I don't believe Margaret is the type to waste that amount of time, and she could have people waiting for us."

"Then two elves are better than one." He leaned down and picked up her bags. "What's it going to be, Lady of Starlight?"

He knew she hated that name. Only Abraxas could call her that, and it was because he'd named her so. That term was an endearment from his lips, but they were worshiping from Draven's. She hated how people called her a goddess. She hated that anyone thought that she had come back from the dead to serve them.

Lore was done serving other people. It was long pastime she did what was best for herself.

Unfortunately, that meant that she had to deal with Draven.

Sighing, she pinched the bridge of her nose and tried to press the headache back into her skull. "Give me my bag."

"Does that mean you're going to take me with you?"

"I think you need to make sure this is what you want to do. Margaret will not forgive this, and if Beauty is right, that woman wants to make herself Queen of Umbra." She took the bag he offered her. "Leaving all of them right now might be a bad idea. You may need to stay."

"I also have no allegiance to these people." The side of his mouth lifted in a smirk. "Besides, I'd rather be with you than I would a pack of humans who can't seem to figure out the right way to run their kingdom."

"Humans?" She grabbed the horse's saddle from the door and strapped it onto the big beast. "Margaret is far from that."

"I think she's closer than you or I would ever know." He stepped closer and let his hands hang loosely over the door to the stall. "Should I grab my own horse?"

"No." She tugged hard on the strap beneath the horse's belly, making sure it hadn't taken a big breath in so she wouldn't slide off the moment she got on top of it.

"Ah, so I'll be riding with you. Likely the smartest move, I'll admit. There will be people searching for us soon enough and neither of us needs to give them too many hints. Fewer tracks means it's harder to follow." He nodded as though that made all the sense in the world.

Lore secured her bag to the side of the saddle and tugged it tight. The last thing she wanted was to lose the bag of supplies. It would make her journey a lot more difficult. Then she placed the bridle onto her chosen horse, clicked her tongue, and led it toward the door.

The elf gave her another flash of a grin. "Allow me."

He opened the door for her and let her bring the horse outside. The heavy strikes of its hooves were too loud, but she supposed now was the time when she had to be loud. People would know there was a horse loose in the stable soon enough, and that meant her time was running out.

She glanced behind her to see that Draven had already situated his bag on the other side of the saddle. He gave his own similar treatment as she had done. Making sure the knots were sound, tugging it a little too hard to make sure it wouldn't come off as they galloped out of the stables.

The moon waited for her beyond the stable doors. She could feel the rays calling out to her, promising that they would fill her stores of power even more than they already were. The moon was her mistress, and Lore had never been able to ignore its beck and call.

She led the horse and Draven to the doors of the stables and patted the beast's side. She swung up into the saddle and looked down at Draven, who held his hand.

"Tell Margaret that I have no intent on helping her. I will find Abraxas. And if she tries to stop me, then she will know just how powerful I can be."

He looked up at her in dumbfound shock. "How are you going to get onto a ship? You need me with you, Lore. You can't do this alone."

She shook her head. "I'll be fine. I have friends in low places."

With a crack of her heels against its heaving sides, the stallion lunged forward and left her friend long behind her.

CHAPTER 7

It was strange to be here among all the other dragons. Abraxas had spent so much of his life without, and he had grown accustomed to living with mortals. Dragons were an entirely different species, with odd wants and needs and expectations in comparison.

He knew his children, of course. They were ever the crazy dragonlings he'd raised. They wanted to explore the entire island and then complained when he told them he wouldn't allow them to wander off on their own. Tanis had laughed at their antics, but Rowan at least saw the nuisance they would become. The elf shook his head and rolled his eyes as though children tired him.

Maybe Abraxas was more like an elf in his old age. He didn't see the reason for Nyx and Hyperion insisting on experiencing "dragon life". They wanted to wander. They wanted answers to all the questions they'd asked him and sometimes he couldn't explain.

But mostly, they wanted to see their new home, and he supposed he couldn't argue with them about that.

They all gathered outside of Tanis and Rowan's cabin most days. Abraxas and his children slept outside those walls in their own dragon forms that were more capable of handling the chill of the outside air. However, he knew that wouldn't be forever. They needed a place of their own soon.

"Father," Nyx whined, lying on her back with her wings spread dramatically underneath her. "Why can't we explore today? You understand that we've been here for ages now, and nothing has happened."

"In this area," he corrected. "This is the place where Tanis and Rowan have made their home and it makes sense that there would be few creatures here. Beasts of the wild know when there is something they need to avoid. They likely smell dragon on the wind and give this place a wide berth."

"So we can go outside of these parameters, check over everything, and come back."

Now he was the one who wanted to roll his eyes. "Listen to me, Nyx. You will not wander through the forests or find another warm pool to lie in without me being by your side."

"But Father—"

"I said no!" He perhaps thundered the words a little too aggressively. Abraxas was just so tired of having to tell them the same thing every day.

Why couldn't they understand the danger of a grounded dragon? Perhaps he hadn't explained it well enough that they were easily targeted. If he made them understand that some creatures, like a bear or a lion, could tear into their soft underbellies at this age, maybe they would see that he wasn't joking when he said they needed to be careful. If he painted enough of a grisly picture, then he might scare them into realizing that he was right.

But as he opened his mouth to do that, Tanis stepped outside of her cabin. She shaded her eyes as the sun hit her, then smiled at the dragonlings. "I have good news for you two."

The children stood at attention. They focused on her so much better than they focused on their father.

He didn't know if that should insult him, or be a relief.

He eyed Tanis though, knowing that she was about to say something he didn't agree with. And if she thought she could get them to stop arguing with him by offering an out, or telling them that they could explore the island without supervision, then he would have to toss her back into her cabin.

"Rowan has agreed to take you around the island. He said he'd happily show you the old ruins and some of the dragon homes. If you're especially good, then he might even bring you to the crystal caverns." She smiled at them, but eyed Abraxas as though she were daring him to say something about her plan.

He didn't like it. Rowan was a good fighter, he was certain of that, but that didn't mean Rowan could defeat a bear or any other creature that attacked his children. After all, the elf was getting old.

But Tanis clearly had plans for them. She intended for Abraxas to come with her, and that meant they needed privacy. His stomach twisted at the thought. He didn't know what she wanted of him yet, only that she required him to hang onto the tattered shreds of his sanity until he'd helped her procure another crimson dragon. Which, the more he thought about it, the more he realized could potentially become rather awkward.

There were only a few ways that they could get another of his kind, after all. He hoped that Tanis had an impressive surprise waiting for him and wasn't about to suggest something he would never agree to.

The two dragonlings looked at him with hope in their eyes, and he knew that he'd been backed into a corner. If he said no, then Tanis would assume he planned to deny helping her. If he said yes, then his children might be in grave danger. He didn't want either of those to occur, therefore, he had to tell them that he would allow them to go with Rowan.

He looked over at the elf who had exited their cabin as well and growled, "If anything happens to them, I will swallow you whole."

"And don't I know just how easy that would be for you." Rowan bowed and then flashed the knives strapped to his waist before gesturing to the bow and arrows on his back. "I might be getting up there in years, but I still know how to fight. I will keep your children safe, Abraxas. You have my word."

The word of an elf was binding. He knew that. They all did. If Rowan vowed to keep them safe, then he would do everything in his power to ensure no harm came to them.

It made his stomach turn, but Abraxas nodded. "Then go off with the elf, children. Give him no trouble. Do you hear me, Hyperion?"

The boy rolled his eyes and loped off after Rowan without saying a word in response. Nyx, however, met his gaze with a solemn expression. "I will keep him out of trouble, father."

"See that you do."

He watched his children meander away and couldn't help but feel a little sorry for it. They were so happy here, and seeing them with another elf made his mind fracture a bit. With a blink, he saw them wandering after Lore while she told them wild tales of her own childhood. Then he blinked again, and it was back to Rowan as he gestured with his bow in the direction they were going.

"You're already seeing things, aren't you?" Tanis asked, stopping next to his leg and crossing her arms over her chest.

"Excuse me?"

"It is the way of it. Every dragon who has lost a mate sees them, you know."

He shook his head to clear it of the sights that only he could see. "Is that so?"

"All the dragons I have known and all the ones who recorded their memories through the crystals. It's a horribly sad thing to happen to us, of course. Everyone wants to see their loved one, even when they know that they are gone. Those sights can be difficult when we cannot tell the difference between reality and our minds. But rest assured, it only means that you loved her as she was meant to be loved." Tanis put her hand on his leg, patting gently. "The feelings you felt for her in your heart were true, Abraxas. You should take great pride in that."

He didn't.

He'd gladly give up all those emotions if it meant he got to see her again. He'd give up that overwhelming sensation of love and release it out into the world if she got to take another breath.

Inhaling, as she would never do again, he sighed. "I hate to tell you this, Tanis, but that doesn't help."

"No, I didn't assume that it would. But comfort is rarely comforting in the moment." She stood back from him, and then added, "You should turn into your mortal form for this."

"Why?"

"Because I want to see your expressions more clearly when I explain to you what has been going on here, and how you can help me." She lifted a brow. "Unless, of course, you believe that you're too vulnerable in your human form. Then you may remain as a dragon."

It was a test. She wanted to know how much he trusted her and if he was willing to be more vulnerable before her, as she had consistently been with him. Abraxas should have expected this game.

He hadn't, though. He didn't want to change out of this form because it was more equipped to handle the riotous emotions that never seemed to leave him. What if he hallucinated that Lore was there again? He'd chase after her as a man. He'd try to find her and then hold her against his heart, and then she'd disappear again.

All that suffering could consume such a weak form. And maybe that was what Tanis knew would happen. Maybe she was trying to test how far gone he really was, and if he could even help her.

Sighing, he let the scales melt away from him. The change took longer than it usually did, almost as though his dragon didn't want to let go of its control. As though it knew the moment he was a man was the moment when everything would fall apart.

He pressed his fists into the ground, feeling the warmth of the soil heated by the sun. He tried to ground himself with that sensation. He was here, in front of Tanis. Not back in Umbra on that battlefield watching as the woman he loved was murdered before his eyes. No one would hurt him. Tanis didn't care that he was weaker than he used to be. She needed him.

His heart thundered in his chest and all he could hear was the sound of his ears ringing. But he wrangled those emotions back into the cage where he kept them and slowly stood.

His spine creaked as he moved, this body not used to being in control.

Abraxas opened and closed his fists, testing to see if they would still work. They did. And the magic had even allowed himself to be dressed as he stood before her. Black pants, black shirt. Suitable for how he felt.

Tanis reached forward and tucked a lock of his dark hair behind his ear. Unlike most women he'd met in this form, she was so tall she looked him in the eyes with ease. "Fitting for a dragon in mourning," she murmured. "You do her spirit proud, warrior."

He didn't feel that way. In fact, he was certain Lore wouldn't feel that way either. She'd tease him for mourning her when she was already gone and couldn't see all the effort he put into missing her. Then she'd tell him to go live his life as he always was meant to.

Without her.

How was he supposed to do that? How was he supposed to survive without her?

Sighing, he cracked his neck to the side and effectively dislodged Tanis's touch. "What is it that you want help with that requires me to be in this form?"

"I already told you, Abraxas. I need to find another crimson dragon to take care of us, otherwise, there will be no guard for this isle. There has to be more of your kind before I can let you go."

The sadness in her expression set his nerves on edge. What did she mean? Why would he need to be in the human form?

He looked her over and blew out a long breath. "I'm afraid what you're searching for is not something I can provide."

"Oh please." She rolled her eyes. "Rowan is the only man for me, Abraxas. You dishonor us both by assuming such a thing."

"You asked me to be in mortal form," he reminded her.

"For a good reason, but we both know you couldn't perform in such a state, regardless." She rolled her eyes once again for good measure before pointing toward the mountain nearby. "I had my own brood, young one. There are still more eggs to hatch, but they are difficult to reach where they are. I need your help, and not the strength of a dragon just yet."

His stomach bottomed out again. In such a short time he'd been told he wasn't the only adult dragon, that he wouldn't have to raise his children on his own, but now… there were even more?

They could really restart the dragon race. This wouldn't end with just him and his children. They wouldn't be forced to make difficult decisions based on bloodlines and necessity. More dragons.

"How many?" he gasped.

"Only three."

"And they all survived?"

Her eyes filled with tears before she glanced away from him. "I do not know. I sealed them inside of a cave nearby, knowing that there would be those who came to destroy them. Or to steal them. But they are the rest that we need. Gold, crimson, and another purple. They are the hope for our species to survive, to continue."

The bloodlines would be raw for a while. They might lose some of their children knowing that it was a risk when they were all potentially related. But these eggs were older than his. Surely there would be enough in their bloodlines to continue the race without fear of... of...

"I will help," he found himself saying without hesitation. "Whatever you need from me, Tanis."

She tucked her hands into the small of her back and turned toward the mountain. "I need you to remain with us, warrior. Crimson dragons were born to suffer great tragedies in their lives and persevere through them. You and your line were always our guardians, protectors, and those who suffered the most."

"It is a cruel fate."

She glanced over her shoulder as she started walking away from him. "You were also the most loved."

The words warmed his chest, even though he knew how wrong that was. Lore had taught him that there was better in this life than constantly sacrificing himself for others. "Is that love enough payment for the amount of torture that we all endured?"

"I don't know." She walked them to a well-worn path that suggested she'd visited her eggs many times and sat outside the cave of her own creation. "Some crimsons would agree that it was. If you could talk with my previous mate, Attor, then I believe he would tell you it was the greatest honor of his life to die for his people. But change is coming to this realm and to the world. So many threads of the web are outside of our control. Perhaps you will teach them another way."

His vision turned foggy, and he heard a voice whisper in his ear, "Go with her, Abraxas."

The words were from Lore. He knew that voice anywhere. But he also knew that she wasn't here. She couldn't be now that she had found her peace.

Sighing, he cast those thoughts aside as he walked down the worn path behind Tanis. "I will not be teaching anyone anything, I'm afraid. The madness has already set into my blood, Tanis. I see her everywhere. I hear her speaking to me, calling for me from the beyond."

"It is my hope that I might convince you there is more to life than tying yourself to a mate." She looked back at him again, those purple eyes wide and sad as they took in his form. "You can be connected to more than one person, Abraxas. You can choose to tie yourself to another. Or many. Become the father these dragon babes need and perhaps you will find that your soul is satisfied with such a change."

He wished it were possible. He really did.

Abraxas would like nothing more than to see the skies full of dragons again. He wanted to see them soaring overhead and calling out his name with laughter, as his own children would do soon.

But he also knew what his heart wanted. And his heart wanted her.

"I will try," he murmured. "But I make no promises when I know what it is like to be merged with another. One woman. One man. One soul. And now mine has been ripped apart."

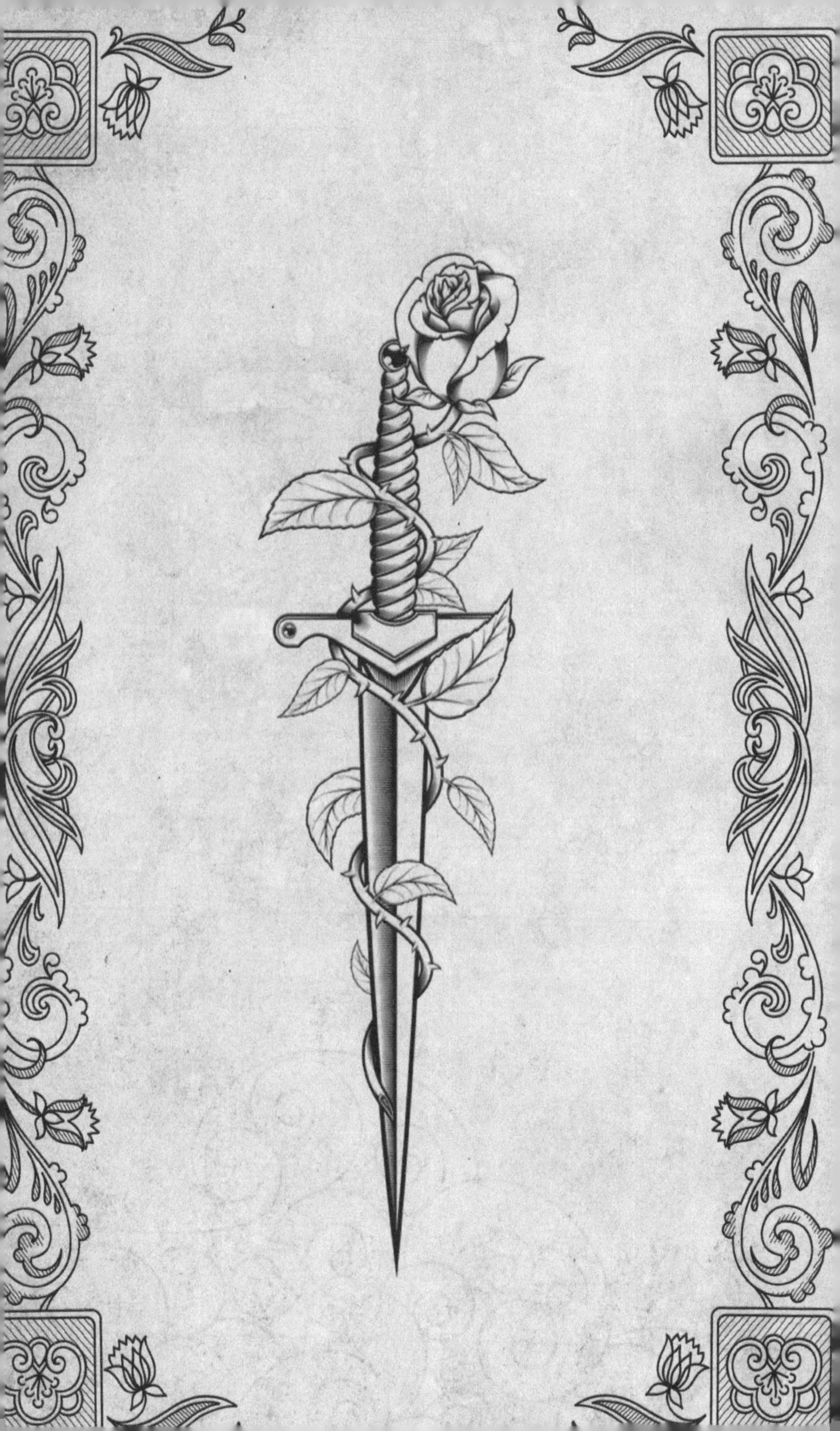

CHAPTER 8

"You've done well," Lore said as she patted down the horse for the night.

She'd known the big beast could manage the speed she wanted, but she hadn't guessed that it would enjoy the grueling pace. She hadn't needed to ask the stallion to go faster. The horse had wanted to go faster. The more she pushed it, the more it seemed to take that as a personal challenge.

They'd ridden the entire night and into the wee hours of the morning. She'd stopped only twice. Once to get water from a local stream and then again when they came upon a lake. Though she didn't want to anger any kelpies that might be there, she also knew the stallion needed to cool off. It waded into the waters without fear. She'd kept a close eye on him while he swam. Just in case.

They were lucky. No kelpie had taken up residence in the pond or lake, and they were swiftly on their way again.

Now, the sun was already setting on the horizon and they were even closer to her goal. The harbor was another day's ride away from them, and they should be able to make it by tomorrow afternoon.

She'd catch the captains as they found their crew for the next sail. Lore hadn't been on a ship in her life, but she learned quickly and no one could ever throw her overboard. All she had to do was get on a ship, and she'd already figured out the best captain to do that with.

Hauling the saddle off her stallion, she set it down on a large rock so it didn't warp overnight. "Go on," she said to the horse. "You've earned a wander. Just come back tomorrow morning."

Somehow, it seemed as though the horse understood her. Perhaps she should have questioned that more, or at least wondered why the beast seemed to nod before it plodded off into the shadows.

These powers were strange. They were new, and she didn't want to question them too much. Otherwise, she feared what other questions she would discover.

The packs already rested next to the circle of stones where she'd marked out her fire for the night. She would like to rest, and the stones would help contain the flames that could get out of hand in a forest like this.

It was strange to feel tired.

She hadn't felt like this since she had returned, and that knowledge made anxiety quake through her bones. What if she had only come back for a few days? What if the unnatural energy that had spread throughout her entire form was simply because she was getting ready to die again?

She didn't want to go back to that quiet place of peace and happiness. It wasn't for her. She was meant to remain by Abraxas's side until they both died after long centuries of enjoying each other's company. That was how the time was supposed to pass and the only way that she would be satisfied with how their story went.

But what if this sleep was her final one, and she had wasted her short amount of time in that stupid castle?

She laid out the blanket on the ground and shook her head. Anxiety over such things was a waste of time. If she only had a few more hours left, then wouldn't she want to spend those in hope rather than fear?

"You're borrowing worry," she muttered as she finished setting up her bedroll.

Lore busied herself so she could keep her hands moving and her mind occupied. She carved out two quick stakes to put into the ground on either side of the fire. Rolling a log closer for a seat, she then set to work scraping the innards out of a rabbit she'd killed on the way here. It wasn't much, but the dinner would keep her going. Tomorrow she could barter for a proper meal once she reached the harbor.

The hair on the back of her neck prickled.

Someone was watching her. She could sense their energy in the woods as they moved quietly through the shadows. They didn't want her to realize they were there. Most people wouldn't have noticed, but Lore was a little more than most people these days.

She reached down into her boot for a knife and whirled. The blade whistled through the air with unnatural speed and she heard the thunk as it struck a tree near where the person had stood. Tilting her head, she listened for the sound she knew would come.

A wheeze of pain. A cough of discomfort, and then a voice.

"Lore," the smooth tones were clearly an attempt to be said in chagrin. "Would you please come take your dagger out of my shoulder?"

Of course. Of course, it was him and not someone else that she actually wanted to see.

"Draven," she snarled as she stood up. "I thought I clarified that I was not to be followed."

"Actually, you said you didn't want anyone to come on the journey with you. Which I didn't. But you had to know that I would not let you go alone." He was pinned to a tree with her dagger through his shoulder. Though the moment he saw her walking through the shadows, he flashed a bright white smile. "There you are. I thought your powers would give you a more accurate shot, but you missed."

"I didn't miss." She wrenched her blade out of his shoulder and didn't care if it tore muscle or flesh on the way out. "I wanted to see who was stupid enough to follow me, and I can't question them if they're dead."

"Ah." He winced and pressed a hand to the wound on his shoulder. Blood already seeped out between his fingers. "Any chance you're also willing to help wrap this before we rest for the night?"

"Absolutely not."

"Lore!" He watched her walk away from him, but then she heard his footsteps following her.

Because of course he followed. Why would he let her go when she wanted to be alone? Obviously, he had to trail along with her to make sure that the "goddess" didn't get into any more trouble and... oh. Die again.

"Go away, Draven," she said as she walked over to her own bedroll and sat down. "I have a fire to watch, food to cook, and sleep to attempt before I try to find a ship tomorrow. The last thing I need is for you to be a distraction."

"I won't be." He sat down next to the packs and pulled his closer. "Thank you for bringing my things, at least. I moved a lot faster without this on my back."

"Did you run after us?"

"I did." He ruffled through the bag, although she caught him looking at her as though he expected to see her surprise at his speed. "You made good time on that beast, though. I nearly caught up when you were at the pool. Just missed you, in fact."

Of all the foolish things to do. He should have left well enough alone and not tried to run after her like an idiot.

"Why would you follow me?" She poked at the fire, coaxing it to burn hotter so that she could get it going a little faster. Her stomach suddenly craved the meat on the stick in front of her. "You realize that I'm not letting you onto the ship?"

"You don't want me on the ship with you, but I fully intend to join you on this mad dash toward saving your dearest dragon." Draven pulled out a long sleeve of fabric and then promptly started about removing his shirt. "You seem to think you can do everything on your own, even though we've all made it very clear that you can't do it all on your own."

"I single handedly defeated an undead King, powered by ancient magic with an entire army of spectral warriors fighting against me. What else do you think I can't do?"

Lore wanted to slap him. If she wanted to run naked through the castle screaming obscenities, then she would. The man had no idea what she had been through, or what she would go through. She'd earned a life of a little more ease than pandering to other people's expectations of her.

He paused. He'd wrapped the gauze once around his shoulder, and his entire body flexed against the pain of it. But he still stared at her with an angry expression, like she'd never seen on his face before. "You died, Lore. You died doing that on your own, and that is exactly why I'm here. You can't be trusted to do anything on your own, or we might lose you again. Don't you see that?"

All the anger in her sailed away on his words. She blew out a long breath and shook her head.

Of course, that was the reason. She was so blinded by wanting to get to Abraxas, and the fear that he might have already succumbed to whatever madness took over dragons when they lost their mate, that she hadn't thought about them.

Particularly Draven. He'd stood there and had to watch her die. She remembered locking eyes with him, seeing him through the bubble of her magic, and she just... hadn't cared.

Perhaps that had been cruel. She'd known how much Draven thought of her, and how that little crush had grown into something like worship the longer he was around her. And here she was, running away again while he feared she would die. Again. And probably thought that this time it wouldn't be right in front of him, so he would never know what happened to her.

She ran her hand over her face and eyed the rabbit. It wouldn't take long to finish cooking, but she could leave it on long enough to take care of his wound.

Standing, she muttered, "Move," and sat down in front of him. Her pack had all the necessities for a wound like this. She pulled out a fine needle and thread that she'd wrapped in a container to make sure it didn't get muddy. Pulling it out of the little metal tin, she set it to the side and gestured for him to move closer.

"I don't need stitches," he protested, but he had to know that was a lie.

"You do. And I need to apologize for ignoring you." She reached forward without asking if he was ready and set to work. The man would have to get over the pain if he wanted to travel with her. She couldn't promise that their journey wouldn't get even more difficult.

"Apologize?" he asked with a wince. "For this? I accept. It's good to know that you haven't lost your touch, however. Even after being dead for a few months."

"I have lost nothing, and no. I won't apologize for stabbing you when you tried to sneak up on me in the woods. You got what you deserved, deepmonger." The needle slid in and out of his ragged flesh a few times before she relented. "I forget that sometimes my actions will affect others. I knew my death would be hard on all of you, and that you had more to mourn than just me. I've been ignoring that guilt in the mad race to get to the isle of Dracomaquia."

He let out a brief hum and his chest vibrated against her fingers with the sound. "You're running away from your own guilt and sorrow, Lore. We all could see that. I just wish you wouldn't put yourself at risk in the process."

"What's one lone elf to a kingdom already freed from hatred of magical creatures?"

Draven gave her such a long look, she wondered if she'd somehow injured herself. Frowning, she looked up into his eyes and waited for him to say something.

He didn't.

"What now?" she asked, tugging on the thread, perhaps a little too hard.

"Everyone knows your face, Lore. The entire kingdom has been talking about the goddess elf who gave her life so that the magical creatures could be free from the tyranny of the King. Do you think they won't remember you? If anything, the legend regarding who you are has gotten even more out of control since you died. The moment you walk onto those docks, everyone will know who you are."

Ah, of course. And if any passerby walked past her campsite, they would likely think that she was an actual goddess waiting for them here. The last thing she needed was that amount of attention when she was trying to leave Umbra.

She sighed again, already frustrated with her predicament and more than a little uncomfortable with how things were going. "Fine, then what would you suggest?"

"Cover up. Stay away from people as much as possible, and try to meet those friends in lower places than normal." He winced as she cut the thread, but glanced down at his shoulder with an impressed expression. "I didn't know you were so neat with your stitches."

"I've had practice." The Umbral Knights used to beat Goliath up rather frequently. He'd return to their home with a bloody cut on his forehead or a new knife wound on his arm and expect her to stitch him up.

Her hands shook as she put the thread and needle back into her pack. Goliath, with all his laughter and happiness that he brought into the world, was gone. Just the thought of him made that guilt he said she was running away from bubble up in her chest.

She shouldn't feel like that. They were at war, and horrible things happened all the time. And yet, she couldn't get it out of her head.

Draven's hand came down on hers over the strap of her bag. "You couldn't have saved him, Lore. His death was an accident and not one you can take on as your fault. War is horrible and death is inevitable for all of us. He knew that. He wanted to save you, and he died a hero."

"Did he?" she asked, her voice a little wobbly. "Or did he give his life for an elf who runs away at every opportunity?"

"You didn't run away, Lore. You saved us all."

She hated that. Was it wrong to feel angry that she had saved these people? She was furious that they had made her become a weapon and that her life hadn't gone the way she'd planned. It was silly, perhaps. Maybe she hadn't worked through everything in her head that needed to be put back onto the correct shelves.

But she was angry.

Lore turned toward the fire and pulled the rabbit off. She laid it out on a small flat stone she'd cleaned off and started slicing it up for the two of them to eat. "How much food did you bring?"

He was silent.

The man who never shut up chose now to be silent.

Grinding her teeth, Lore held out the flat stone for him. "Eat as much as you need then, deepmonger. I'll find another rabbit to cook."

As she stood, Draven sat up a little straighter with the stone and rabbit in his hands. "Lore, you don't have to go find another one. I can eat half, and you can eat half. It's enough."

"It's not. You've been running for nearly two days now, straight. You need more food, or I'll be dragging you to the harbor." And she needed to get away from him. Her thoughts and emotions were already getting out of hand. She could feel that power rocking through her, bouncing in between her ribs like her heart was a beast trying to get out of her body.

Lore wanted to let that power out. She wanted to feel it rip through the universe with her anger and sorrow and guilt.

All that guilt had to come out somehow, and she'd prefer it not to be around him.

"I can feel them," she whispered. "I can feel all their souls out there.

From the grasshoppers hanging onto the green blades, to the rabbits in their dens, to the birds nesting in the trees. I can feel all of them, Draven, even you. Your heart is beating faster because you see something else inside me that shouldn't be there. And it's all very distracting."

He swallowed hard, then turned his attention to the plate in his hands. "Then I'll eat."

She turned away from him before she lost control and took it out on him. But deep inside, Lore shuddered.

What was she becoming?

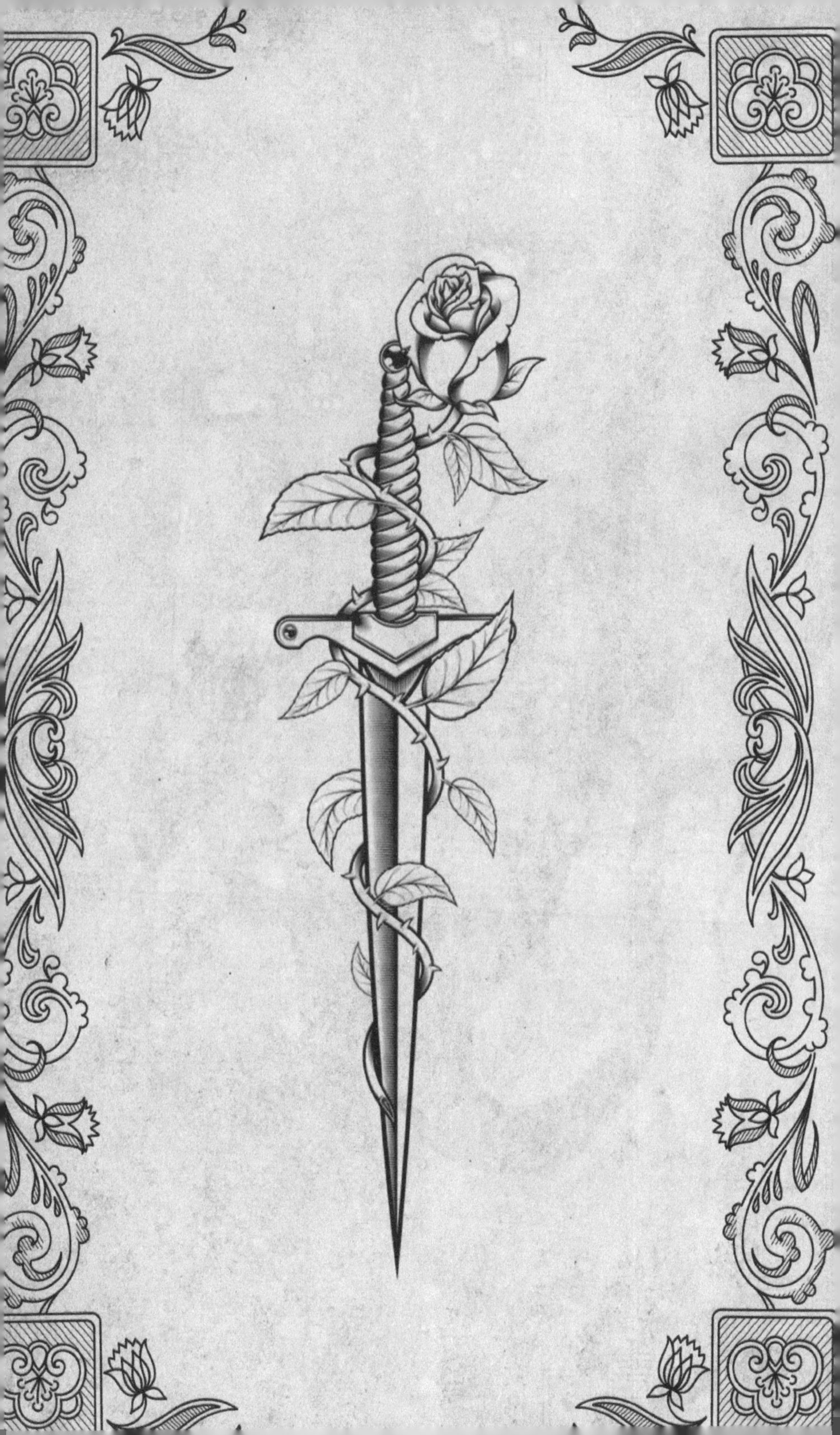

CHAPTER 9

He followed Tanis up the path to the base of the mountain, not because he thought this would change anything, but because his heart wanted to see the truth. If she had actually buried her eggs, then they could all continue into the future with a little more hope.

What he hadn't expected to find was a rocky path that continued up the mountain until he rather felt like a goat. The stones cut into his palms and his fingers gripped the ragged cliff edges with what he hoped might be renewed vigor.

He hadn't used his body like this in a long time. Staying in his dragon form wasn't entirely easy. He wanted to be both the man and the dragon, but he'd only been the dragon for a very long while now.

His biceps flexed as he hauled himself along the path. His thighs burned and his heart thundered in his chest. It was almost enough to distract him from the thought that he was adventuring without her.

But then he tilted his head to look at the sun and saw another person clambering along the rocks beside him.

He was almost certain he'd never seen Lore like this. They'd shared many journeys with each other, but they hadn't ever climbed a mountain like this. He couldn't know that her hair would stick to her sweaty shoulders, or that her cheeks would turn bright red with exertion.

Though, the wild grin on her face was one he knew well. She only wore that expression when they were on the best of adventures. Ones that they should have been able to enjoy. Just the two of them.

"Why'd you stop?" she called out. The wind caught at the remaining dry hair on her head and whipped it towards him.

He could smell her. That earthy scent with the bitter bite of citrus. She always smelled like an island in the middle of the ocean and he could almost taste it. She was so perfect for him that sometimes he wondered if the gods hadn't made her for him and him alone.

"Just looking," he whispered, even though his mind knew she wasn't real. "I miss you."

"Of course you do." She leaned back, one arm holding onto the rock, and she dangled into the air. So free. Without a spark of fear or anxiety. "You're doing this all alone, Abraxas, and I hope you know how impressive that is."

"Sometimes."

"You should take a few moments to look around yourself. You're home. There are more dragons now, and even more on the way if you do this right. You have done all the things we wanted, even without me." She frowned slightly. "Although, I do wish I was here."

"You are," he whispered. His voice stuck in his throat with emotion. "You're always here."

Lore hummed in the back of her throat before shrugging. "I'm not.

I'm back there, where you can't find me. And I'm sorry for that."

Tears burned in his eyes and his chest squeezed tightly. "Please don't go. Please don't leave me here."

The wind blew through her form and he heard another voice call out. "Abraxas! Return to me."

He didn't want to. He wanted to look at Lore and release his hold on the rocks so they could fall together. They'd tumble through the clouds as they had when she first rode upon his back and he could hear her shriek of glee mixed with fear one last time before the ground met him.

A strong hand wrapped around his wrist as his fingers lost their grip on the stone.

Tanis stared down at him, not with disappointment as he might expect, but with a sadness that came from bone deep within her. She hauled him up the cliff herself. He knew dragons were strong in this form, but he was no small man. Having an elderly woman pull him up as though he weighed little more than a child was humbling, to say the least.

She helped him sit down on the stones and then plopped down beside him. "You saw her again, I take it?"

He shook himself as though trying to clear the haunting memory from his mind. How was he supposed to do that, though? Lore existed in his heart, not his head.

Abraxas took a deep breath, blew it out, and then did it again for good measure. "I see her everywhere, but it seems as though I'm seeing her more often."

"I still see them all as well," she murmured.

"Who?"

"The other dragons who lived here with me." Tanis lifted a flat hand

and glided it through the air as though tracing the path of a dragon's flight. "They soar through my memories because those are what keeps us going. The mind of a dragon is so powerful that we can conjure the past before us. You need to remember that they are just memories. You are not seeing her spirit, nor is she calling for you from the grave."

"I've never seen her like that before." His mind flickered again, and for a moment he swore he saw a hand come up over the edge of the outcropping they sat upon. But then, with a blink, it disappeared. "We've never climbed a mountain, nor have I seen the sweat glistening on her shoulders like that. She was more than a memory. She felt so real."

"Sometimes they do." Tanis nodded. "I remember climbing up here on my own for the first time. I saw a golden dragon at the top, just resting. Waiting for me to find her. I was so excited that I nearly tumbled over the edge of this cliff before I caught myself and realized it wasn't there. If I hadn't brought myself back to reality, then I would have met my end."

It was very similar to what he'd experienced. Abraxas knew without a doubt that without Tanis, he would have let go of his hold and tumbled down the mountainside with Lore's image in his mind.

Perhaps the thought should have been tragic. It should have scared him. But his soul knew there was only one way for it to reunite with hers.

"I will admit, it's a terrible feeling." He stared off at the clouds, squinting his eyes to get a better hold of himself. "I wasn't like this before her. And I certainly didn't expect to feel this way after."

"A mate bond is powerful magic. Your heart is telling you to stay for your children, but your soul knows there is nothing left. We are, at our cores, still animals. Perhaps a human might find another wife or an elf might find purpose in some philanthropic ploy at soothing the aches in their hearts." She pounded her fist against her chest. "But we dragons are still part of a wildness that runs through this land. We know at our core that there is no life without a mate bond once we have experienced it."

"Are we wrong for that?"

She set her hand on top of his. "No, we are not wrong. Merely different."

Abraxas felt his shoulders curve inward and some tension leave his body. He wasn't wrong to feel this way. It was natural. Dragons had felt like this for centuries before him, and he could only hope that his children would be spared the anguish.

Somehow, that made him feel a little better. At the very least, he wasn't some weakling who was incapable of dealing with the emotions that had led him to this point. Exhaustion had him settling a little more firmly against the stones.

He did not fear that he would throw himself from the summit anymore, at least. And that should frighten him more that he'd ever thought such a thing. Instead, all he felt was even more tired. There was so much he battled every single day.

Tanis lifted her hand and pointed. "There, do you see it?"

He followed the line of her finger and noted a large cave not far beyond the mountain range. "I do."

"That's where I buried the eggs centuries ago. Nothing could go in or out, so I know no beast has tried to steal or eat my eggs. There were three of them, but it's a start. I'm certain there are other nests we might find as well. But I'd prefer to hatch the eggs we know are near first. The fewer mouths we have to feed will probably benefit us."

Blinking away the sudden confusion from the swift change in subject, he nodded. "Understood. Did you make me climb a mountain to point out a cave even farther away?"

"No, I made you climb the mountain because you needed to move." Tanis eyed him and then shrugged. "And also because I know you wanted to see your children wandering around with Rowan. This was my way of proving to you that we are all safe here. If you wish, you can climb this mountain every day to survey the landscape. We've never had any troubles in Dracomaquia. Not like you fear."

He wasn't paying attention to her words. The moment she'd said he could see his children, Abraxas had turned his attention to the trees.

There, in the distance, he could see his dragons trailing after Rowan. There was nothing around them but a field of bright green grass and sun in the sky. None of them seemed afraid. No one was looking out for creatures that might stalk them because there were none. His children, although foolish and likely to take risks an adult wouldn't, were happy here. They had space to grow and to learn so much from the two creatures who had always been here. From a dragon who was a real dragon and not one who had learned how to be who he was from legends and stories.

Sighing, he felt some of the tension in his shoulders ease. "It is good to see them like that. To see how easily they fit in here."

"And you will as well." She nudged his shoulder with her own. "You're still so young, Abraxas. There are centuries of learning ahead of you, and I hope you give me at least a little time to teach you more of what it means to be like us. You're a good young man, but there's more to life than finding a mate."

"Is that so?" He arched a brow and stared at her. "Then you won't mind if I suggest that Rowan return to Umbra, as they have great need of a wise elf to guide them."

Immediately, she frowned. "You're not playing fair."

"Merely parroting back what you said." Two could play at that game. He had no interest in learning more about this world if he had to walk through it alone. Still, he found it amusing to catch Tanis in her own web.

She gave him an unimpressed look but ignored his sarcasm. A feat he greatly admired, considering how her hands curled into fists. She wanted to hit him, he thought, and that might be the appropriate response to his sass. He had no idea how dragons should treat their elders.

Leaning back on his arms, he watched the clouds pass over their heads. "So what would you have me do?

"Clear the pathway into the tunnel for me. Unfortunately, these old bones aren't quite strong enough to move those heavy stones."

"You lifted me with ease."

She rolled her eyes, the exasperation clear in her next words. "There's a difference between lifting a man and lifting boulders larger than four of us put together. It will be a long and difficult project, but I think you're more than capable of doing so. If you don't mind, it would be a great help to both Rowan and I. Then we can get those eggs, and we can hatch them into this world. They'll be younger than your children, so we'll have to wait a while for more eggs. But I think it would be the start of something incredible. The two of us can welcome our race back into existence. Together."

She was right, of course, but he enjoyed giving her a little trouble about it. Abraxas weighed his decision, letting his gaze meander over the clouds rather easily until he nodded. "I'll do it, then. Shouldn't take too long."

He had spoken too soon.

The next week was spent clearing out stone after stone. Most were small enough that he could wrap his jaws around them and pull them out of place. The unfortunate part was that each stone seemed connected to a possible cave in. He had to be so careful as he moved each piece of the puzzle. They had no way of knowing if any movement continued throughout the entire cave system beyond. If they were unlucky, then the eggs were already crushed.

But, it felt good to use his body like this. Every morning he got up with a purpose. Each night, he returned to the cabin exhausted but unable to think of anything else. He was so busy it was hard to think of what he had lost or what had happened this past year. There were only the rocks that needed to be moved, and the future that he desperately tried to preserve.

Until the day came when he moved the very last stone out of the way and saw the tunnel emerge. A cold wind whistled out of it, as though the air had been waiting to escape. It came with a sense of expectation. He knew there was something waiting for him on the other side. Those souls had been waiting for a very long time.

He should have called out for Tanis, perhaps. They were her children. But something in him knew that there was more beyond. More for him to see and that these eggs wanted to see him right now.

He slipped into the tunnel and felt the wet plops of water hitting his back. This was a labyrinth of a cave system, disappearing deeper and deeper into the mountains in all directions. But the eggs were to his right, so he followed their siren song. Lured by a promise of a future that saw more than just sadness and strife.

The eggs were nestled against the wall of a distant cave. And as he stood there, staring at the many colors of the eggs that still gleamed as though even dust couldn't touch them, he saw Lore again.

She leaned over them with a bright smile on her face, wearing a grin that rivaled the stars.

"They're beautiful," she whispered as she lifted the red egg. "This one looks just like you, Abraxas."

His heart thudded hard in his chest, once, twice, three times. And then she disappeared.?

CHAPTER 10

"I don't have any special powers, Draven," Lore hissed as she drew her hood lower over her face. "But if you don't shut up, then someone is going to notice that we're skulking about, and then we're going to have issues."

"You do have special powers, though. I have seen you use them at the castle, and you can't convince me that your stallion followed us simply because it was a good beast. I saw how he treated everyone else at the castle." Draven stopped in front of her and wildly gestured with his arms. "You can do a lot more than you're letting on, Lore."

The docks were busy today, as she'd expected. Many of the captains were trying to hire their crews before the winter hit. One last sail before they all had to either go further out to sea—and maybe not return—or hole up for the winter and hoped they'd saved enough money for the next season. She wished it were an easier life for them.

This place was little more than shambles. The docks were old and rotting. The buildings dotted around the harbor were weathered with the salty air and paled to a strange gray color. Few people here lived, but they were comfortable enough. The crowds certainly suggested that there was some magical reason to stay close to the sea.

But she knew the truth. Those who fell in love with the sea found their calling long before they were even born. The waves and the salty air were the only place where they could feel true happiness. Unfortunately, that also came with a life of hardship.

A man wandered past them, arms laden with ropes and a lobster trap dangling off one arm. The trap was broken in four places, though she couldn't imagine that a lobster had done such damage.

Lore shivered. It was easy to forget that the sea between Dracomaquia and Umbra was filled with more than just sea creatures. Monsters lived in those depths, if the sailors' stories were true.

As the man passed by then, Draven pointed at him. "You see? That would have been a good one. You could have used your magic on him, got us on a ship, and we'd be out of this place easier than you could imagine."

"I can't control them, Draven."

"Well, you could at least try! I'm willing to do whatever it takes to get us onto one of those ships, are you?" He eyed her with a faux disgusted look. "It's like you think the only way we're going to get hired onto a ship is the honorable way, and let me tell you, no one is going to hire us. We don't have any experience being on a ship."

"I don't intend to be honorable," she grumbled as they walked between a few houses that leaned drastically to the left. "I'm looking for someone."

"Oh, how lovely? You said you had friends in low places, but I don't think even they are going to give you much of a break." He sidestepped a pile of fish entrails that smelled worse than they looked. "Lore, if you told me your plan, then I might be able to look for this person, too."

She was so tired of him. Draven meant well. She understood that. He wanted to help her. Sure. He could try. But somehow he refused to acknowledge that some things she had to do alone.

Like finding the captain no one wanted to work for and convince her to take two extra people onto her boat.

Sighing, Lore pinched the bridge of her nose and reminded herself that lying wasn't necessarily the worst thing she could do to him. She could break his nose. Besides, Draven had to learn that she could be on her own for a while without dying, and maybe he'd find some information out in the wilds of this place that would be useful.

"We're looking for a male captain with hair the color of snow," she lied. "I met him on one of my travels early on in my life. He goes by Bones or Alabaster, one or the other, depending on the day. I assume that he'll be more likely to be in the food market, but it's best if we split up. Sometimes he's in the taverns."

She reached into her pocket and pulled out a few of their meager coins. She really should have raided the castle's coffers before she took off on her own. Counting four silver coins out, she placed them in Draven's hand and then nodded in the direction of the food market.

He repeated everything she'd said and then gave her a nod. "Understood. I'll find him, and if I can't, then I'll get us something to eat."

"That sounds like a good plan."

"And Lore?" he said as she turned away from him. "Stay safe."

Lore glanced over her shoulder and tried not to feel too guilty about the expression on his face. Worry, fear, a little sadness as well. As though he feared this was again a goodbye between them and he hadn't guessed it would feel like this.

She gave him a curt nod. "I'll be fine, Draven. It's not my first time here."

Or well, it was actually. She'd met this captain on one of the dastardly woman's treks to the interior of Umbra. But, while Draven went on a wild goose chase for a man who didn't exist, Lore could only hope that this lady captain would remember her.

After all, sirens were notoriously finicky about who they spent company with.

Finding the tavern took little effort. All she had to do was follow the line of drunken people who staggered through the streets, and that led her right to the tavern's door. The Broken Arrow. She'd heard it was a favorite among most of the captains and all the sailors.

Lore knew better than to walk inside. Her face was too recognizable. Instead, she leaned against the wall of the building opposite the tavern and stuck to the shadows. Propping her foot on the rickety boards behind her, she settled in to wait. Thankfully, someone had left a length of rope on the ground next to her foot. Lore thought that would come in handy.

To her surprise and pleasure, she didn't have to wait very long.

Allura was a siren very true to her name. The woman's beauty was unparalleled with her dark, bottomless eyes and hair like the purest of ink. Her sun tanned skin was the fine color of honey and glistened as though she were always just slightly dewy. She moved like a professional dancer, but Lore knew why she really moved like that.

A siren was a deadly creature with the power to kill a man with just one finger. If she wanted, she could inject her poison into the skin of any person who tried to attack her. The paralytic effect happened almost instantly. Then, as any woman would with an attacker, Allura was more likely to kill the person than she was to ask what they wanted. She was as deadly as she was beautiful.

Which meant Lore had to tread carefully with this one. If she wanted to keep her head attached to her shoulders, which she very much did, then Lore had to be assured that the deadly poison was taken care of before she grabbed the captain.

Lore could cut off Allura's hands, but she wasn't sure that would endear her to the other woman.

Instead, she opted for a slight whistle that drew Allura's attention to her. A thin strand of hair slid over the siren's face, obscuring the beauty there for a moment before revealing a wicked glare.

"Who goes there?" Allura snarled.

Lore had no intent on letting her know that. The siren would have to come closer to see who had whistled at her like she was a dog to be called. It was one of the siren's weaknesses, Lore supposed. That woman would no more allow a man to treat her inappropriately than she would allow a shark to steal her catch.

Predictably, the siren stomped toward her. "Do you know what happens to men who catcall me?" Allura asked. "They lose their lips so they can no longer whistle."

At the last moment, Lore moved. She used the back of the building she leaned on as a jumping point and leapt up higher than Allura had likely anticipated. With a lithe movement, she arched her body over the other woman, caught her wrists with the rope, and forced her hands behind her back. Then Lore shoved her into the wall face first.

Hard.

Barely out of breath, and more than a little impressed with herself,

Lore whispered against the back of Allura's neck, "But I so enjoy my lips, Allura. Surely you won't mind if I keep them?"

The siren froze against the wall, likely trying to think of her escape before the sound of Lore's voice actually clicked in her mind. A few long moments passed as Allura tried to place the voice that sounded so familiar.

Lore knew the moment she remembered who she was. Allura's hands went lax in her grip and she sagged against the building with obvious relief. "Elf? Is that you?"

"I said I would come back for that debt." Lore released Allura's hands and side stepped. The siren swiped at her with those deadly claws before she leaned against the building, rubbing at her rope burned wrists.

The siren always liked to have the last attack. Lore was just lucky she'd stepped far enough away.

Allura blew hair out of her face before looking Lore up and down. "I heard you died."

"I heard the same about you."

"And that you'd turned into a goddess."

Lore lifted one shoulder and shrugged. "Someone had to have ambition."

Though they glared at each other for a few moments longer, neither woman could stay angry for very long. They dissolved into chuckles and both of their postures relaxed. Lore even took her hand off the dagger at her belt.

"What are you doing here?" Allura asked. "I thought you said you hated the ocean."

"I do. All that constant movement makes my stomach sick, and that's just looking at it. I'm sure being on the waves will be even worse."

And she wasn't looking forward to the long weeks of vomiting. "Still, I need transport and you're the only one mad enough to take me there."

Allura lifted a dark brow. "Mad enough? I'll admit, I'm intrigued. Shall we talk about this adventure of yours over a drink?"

If only. Lore would have given her right arm for a strong absinthe and a blunt of elfweed to take the edge off. She shook her head. "'Fraid not. Too many people recognize my face these days, and I'd rather stay hidden if possible."

"In trouble again, Lore?"

"Less in trouble and more looking to stay away from those who would cause it for me." Though Allura didn't need to know about Margaret and that foolish woman's plans, Lore found herself wanting to tell the siren everything. She'd always thought of Allura as a woman with a good head on her shoulders.

There was no one else to talk to. No one else for her to purge these horrible thoughts in her mind. If there was anyone here who would put up with her rambling story, it was Allura.

Gesturing with her hand, Lore asked, "Walk with me?"

"Let me get a drink first. You want anything?"

"Whiskey."

Allura disappeared into the Broken Arrow, only to return rather quickly with two golden goblets. They were both heavy with a whiskey that smelled of caramel and charred wood. Good whiskey for these parts, surprising considering where they were.

"They let you leave with these?" she asked.

"They let me do whatever I want here. This is my town, Lore, just as that castle is now yours." Allura clinked their goblets together. "We've all got to be queen of something, I suppose. To the Goddess of Umbra."

"To the Queen of Rats."

They laughed some more as they wandered through the streets. Lore hadn't realized how out of place she'd felt in the castle and for a long time now. Here, she was just another woman in the slums of the world, where she belonged. She knew how to avoid the stares of people who were hungry, or when to offer them help. It was natural to pull her hood over her face when a guard walked by. This was closer to her home and comfort than she'd been in for a very long time.

"So why are you here?" Allura finally asked. "You've never sought me out after all these years. What has it been, nearly a hundred?"

"Hm," Lore hummed in agreement. "A long time."

"And you found yourself a little nostalgic for the old times, is that it?" Allura finished her drink and set the goblet now next to a beggar. "Or did you want something more from me?"

"I need someone willing to go on an adventure of a lifetime that may end in certain death." A wild grin spread across her face. "And of all the captains insane enough to agree to it, I think you're at the top of the list."

"And just where do you expect me to go?" Allura asked with her hands on her hips.

This was when the siren might cut and run. Allura would hear where Lore wanted her to go, and that would likely be the end of it. No sane person would try to sail to Dracomaquia. It wasn't done.

Partly because the rough seas could tear a boat apart. Partly because the isle was rumored to be haunted. No one wanted to go to the old home of the dragons and risk their lives on whatever had taken up residence there. Apparently, the last boat that went, hoping to find some of the dragon's old treasure, had sunk long before it ever reached the place. And the boat before that had been seen on the far shores of the isle, a skeleton of a ship floating on the empty waves without a single sailor aboard.

Lore took a deep breath and dove underneath the waves of uncertainty. "I need someone to take me to Dracomaquia."

The echoing silence was nearly her answer.

Allura let out a little cough, then a laugh, and then tossed her head back as though that was the funniest thing she'd ever heard. The siren laughed so hard it was drawing attention, and Lore had to put her hand over her friend's mouth and squeeze hard.

"What are you doing?" she hissed. "Shut up."

"I just thought for a second you said you wanted me to bring you to Dracomaquia and that is the most ridiculous thing I've heard all day." Allura straightened and pressed her hands to her belly. "Whew, that was a good one, Lore."

"I'm not joking."

Allura's expression fell. "You're not?"

"Not at all."

"I'm not insane, Lore. Do you know how hard it was for me to even get a ship? I'm not going to beach that beauty just because you're on some treasure hunt or looking for the next spell to make you even more powerful." And with that, the siren started to walk away.

Lore reached out and grabbed her arm, holding her in place. "The man I love is there. He waits for me and every second we waste is another when he might die. I need you to help me, Allura. And I will pay anything."

And there it was. The glint of greed in Allura's eyes. "Anything?"

Lore nodded, although her stomach twisted in worry. "Whatever you want."

CHAPTER 11

They all sat around a fire after a day of adventuring and exploration. Abraxas grinned at his family as they all chattered about what they'd discovered. He hadn't seen his children this happy since he'd left them on the shore with their mother.

They leapt over the bonfire, giggling and pushing each other as though it might hurt if they fell in. Their tails lashed behind them, and he hoped they'd keep their balance or they would destroy the fire that Rowan had worked hard to build. The elf insisted he knew how to start a flame, even if he was surrounded by dragons.

Tanis watched his children with a soft gaze and he knew she was already fantasizing over what her own children would look like. They'd differ greatly from his, certainly, but they would be beautiful in their own right. Soon there would be so many dragonlings around, she wouldn't know how to keep her head on straight.

Her elf partner, however, was not nervous at all. Rowan had even built a small chest to keep the three eggs in and lined it with soft rabbit skins he'd killed and tanned himself. Almost as though the man were nesting.

Snorting at the thought, Abraxas laid his tail over his nose to hide his mirth. The elf would soon realize that being a father was more than just a comfortable place to lay them to sleep.

Speaking of, Hyperion bumped into him hard enough to rock his scales. Grumbling, Abraxas lifted his head to glare at his boy.

"Sorry," Hyperion said with a laugh. "I didn't see you."

"You what?"

"Well, I... I..." His son sat up on his back legs, balanced on his wings as his beard tendrils twitched. "You looked a bit like the mountain, so I thought you were just a shadow."

"That's a terrible excuse. Go chase your sister. Maybe she can teach you a more believable story for why you'd walk into a dragon of my size." Abraxas swept the boy's wings out from underneath him, sending his son tumbling onto his back while his sister laughed.

Hyperion cursed—where had he learned that word?—before racing after his sister with snarls that lit up the entire night sky with noise.

Though they were annoying at times, he still shook his head with a slight smile. Those children were so important to him. And it was a relief to know that they would be taken care of here, with more of their kind and the world unfurling before them.

"How did you hatch them?" Tanis asked, her gaze curious upon him as she worked with Rowan to line up their dinners. She carried the deer carcasses with ease, even in her mortal form.

He'd noticed she preferred to stay that way rather than the dragon he knew she could be. Abraxas had long wondered why, but now he thought he understood. She wanted to be in a human form so she could be closer to Rowan. It made some kind of sense, although it reminded him how often he'd been in his own mortal form when he'd had Lore.

"Abraxas?" Tanis asked again. "Are you still with us?"

She worried too much. He was rarely with her, but he wasn't about to do something insane. At least, he didn't think he would.

Abraxas sighed and nodded. "I am here, Tanis. What question did you ask of me?"

Her lips pressed into a thin line. "How did you hatch the eggs without a female dragon?"

"Ah, that's a story and a half." He was quite proud of himself for figuring it out, even if it seemed like an impossible tale. "I spent a few centuries thinking about it and trying to remember exactly what it was that my mother had tried to do with her last batch of eggs. None of them hatched, but I knew they had to be kept close to the belly of a female dragon and that a male belly won't do."

Tanis nodded. "We've tried to hatch eggs with males before, and they never hatched. Which is precisely why I'm asking. I've never heard of a male dragon successfully bringing eggs into the world. At least, until you."

Even his two children settled down to listen to the story, although they must have heard it at least once before.

Abraxas took his time thinking about the perfect way to weave this web. And partially because he enjoyed watching Tanis squirm a bit in her seat as she waited for him to begin.

"A female dragon's belly is warm and safe, and I had read in a warlock's journal that the heat needed to reach impossible temperatures that no mortal could replicate. Then, about fifty years later, I was on the beach when lightning struck. The way the sand turned molten and how hot it felt to the touch, even to me, gave me the idea." Abraxas settled his head next to the bonfire and stared into it. "I didn't know if it would work, but I also was unaware that there was a female dragon available to hatch the eggs. I used my own flames to melt the sand that held onto my flames as it had with the lightning."

"So you melted sand into molten glass and... what? Sank the eggs into that mixture?"

"I did." His huff of a laugh nearly extinguished the fire. He waited until it roared again before he elaborated. "I allowed them to stay there for a very long time. Nearly an entire day before the glass cooled. And then the eggs, they rose to the top before the dragonlings hatched. It worked, and I'll admit, it's still surprising."

Tanis shook her head in what must be disbelief. "I'm shocked that it worked as well. And that we haven't thought of that before. When the dragons were still here, nesting mothers were dangerous to leave alone. They were so vulnerable when they were trying to hatch the eggs. They couldn't move around, couldn't even leave their cave if they wanted the eggs to actually hatch. Some died of starvation if their mates didn't bring them food."

What a cruel way to treat someone more important than life itself. Abraxas knew there were some who abused their mates, but he never would have guessed such a thing as that could happen.

Sighing, he shook his head. "None of us knew the ease with which we could fix all our problems. I breathed my fire into the sands and my children were born from the glass."

"How fascinating." Tanis shook her head as though she could hardly understand how he'd done it. "I am shocked that you managed. But I'm so pleased that everything went according to your, albeit limited, plan."

"It was a desperate attempt to no longer be alone." He looked over at his children and smiled. "And now I am not."

He expected them to grin back at him, but both of his children wore matching expressions of sadness. He'd thought they would enjoy the stories, but instead, the tale appeared to have made them sad.

"What is it?" he asked, leaning closer to them in case they didn't want Tanis to hear their complaints.

Nyx, his precious daughter with a heart of gold, was the one to answer. "I remember my mother was there."

Her words danced around the fire and he felt the heat of the flames lick at his face. Of course Lore had been there, but he didn't want to bring her up. Not when his children were so sensitive right now. When they needed to think of happier memories and forget the darkness of their past. Apparently, he was wrong to have hidden that part of the story.

Tanis looked between the two of them, her mouth slightly open.

But it was Rowan who spoke first. "Your elf was at the hatching?"

He couldn't tell them. He couldn't speak her name or let the story drip from his tongue when he feared what state of mind he would be in afterward. His daughter, however, did not hesitate to tell the rest of the story that he had hidden from them.

"I didn't want to hatch," she mumbled, taking her turn to stare into the flames and ignore the world as she lost herself in the words. The story ripped out of her, dark as the night she was born. "My mother sat with me in her lap. I remember how warm her legs were, and how she wrapped her whole body around me and promised that she would take care of me. We would face the world together, even though it was terrifying. She made promises she couldn't keep."

"Hold your tongue, girl," Abraxas snarled in response.

"It's the truth." Nyx met his angry gaze with one of her own. "She didn't have to die. She could have left that kingdom to rot and come with us here. We all could have started a new life and she would still be alive. But she couldn't. She chose to stay there, with them, to fight their King, and then she died."

"Because she was a good woman with a pure heart who refused to let a kingdom fall when she could stop it from happening. Because she knew if she didn't stop that King then he would track us to the ends of the earth itself to make sure we were all dead." He had to remind himself to be softer. Kinder. His daughter was young, and she didn't know the whole story.

She didn't know how much Lore had struggled, and how it had made her heart bleed to leave her children behind.

He shouldn't get so angry with his daughter. But the rage in him that surged the moment she dared to insult Lore made his heart race in his chest. He wanted to lunge across the fire and defend his mate, even from his own daughter.

That same racing heart would never let him lift even a single claw in Nyx's direction, however. She was his child and there was no anger that would ever turn him so far down a path of rage that he wouldn't remember who she was.

Taking a deep breath, he turned his attention away from his daughter and to the amethyst dragon. "Lore was the first person Nyx saw, and I can confirm that Lore made many promises to our children. She helped break apart Nyx's egg. And from what I know of our people, that is something that has never been done before."

The Memory Keeper looked at them all with a thoughtful expression. "Your family is strange, Abraxas. You've all rebuked all tradition, but I find everything you tell me to be a softer way of living. Perhaps our people have adhered to the harder way of life because it was familiar, and not because it was necessary."

He hummed low in his throat. "Indeed."

The heat from the fire surged again, although this time he felt it in his cheeks and down his throat. The strange sensation was not what he'd expected tonight. After all, fire had always been somewhere he could find peace and comfort.

Clearing his throat, Abraxas leaned a little farther away from the flames, hoping to find some reprieve from the heat. "She was a remarkable woman, and one who changed the fabric of time itself."

Tanis looked thoughtful at his words. "I've heard that term before, but I can't remember where or how. The words are familiar, though."

"Many have heard the same." He wished he could tell her that there were hundreds of people who had heard of the elf that would change their world. The humans had been afraid of her legend. The elves, too.

Even Rowan now wore a peculiar expression that made him wonder just how many of the old legends he remembered. It would make sense that the elves of old had talked about the day the world would spin on its axis and everything would change. Perhaps that's how Tanis remembered it.

He cleared his throat again, the heat spreading throughout his entire body now. Was something wrong with him? It felt wrong. There was a fire in his chest that didn't seem right. Of course, he always had a fire burning, ready for use, but this felt wrong. Different.

Tanis clapped her hands loudly. "Children! Have you fished before?"

Both of his dragonlings looked at her in shock, then at each other. "No?" They said in unison.

"Rowan, go teach them how to catch the fish in the pools. I think I'd like something different from gamey meat tonight." She shooed them away with her hands. "Night fishing is the best. Perhaps you'll catch us a few giant squid."

No one looked at Abraxas after that. Rowan leapt up, as though the elf knew something was wrong. He ushered the dragonlings toward the woods, talking about how giant squid were massive and how terrifying they were. Abraxas hoped they wouldn't actually fight one of them. The last thing he needed to fight was a creature with multiple arms.

Tanis knelt beside him and patted his cheek, staring into his eye on that side of his head. "Change into something more manageable, Abraxas. There's not much I can do for you in this form."

Sighing, he let the scales melt away into something much softer. His flesh burned and ached. It felt as though he'd been run over by an entire stampede of horses, and he didn't know why.

Groaning, he held onto his skull as something tried to split it open. "My entire body hurts. I feel so hot, and I've never felt like this before."

She pressed the back of her hand to his forehead. "You're ill, Abraxas."

"Dragons can't get sick."

"We can if something goes wrong. Like losing our mate." She sucked in a breath through her teeth, then leaned back on her haunches. "There's not much we can do for you here."

"It's all right," he said, slightly panting now through the pain in his skull. "It's as it should be. I know she's waiting for me, and I know the children are in good hands."

Tanis smoothed her hand over his sweaty forehead. "You need to go into the cabin. We can watch over you there. I can help ease your pain."

"I don't mind it."

"Well, I do." She stood, dragging him with her and helping him move toward the cabin. "You'll take the bed. Rowan and I have slept in worse conditions. I'll get some cool cloth to put on your forehead and that'll get you through the night."

He couldn't help but feel as though she were fighting to slow down the inevitable. The idea of death didn't frighten him so much. Especially not as he looked up and saw Lore holding the door open to the cabin. She would wait for him, he supposed. And if he couldn't find her there, then he would usher himself into the next life for them to be together.

"I miss her," he whispered, his voice hoarse and gruff. "I'm ready to see her again, Tanis."

"You'll have to wait for that. You need to see my eggs hatch, don't you remember?" She gave him a little shake. "There are more dragons coming, Abraxas. You have to wait until that."

He held onto the door frame for a moment, peering into the shadows where he now saw the figure of Lore smoothing back the covers. "I can wait for a bit," he muttered as he lurched toward the bed. "But not much longer."

CHAPTER 12

"So you sent me on a wild chase to find a captain who doesn't exist?" Draven asked as they stood on the docks together. At least he was wearing his own pack today, although he only had one strap over his unwounded shoulder.

"I did."

"Why did you do that?"

"Because I needed to talk with Allura on my own. If you were there, then everything would have gotten muddled." She refused to admit that Allura had a hard time focusing when there was a man around. Particularly someone who looked like Draven.

If the dark elf had been there with them, then he would have caused an argument between her and the siren captain. No one was more talented at sailing the seas, and Lore refused to have another person take them anywhere near that dangerous isle. But if Allura had tried to tempt Draven over to her side, or distract him with her wiles, then Lore would have to punch her in the throat and that was bad for business.

Draven sighed and looked back in the direction they'd come from. "Are you sure that horse will be all right here? It seems like a lot of people are looking at him for meat rather than as a stabled beast."

"He'll be fine." She'd already paid a young boy to release the horse from the stall tonight. No one would buy him today. They needed to get enough money first, and the stallion would return to the castle long before anyone scrounged enough to buy his weight.

"Then we're really getting on a ship that's sailing to Dracomaquia." Draven shook his head. "Never thought I'd say that in my life."

"Me either."

Lore put her foot on the gangplank up to Allura's ship and stared up at it. Savoring the moment. She was one step closer to Abraxas. Lore hadn't really let herself think about it. All she'd done was rush forward into this mad plan, not allowing herself to think even for a second about how much she missed him.

Allura's ship wasn't the largest one in the harbor, but it was sturdy. Wide and low, it was made to ride on top of the waves like a feather. Three giant masts held up massive sails that fluttered in the wind, ready to take them to their next adventure. And, of course, the signature mermaid figurehead that led them all throughout the storms.

Allura wasn't a mermaid herself. Sirens and merfolk were vastly different, after all. Sirens lived closer to the shore, and they rarely dove into the dark depths. And they looked like mortals, although more beautiful and deadly. Merfolk were rather different with those massive tails that made it hard for them to appear human at all.

"There you are!" the siren called out. "You're the last one to board, so hurry up, would you?"

Lore made her way up the plank with a lifted brow. "Waiting for us for a while, were you? The sun just came up."

"And we usually set sail before the sun is on the horizon." Allura turned and called out her orders. Men appeared from every nook and cranny of the ship. Some women as well, Lore realized, although they all wore their hair cut short or tucked beneath hats.

She and Draven stepped out of the way and followed Allura through the entire ship. People moved as a unit here. Not a single sailor bumped into another, nor did they ever have to tell another to move. They moved, perhaps a bit like the sea itself. And it was a beautiful thing to see.

"There's a cabin for the both of you. We use it for storage, but apparently the intent was for guests when the ship was originally built. You two can set up here." Allura looked Draven up and down, then licked her lips. "I didn't think you'd be bringing such a fine elf with you, Lore. It's unlike you to keep such company."

"Wait until you see the dragon we're looking for." Lore had filled her in on the entire story yesterday evening, so Allura had no reason to look surprised when she saw Draven. "We'll put our things here, and then is there any way we can help?"

"Stay out of our way." Allura grinned. "Although I wouldn't mind seeing this one all sweaty and pulling up the sails."

Lore hadn't thought it possible for Draven to be embarrassed, but the tips of his ears darkened and he looked anywhere but at the siren in front of him. "I'm afraid I know nothing about sailing."

"How interesting." The siren trailed a finger down his arm. "Perhaps I could teach you."

The door in front of them was below the upper level of the ship. Lore assumed this was their room and immediately opened it before tossing her things in. Then she grabbed poor Draven by the arm and shoved him in, as well. "Thank you for the hospitality, Allura."

"But I wasn't done—"

Lore slammed the door in her face. "Of all the ridiculous women," she muttered, then turned her attention to Draven. "Are you all right?"

He still wore a rather stunned expression. "Who was that?"

"The captain."

"The captain?" He blinked a few times as though his body needed the motion so that it could commit the words to memory. "I've never seen a captain like that before."

Lore snapped her fingers in front of his face. He seemed to come out of the stupor, but not completely. "Oh, right. She touched you."

And, just as she expected, he lifted his hand to point at his arm. "Right here, actually. She touched me and it was... it was..."

"I don't have enough patience for this." Lore looked around for anything she could use to douse him in water. Allura must have put some magic into that touch and that's why he couldn't get her out of his head.

Draven would snap out of it, but a siren's spell was difficult to shake off. Especially for the opposite sex. He'd probably spend the better part of the day mooning over her now.

Of course, Allura hadn't given them a drop of water or rum in their room. Nothing to wash off the taint of her magical skin or the way she could so easily put men under her spell. There was a key on the top of what looked like a built-in dresser though. Two cots on either side of the room were bolted to the wall, and that was it. Not much of a room, but it had been stripped to make space for storage.

"Draven, can you check your bag to make sure you have everything?"

Lore had to distract him so she could get the key and lock him in here for a couple of hours.

"I think I should go find her, don't you?" He already turned toward the door before she gave her response. "She probably needs me."

Lore's eyes rolled so hard in her head, she thought she could see the back of her own skull. "Allura gave me something for you. It's in my bag on the bed if you want to see it."

There it was.

He spun around on his heel like she'd offered him a kingdom. "She gave you something? For me?"

"Mhm." She pointed to the bed. "It's at the bottom of my bag, though. I had to keep it safe."

He staggered toward the cot, sat down hard on it, and slowly dragged her bag into his lap like he was drunk. Draven didn't even notice the scrape of the key from the dresser or that she'd walked to the door. His mind wouldn't let him, after all. That curse would take a long time to wear off.

Lore slipped out of the room and locked the door behind her. He'd be fine in there by himself. There was food in their bags if he got hungry, and besides, twelve hours locked in that room would only make him appreciate how much nicer it was to be out on the deck.

The boat rocked beneath her feet and she noticed that they'd already drifted away from the docks. The land she knew so well moved away from her. Or well, that's what it looked like. She had to let Umbra go on its own, even though it felt rather strange to leave it behind. Her home. Her land. Her legacy. All of it was on that part of the kingdom, and soon, she wouldn't even be able to see it at all.

"Sails!" A shout came from somewhere else on the ship.

The flutter of fabric snapped in the wind and suddenly they were moving even faster. They soared over the waves, riding atop them with a grace she hadn't realized a ship could have. The salty wind blew in her hair and the sun rose on the horizon to send sparkling lights glimmering over the surface. She hadn't expected it to be quite so beautiful here. The sea had always made her feel ill. But today? All she felt was the rush of adventure.

Lore traced her hand along the railing of the ship and made her way to the second level. Four people stood here surrounding Allura, each one with questions to ask her. They all muttered about the stars in the sky and the direction they had to go. Someone had brought a map and spread it out on a small table in the center of the upper area, while Allura herself poured over whatever had been etched on the page.

The wind shifted, drawing Lore's strands of blonde hair across her eyes. Then, surprisingly, a young man stood in front of her as though he'd been summoned by magic.

"Hello," he said. His eyes were wide and expectant, as though she had to say something in response.

"Hello."

"You're the elf that we're transporting, aren't you?" His nose was peeling from a sunburn and his hair was once brown, but now had blonde streaks from hours upon hours on deck. He would have been a handsome young man if he wasn't quite so forward.

"I am," she replied, leaning around him to see Allura.

"I heard there was an elf in Umbra that came back from the dead. Surprised everyone. That you?" He narrowed his gaze, eyeing her with no small amount of suspicion.

As if she would tell him the truth. "No."

"You sure?"

She glanced back at him again, seeing that Allura was finishing up with the map. "No."

Lore left the young man standing there with his mouth open and his eyes perhaps a little too bright. If they thought they were transporting a hero to Dracomaquia, then they could all think what they wanted. As of right now, the freedom this ship offered gave her a little more confidence than before. No one had to know who she was here. She was just another passenger on a perilous journey.

Placing her hand on Allura's back, she leaned over the map with the siren. "Do you see the stones that have given everyone trouble?"

"The problem is that no one has ever mapped where those stones are. We'll have to tie someone to the figurehead at this point to help direct." Allura turned her grin toward Lore. "How's that young man of yours doing?"

"Currently locked in the cabin you gave us because I'm not about to deal with him when he's in that state. Rather cruel of you to do that, Allura."

"Couldn't help myself."

"We all have our battles to fight, I suppose." Lore still wanted to slam Allura's head into the table for playing that game. Draven didn't deserve the hours of torment he was about to go through. "Now, if you don't know where the rocks are, do you at least know how to get there?"

Allura gestured to the wide open seas of the map. "Uncharted waters for real this time, elf. There's a lot of space between us and Dracomaquia, and no one really knows what's in there. We've already set up a schedule for the watch. I want to make sure there isn't a single moment where there aren't at least two sets of eyes on those waters. It'll be slow going."

Lore appreciated that. She knew how fickle the seas were, and how easy it was for a ship like this to run up on a sandbar and be stuck for months. No one would sail in the same direction and come across them. They were alone and therefore had to figure out all of this without the safety net of a shipping path.

She looked down at the map herself and tried to make some sense of the squiggly marks. "Are we going straight there, then?"

"An old sailor's tale claims there are sea monsters who guard this path. We're going the roundabout way, but it will set us right here." Allura tapped her finger against the jutting shore of Dracomachia. "Apparently that's where most of the ships landed when they attacked the isle all those centuries ago."

"You sure?"

"Not in the slightest."

What an adventure indeed. No one knew if they were going to make it out alive. And yet, Lore hadn't felt this excited since the first moment she realized she might fight against the King. This exhilaration filled her from the bottom of her toes to the top of her head. She was really free.

Free from all the people who wanted to tell her what to do. From the orders to put her kingdom before herself. After all this time fighting and scraping to get by, she'd done it. She'd broken out of the box they'd put her in and now she could breathe.

"Lore," Allura murmured, moving so she stood between her men and the elf. "Your hands."

She looked down at her fingers that had disappeared. Or maybe not quite. She could see the map through the outline of her body, but there was more to it there. Like her fingers had turned into warped glass that changed the image seen through them.

Instead of a clear line on the map, there were now other etchings when she looked through her hands. Markers that must have come from somewhere.

"Do you see that?" she asked, ignoring that Allura didn't want her men to see what was happening. "Through my hands."

Allura blocked her from the view of others, then leaned over to peer through Lore's hands. Her jaw dropped open. "That's a marker to tell sailors not to go through that part of the sea. Rocks. That's what it's saying."

Lore moved her hands around the map, finding more and more markers beneath her skin. Some were written in the same hand, others were clearly by someone else. It was like the magic inside her had reached out to everyone who had ever noted this path and brought them all together for this purpose.

"Give me a quill," Allura shouted, gesturing wildly with her hands until someone placed the quill between her fingers. "You're handy to have around there, Goddess."

"Don't call me that."

"What else am I supposed to call you?" Allura moved Lore's hands on her own now, like her palms were a paperweight to be shifted so the siren could mark the map correctly. "You see the future through these hands. You come back from the dead. You're not telling me everything, and I'm not saying you have to. But you should at least acknowledge that you're no longer just an elf, Lore."

While she spoke, Lore found her eyes lingering on the young man who'd spoken with her before. He'd looked more and more shocked until all the blood drained out of his face. His eyes rolled up in his head as she called out, "That one is going to faint."

The other sailors caught him before he hit the ground, and Lore had to admit that Allura was right.

She wasn't just an elf anymore.

CHAPTER 13

Tanis had warned him that everything would worsen soon. He would feel the very fires of his dragon form trying to eat him alive, and he had scoffed at the thought. But then the fevers set in. He learned what it meant when humans said they had night sweats.

He discovered what illness felt like.

Abraxas wasn't sure how long he'd suffered through it. Time bled together until he wasn't sure what day it was. His breathing grew labored, even though he thought perhaps some of that was in his mind. Regardless, he had a hard time focusing. His chest grew too heavy to fight through each inhalation, but he managed.

He had to. Tanis had made it very clear that he was to be around when his replacement was born, and he would do that for her.

After all, a dying man could fight for a few more moments of breath. Thankfully, the illness had all but banished the visions of

Lore. Some part of him mourned that. He longed to see her again. One last time.

Then, that horrible voice in his head whispered that he would see her again soon. Of course he would. She waited for him on the other side of the realms. The dead always got to see each other again, and he was a fool for thinking that he wouldn't see her.

Sighing, he rolled onto his side on the small cot that Tanis and Rowan had made for him. Tanis didn't want him too far away from her. She claimed it was so she could get him water or check on his temperature. But he had a feeling the dragon wanted to keep a closer eye on him. She'd know if he wandered out of the cabin in the middle of the night. And they would also know to follow him.

Every fiber of his being wanted to rest. He'd earned that, hadn't he? After all the years of serving his people and ensuring that the dragon kind saw the light of day again, he should be able to walk out of this cabin on his own and seek an end he desired.

And now, in the last of his moments, he didn't even have that dignity.

Sighing again, he pushed himself upright. It took a while. His arms shook with the effort and his vision skewed to the side. Exhaustion rode his shoulders like a well-worn coat. He wanted to sleep, but woke constantly as his dreams turned dark. Thirst plagued him, but water made it feel as though steam was running up his throat and he coughed through every mouthful.

"So it is soon," he muttered, his voice a deep baritone in his chest.

Soon he would let go and his children would have to say their goodbyes. But, he supposed, not quite yet.

Through the illness, he heard them. Their footsteps pattering outside and the quiet whispers they thought he couldn't hear. His children stood outside the door, arguing that Tanis had told them to leave him alone, but their natural desire to see their father overwhelmed him.

He wanted to see them as well. Tanis hadn't been keeping them away from him, not really. She just didn't want them to disturb him, either. In a way, she kept him alive for her own means to an end.

"Come in," he said. The words were a harsh croak in the darkness. "I can hear you two."

"You were too loud!" Nyx hissed, followed by the sound of a quick snap and a yelp from his son.

He really needed to have a conversation with her about using her words more and her jaws less. She'd gotten a little too surly since they moved here, and he feared that would continue throughout her life. Someone had to inform her that she would be more likely to get what she wanted if she simply asked, rather than ordered.

But he saw a bit of Lore in her. Perhaps too much, now that he thought about it. Nyx wanted to bend the world to her whims, and she refused any other reality than that.

The door creaked open and one giant green eye filled the opening.

"Father?" Hyperion asked, his voice hesitant. "Are you awake?"

Abraxas told himself not to heave a sigh. Of course he was awake. He'd told them to come inside, hadn't he?

"I am." He leaned forward onto his knees, bracing himself as he watched them. "You knew I was awake."

"Well, we hoped." Hyperion cleared his throat and then stepped away from the opening. "Could you come outside, please? Tanis has been teaching us many new tricks and how to be better dragons. We thought you might want to see the progress that we've made."

"He can't come outside," Nyx said again. "He's sick."

"I'll come outside," he interrupted. "You two need to work on your communication skills."

"I will not communicate with a child," his daughter said.

"And you only think of him as a child because you absorbed the memory crystals we found in Umbra." He staggered over to the front door and braced himself on the door jamb. With a wry grin on his face, he stared her down. "If he were the lucky one instead of you, then perhaps he would consider you to be the child."

All the scales along her back lifted, as though he'd insulted her by the mere suggestion. She didn't want him to think less of her. Nyx had always been self-obsessed like that. But she also hated the idea of her brother being the smarter one.

The history between the two of them could have so easily changed. Abraxas needed to remind her that she should be happy with what she'd been given, and not use it to her advantage too much.

"Besides," he said as he walked over to Hyperion. Placing a hand against the emerald hide before him, he patted his son's shoulder. "You should enjoy being children for as long as you have time to. Soon, you will have responsibilities and expectations. No one wants to waste their childhood when they could have enjoyed it."

Nyx rolled her eyes. "Tanis says the same thing, but I think it's much more interesting to be an adult. You get to do what you want, when you want. You don't have to follow any rules or care about what anyone else thinks."

He thought about her words, mulling them over in his mind. Abraxas supposed she might be right. He had certain abilities as an adult that his children didn't. However, he would give anything to go back to a time when he was just as innocent as them. When he didn't know all the things that he did about this world.

"I still follow rules," he replied. "They just aren't as apparent as yours. No one tells me what the rules are, or how to live my life. The choices are perhaps a little more freeing, but that doesn't make them any easier."

Nyx eyed him with no small amount of distrust. "If you say so."

"I do."

True to his nature, Hyperion appeared to ignore the conversation that they were having and instead, had made up a new conversation in his own head. "Did you hear us when we said Tanis had taught us new tricks?"

Of course he had. And Abraxas had commented on it, so the boy knew. Sighing, he turned to his son and gravely nodded. "Indeed, I did. Tanis has a great many talents, so I am curious to hear what she taught you. You're both rather young for a lot of the magic that dragons can cast."

Although, they weren't anymore. They'd eaten so much here that his children were nearly full grown. It felt like he'd blinked in the time since they hatched and now they were teenagers. They were larger than the cabin, at least. Their growth would slow down for the next couple years, although they would continue to grow for likely the next twenty. Still, they were large enough to be considered actual dragons now.

If any human had seen them, they would think the children were adults. Full grown and giant in size, they could have destroyed an entire village if they wanted to.

Oh, it made his heart hurt to look at them. How quickly things changed.

He groped for the bench in front of the cabin and then sank down onto it. The sun was halfway across the sky. They were well into the afternoon at this point. And the golden rays danced upon his children's wings, glowing through the thin membranes of their wings.

"I'm ready," he said with a small smile. "Show me what Tanis has taught you."

He thought that they would do something with fire. He'd played with his breath enough at their age to know how to blow different shapes of flames. In fact, he remembered a time when he'd taught himself how to blow fire into his closed mouth, extinguish it, and then let the smoke billow out through his nose. It was a rather terrifying effect, and the King's father had always thought it meant Abraxas was angry. He'd just been bored.

Someday he'd tell that story to his children. But first, he wanted them to feel like they were the ones telling stories.

"I want to show him first," Nyx said, shouldering her brother out of the way.

Hyperion rolled his eyes, shoved his sister back, and then reared up onto his legs. He spread his wings wide, and Abraxas thought for a moment maybe Tanis had taught them to fly. He'd yet to see his children do such a thing.

But then...

Hyperion's form warped. Changed. Cracked and snapped into something else, and then a young man stood in front of him. A mortal man, with a chiseled jaw, round cheeks, and bright green eyes that glittered with laughter. He was tall, as most dragons were, and his shoulders were broad. His whole body looked rather like a twig, lean, long, with feathery, dark hair at the top, like he had sprouted some giant plume from the top of his head.

"I wanted to go first!" Nyx snapped. "I'm better at it than you!"

And then she changed as well. Warping out of the bright blue dragon skin and into that of a young woman. Her dark hair was the same color as her brother's, although with streaks of darkness rather than sun staining like Hyperion. Her long, lean body was more muscular as well, and her blue eyes rivaled that of the sky. She was remarkably stunning, with pretty bow lips and a grin that made her seem far more intimidating than it did happy.

He'd never seen more beautiful people in his life. Perhaps their mother rivaled their looks, but he was having a hard time remembering what Lore looked like.

Both children waited for him to say something, but all he could see was that they weren't children anymore. They were likely the equivalent of an eighteen-year-old to the humans, and they were so impressive that it made his eyes water.

Or perhaps it wasn't that they were impressive, and it was that they were right here and looked like him. Not just dragons.

Just like him.

"Father?" Hyperion asked, his pleased expression warping with worry. "Should we bring you back inside? We only wanted to show you because we thought it would make you feel better."

"I told you we shouldn't push him," Nyx whispered. "We should have waited for tomorrow. He's probably too tired for this."

"I'm never too tired for you," Abraxas replied, his voice thick.

He just didn't know how to stand up when his children were

right in front of them and they'd performed magic that dragons his age struggled to do. They were more than just the dragons who would save their kind. They were the dragons who would change the world.

Struggling to stand, he made his way over to them and hooked an arm around each of their shoulders. "Come here," he gruffly said. "Both of you."

At first, they were both stiff. He thought perhaps that had to do with their proximity to each other. Neither of them seemed to want to hug the other sibling until they realized how nice a warm hug was. They couldn't do this in their dragon form, and Abraxas himself hadn't realized how nice a hug was until Lore wrapped her arms around his waist.

A hug was more than a quick squeeze. It was the feeling of his heart beating in unison with another, feeling their breath taken through his lungs. He knew how soft a hug could feel, and how little softness a dragon experienced.

Hyperion sank into his side and then wrapped his arm around Abraxas as well. That clap of a hand against Abraxas's shoulder fueled something deep inside him. As though his son had given him some of his own endless energy.

Then Nyx heaved a sigh, and he felt her entire weight ease against him. All three of them leaned against each other, and he took the moment to soak in this sense of peace. Happiness.

He tilted his head and leaned his cheek against Nyx's hair. "You both look so much like yourselves, it's startling."

"I look nothing like myself," Nyx grumbled. "But I suppose it is a suitable form."

"You look like Father," Hyperion corrected. "The two of you

standing together are certainly father and daughter."

Well, that would be impossible. But Abraxas didn't know where their eggs had come from. For all he knew, there might be some blood relation between them. He supposed that would only muddy their understanding of each other and he didn't want to make all of this even more confusing than it already was for them. He was their father. They were his children. That's all that mattered.

With a smile on his face, he leaned back to look at them both a little more. "You look exactly as I'd imagined. Handsome, beautiful, but still with a dragon in those eyes that is unmistakable. If you walked into a city full of mortals, they would all know you were something vastly unlike them."

Both of them swelled with pride. They looked up at him with those big, wide eyes, and he knew they wanted him to stay with them. They wanted him to choose to live alongside them without Lore, in the hopes that he would see just how much they wanted to be with him.

He knew what they were thinking without having to ask.

"Choose us. Please."

He wished he could. They didn't get the luxury of choice like other species. He could fight against this for a long time, and he would. Every part of him would battle against the instinct to seek out his mate until the lingering dark was too much for him to deny. He'd fight for them.

But, as he drew them against his heart again with a fake sounding laugh, he feared there wasn't as much time left as they hoped.

CHAPTER 14

She did not know how long they had traveled. The nights bled into each other, and Lore realized the truth of how difficult it was to tell time at sea. The stars never seemed to change over their heads. The sun rose and blistered their skin, then sank to leave them freezing in their beds at night.

The sailors' work never ended, and they took their time with every task that they were given. First, she had thought they were lazy. The anger and rage that always bubbled underneath her skin slowly gave way, however, when she realized they were being careful. One wrong move and they would be cast overboard. Or worse, the ship itself would sink.

They took their jobs seriously, because their lives depended on it.

She and Draven were more in the way than they were helpful. Lore had taken to staying inside the cabin during the day unless there was food to be had. She pored over documents that Allura had given her. The siren's travels had brought her to unknown lands. Every detail she journaled as she went, and Lore found herself quite interested in these adventures in far-off places.

Allura had led a very different life than Lore had. And in a way, that made Lore jealous. Her heart had always been in Umbra, her soul tied to the very earth there as generations of her kind had poured their blood, sweat, and tears into making the kingdom what it is now. But her heart whispered that maybe she could have left it behind sooner. She could have escaped. Traveled the seas and found new lands, new realms where she could have been happier.

At night, Lore found a new purpose. She did not sleep, for she found she no longer needed rest. Instead, she nimbly climbed to the top of the figurehead and straddled the woman's shoulders. She stayed there, watching the waves and the sea as if she were waiting for something.

And she was. Lore's eyes could see farther and better than any of the mortal men in the small basket at the top of the masts. They would take much longer to see land, but Lore? She would see it leagues away.

Even now, as she resumed her normal position upon the figurehead with her elbows braced on its knotted head, she swung her feet above the waves and stared, unblinking, toward what she hoped was her salvation.

Her heart whispered, "Wait for me", as if the words could reach all the way across the ocean to him. Surely he could hear her. Abraxas was too dear to her very soul to have given up so soon, and he must be able to feel that she was closer. She was coming.

Footsteps approached. Their hesitancy suggested it was not Draven or Allura, but she could already feel the energy that warped around his body. and shivered the closer it got to her.

The young sailor stalked her every move, it seemed. She'd seen him watching her for weeks now. His eyes rarely strayed from her form, even when he was working on deck.

If she didn't know better, she'd wonder if someone had sent him to kill her. Margaret had enough connections to send a young man like him on the same ship, and her ravens must have seen that they were leaving. For a while, Lore had assumed the old woman had been pleased to get rid of her. Then she wondered if this young man was an assassin.

But on the tails of that thought, she'd seen him tripping over the ropes and how he nearly tossed himself into the ocean, and she'd dismissed the idea. He was interested in the legends about a woman like her, and he was merely intrigued that she'd somehow come back from the edge of death.

"You're out here every night," he said, his voice floating along the wind toward her. "I don't... I don't understand why."

"I'm looking for something."

"What are you looking for?" As if her response gave him permission, the young man pressed his belly to the railing of the ship and leaned over the edge. As though if he got a little closer to the horizon, he might see what she did.

"Land."

"Why?"

Lore rolled her eyes up to the sky. "I'm looking for someone. That's where we're going. To find him."

"Ah." He nodded and then waited in silence until she looked over at him.

He was so young. This sailor who had barely seen the sun rise on the horizon enough times to make him less than a child. His eyes followed her every move in a way that she recognized. Hope. There was so much hope inside him that he dreamed of her saving the realm he knew and turning it into something better. She wished she had an option for him that didn't end in blood.

"You didn't die, did you?" he asked, his voice quiet. "They said you died on that battlefield and that you came back as you are now. Not quite an elf anymore, but something that could save us all."

"That's a gross exaggeration," Lore muttered before looping one of her thighs over the figurehead's neck. Sitting side saddle now, she crossed her legs and focused on the young man. "What is your name?"

"Edmund," he replied instantly. His shoulders straightened as though he were being addressed by a military leader.

"Edmund," Lore repeated. "Why are you on this ship?"

"To seek adventure."

"Why are you really on this ship?"

His shoulders curved inward. "My father beats his children. My mother died in childbirth a few years ago and after he started drinking, he stopped working. The rest of us tried to get enough money to keep the house from getting taken, but it was anyway. Sailing makes good money, even if I'm not there to protect them any more."

This sweet young man. He'd done all he could for his family, and now he stood before a living god while trying his best not to shake. She could admire that bravery, even if it was a little foolish. He needed to learn how to stay quiet and not watch her so closely.

Although, she supposed, she was the only person who could teach him how to survive like the elves did. And if he wanted to learn how to hit his father back, then she would teach him that as well.

She opened her mouth to tell him just that, but thunder rolled in the distance. The sound overpowered anything she might have said. Lore turned with a frown, eyeing the strange cloud that had appeared in the distance. It did not move as a cloud should move. Lightning rippled within it, but never reached out to the waves to strike. Unnatural, that, magical in origin although she couldn't guess what had caused it.

Edmund froze, his body tensing, and she could smell the fear that wafted off his body. "What is it? What do you see?"

"I do not know." The ocean was not and never would be, her home. "A storm on the horizon, but no natural storm in the slightest."

The young man gulped. "Why do you say it seems unnatural?"

Even Lore had to squint her eyes to see the details. Her heart flipped over in her chest, strange thuds against her rib cage telling her that something was wrong. Something was very wrong.

"There is a cloud that moves against the wind," she said. "Beneath it, the waves are boiling. But no steam rises from them, as though there is something underneath the water that makes it churn like that." She had no idea what could cause such a thing.

She turned her attention back to the boy who stood beside her and saw that his face had gone white. Pale as the moon, he swallowed hard, as though his mouth had gone dry. "The water moves on its own?"

"There are white caps underneath it but nowhere else out to sea." She thought back to her meager knowledge of sailing and asked, "Is it a whirlpool?"

"No." He reached for her.

Lore stared at his fingers wrapped around her arm as he tried to tug her back to the boat. His fear sank through her skin, sticking against her like a fine layer of oil. He dared to touch her? This strange phenomenon was enough for him to get past his fear of her and try to pull her back onto the boat?

She allowed him, but only because she was so surprised that he'd be this forward. The young man had always seemed to stay far away from her, but now he didn't hesitate to grab her.

Why?

"What is it?" she asked. "Why are you so afraid?"

"Get to your cabin," he ordered. "Don't come back out. Not for anything."

"Edmund, what is going on?"

He shoved her then, surprisingly strong, as he raced away from her. The boy clambered up the nearest mast to a bell she hadn't noticed. As he rang it with more vigor than she had thought possible this late at night, she realized there were bells on every mast. No matter where she looked, they were everywhere. Bells. Tens of bells.

"Leviathan!" Edmund screamed into the night. "Awaken! Leviathan!"

The entire ship came alive underneath her feet. All the sailors streamed out onto the deck and Allura herself shoved through them. The temptress of the seas blended into the night as she strode to the figurehead herself. The siren leapt with all the grace the sea had given her, balancing atop the figure's head as she peered out to sea.

All the sailors fell deathly silent after the raucous the bell had made. They barely even breathed as they watched their captain for signs that the boy was mistaken.

"Leviathan," Allura snarled, her face twisted into a mockery of beauty. "Twenty minutes, men."

Twenty minutes until what? Lore glanced around to see that so many of these men had frozen where they were. The terror in their eyes was no laughing matter, and neither was the hesitant way that Allura stepped off the figurehead and searched for Lore.

The two of them held their gazes. Lore had no idea what was happening and wanted the other woman to clue her in. Allura, on the other hand, could barely hold Lore's gaze without trembling.

Whatever this leviathan was, it was something to fear.

"What can we do?" she asked, her voice pitched low as Allura staggered toward her. She caught the siren's shoulders and clasped them. "You are the captain, Allura. What can we do?"

"Run," Allura said. "All we can do is run."

"Then hoist the sails, Captain. We will flee across these waters as though a demon runs behind us."

"We cannot." Allura looked up at the limp sails and didn't so much as move in a single wind. "We are dead in the water, Lore. Leviathans take all the wind out of the air and all the waves out of the sea. They drag all that power to themselves until it is too late for a ship to run. We will make our last stance here, but there is no way to escape it. Not in the middle of the night with a dead ship."

Lore grinned and knew her teeth flashed in the moonlight. "You've never had me to help. Hoist the sails, Captain, and I will be your wind."

Though the siren clearly didn't think it possible, she stared up into Lore's eyes with a new fire in her own. "You think you can call a storm?"

"I can do better than that." Lore stepped away from her, arms already glowing with power. "I am the storm."

Allura swallowed hard, but it was as though some hope bloomed in her chest. "Men!" she shouted as she spun toward her crew. "We've been given a second chance at adventure this night. It appears a leviathan believes it can take this ship to the deep with it and we are here to say that will not happen. Hoist the sails, we have our own wind tonight!"

They hesitated for a brief moment, looking between Allura and Lore. The siren, apparently, didn't appreciate that they would question her.

With a slap of her hands against the railing, she shouted out into the sea, "Come and get us, you bastard! See if you can keep up with my ship!"

The storm on the horizon turned toward them. Lore knew the beast had already sighted them. That was why it stayed out to sea, hesitating, waiting to see if there was enough of a meal aboard their ship for it to bother. It had already decided it would attack. It was simply waiting for the right time.

Now, it hurtled toward them. The seas parted at its sides and even from this great a distance Lore could see the scales that reflected the lightning above it. The monster was enormous. It glided through the water with an ease that suggested there was a lot more of it underneath that she couldn't see. A lot more.

Lore spun on her heel and ran. She vaulted up the second level of the ship until she balanced on the back side. Holding onto the ropes there, she turned her attention to the skies. The power inside her thrummed.

It echoed around her like the beat of a drum, or perhaps like a sound wave that moved with each of her breaths. The power inside her wanted to be used. It wanted to stretch its wings and take flight into the sky. All she had to do was ask.

"Wind," she called out, and her words were ripped from her mouth as a tempest blew into life behind them. "More," she called out, her voice deepening into a low growl.

The sound echoed through the storm beside them, and then another blew to life. Another. Three storms merging together to conjure up a gale that the sea had not seen in a long time.

"Careful!" Allura called out behind her. "The ship cannot sustain a hurricane!"

But already the power inside her swelled again. It knew what the ship could withstand. And that power beckoned her to let it flow through the ship itself. The magic inside her could solidify the ship's boards. It could hold together the wood that already hurtled away from the leviathan with a speed similar to a rock skidding across the surface of the waves.

A small spike of fear made her chest tighten. What if she lost control? What if the power inside her sank this ship when she was done? The boards would all fall apart like a child's toy that had been cast aside at the very end. This magic was not hers, and even now it didn't feel like Lore. It felt as though another person lingered underneath her skin, whispering for her to do what it wanted.

But she couldn't stop now. Not when the leviathan had already seen them fleeing, and the creature looked at their ship as a challenge.

That strange power felt the creature's hunger. It was not good nor evil, only hungry. It starved in these oceans where there was little to hunt and even less it could find. A ship was more than just the mortals inside it. The ship itself would be consumed as its hunger made the beast devour any and everything it could get its tentacles on.

How did she know what it looked like?

Lightning struck beside her and Lore could see the beast even though it was some distance away. The lightning illuminated its form underneath the waves. The strangely elongated body, the many eyes that trailed down its sides, the great tail that lashed behind it even as it dragged countless tentacles through the deep.

It would be nearly impossible to kill if it ever caught their ship. And so... Lore would make sure that it didn't.

CHAPTER 15

He stood before the egg cavern they had discovered and let the change ripple through him. Abraxas had not been in his dragon form for a long time now, and it took a while for him to change back. His muscles stuck together as though they didn't want to be larger. As though being in this bigger form was dangerous in a way he did not understand or comprehend.

Now, he felt the heated scales along his body and he knew why the dragon in him hadn't wanted to change. He was tired. So damned tired.

This bigger body was harder to move. His wings drooped behind his back, large and burdensome as he tried to shift past the stones. His back legs shivered with the effort, but he knew there was no option. He had to go on. He had to stay in this form for as long as he could.

The time for this crimson dragon had almost ended, he mused. And though he'd thought that many times in the past few months, he now knew how true it had become.

The fight in him was what kept him going. The desire to live for those that he loved and for the world that needed him when it was at its worst. But now, there was so much hope, and they no longer needed his guidance, nor his protection.

Lifting his heavy head, he snaked his neck into the cave one more time.

Tanis lay deep within. She'd taken the past week to make the perfect nest for her and the eggs. Rowan had brought them to her one by one, making sure they were all nestled within the thick layers of moss and grass and hay that she had woven into a thick cushion for them.

The eggs were carefully set amongst all that comfort and they would remain against her belly now. Already the thin scales there glowed with an inner heat. Soon, the nest she had built would burst into flame around them. Hopefully, she had built it thick enough to remain on fire for a long time. If she hadn't, then Rowan already knew he would bring her more kindling to keep the fires around her and her children roaring for enough time. They would hatch within a few days, he hoped, but some eggs took longer than that. Until it was over, Tanis insisted she would not eat.

Rowan would see that she did. There was no more room for the old ways. They needed all the dragons they could get, even if that meant casting aside the traditions that had served them for centuries. Until they didn't any longer.

"Abraxas," she called out the moment she saw his head poke through the cave odor. "You're here."

As if she was surprised.

"I have hatched children myself. I wanted to make sure you were comfortable." And perhaps to see how it was meant to be done. He'd never seen a real nest or another dragon female who took the time to ensure that her children were safe.

The softness in her gaze when she looked at the eggs warmed him to the very core. He'd always thought he would have a dragon mate of his own, considering he hadn't ever thought anyone would find him useful. No human had. Nor elf. Or any species, really. He'd been hated in Umbra for so many years. So of course his mind wandered to a future where someone like him, who understood him, would eventually have their own nest.

And though his heart softened at the look in her eyes and the way she moved around the eggs, all he saw was Lore as she picked up their dragon eggs. She'd been so gentle with them, helping Nyx out of her egg as though that was natural to do.

Lore had protected them to her last breath, knowing that the King would never stop hunting them. She'd given her life for their children. For the kingdom.

"Abraxas?" Tanis's voice broke through the ragged sound of his breathing. "You are here, warrior. Here with me and not wherever your mind has gone."

His mind had wandered again. There was no war in front of him. Lore wasn't lying at his feet while her blood pooled around her body. Or worse, just gone. Disappeared before he could ever say goodbye.

He swallowed hard. "I am here."

"You were not for a few moments there." She shifted, and he realized that Tanis had almost stood. The eggs rolled against her belly, clinking against her scales before settling back in place. "We still need you, Abraxas."

"Part of me rejoices that I still have use," he replied, then set his head on the stones at her feet. "But I grow tired, Tanis. I have been needed my entire life, forced to recognize that my duty came before myself. Always. Regardless of my own wants or desires."

The hard expression on her face softened. "You have not lived an easy life, warrior. I know how hard it is to dedicate your entire life to your people. It was how I lived before Rowan as well."

The darkness seeped into his mind again. Of course, she had lived like that before Rowan. Before she knew love. But she did not know how hard it was to let go of.

"You do not know a life after him, Tanis." His voice filled the cave with the same ache that never left his breast. The wound that would not heal. "You do not know what it feels like to live without them, as though you have cut off a limb and no matter how much you burn the wound, it always cracks open and bleeds."

"I have lost many."

"It is not the same." He met her gaze and hoped she could see the sincerity in his. "It is not the same to lose those you have loved before, when they were not part of you. When they were not the reason you woke in the morning and the last thought in your mind before you slept."

"This illness is in your mind, Abraxas." Her words cracked through the cave like a whip. "I have tried to be gentle with you, but you will not see it. There is nothing wrong with you other than the loss of this mate, and I know it is hard. I know the wound bleeds incessantly, but there are others here who need you!"

He let her shout linger in the air between them.

Abraxas knew what she meant. There were more dragons they needed to bring into this world. She would sacrifice herself if she could, and would, to see more dragons. More creations.

"You have a mate, Tanis." He lifted his head slightly, as though her words disgusted him. "You have a future here that I do not."

"We have five dragonlings," she replied with a low hiss. "Five. That is all. I know you've thought the same as I. That is not enough diversity to create dragons that will survive as we did. Not in the long term. Five lineages will only cause doom in the bloodlines later on. We need more eggs."

"And you still have a mate."

"We have spoken." She folded her wing gently over the eggs and tucked them closer to her. "If it is a choice between our bond and the future of dragonkind, then sacrifices must be made. Broken bonds can be mended. The future is much more difficult to weave."

"I will not listen to this folly."

"And why not?"

"Because I will not sully her memory by even speaking of—"

"She is dead!" Tanis roared, her voice splintering through the delicate peace he'd woven through his mind. "She is gone, Abraxas. You honor a memory and nothing more. What use is there to remain loyal to someone who is no longer here?"

He had no words for her desperation. For that was where these words came from. She wouldn't have shouted at him otherwise. Fear made her desire for change and a way to keep their people alive. And while he knew there was a level of truth to what she said, she asked for the impossible.

"There will never be another," he replied quietly. "She is the beginning of my life and the end of it. Perhaps I choose to let my fires overtake me, and perhaps you are correct, that is the wrong choice. But I tell you now, Tanis, what you ask is not something I can give."

She wilted where she was. Tanis turned her scales to the eggs at her side and sighed. "Then what kind of life will we give them? What future can we promise to these children who have only known hardship?"

He thought about the question for a few moments as his mind struggled to keep up with the change in conversation. He still bristled at her tone, and how much it hurt for him to even consider that Lore might not be the only person he would be with. She asked for too much and if Lore was still here... he might have killed Tanis for that suggestion.

As it was, he could only look at her with sadness in his gaze. She was scared and wanted him to help her. She wanted her children to have a good life, and that was not something he could promise.

And wouldn't he have done the same for Nyx and Hyperion?

"We will give them all that we can," he replied. "You will love them and show them that the world is worth protecting. You will show them how to be dragons and never let them give up hope that there are more nests out there for them to find. You will prove to them that the world needs us."

"It is all in vain if we cannot show the world that it needs them." She turned her face away from him and he knew that he had been dismissed. She did not want to see him if he would no longer help her.

As Abraxas left the cave, he mused how the last chain around his shoulders fell away. The weight of responsibility for her had loosened and now, there were only two more tethering him to this place. Nyx and Hyperion.

His children needed him still. They were young, and they were vulnerable. They had Tanis, but she would soon have other younglings to focus on. Though dragons grew quickly, it was easy to forget they were still children. They still wanted a father, to show him their new tricks that they had learned and to have him say how proud he was of them.

Leaving this early would also end with them fatherless. Losing both parents in such a short amount of time was sure to weigh heavy on their young minds.

And yet...

He sighed and turned his attention to the cliffs where Tanis had said the crimson dragons lingered. It took him the better part of the afternoon to make the journey. But once he reached the peak, he understood why so many of his brethren had stood here before.

The entire world spread out before him like a blanket sewn with godly hands.

The clouds floated near his head, just out of reach. The water rolled beneath him, so far down the cliff's edge it appeared like faint rolls of grass as the wind played over it. But the sky that unfolded before him was so lovely, and the sun was so close to his skin that he could feel its heat against his sides.

And for the first time in a while, he didn't mind being warm again. Settling on the edge of the cliff, he let a wing dangle over it and rested his head on his claws. He watched the skies and the waves alone for a long time.

The birds chirped around him and seagulls screamed as they hunted. The music of nature lulled him into a state of near sleep. He rested, certainly, and he felt so calm. He could breathe again, and he didn't know when the air had become so laborious.

The sun set on the horizon, and he watched as pinks and reds streaked across the sky. Lovely, he mused. He had forgotten how much he loved a sunset, even watching one on his own. Stars twinkled in the sky, slowly blinking into existence again.

He missed those stars, he realized. Because they looked like her.

They sparkled with an inner power he couldn't deny. They spread across the sky in a thousand sparkles and he knew he would never understand them. But he didn't want to. All he wanted was to look at the stars every night for the rest of his life and know, without a doubt, that they would always be there.

Abraxas stared up at them for a long while. He let the feeling of love and hope envelop his entire body for the longest moment since she'd died. In some strange way, it felt as though she were there with him.

The wounds on his soul eased, patching together as though someone had placed a cool ointment over those aching spots. He could think clearly again, even though he was so certain it would be impossible to do so. And for a while, he thought it was the stars.

If he could stay like this, as himself, eased from the torment of loss, then he would turn to the night sky every evening. He would languish under the bright lights of the stars and then he would heal. His family wouldn't worry about what he might do out of their sight, and he could feel some measure of peace from the nightmarish torment of loss.

Sighing, he looked up at the stars one last time before returning to his family. "If only this feeling could last."

His gaze moved over the sea and in the distance, he saw a ship. It rocked on a wind he could not feel while a storm chased it. And though that would not be surprising out to sea, he wondered why that storm appeared to move on its own.

Was a warlock on that ship? If they thought to attack his island, then it would be the last thing they tried. One final battle he fought for his family.

Spines raised along his back, he stood and braced himself on his wings. But then he realized the storm wasn't magical at all. There was no warlock casting a spell to create it. A great beast of old followed the ship, its massive weight underneath the waves.

His eyes saw the tentacles that rose out of the water and wrapped around the hull of the ship. The beast was massive, and it would crush that tiny boat as though it were little more than a child's toy in the bathtub.

And yet... Some part of himself reached out. A tendril of his soul that scented something in the air that he hadn't thought he would smell again.

The sea. Green things growing through loam. Citrus.

Her scent.

"Lady of Starlight," he muttered. "You mock me even in death."

But he settled back onto the cliffs to watch the battle unfold before him. Because he felt more like himself than he had in ages, and Abraxas refused to let that feeling go so easily.

CHAPTER 16

"It's coming!" Allura shouted behind her.

The storm had already reached them. Lore knew the beast wouldn't be far behind.

She tightened her grip on the daggers in her hands and looked back at the siren. They'd failed to outrun the leviathan, and now they didn't know where they were going. The wind had brought them so far away from the original site where they had seen the creature. They had fled for a long time.

But the beast had endless energy. The leviathan seemed to have an unending energy as it tracked them through the seas. It didn't stop. Didn't slow. And the surrounding storm only grew larger as it chased them. As if the creature had grown excited at the challenge.

Allura had stood beside Lore where she had summoned her own tempest to them, and the siren had said to let the beast catch them. They had no other choice. They could not run the ship onto the beach because the creature would follow them onto the land.

Only one option remained. Fight, and hope they won.

Lore kept the ship moving for as long as they needed and then she let her own storm die out. It only took a few moments until the leviathan's tempest overtook them. The ship rocked side to side in the rolling waters. White caps rose over the edge of their ship, threatening to toss sailors into the deep.

Now, Lore and the others stood in the center of the ship, waiting for when the leviathan would attack.

They didn't have to wait long.

The first tentacle reached over the side of the boat, lifting out of the waves even taller than a building before it slammed down on the deck. The wood bowed under the weight and Lore leaned down to press her hands against the wood. Her magic flowed through it, the glow of the moon holding it together as the beast tried to snap the ship in half.

Its limbs seemed to tense for a moment, and then it squeezed harder until it released. Surprised, perhaps, that this ship was more resistant to its strength. It would soon learn that they would be more difficult to kill than most.

However, Lore looked up as another tentacle slammed down to her right, and realized staying alive might be a little harder than she'd originally thought.

"Watch out!" Came a scream above her.

She'd forgotten the masts.

Damn it.

The main mast cracked in half and came down upon them. The fabric tangled a few sailors up in it, only for them to slide into the waves as one of the leviathan's tentacles dragged it into the water. Their screams echoed in her ears as Lore found her mind flashing back to another time when she had fought. Another time when she had lost a dear friend.

Goliath, the name whispered through her mind. You lost him too.

Sprinting away from the others, she braced a hand against a tentacle and vaulted over it. Lore skidded over the wet boards and slammed her side against the door that had trapped her other friend this entire journey.

"Draven?" she called out, her back against the door. "Are you yourself yet?"

There was silence from the other side, before she heard a dark voice mutter, "I've been myself for a while, Lore."

"Wonderful." She hacked at a tentacle as it came too close to her, but the beast didn't seem to mind in the slightest. At least, until she wedged her knife under one of the suction cups and ripped it off. "Do you want to work your anger off on a creature bigger than either of us has ever seen before?"

"I have half a mind to kill you first," he snarled.

She fumbled for the key that she'd hung next to the door, pulling it out of the bag and quickly twisted it in the lock. Slamming the door open, she braced herself on the frame and gave him a wild smile. "You'll have to get in line, I'm afraid."

Draven wasted no time. He reached for her and tossed her out of the way before a tentacle could grab onto her. The suction cup very nearly struck her back, but instead hit empty air as the two elves rolled across the deck.

Lore spun across the slick surface, catching herself on the edge of the railing as the ship tipped up on its side.

Hanging onto the railing and dangly over open air for a few moments, she stared into the sea. The waves parted around a thick, rubbery hide.

White caps rolled to reveal an eye larger than her torso. And it was staring right at her.

The leviathan had a bulbous body underneath the waves, like an octopus. But those eyes... Those black eyes were larger than she could stretch her arms wide and they saw right into her very soul. The beast never blinked. It stared at her with a hunger that she had never felt in her life. Would never feel. It could never be satisfied and as the waves smashed over its sight, she knew that it would not stop. No matter how hard they fought.

In the water's reflection, she saw a tentacle lift behind her as it readied itself to throw her into the water. Deeper still, she could see the beak-like mouth that chomped, ready to devour.

"I'm sorry," she whispered.

She'd killed before, and would again, but killing something like this made her heart ache. The beast did not deserve the death she was about to give it. The creature had lived for a very long time, and it was old. Older than most.

But she was not ready to die again.

Bunching her legs underneath her, Lore leapt from the railing and back onto the deck. She dodged the flying limbs of the beast that wanted to knock her off course, almost as though it knew what she planned to do. There were no masts for her to climb, no easy way for her to get into the air. But that didn't matter. She'd find the highest point for her plan.

"Lore!" Draven called out, his voice carrying over the storm. "What are you doing?"

He'd taken a sword from another sailor. She could only hope from a dead man, and was hacking at a tentacle. Every bolt of lightning illuminated his dark skin, highlighting the muscles that flexed with each powerful blow. And unlike the mortals aboard the ship, he was actually cutting through it. He brought his blade down into the flesh of the beast, over and over, until they all heard a deep roar from below.

He'd severed the leviathan's limb.

Even Lore gaped at what he'd done. Draven stood there, covered in the beast's blood, while rain sluiced down his chest. Lungs heaving, shoulders rocking with each movement, he glared at her from where she stood hanging onto a rope from the splintered half of a mast.

"Get going!" he screamed at her. "If you have a plan, then stop staring!"

She shook herself free from the haze of shock. She had to get moving.

Lore wrapped the rope around her fist and then jumped. She swung over the crowds of people and the beast's limbs. The ship was cracking. Her magic would only last so long. Landing hard on the second tier of the ship, she rolled to the back, where she had summoned the storm. It was the best she could do. If she could climb the mast, she would, but the beast would see her. And she needed all of its attention on the sailors.

Allura thundered into view. The siren held two pistols in her hands that she fired at a tentacle nearby. "What's the plan?"

"I'm going to cook it," she muttered as she crouched low. "But I need you all to hold its focus."

"That's what we have been doing, Lore."

"Do better, then," she snarled as she traced lines on the floorboards. Usually magic like this would require at least chalk to mark the runes she drew, but Lore didn't need chalk. Her power seared the runes into the boards of the ship until she had a small casting circle drawn. Earth, air, fire, and water, all of it were now at her beck and call.

"Do it now, Lore! If you're going to do something, then do it now!"

Allura's pistols clicked as the last of her bullets were spent. Hissing, the siren drew out a wicked serrated blade and held it aloft.

Lore looked up and saw there were few of the crew left. Edmund stood back to back with Draven as they both fought off the tentacles. Another man screamed as one grabbed onto him and drew him into the ocean.

Her muscles locked as anxiety pressed against her neck. What if this didn't work?

What if she lost someone again?

She couldn't, she realized. She couldn't lose anyone like that because no one deserved to die. No one deserved to put their lives on the line for her and then lose it because she couldn't save them. No one would, again. Ever.

Slamming her palm into the middle of the rune circle, she poured all her rage and sadness into it. She heaved all those emotions into the dark abyss of her spell until she couldn't see anything other than a blinding white light. It burned through her eyes, into her brain, and pulsed with every rapid heart beat. She was death and death had become her.

Lightning arced down from the sky, not from the beast's power, but from something new. It struck the leviathan on its side, sizzling through the skin and leaving a hole that steamed as though someone had cooked a piece of meat over a fire. The leviathan's roar echoed through the waters and sent a bellow through the air. The sailors dropped onto their hands and knees as screams echoed all around them.

Lore answered its pain-filled cry with a shriek of her own as she fed her newfound power through the world and summoned raw magic to her.

One tentacle released its grip on the ship and slapped into the water.

Then another. All the limbs slowly loosened their holds, incapable of grasping onto the ship as the beast's body sank into the depths below.

The sudden silence rang through the air. Even the storm above them let go of its water, a faint mist raining down upon them with no more thunder or lightning. Just a light drizzle that covered their hair in fine water drops, like spiderwebs after a delicate rain.

Breath shaking in her chest, Lore stood and surveyed the damage on the ship. It was more than she would have liked to see. Too many sailors lost. Too many lives gone.

Draven leaned back against Edmund, who did the same to his counterpart. They both helped each other remain standing as they tried to catch their breath, so covered in blood it was hard to tell who was who. Allura stood still beside her, watching the other sailors as they sought each other out.

This was too much of a task to beg from them, Lore realized. She had led them into danger and they did not deserve it. She should have gotten a ship on her own and sailed by herself to this isle.

Lore lifted her gaze in the direction they still needed to go and felt her breath catch in her throat. The sun rose, barely giving her enough light to see. But there, on the horizon, were cliffs. Cliffs that were jagged and rocky, just as the legends had claimed they would be. They were not a welcoming sight, and she knew this was Dracomaquia. It had to be.

And at the top of those cliffs was the silhouette of a dragon.

She'd know him anywhere. Those long wings. The prideful length of his neck as he stretched it up toward the sky.

He'd waited for her, she realized. Her heart thudded hard in her chest and her palms suddenly turned sweaty. He knew she was coming, or he had stayed there for ages, waiting for her to return to him.

He had to know that she wasn't dead. Abraxas wouldn't give up on her because one battle made her disappear.

Taking a step forward, she pressed her hands against her heart, willing it to stop thundering so wildly. Didn't it know how happy she was? How he stood there, waiting for her, and she had been here not long enough to even breathe?

But it all hit her at once. She'd been pushing those feelings aside for such a long time in her wild dash to get to him. And now? Now it all hit her instantly.

He was right there. Within her reach. Her heart squeezed, and it felt like someone had wrapped a hand around her throat so she couldn't breathe. Tears burned in her eyes, hot and acidic where she didn't want them.

Gods. She'd missed him.

"Lore?" Allura asked. "It is done."

She knew it was done, but that didn't mean she was done. The seas could have any manner of creatures within them, waiting for them to move, but Lore didn't care. He was there. He was alive and she could think of nothing else.

Without thought, she stepped off the second tier and landed in a crouch on the first. Then she started forward again, her eyes never moving from her dragon.

"Lore?" Draven said, his voice carrying across the wind. "What are you doing?"

She was running. And then Lore leapt off the edge of the ship and dove into the waves beyond. She felt the power inside her swell, propelling her through the waves like a shooting star that sliced through anything that stood in her way.

The waves parted before her. Nothing prevented her from spearing through the water all the way to the shore while her mind and her heart screamed he was here. He was waiting. He had known she would reach him and he'd never given up.

Her soul screamed for him to hear.

"I survived."

"I am here."

And as she swam through the waves, she looked up at the cliff's edge to see the great crimson dragon leap off the cliff's edge. He spread his wings wide and glided through the air, graceful. With so much ease she marveled at how he could move like that. Like a piece of paper floating through the sky, waiting to meet her on the shore.

Lore's feet hit the rocks beneath her and she stood. Seawater plastered her hair to the sides of her head and her clothing clung to her form. She didn't have to look down to see that her entire body sparkled and glowed with moon magic. So much brighter than before.

Abraxas landed on the shoreline hard, and then the change shimmered over him. He stood there on the sands, his hair lank and his face far too thin. He stared at her with haunted eyes, dark orbs that had seen too much.

Then he took a step.

Another.

He staggered toward her into the waves with torment on his face before he stopped just out of her reach.

Her breath caught in her throat. She didn't know what to say. How did she tell him that her heart broke looking at him and then mended together the moment their eyes met?

"Is it you?" he asked, his voice breaking. "Are you really here?"

Oh, her dragon had suffered. Lore couldn't speak. She couldn't reassure him that of course she was here, she would never leave him. Didn't he know that?

Instead, she sloshed through the waves and threw herself into his arms.

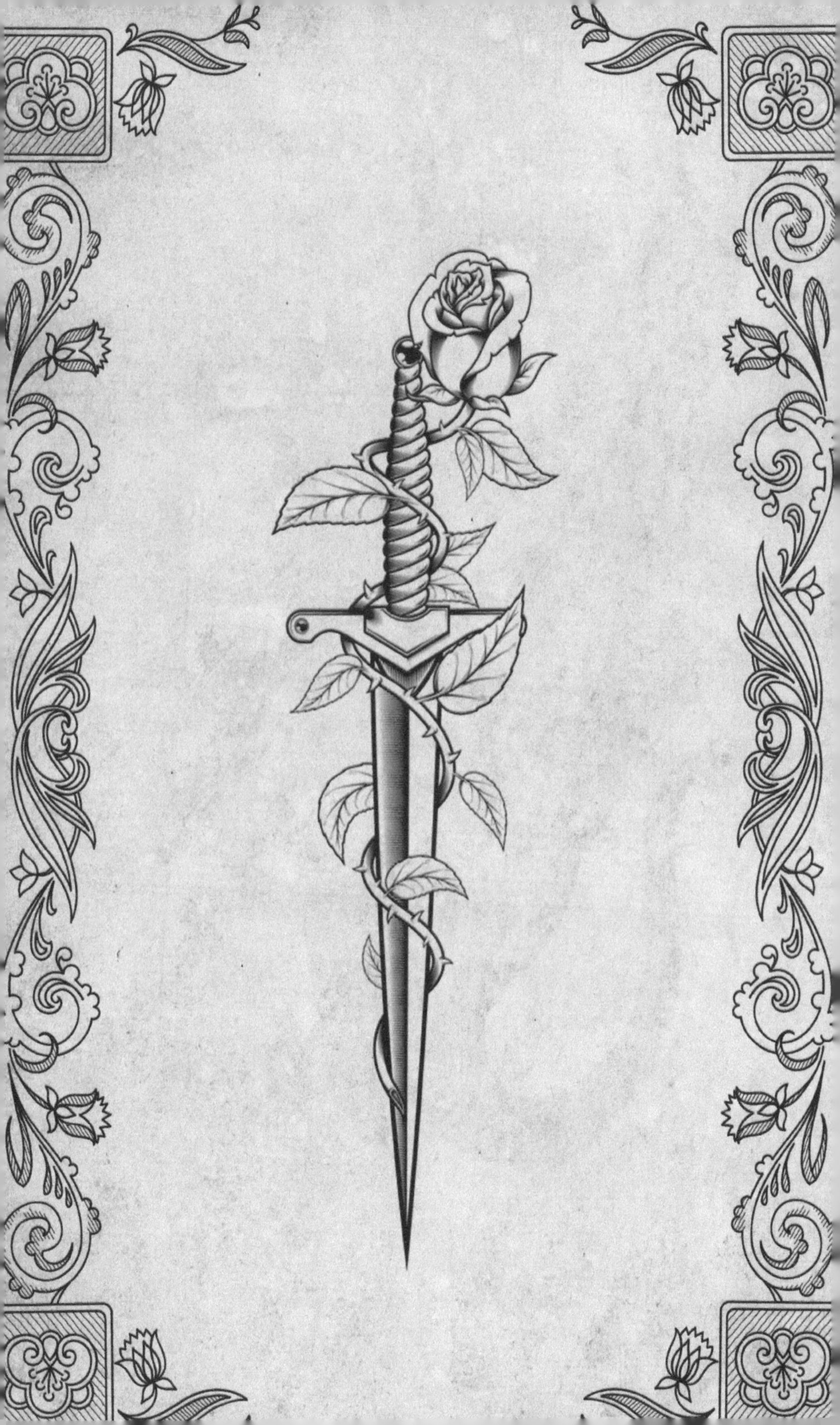

CHAPTER 17

He saw light hit the waves and then travel underneath it. A falling star, he thought, that traveled across the sky and played through the waves as the ship celebrated their victory. He'd seen such marvelous things before, although never from the peak of a cliff.

But then he looked up into the sky and he did not see a mirroring glimmer. The light that speared through the waves and underneath the water had come from the ship itself. A light that glowed with more power than anything he'd ever seen before.

His heart flipped in his chest. Something inside him knew that there was more to what he saw. His soul stretched out its wings inside him and there was almost a roar in his mind, as though a dragon had awakened again. The fires that had been trying to consume him for months eased. Not extinguished, but banked to see what waited for them.

Abraxas eased off the cliff and let the wind take him onto the sands below. There was no rush. The light moved quickly, but not so fast that it would attack his family before he could stop it.

And he would stop it. He had no doubt in his mind that if he wanted to murder anything that came to this island, he still could. In one last blaze of glory, he would keep his family and his people safe, no matter the cost.

But then he landed on the shore and watched as a goddess stepped out of the waves.

She was still tall; he noted. No matter how his mind conjured her, she was always tall. Her clothing stuck to her body, and it was the same as he remembered it. Strong. Not an inch of softness to her. Just as powerful and lethal as the day he'd met her.

His soul ached for her, and he recognized the feeling in his chest. It was as if he was seeing her again for the first time. He'd stumbled upon her in the woods, glowing in the moonlight and watching the magical butterflies over her head. He should have known then that she would change his life.

Abraxas staggered toward her, moving through the waves that tried to shove him back until a little voice in his head whispered, "What if she's still not real?"

All those conjured images in his mind had led him astray so many times. He'd reach for her and she would disappear between his fingertips again. He wasn't certain he could survive such a disappointment, not after all that had happened.

Sighing, he paused. The cold water already turned his toes to ice and his hair hung over his face as he stared at her through the locks. "Is it you?" he asked. "Are you really here?"

A mirage wouldn't respond to him. He knew that. He asked the impossible of his mind to conjure her voice when he was so certain he'd forgotten it. She didn't respond, only looked at him with those sad eyes, and his mind fractured again.

But then she ran through the waves and he instinctively lifted his arms for her. Even if she disappeared the moment he touched her, he would give anything to hold her just one last time.

Lore ran straight into him, hard. He felt the breath leave his lungs in a loud "oof" and then stumbled backward three steps from her sudden, unexpected weight. She wrapped her arms around him and the cold slap of her hair against his face proved she was real.

This was real.

Lifting shaking hands, he touched the tips of his fingers to her back. She held him in a viselike grip, squeezing around his neck so hard he could hardly breathe. But him? He touched her lightly, as though at any moment she might disappear.

She couldn't be real. He'd dreamt her up and somehow his mind had gotten more powerful in his madness.

But then he lowered his head to her neck and breathed in her scent. Saltwater and pine. He hadn't smelled that in any of his conjured visions. Not a single one.

Tears burned his eyes, and he swallowed hard. Once, twice, then his arms spasmed. He held her to his heart in a grip that must have hurt, but she didn't struggle. A chuff of breath escaped him, a sob perhaps, before he turned and dragged them both out of the water. He barely made it to the sands before he fell onto his knees with her in his arms.

She was here. She was real. Lore had somehow beaten death itself and now she was pressed against his heart, where she always should have been.

His entire being felt a little weak. As though she might shatter him with the barest of touches. He had to be careful, or he would... he would...

Break.

He'd always been strong. Powerful. The dragon who could handle the world on his shoulders. But having her back in his arms was suddenly too much.

Gods, he loved her. More than life itself, and now that love bubbled up into him and overflowed.

He dragged his fingernails down her back, holding her closer even though she could get no more close than she already was. Abraxas touched every part of her he could. Her thighs, her hair, her shoulders that flexed as she held onto him tighter as well.

She was here. Gods, she was here, and he was shattered.

Lore leaned back in his arms. She traced her fingers over his face, following the lines of worry that had permanently wrinkled his forehead and month.

"It's been too long," she whispered as she traced her thumb over his lips. "I'm sorry for leaving."

A hard lump formed in his throat, but he nodded through it. "I'm sorry for not waiting."

They stared at each other for a few heartbeats, tracing the new wrinkles, lines, and scars, and then he moved. Or maybe she did. They tangled around each other again and he kissed her as he'd been dying to do for months on end. He poured all his anger and sadness into that kiss, forcing her to endure the worry and the heartbreak that had consumed him from the inside out. Lore took it all. She eased that torment with her lips and tongue until he realized she was healing him with a single kiss. One that did not stop until they both were gasping for breath.

Her legs wrapped around his waist, her arms around his neck. He had never been happier than in this moment, knowing she was safe.

When he caught his breath, he traced a line over her eyebrow. "Your eye, Lore."

"I know." She smiled, but happiness didn't reach her eyes. "It's one of many things that has changed since I came back."

"So you were dead, then."

"Not for long." Another flash of a grin that he knew she didn't feel. "I don't know what happened, or how I came back. Only that I needed to return to you."

His heart squeezed again. So she'd felt it too, then. That horrible ripping and tearing the moment they'd parted.

It was still hard to imagine that she was here. That she hadn't died and now she stood before him, strong and confident as ever. He didn't want to let go of her, but knew they couldn't remain kneeling in the sands either.

"Your companions?" he asked, not having to look over his shoulder to know the ship would soon come toward them.

"They'll be fine."

"We should wait for them."

"I'd rather not." Lore smiled at him, that soft look finally reaching her eyes. "I have spent too long wondering where you were and why I wasn't in your arms at night. Take me somewhere, Abraxas. I have longed for you, and I am tired of waiting."

He needed no other encouragement. Abraxas stood still clutching her to his chest, because he refused to put her down for even a moment. His feet moved as though he'd known this land for years rather than months. Though he did not know where to bring her, his body apparently did.

The ground beneath him felt as though a thousand years of dragons were guiding him to the right place. The only spot on the entire isle that would allow him to be alone with his beloved who had somehow beaten death. For him. And only for him.

The sand gave way into rocky terrain, far from the woods where he'd brought Hyperion and the lakes where Nyx would languish. There was time for them to see the children. Soon she would reunite with the rest of her family. But for now, he wanted to remember what it felt like to be alive. They both did.

His feet and the legacy of a hundred other crimson dragons brought him to a cave where he had never been. He walked through the mouth of it, seemingly large in his mortal form, though he knew it would barely fit him if he were a dragon.

He stepped into the cave and the ground hummed. It welcomed him, the last crimson dragon, with a shake that rumbled through the entire structure. The stones themselves sang for him and his beloved, who had draped herself across his body.

Lore never stopped touching him, even as he moved through the cave. Her hands untangled the long locks of his hair and deftly twisted them into a single braid. She dug her fingers into the knots of his shoulders, caring for him even as he walked. She traced the outlines of new scars that she had never felt and the aches of old pains that she knew existed.

And through it all, his soul sang. She was home. She was with him. They were not alone any longer.

The ancestors had guided him to a part of the cave which had once collapsed with sand. The outside had poured in through a small rift in the ceiling, filling it nearly to the brim. But the crimson dragons had seen this as the opportunity it was. With their breath, they melted the sand into a perfect pool of glass. And as he walked out onto it from a smaller tunnel into the room, it looked as though he walked on air.

Abraxas let Lore slide down his body then, his hands lingering on every curve and valley of her body. "I have missed you," he said, fierce and true. "Your memory was the only thing that kept me going, and though I fought to join you, something held me back."

"I heard that you feared madness would take you." She framed his face with her hands. "That you feared what you would do if you remained in Umbra."

"It was more than that. A mad dragon will destroy so much, but a life without my mate?" He hissed. "That is no life."

"And a death without mine was unbearable." Her thumbs traced over his cheeks, and he felt that flutter in his stomach again.

He'd almost made the worst mistake he could. He had almost given up his life in the hopes to join her, but she was here. And he hadn't taken the time to look for her.

Abraxas sank to his knees before her and wrapped his arms around her waist. Drawing her close, he pressed his cheek to her belly. "I am a flawed man who worships at your feet, and you are the goddess who returned from death itself to find me."

In his arms, she slid down until they faced each other once more. "You did what you thought was right while I languished in the realms beyond. I gave you no option, Abraxas. Do not think I have forgotten that. You were forced to watch me die, our friends die, to see the world as you knew it upended and torn apart. Our hearts knew that the other half no longer remained in the same realm, and we both fought to reach each other. There is no disgrace in that."

She was too forgiving. Too kind. She did not know what he had almost done so many times in her absence, and how that would have left their children alone.

He opened his mouth to tell her just that, only to feel her hand press against his mouth.

"No," she whispered, shaking her head in denial of whatever he was about to say. "If it is not dishonorable for me to claw my way back to the realm of the living, then it was not dishonorable for you to seek me out in the realm of the dead."

Tears shone in her mis-matched eyes and he knew they shone in his as well. Though they had both fought for months on end, they had found each other again.

Against all odds.

How could he not kiss her when she looked at him like that? When she forgave him for being who he was, and never once questioned why he suffered. She knew it was hard for him without her. She understood their children were difficult, but that he hadn't given up on his life simply because she was gone. There had been choices. He had to... had to...

Oh, Abraxas had to stop thinking about everything so much and just enjoy the vision of a woman who was before him.

Their lips lingered, their kisses grew deeper, and he took his time exploring this new version of Lore. Though his mind lingered on the change in her eye, he didn't mind it. And he realized his original vision of her as being the same person was wrong. Her body had changed, too.

Like him, she'd grown thinner. Whether that was the journey across the sea to find him, or the hardship of whatever she'd done to come back to him. His fingers skated over her revealed ribs, and he planned on a hunt to feed her. Then he licked his way down her neck and realized there was an unfamiliar taste of power. She hadn't come back entirely as his Lore, and he should have guessed that. A woman who did what she did wouldn't come back the same.

But to him, even with the power and the strangeness and the eye, she was still Lore. Just his Lore.

And as they came together, he remembered how it felt to really live. The spark of their love bloomed in his chest and the breath in his lungs returned. This was why he had fought for so many years.

For her.

For this moment, to be with her as they floated above a sea of glass. Together, as they should have always been. No kingdom to save. No king to kill. Just them.

Sighing, he leaned over her in the aftermath and stared down into her mismatched eyes. "I love you," he said, his words echoing in the cave. "I love you and I will follow you until the ends of the earth. You are my heart, Lady of Starlight. You are my reason for breath."

The smile on her face finally reached her eyes. "I love you." Twin tears slid out of her eyes and down her temples. "I do not know what the future brings for us, or what we will do after this. But I never wish to be parted from you again, Abraxas. Never."

He leaned down and pressed their foreheads together. Then he lifted a hand and held it over her heart, feeling the steady beat there. "You are mine, and I am yours."

"Forever," she replied. "I will not suffer a torn heart for any longer."

"Neither will I."

CHAPTER 18

Lore cushioned her head on his chest, feeling herself rise and fall with every heave of breath as he inhaled. She had missed this. Just laying on him without worrying about what was going to happen to them.

A little huff of breath rocked through her.

"What is it?" he demanded, tilting his head to look down at her. "You find amusement somehow?"

"I had a thought that I had missed laying with you like this." Lore sat up with her forearm across his chest. "And then I realized we've never gotten this before. There has never been a time between us when we could relax like right now. There was always a war or someone hunting us down. Even before you, I never knew what it felt like to be safe."

His eyes searched hers for something she couldn't quite understand, but then he let out his own little chuckle. "I suppose you are right."

"It's hard to believe that all of it is over. Don't you think?"

And some small part of her whispered that it wasn't. She didn't know how to be Lorelei of Dracomachia. She only knew how to be the scrappy elf who had survived in a kingdom that hated her, and then the elf who was determined to save her people from a coming evil that none of them could understand. She'd never been anything else, and now, to think that she had earned a life of... boredom?

Oh dear.

She worried her lip with her teeth, watching him and hoping he would know why she'd hesitated. Abraxas had always seen into her mind so easily. But now, there had been months of space. Neither of them were the same person after so long.

He let out a little hum that she felt vibrating through his bare chest. "We will be able to start a little farm here. You and I, together, every day. We will rise at the same time and we will have the same tasks. It will be a life of certainty and repetition."

How she hated that idea. The mere notion of having the same duties repeated throughout her life, over and over again... Lore thought she'd rather put a knife through her eyeball than subject herself to that.

He chuckled again and wrapped his arms around her. Abraxas drew her back down to his heart, and then eased her worries with his words. "We will not live a boring life, Lore. Just because we are here does not mean that we will become mundane creatures who follow a predictable pattern."

"You did just say we were going to do that."

"I tease." Abraxas stroked the back of his knuckles down her spine. "There are dragons to train. You will stand on the cliff tops with a crimson dragon as it soars through the clouds. You will dive deep into the oceans with sapphire dragons and teach them how to hunt the creatures you just fought. The leviathans will be wiped away from these waters again, as they should have been centuries ago. You will run through the forests with emerald dragons above your head and fly high toward the sun to greet it every morning. So much is required of you here, Lore. I fear you will be weary for the rest of your life."

And though some of those options sounded terrifying, Lore felt the knot in her chest ease. She didn't have to be so worried about what her life would become.

She had not been born to be a young woman who stood before a kitchen and waited for her husband to come home. The idea of even having children running around her feet used to terrify her. But now? Now she wanted to live a life of adventure with the man she loved by her side.

Lore traced a circle over his heart, watching his skin as it moved, supple against her touch. "I was dead for six months," she whispered. "That's what Beauty said. Gone for that long and I don't feel like it was more than a few seconds."

"Do you remember it?"

A flash of memory pulsed in her mind with a spike of a headache that bloomed behind her eyes. "No."

But she did.

She remembered that dark void of nothing where she couldn't see or think or feel. She was at peace there, of course, but there was another sinister quality to it. A pressure to make her choice because there was something dire that needed to happen. It was either her responsibility to go back and fix something she'd broken, or she had to let it go.

Lore didn't know what she was supposed to fix, or how she was going to fix it now that she was back. But she knew that her powers, though deadly and lethal, were getting out of control.

Her fingers shook as the thoughts took over her. Abraxas covered her shaking hand with his own and held it still. "You don't have to talk about it."

"I do." She swallowed hard. "These powers are not my own, but you know that. You've seen what I can do, and this is different. This isn't right. I made that boat solid as stone and I killed a leviathan with lightning. None of this magic is mine, and I do not know what to do with it."

"You let it go back to wherever it came from."

A pulse of energy thrummed from her neck down into her hand. He must have felt it. He must have realized that the electricity in her hand he held wasn't the same as before, and it wasn't something she had summoned or sent out to him.

The magic didn't listen to her. It did what it wanted and sometimes it helped her. Other times, it did the exact opposite of that.

Again she swallowed, as though she could gulp down the horrible feeling in her chest. "It grows stronger, Abraxas. Every day it does things that I cannot control. Even with the leviathan, I felt as though someone else was in my head, telling me what to do and how to kill it."

"That sounds helpful."

"It is other and therefore terrifying." But she hadn't wanted to talk about this right now. She'd wanted to enjoy him as she hadn't in long months. She'd wanted to see him as he was, to feel him against her heart and to hold his skin against hers.

He was alive, and she'd been so afraid that she would arrive on this isle and find him dead. And here she was, talking about her own fears rather than enjoying the moment with him.

She worried he might learn to fear her. But that was nonsense. He didn't need her to change for him. He loved her exactly as she was. And though they had been apart for such a long time, he'd never wavered from that love.

At least, she didn't think he had.

Lore smoothed her fingers over his heart and pressed her palm above it. "You've been gone for a long time, Abraxas. The journey must have been difficult."

"It was not so bad when one can fly." His knuckles resumed their bumping journey over her spine and then back down. "The cages with our young were heavier than I had carried before, and we stopped many times. But there are islands that only the dragons know of. It gave us time to rest and to feast."

"They hunted?" She couldn't imagine them hunting on their own. They were so little.

"They did more than hunt. They terrorized the inhabitants of every island we stopped at. The creatures of those places did not know what it meant to feel fear until they saw our children."

Lore felt his chest inflate with pride, and she knew he'd done his job as a dragon father. Abraxas had taught them much, it seemed, and a part of her chest ached with it.

She should have been there to see them hunt for the first time. To run alongside them as they found their first deer and to make the final kill if they couldn't do so. She could have eased them into the reality of death as the world forced them to find food on their own. Or she would have hunted for them, so that they never had to see the glassy eyes of an animal that had given its life.

But she hadn't been there. And for that, she would always feel some measure of guilt.

"I missed them," she whispered quietly. "I know there was a part of me that returned because I know what it is to grow up without a mother. To know that she died for you and how selfishly it still aches, as though she gave you up willingly. I didn't want them to suffer as I did all those years ago."

"They may not have known that," he replied. "But they know how much you loved them and that you had no other choice."

Lore let herself feel the disappointment. Finally. It had taken an entire journey across continents to get to this point, but his voice softened the hard case of ice that she'd put around her heart. She felt the loss of so many people. She mourned the loss of a dear friend who had been with her for ages.

Unfortunately, it all hit her at the same time.

Abraxas's eyes widened in shock as the first bubble of a sob erupted out of her. Then he sat up with her in his arms, and Lore tucked herself underneath his chin as the sobs wracked through her.

"What is it?" he asked, his hands dancing up and down her back. "You have to talk to me, Lore."

"I should have been here," she tried to say. "I shouldn't have taken that risk and lost so many of the people I love. But I didn't see another way, Abraxas! The King wouldn't have stopped, and I was just so angry. I wanted him dead and I could see nothing other than the end."

Her rage and anger had cost all of them so much. Goliath had lost his life. Abraxas had lost his mate. Her children had lost their mother and now she expected to waltz back into their lives as though none of it had happened? This was all her fault!

As always, Abraxas seemed to understand why she was upset. He hissed out a long breath against her shoulder, the heat of it warming her in the cold cave room. "This is not your fault, Lorelei. The wheels of fate turned, so that we were all led here. Nothing you could have done would have changed that."

"Why?" she whispered, her words thick and her nose already stuffed. "Because some fool of an elf made a prophecy years ago that a woman like me would come and change the world? Is it right that I was the one to do this when there were so many others who fought before me?"

"We do not get to question what has been done or what will occur." He pulled back and smoothed his thumbs underneath her eyes. "You did what was right, Lore. And though it ripped my heart out of my chest to know that you had died without me, far from my grip, you are here now."

"Does that change a single thing that happened, though? Can you forgive me for what I have done?" Lore looked up at him as though he had all the answers to her fears. As though he was the only one who could speak to her and ease the pain in her chest. "I am here, yes. I would run to you a thousand times over because I love you more than my own soul. More than the peace I felt in that dark place. But that does not change what I have done to you or to our children."

His expression softened. She'd seen him angry, and she'd seen the look of love on his features before. But Lore had never seen this expression of sadness and softness on his face.

Abraxas took his time as he wiped every single tear from her cheeks. He chased after the few that fell after as well until he gripped her jaw with both of his hands. "You are the fire in my lungs. The wind that rustles through my wings. My mate in all things and throughout the journey of life. Without you, I am nothing. You have returned to me and our family, Lore. That is all we will ever ask of you."

Damn it, the tears started up again. He was so sweet and understanding, and she hated that she couldn't be the same with herself. Abraxas always knew exactly what to say.

Sighing, she let her head fall forward and pressed their foreheads together. "I love you, you know."

"I know."

"And I will never give up my life for anyone other than you again. I don't want to die, my love. All I want is to stay here, with you and our children, and to live the life that only you can give me."

"I know that too." He chuckled. "Do you have more apologies?"

"Countless."

"Is that so? Then we will be in this cave all day, and I'm afraid we cannot stay in this little bubble forever. There are people to see."

She took a deep breath and nodded. Of course there were. She needed to see her children, after all, and the anxiety of not seeing them yet had already made her throat close up. "Nyx and Hyperion must look different than I remember."

"That is not entirely of whom I speak." Abraxas untangled their bodies and stood.

Lore couldn't help but stare up the length of him. He'd changed, as people did when time moved on. His body was thinner, but his shoulders were still broad. And though his features had wrinkled with worry and anxiety, she also saw how handsome he was beneath all of it. No matter how much time changed him, Abraxas would forever be her handsome dragon.

She put her hand in his and let him draw her to standing. "Then who are you talking about?"

"You had an entire ship full of people that came to this isle, and I believe they will need some direction on where to go." He lifted a brow. "Just who are they and should I worry about what they will do here?"

"I might have promised the captain whatever gold was left on this island." Lore sheepishly grinned at him. "It's my hope that the rumors of dragons are not true."

Abraxas tilted his head back and laughed. The long cords of his throat stood out in stark relief with his mirth. "Dragons do not hoard gold on Dracomachia, although she is welcome to whatever the crimson dragons took a liking to. Your captain may search this entire place for whatever is of value here."

"Really?"

"Yes." Abraxas tucked her underneath his arm and squeezed her shoulders hard. "She brought back the love of my life, Lore. She can take whatever she wants."

CHAPTER 19

He hadn't realized how incredibly intimate it could be to dress her. Lore had always taken her clothes off before they explored each other. He'd thought that was intimate. But helping her slide the clothing back on, making sure her leather armor was back in place, that her buttons and ties were secure. It felt like he became her armor as he ensured she was safe and well.

Leaning down, he pressed a kiss to her bare shoulder as he slid her sleeve up her arm. "It's good to have you back."

"I imagine it is," she said with a little chuckle, but then turned in his arms. "The only thought that has kept me going is knowing that you were waiting for me here. I was so afraid when Beauty told me you might have... Well. Decided to go where I could not follow."

He almost had. Many times. But Abraxas hoped he had stuck around because his soul recognized the moment she'd returned. It had certainly known the moment she was within his reach.

Sighing, he settled his forehead against hers and breathed in her scent. Every time he did that, it assured him how real she was. She stood right in front of him, and this wasn't some horrible trick of madness to make him believe she was here.

Although, part of him still feared that she would disappear at any moment.

"I saw you," he said quietly. "Almost every day. You were in the trees, climbing a mountain beside me, in the reflection of streams. I could never get away from your image, which Tanis said is normal when one loses a mate, but..."

He felt her stiffen in his arms. "Tanis?"

"Ah. I have not told you everything yet, dear elf of mine." He should have told her right away that there was another dragon here. That their children had grown to monstrous heights and another elf still lived with more knowledge about their people than she could have guessed.

Selfishly, he'd wanted her to himself for a while, before they had to rush out into the real world and explain away what had happened. He'd wanted her to focus on him, and him alone. They'd earned that after everything they had been through.

Blowing out a little breath, he took a step away from her and avoided the look in her eyes. "Come with me," he said. "We have to leave the cave if you want to see everything that has happened."

"Who is Tanis?" she asked again. This time, her voice rang with an iron core.

Was she jealous? He wondered what she must think when he brought up another woman's name regarding his own health and the madness at losing her. He had lost his mind because he'd lost Lore, not this other woman. Surely she must know that meant he'd been focused on her memory and not another.

But he enjoyed this side of her. Abraxas would be a fool if he didn't like the way jealousy flashed in her eyes and how angry she was as she stared at him. It meant she still cared, even if it was a little cruel to let her sit in wait.

"There is so much you don't know about this isle, and so many mysteries to reveal." He held his arm out for her to take. "And I would rather show you all of them than tell you. I think you'd prefer it as well."

Her eyes narrowed on him as though he'd suggested that they take a stroll and ignore all her feelings. Which, he supposed, he had.

She still placed her hand on top of his arm as she had done so long ago in a glade of silver moonlight while the laughter of nobility trickled over them. He couldn't imagine what she had thought then, alone and terrified, knowing that she'd been tasked with killing a king. And, he supposed, he couldn't fathom how she felt right now either. He led her off into a world of the unknown.

Lore had changed since that fateful meeting between them, though. She held herself straighter, more like nobility herself. She didn't fear what the world might bring to her, and instead, she met it head on.

Although, he noticed the rocks at her feet started to float as they passed by them, clattering to the ground when she stepped out of reach. Her power? He'd have to ask her about that. Rowan might know some secrets about the prophecy as well. He'd been around when it had first been uttered. Perhaps he would know what was happening to her.

Right now, he merely wanted to get her out of this cave and into the sun.

Abraxas led her through the gap they'd staggered through, wrapped in each other and the wonder of finding their souls once again bond. He stared at her as the beams of sunlight struck her hair. He hadn't forgotten the golden strands, or how they tangled around her face in the wind. He hadn't forgotten a single instance of the way light played along the columns of her neck or how her skin seemed to sparkle.

She was everything he remembered and more. Everything he loved so much that it made his heart twist in his chest.

Anxiety replaced that happy feeling. What if he brought her out of the cave and no one else saw her? What if this all was some twisted game of his mind?

He didn't know what he'd do if everyone stared at him with sad, drawn expressions as he insisted that Lore had swum in a beam of light from the depths of the ocean and found him again. It made him nervous. So nervous his palms turned slick with sweat and his heart thundered in his chest.

"Lore," he rasped, flipping his hand in her grip so he could hold her a little more tightly.

She frowned at him, the tiny furrows between her eyes both familiar and worrisome. "What is it?"

He couldn't tell her how he feared she might disappear. He couldn't say how he worried the others would think him insane for holding onto a mirage of a woman who had died a long time ago. The sea had brought her back to him, and yet... He still dreaded all of this was in his mind.

Abraxas kissed her and breathed in her beloved scent. Just enough to remind himself that he'd never smelled her like this. Not so strong. She'd always had the faintest presence on the wind, but that didn't mean she was there. Not on the tiny island between Umbra and Dracomaquia. Not when he was on that cliff and he swore he could smell the perfume of her body.

This was different.

She trailed her fingers over his face, gently touching his cheeks before tilting his chin so she could see his expression. "What is wrong, my dragon?"

"I do not know that you are real." He couldn't even look her in the eyes as he said it. He kept his gaze cast down on her arms, waiting for them to disappear. "I fear that I will bring you to my companions and you will float away in the wind. As you have done many times since I left."

Her breath caught in her chest. Lore drew him down for another kiss, a chaste lingering movement that he used to remind him all of this was absolutely real. He wouldn't be able to feel the warmth of her against his skin, or the breath that lingered on his lips even as she drew away.

Eyes closed, that spike of anxiety whispered for him not to open them. If he did, then she'd be gone and he would be alone. Again.

The part of him that was more dragon than man wailed in his mind and he had the sudden fear he might change without warning. He hadn't ever changed without wanting to, but the dragon in him wanted to battle to keep her beside him. And if that required him to burn down the entire world, he would. He would do it for her.

"Abraxas," she whispered, her voice bringing him back from the edge of madness. "I'm right here. I'm not going anywhere."

"The wind always took you."

"Why the wind?"

He shook his head, then swallowed hard. "When you died, you left behind a circle of glowing runes and power. I stepped up to it as the lights dimmed and I felt you in the wind. I felt your soul as you touched my face and then you were gone."

The memory still scared him. He'd known the wind was her. He'd felt her hand, even in the worst loss of his life. She'd touched him so gently, a goodbye that was burned into his flesh for the rest of eternity.

There it was again. Her fingers on his face, cupping his jaw, tracing the outline of his lips.

"I remember that," she whispered, her words floating through the air and shattering his heart. "I remember seeing you, but I hadn't... I didn't know that I had seen you until you said it. You were standing in that circle of runes and I remember how broken you looked."

"I had lost you."

"It was more than that." Her hand tightened on his jaw. "You were feeling my loss as well."

Finally, he opened his eyes. And his stomach dropped out of his chest as he looked between them and saw nothing. He could feel her hand on his face. He knew that she was touching him. But there were no arms before him.

Panic spiked through him as he snapped his gaze up. Still there. He could feel the heat from her body and see her face tightened with anger. But she no longer had arms.

"Lore?" he asked. "Are you..."

She blinked, and the strange expression fell from her face. She looked down between them and let out a little sound of surprise. "Oh, they've been doing that. I'm sorry, they'll come back."

"Why are they—"

"I don't know." She shook her head, interrupting him as though talking about her missing hands made her uncomfortable. "It's part of what I was telling you about. The power has a mind of its own, and I don't know how to control it."

He lifted his hands and grabbed her wrists that he could feel but not see. And then he realized he could see them, at least a little. Her arms might be see through, but they warped the air around them.

"Like glass," he murmured as he looked down at them. "We'll have to see what can be done about this."

"I don't think anything can." She tried to tug her arms free from his grip. "They are going to be like this for a while yet, Abraxas. I'm not interested in figuring this out until we're all safe. Then I can let go of this magic and I don't care where it disappears off to."

His hands spasmed, gripping her perhaps a little too tight. The slight wheeze she let out warned him to be more careful, but then her hands came back into view.

They were cold. So cold they almost burned his hands where he gripped her. Rubbing them, he brought her fingers to his lips and blew upon them, letting the heat of his breath warm her fingers until they felt more like flesh and less like... glass.

She still felt like glass. Delicate and ready to shatter at any moment.

He drew her against his heart and set his chin on top of her head. "We'll figure this out, Lore. Together."

"I'm fine," she muttered against his collarbone. "Nothing to worry about. It got us here, didn't it?"

He wasn't so sure about that. Magic had a way of taking rather than giving. Nothing was free in their world, and he feared what it was taking from her. He wouldn't allow for anything to happen, nothing that would shorten her life any longer than at least three thousand years.

Abraxas wanted a long and happy life with her. No matter how much they had to fight to get that.

But they couldn't stay in this cave forever, no matter how much he wanted to.

Sighing, he squeezed her one last time before he drew back. "Come. I'm sure the others have realized that you are here, and they don't need to wait any longer to see you."

"I'm a little afraid to see how big they've gotten." She tucked a strand of hair behind her ear. "What if they don't recognize me?"

"Oh, they would know you anywhere, just as I would."

She had nothing to fear in that regard. His children and he had never forgotten the mother who had given her life for them. If anything, Lore had become someone to worship in their eyes. Someone who, despite all the odds, had loved them and them alone.

He settled her hand back on his forearm and promised himself that he wouldn't be afraid any longer. She was here, and even if others didn't see her, that didn't matter. He had her, and no one could take that away from him.

Drawing her onto the sands was as natural as though they'd done this a thousand times in their lives. She held onto him with a light grip, her eyes turning toward the sky as though ready to see dragons soaring above her. They weren't quite ready for that yet. He wanted to tell her, but of course, how would she know? Dragons hadn't been around for centuries now. So long that people had forgotten the old myths and the old ways.

Abraxas had expected his children to have gathered near the forest's edge. They would have scented where he was, and likely had smelled her as well. He wouldn't put it past them to believe that something was wrong. So it didn't surprise him to see them lingering by the tree line.

What he didn't expect was for Nyx's hackles to be raised. She'd lowered herself nearly flat to the ground, with her spines poking in all directions. Teeth bared, she stared toward the sea and looked quite terrifying. Hyperion, on the other hand, paced in front of her. His long tendrils of mustache twitched as he walked back and forth before his sister, hissing out a low breath that sounded like the rumble of thunder. Impressive for such a young beast.

Then he turned his attention to the water and realized that Lore's ship had beached itself. A good thing too. He could see that the masts were all broken and the deck itself had crumbled. Lore said her magic had held it together, and her magic had disappeared when Lore left the boat.

"Your people?" he asked, making sure this was the same ship.

"Yes."

And then he saw him.

Draven.

Abraxas bared his teeth with a deep growl. The words ripped from the depths of his being as he snarled, "What is he doing here?"

The last person he expected to see traveling with Lore was that idiot who had tried to take her from his side multiple times. What was she thinking? Draven could not be trusted with her alone, especially not when that elf wanted her for his own.

"Lore," he snarled, but he noticed her attention was not on the dark elf. No, she stared at her children with equal parts horror and awe.

"Nyx?" she whispered, and the wind caught her words. "Hyperion?"

Without thinking, she sprinted toward the hissing dragons. A call went up amongst her people, who all raised their weapons before arrows were notched and a shout echoed down the beach.

Battle broke out before Abraxas could even take a breath.

CHAPTER 20

She didn't care that the sailors were likely terrified of seeing not only one dragon but three standing before them. Perhaps she should have insisted that Allura tell them where they were going or why they were doing it, but part of her still didn't care.

Her children were right there. Within reach. All she had to do was run towards them and she would have them in her arms. Or at least, within her grasp.

They were so much bigger than they had been. Nyx glistened in the afternoon light, her scales so lovely that they looked like chips of gemstones. And Hyperion! He'd changed the most, and she didn't know where to look with him. She remembered him being a bouncy little ball of dragonling and now he was long and lean and oh, so terrifying when he hissed like that.

It was wonderful. Remarkable. They were alive, and she was

alive and her thoughts wouldn't stop racing through her head with a million questions she wanted to ask them.

Had their father behaved? He was supposed to treat them well, and if he hadn't, then she would have his head. Had they been safe on their journey? Abraxas had better not have put them in any danger whatsoever. Otherwise she'd... have his head again, she supposed. The power inside her might even make that possible if she tried hard.

A part of her heard the nocking of arrows and the whistles as they flew through the air. Arrows that would tear the thin membranes of her children's wings.

The power inside her flexed, and she only had to lift a hand toward those weapons that zinged toward them. She didn't have to look. She could feel what happened. Lore knew that the metal tips turned to dust the moment they hit the barrier she'd thrown up. She knew the instant the wood shattered into a million tiny splinters like sawdust in a mill.

Nothing would touch her children. No one but herself.

Lore skidded to a stop in front of her dragon children and pressed those dangerous hands to her heart. "You're here," she whispered, her eyes wide as though in doing so she could see more of them at once. "You're okay."

The children blinked at her, then looked at each other. Nyx was the first to step forward, her movement hesitant until she said, "Mother?"

Oh.

Oh, they could speak now.

Her heart thundered in her chest at the rare pleasure of hearing her child's voice. She'd spoken with Nyx once, but only that one time. They were old enough to use those vocal cords when they were in their dragon form and it broke her heart.

Tears gathered in her eyes, then dripped down her cheeks as she nodded and opened her arms. "It's me. I'm so sorry it took me so long to find you."

The dragon children wasted no time. They ran for her like little puppies, but they were so large they'd knock her over. Lore felt the power flex inside her and though she stiffened with worry, it wasn't aimed toward her children. Instead, she felt it flex down into the ground and solidify her stance so her children couldn't knock her over. They nuzzled their heads against her, and all she could see was the flashing of scales and the wide stretch of wings as they descended upon her.

A boom of answering magic rocked the ground, and she had to move away from the mound of dragon wings to peer through it. Abraxas had changed back into his dragon form and she swore he'd gotten bigger since she saw him last. He was larger than a building with his wings spread between her people and that of their children. He snarled at them, the fires in his throat already glowing and vibrating with a sound like thunder. A warning, she knew, but also a test.

Allura and her crew had been gearing up for another attack. Likely because they thought Lore needed to be saved from the terrifying dragons who had attacked her with flailing wings and flashing scales.

They didn't know, she remembered. They had no idea.

"Stop," she said with a laugh. "I have to get up before they all descend upon us. The last thing we need is another war, don't you think?"

Hyperion snorted, then licked her entire body with a tongue that was sharper than sandpaper. "Let them fight Father. He never loses."

But their father was tired, she wanted to point out. He'd been fighting for his entire life and he deserved a few moments where he wasn't trying to piece himself back together. The last thing Abraxas needed was to pour his energy into keeping the sailors she'd brought here at bay.

She shook her head with a laugh and then shoved at them. "Enough, you two. Let me stop your father from killing all the people I brought here with me."

"They'll learn," Nyx replied. "They will flee or they will stop trying to stick little arrows into us. It's quite annoying."

The dragons had no fear of weapons or humans, she realized. And though she admired that strength, she also knew how dangerous that confidence was.

It was humans, after all, who had destroyed this place to begin with.

Lore untangled herself from her dragon children who wanted to keep her with them, laughing the entire time before she waltzed across the sands to Abraxas. He kept his wing spread wide, carefully hiding them from the sight of those terrible beings that wanted to hurt them. But he arched his neck at the sight of her, tilting his head down so she could put her hand on his nose.

"Let me through," she said.

"They're still shooting arrows." But he didn't wince even once. As though those arrows weren't sticking through his wings. She could already see the head of one through the web of veins and dim red light.

"And none will touch me." Lore didn't know how she could be so certain of that, but her words felt as though they were law.

And the moment she thought about it, she heard the arrows stop hitting Abraxas as well. His eyes widened, surprise running through him as she knew it would.

"Was that you?" he asked.

"I told you the powers are uncontrollable." Although, this time, her words were a slight lie. They were very much uncontrollable, but they seemed to listen to her requests as her other magic would. They knew when she wanted something or needed it, and that was what happened.

Perhaps this was what life as a goddess was like. She could ask the world to give her something and it would bend to her will in that way. Although, she supposed that was a dangerous game to play as well. The world didn't like to bend, and asking too much would break it.

Lore patted his wing and gestured for him to move. "Let me see them, please. I think they also need to see that I am alive and not down the gullet of a monstrous dragon."

"Monstrous?" he repeated with a snort, but lowered his wing. "I'll admit, your size makes you easy to swallow."

"A horse is easy for you to swallow."

Abraxas lowered his head so his eye was level with her, moving his neck as though he were walking beside her, even though she knew the movement was slight on his part. "Are you teasing me, Lady of Starlight? I could eat a horse to show you it would get stuck in my throat. It's at least two bites unless one has terrible table manners."

"And you have lovely manners."

"I spent most of my time in a palace, after all."

She'd missed this. Bantering with him back and forth as only two ancient beings could do. Neither of them were overly concerned by the amount of weapons aimed at them, nor even the cannon someone had dragged out of the ship's bowels to point at his head. The worst it would do was dent one of his scales if it ever reached him. Lore would make sure it didn't.

Allura walked forward, hesitant with her steps. "Lore? Are you still alive?"

She held her arms out and patted herself down. "I seem fine."

No one seemed apt to believe her until Draven took a couple of steps forward. He was slow as he approached, although his eyes never strayed from Abraxas. The dark elf knew how much history was between them, and he had to know that Abraxas didn't want to see him here.

Lore had forgotten the two of them didn't like each other. And she'd also forgotten that Draven had been so interested in her in the first place. He'd kept his hands to himself, and those wandering eyes of his had stilled in the time since she'd been gone.

Abraxas didn't know that, though.

She watched the two of them glare at each other with an amused expression on her face. She should step in, just to make sure they were aware they couldn't kill each other. But also she quite enjoyed knowing that both of them were angry at each other just for existing in her life.

The jealousy was a pleasant reminder that he still felt as strongly about her as he had all those months ago.

"Draven didn't give me much choice but to bring him," she said.

"Of course he didn't," Abraxas snarled. "He'd walk to the ends of the earth for you, even if a dragon's maw waited for him at the end."

"It would take a lot for the dragon to eat someone like me." Draven flashed him a feral smile. "Swallowing a sword is difficult, after all."

"Swallowing anything as little as you is not very hard." Abraxas picked his head up, looming over the tiny people below him. Just so that Draven could see how large he actually was. "You don't have a healthy enough fear of me, elf."

Lore would be happy to let them continue, but she could see the sailors were getting all riled up again. They put their hands on their weapons and eyed the two dragons behind Abraxas as well.

Most people know of the King's crimson dragon. They knew Abraxas existed, and some had seen him flying over their ships or towns. But they didn't know what to do with two other dragons they hadn't known about. Perhaps some of these sailors thought they could kill a single dragon. Together. But three? That was suicide.

If she didn't stop them from arguing, then they would all stand in the middle of an arrow hailstorm again and she'd gotten tired of that.

"Stop it, you two. You'll scare my children and then I will get involved. Neither of you wants that. Put it behind the two of you or fight it out later. Right now, we all need to act like adults."

They both glared at her for calling them children, but it was Allura who stepped forward and put her sword back in its holster at her side. "Children?"

"They are." Lore looked her in the eye and gestured back at the dragons. "And those are mine."

"Yours," Allura repeated, her brows furrowed in confusion. "How can they be yours?"

Lore felt the stares of her dragons on her back and she knew this moment was as important to them as it was to the siren. She had to choose her words carefully, and therefore, she chose them from the heart. "I was there when they were born. I carried them across all of Umbra to watch them hatch and carved away their shells. They are my children, Allura, and I should have been here to raise them. Why did you think I wanted to cross that nightmarish sea?"

"For him." Allura pointed to Abraxas with a shaking finger. "You didn't tell me there were more of them."

"There should be more of them. There should be an entire island full of dragons and a good reason for us to stay away and instead, look at this place." Her heart shattered looking around them. Lore hated knowing that there once were countless dragons here, and now was only a haunted shell. "We did this. People like us did this. And I'm here to fix it."

"What makes you think it can be fixed?" the siren hissed. "The dragons died out for a reason, Lore. There were so few of them left according to the recounts, and why would I ever think that someone like me can help them? There's only three dragons left, Lore. You helped make there be three of them. Why isn't that enough?"

Rage shivered underneath her skin. "Because they deserve better than that, Allura. We all did. And if I can help make their lives easier than mine was, then I will do it."

"Why? You're not the goddess everyone claims you are. You're an elf who happened to fall into the wrong plan."

The ground shook underneath her and Lore knew it was her anger getting out of control. She needed to rein herself in. If she didn't, then she could very well drag all of them into the pits of the earth itself. She'd bury them all and would feel better for it.

Until a hand came down on her shoulder. From behind her. A hand where there had not been a person before. She stilled, looking up at Abraxas to confirm that he was still in his dragon form. And her children couldn't turn yet, could they?

Lore glanced over her shoulder and into the eyes of a very old elf. There were even wrinkles in the corners of his eyes and wings of gray at his temples. His skin was burnished by the sun, stretched over rippling muscle as much of her kind still had in their elderly years.

He smiled at her, bright teeth gleaming in the sun. And that kindness made her shiver, although she didn't know why. The elves had never been kind to her. Perhaps that was the fear that burst into gooseflesh all along her body, of what he would do to her for seeing that kindness.

"I can see now why the prophecy claimed you would change much. Your voice is well heard, young elf. But I fear you have a lot to learn in how to speak without shouting at people." His smile crinkled his face into well-worn lines of laughter and happiness. "But it is good to meet you, regardless. We've been waiting a long time."

"Excuse me?" Lore replied. "I have no idea who you are."

"As most prophets are forgotten, so am I." He bowed low, and then grinned up at her again. "Although I'll admit, I was a terrible prophet and much better at being a farmer. I'm glad my sister was a good artist, though. Abraxas informed me you saw her work in the mountains."

She felt faint. This was the elf who had created the prophecy about her? Or did he only know of it?

Her vision skewed, and she had to balance herself on his shoulder. "You have a lot of explaining to do," she whispered.

"I imagined that I might."

CHAPTER 21

Abraxas led them all toward the camp, wondering exactly how they were going to fit all these new bodies and feed all these new mouths. He'd been so lost in the fog of his own mind, it was hard for him to remember what their food situation even was here.

Likely, they would need to hunt. Abraxas felt more like himself, though, and he knew Lore could hunt with the best. Between the two of them, they could feed this entire village of people for a few weeks.

The sailors could not stay, however. He'd already made that decision before they hit the shore. While he understood they were looking for treasure, he also knew the heart of a siren captain like Lore's friend. The woman had no ability to stay in one place for very long. Her restless spirit would send her wandering for ages before the sea swallowed her up. That was the only fitting end for a woman like her.

Grumbling, he moved his tail a little aggressively and knocked a few of the soldiers over. They stumbled to the side and then remembered what he'd said. They could follow, but don't get too close.

Thankfully, he was still in his dragon form or they would have seen his grin. Instead, all they saw was a dragon baring its teeth at them.

Their faces all went white and the three men gave him a little more room. Good. They should fear him, even though he had vowed to help them. Soon, they would understand that dragons were terrifying beings with fickle minds.

A soft snort interrupted his musings and Lore looked up at him where she strode beside his shoulder. "You're doing that on purpose."

"Doing what?" he asked, although he knew what she meant.

"Give them a little time to get used to even seeing a dragon, let alone three." The smile on her face never wavered when she looked at him, as though the expression was unbidden and one she couldn't control. "They're not staying long, anyway. I promised them gold. That's the only reason they're even on this shore."

"And because their ship is broken."

"They will fix it."

He tilted his head to the side, peering down at her with one eye. "Why does that feel as though you volunteered me to help them fix it?"

"You are the largest person here. I'm sure knocking down a few trees would be so easy for you." That wry grin twisted a little. "Besides, I wouldn't mind watching you work. It's been a long time since I've witnessed the true power of a dragon."

He knew she was manipulating him. But he wouldn't mind flexing his muscles and showing his wings off a little if it made her look at him like that for a little longer. He'd missed that look. The one that said she couldn't stop staring at him, with the heat in her eyes that whispered she wanted more time with him. Alone.

Oh, how he'd missed her. Life simply wasn't the same without his Lore.

Grumbling a little, he flicked his tail again. This time missing all the men who stood behind him. "Fine," he replied, lifting his head up as they got close to the clearing. "I'll help them get their ship ready, only to see them gone sooner from this isle."

"Of course. That's the only reason."

"The only one."

How did she make his heart feel so light? All it took was a little bantering, a laugh startled out of her as though she hadn't expected the sound, and he felt like a god. He was the only one who could make her feel like that. And knowing she'd traveled over half the world to get to him? Abraxas had never felt so lucky in his life. This woman had dug her fingers deep into his heart and reminded him how much he loved her.

As if he had ever forgotten.

They reached the encampment far too quickly, and Abraxas let the dragon melt away from his body. It was easier this time. As though just being that large and powerful had given his human form the health that it needed. His power had already started to heal what his loss and mourning had taken from him. Soon he would be back to his full strength.

Having Lore near him gave him all that. Though there was still a lingering sense of guilt inside him. One that he couldn't quite shake off.

He hadn't known she was alive. He hadn't felt when she'd come back and in lacking that ability, he had nearly made her go on another journey to find him.

Her hand came down on his back, smoothing up and down as he used to do so often for her. Her touch then trailed down his arm. Lore tangled their fingers together, weaving their touch so he could feel the tight squeeze and strength of her hand.

"Thank you for bringing them here," she whispered. "Even him."

She thought he was still angry about Draven. In a way, he was. He didn't like the deepmonger and certainly didn't want him anywhere near his children. But Draven had proven himself in that war. He'd taken care of Lore in the moments where Abraxas couldn't.

Begrudgingly, he shrugged. "He can stay if he wishes. Let me speak with Rowan, my love. We need to figure out where to put all these people."

Rowan and Tanis hadn't expected an entire horde of humans to descend upon their quiet home. That much was certain.

He strode toward the aging elf, who wore a smile on his face that didn't quite reach his eyes. Of course, Rowan would want to welcome everyone into the glade and make sure they were all settled. But he had a feeling the elf also had a hard time imagining where to place them.

"There is always the old town," Abraxas said as he strode up to the old man.

"You mean the town which has been in ruins for ages now?" Rowan shook his head. "Only shambles remain there."

That could become a problem then. Abraxas glanced around the clearing and knew this wasn't enough room. Perhaps the sailors had tents back on that ship so they could set up, but that wouldn't give them enough room to even move in this small space. And then there was the problem of Tanis.

He glanced over at the elf and knew that Rowan had the same

thought. Tanis wouldn't want so many people next to the nest she hatched.

"Will she be all right?" he asked, but Abraxas already knew the answer.

"She grows... testy," Rowan replied. "Her anger is quick these days as the eggs get closer to hatching. It should be any day now, but I fear what might happen if we push her too far."

As did he.

Abraxas knew a dragon female would get overly protective in the last stages of hatching. The rumors of their wrath ran deep in the lore of dragons. He'd heard of females killing their mates if the male got too close to the nest. They were swift in ripping out the throats of the male they loved, hissing with all their spines raised. As though they couldn't even see the male who had once dreamt of a future with them.

Keeping anyone so close would only end in folly. The sailors would need to return to the shore.

"I'll inform them," he muttered, casting his gaze over the multitude of people who had just made a rather long journey. Again. "But we should feed them first."

"There is plenty of dried deer meat. I believe there should be some bread as well, and ale." Rowan hesitated to say the last part. "Though I had hoped to keep that for myself."

Abraxas clapped his hand down on the elf's shoulder. "Then you should drink it, my friend. We'll keep that our little secret."

The relief on Rowan's face proved how important it had been to him. The man didn't have to share all of himself every time there was someone in need. But apparently, the elf felt as though such sacrifice was necessary.

Perhaps it was because he hadn't seen other people who looked like him in such a long time. Tanis had been his only companion for centuries, as they told it. And that had to wear on a man. Even though he loved Tanis and that woman was everything he'd ever wanted, having other friends was important.

And apparently, that had manifested into him trying to please everyone who arrived on his isle.

"It'll be fine," Abraxas added, unsure of what was the best way to comfort an ancient being. "Food and fresh water should be more than enough to satisfy their bellies."

"If you say so."

"I do." Abraxas squeezed the other man's shoulder and then froze when he heard gasps erupting from behind him.

The entire crowd of people seemed to freeze, and then shouts rose. Abraxas spun, the knot in his chest twisting tighter even before he saw what had happened. He knew. Of course he did.

Lore seized in Draven's arms. The deepmonger was trying to lower her onto the ground. It appeared she wasn't standing on her own, and she was convulsing so violently that Draven couldn't let go of her. He had one arm around her back, the other trying to catch her hands that were already curling to her chest.

Abraxas didn't know how he moved so fast. One breath he stood beside Rowan, the next he was sprinting toward Lore with his heart in his throat. He wouldn't lose her this soon. He couldn't.

Dropping to his knees beside them, he reached for her.

"What happened?" he hissed as he gathered her up in his arms.

Draven shook his head. "I don't know. She was fine standing next to me and then this happened."

Sweat already beaded on her brow and her eyes had rolled back in her head. All he could see was the whites of her eyes and the listless movement behind her lids as she shook. Draven didn't let go of her hands, and Abraxas stared in horror at the reason. She was curling her wrists so forcefully that she was in danger of breaking them. Draven's biceps already shook as he tried to keep her hands still. Even at the uncomfortable angle, it was better than broken.

Rowan shouted from the cabin, "Bring her here!"

He didn't know what to do. Would cold water help? Could he dunk her into the ocean and perhaps that would stop it?

Too many eyes were on them. He couldn't breathe. Couldn't think. All he knew was that his mate was in his arms, in pain, and he had frozen with the fear of what might happen.

"Abraxas," Draven whispered, his voice pitched low so no one would hear their conversation. "Let's bring her into the cabin. It's safe enough there for now. She's going to come out of this on her own."

He looked into the other man's eyes and found a steady calm staring back at him. Draven wasn't afraid. He wasn't terrified, nor did he think they were going to lose Lore.

It was enough.

Abraxas nodded and then stalked toward the cabin. Together, they drew Lore into the shadows of the home where Abraxas had just laid, thinking he was about to die. Had nearly died.

He laid her down on that same cot, hoping that maybe the scent of his blankets would bring her back.

"Here," Draven said, holding her wrists out to him. "I can't hold her much longer. We'll take turns."

Grabbing onto her hands, he was surprised at the power there. Abraxas lurched forward as her hands tried to twist before he got control over her.

"Lore," he whispered, staring down at her face that looked unfamiliar in pain. "Come back to me."

"Get out of the way," Rowan snapped. He shoved Draven aside and then dumped a pile of herbs and pots on top of Lore's stomach. At Abraxas's growl, he muttered, "Oh stop, she can't feel anything right now and I need to get the right medicine."

It never ceased to amaze Abraxas how little the elf feared dragons. He should at least know better than to tempt a dragon male when his mate was in pain. But what could Abraxas do? He had to hold her hands.

Lore's back bent in pain, her heels digging into the cot as her spine curved far too much.

"Hold her," Rowan said as he plucked the right pot off her. "I need to get this into her mouth."

Draven rounded the cot and placed his hands on her shoulders. With a firm grip, he forced Lore's head to stop moving and held it still for Rowan to walk over to. The elderly elf took a deep, steadying breath before he unstopped the jar.

"This is going to get worse before it gets better," Rowan said. "But this at least will keep her still."

The vile liquid looked like blood. The black ooze dripped out of it and hit her closed mouth. Abraxas thought it would dribble down her cheeks, but instead, it seeped into her skin wherever it touched.

"What is it?" he asked.

"Poison," Rowan replied before he grabbed a handful of what looked like laurel leaves. He then pried Lore's mouth open and packed it full with the leaves before letting her jaw clamp shut again with a snap. "The magic inside her will have to deal with the poison before it can continue harming her body. Hopefully she'll snap out of it before that happens."

Stunned silence filled the room before Abraxas growled, "You poisoned her?"

The elf took his time replying. He sat down, breathing heavily, his back braced against the wall. "The elders used to whisper about elves like her. Elves with power beyond any reckoning. That magic could save a village from starvation or bring a dragon out of the sky. But it always came with a price."

Lore's hands loosened in his grip. No longer trying to break her own hands, she seemed to relax into the cot. But her eyes never settled, moving behind her lids as though she dreamed.

"A price?" he rasped.

"We cannot bend the world to our whims without paying for it." Rowan shook his head. "She used that power too much, and now the ancient ones will extract whatever price they require from her. And it may be a price she does not want to pay."

His heart ached. Abraxas rubbed his hand over his chest, trying to still the thudding behind his ribs. "Just what will that price be?"

"None of us know."

Draven hissed out a long breath. "She only used her magic to stop arrows. Hardly a parlor trick to the Silverfells."

"That was not all she did." Rowan's eyes seemed to glow in the darkness. "She killed a leviathan, deepmonger. A creature as old as the gods themselves. There is always a price for such a death."

Settling in beside her, all three of them stared at the woman who remained so far out of their reach. Every time she twitched, they all leaned forward, only to slump back as she settled again.

Abraxas knew that his heart would not find peace until she opened her eyes again.

CHAPTER 22

Lore was awake, but not. Asleep, but aware in the land of the dreaming. The power inside her had grown so painfully wide that it felt as though it would burst out of her skin.

A dull discomfort ached through her entire body, and she had the thought that her physical form might be in immense pain. If she could feel it in the dreaming, then it would hurt to return.

That whispering power in her mind said she didn't have to return. She could leave that form behind and go back to that realm she'd originally left. The one where she had waited. The realm where there was only peace and rest and something beyond that which both terrified and excited her.

It seemed, for the time being, at least, she could choose which realm she wanted. If she let go of the painful life she left behind, then she could continue on. Without a thought.

Dying seemed too harsh a word for what it would be. It wasn't death. She'd already seen that and it was bloody and hard. Death meant that she experienced all that pain willingly while she fought to free herself from its clutches. But this was not that struggle. It was... moving on.

Blinking her eyes open, she refused that desire. That need. She wouldn't let it cajole her into leaving behind all those she loved so very much. Abraxas. Her children. Draven. Beauty. Even young Zephyr, who she'd barely had time to speak with. None of them deserved to have her die again. At least not so soon.

Lore sat up and pressed the heels of her palms into her eyes. They ached as though there was a headache throbbing there, but she couldn't quite feel the same amount of pain she knew her physical body experienced. In the dreaming, it merely made her feel a little slower. A little less like herself.

She'd get better if she moved, she decided. Lore slowly stood and looked around herself. The power must have placed her somewhere pleasant to hide from all that pain.

But this was not a pleasant place in the slightest.

Lore straightened as she surveyed the great hall of the Umbral castle. Just as it had been the first time she ever seen it.

The beautiful flowers grew in abundance here. They spilled over the railings of the stairs in a thousand colors that shouldn't exist and yet did. They stretched up to the ceiling, violet wisteria hanging down from the ceiling and glistening with magical orbs. Even the hanging lanterns were still there with the tiny pixies stuck inside them.

She reached for the one that was so familiar. It was the first moment she'd met Abraxas, she mused as she opened up the small cage. The pixie inside was so tired. It had been fighting to breathe inside the glass, and it rested against her palms, its wings shuddering.

"It's all right," she whispered. "You're going to be fine."

And in some strange way, she wondered if this was an alternate dimension. If she'd somehow thrown herself into a different timeline to relive the moments that meant so much to her all over again. If only so that she could see him in all his glory, before she'd known the dragon lurked underneath his skin. To feel that she was falling in love all over again.

A soft smile on her face, she listened for the movement behind her. The movement she knew would come.

Footsteps. She'd heard them a hundred times in her dreams as she remembered this exact moment, but turning around made her feel as though she were about to experience something magical all over again.

But the shadows at the back of the room weren't tall enough. They didn't stretch to his great height, nor did they seem to cling to his shoulders as they used to. The lingering effects of the King's magic had always tried to hold on to him, as though even the King had known that Abraxas wasn't his loyal servant.

The shadows twisted and warped into a different figure all together. Her mother stepped out of the shadows, exactly as Lore had remembered her in those last moments.

Her mother used to wear leather. Every day, in fact. Lore remembered seeing her in those tight leggings and a leather corset that hugged her waist tight. Straps had decorated her legs, usually used for holding weapons, but as a child, she'd never seen those.

In the moments before her mother's death, she hadn't been wearing her usual garb. The Umbral Knights had tossed her into a dungeon where they had stripped her of all that. They'd thrown her into a gray dress that barely hit her shins, with no arms to help keep her warm. It had looked more like a sack.

She remembered how proud her mother had looked, even tied to a stake glaring into the eyes of a dragon. She'd tilted her head back and stared him down with a knowing scowl. As though accusing him of all he had done and all he would do for the King.

Lore could look back at the memory without anguish. Watching it play again, she realized that Abraxas had hesitated. He'd looked into her mother's eyes with something similar to sadness. Or perhaps a kinship of two creatures who knew they were about to do something they didn't want to do.

She shuddered, staring at the visage of her mother and not knowing what this memory wanted from her. This dream had gotten out of hand. The wavering image of her memory shattered, and she returned to the Great Hall.

Tears blurred her vision as her mother walked forward, holding out her hands. Just as she had when Lore had been very little and hadn't seen her mother in a very long time.

"Hello, Buttercup," her mother whispered.

That nickname.

Lore hadn't heard it in years. She'd almost forgotten about it. Her mother used to call her that. They had gone into a field when she was very little and Lore laughed when her mother placed the yellow blooms under her chin too... too...

Brows twisting, she asked the mirage, "What were the rules of buttercup flowers again?"

"It meant you liked butter."

"I didn't like butter," she replied with a shake of her head. "I hated it, actually. The color always made me think it was unnatural."

Her mother's face creased in a smile and Lore's eyes burned again. Her mother's smile had always been warm, even in the darkest of days. The smooth waterfall of her pale hair was tucked behind her pointed ears, just like Lore's. And though there were wrinkles of time at the corners of her eyes, she'd always focused on the high arches of her mother's cheekbones, the way her lips always pointed into a lovely pink bow, and the determination in the set of her brows.

How had she conjured up her mother's memory so well? Lore barely remembered what she looked like outside of this dreaming world, and yet, now she remembered in exquisite detail. This was her mother, without question or fail.

Sniffing hard, Lore wiped her nose on the back of her sleeve. "It's good to see you."

"You think this is a dream, don't you?" Her mother took another step closer, still holding out her hands. "Touch me, daughter of mine. Feel my hands in yours and know this is no dream."

Lore couldn't. What if her hands went right through her? And in that moment, she experienced the fear that had jolted through Abraxas the moment he'd seen her. Alive. Well. Still whole.

She shook her head and took a step away from her mother. "I can't. I cannot touch you and know for certain that I can see you in this place. I'll never leave."

A soft chuckle was her answer. "Oh, I think you'll leave. You have someone waiting for you, don't you? I might not be able to see everything in the land of the living, but a mother knows when her daughter meets her soulmate."

Lore's stomach churned with a flash of guilt. The man who she knew was more than just a mate, but a soulmate, was the same person who had killed her mother. The woman standing in front of her had every right to hate him. And Lore didn't know what she would do if her mother disapproved of him.

But this wasn't her mother. This was a conjuring of her own mind to make her feel better about losing the woman she desperately wanted to see right now.

"He's a good man," she whispered. "I love him very much."

"Yes, I know. That's why I'm here." Her mother took the choice away from her. She reached forward and gathered her daughter's hands with her own, real and warm and solid. Squeezing tight, her mother shook her head with a smile. "I forgave him long ago, Buttercup."

Hearing those words broke something in her. Lore launched forward and wrapped her arms around her mother's shoulders. Lore held onto the woman who had given her life and sobbed into her hair. Because she still smelled like her mother. She still felt like the woman who had rocked her to sleep at night and even though that broke Lore's heart to know that she'd never have this again while awake.

Lore didn't know how long she cried. All she knew was that when she finally stepped back, she felt so much better. As though she'd purged a darker side of herself that she hadn't realized she had carried for a very long time.

Her mother smiled at her and patted her sides a few times. "Better?"

"Better."

"Good, because as much as I'd love to say this is a visit, I'm here for a reason."

Of course. Lore never experienced good things in her life without them happening for a reason. Though visiting with the woman she'd lost so long ago would have been a gift from the heavens themselves, she knew this was part of a bigger plan.

Clearing her throat, she tried to dash all the tears from her eyes and focus on the now. "What news do you have from the land of the dead?"

"You know your body is..." Her mother hesitated, as though she didn't want to point out the obvious.

Another twinge echoed down her spine. Lore wondered what her body endured out there, the belated dull ache spreading through her entire being for a moment before loosening again. She looked down at her hands especially, noting the pain in her wrists.

Then everything eased a bit. The pain dulled until she couldn't feel it at all.

Lore nodded. "I know there is something happening to my physical form, yes. I can feel the pain if I focus."

"We feel little here, I'm afraid." Her mother shrugged. "Everything is a little dull in the dreaming."

"How are you even here?" Lore knew there were more important questions to ask, but this felt like she finally had a chance to converse with her mother again. Like they had when she was little and she asked a thousand questions every night before falling asleep. "I didn't think the dead could dream."

"There is so much you do not know about the world, Buttercup. But there is so much I cannot tell you, either." Her mother winked. "The lands beyond life are a secret for a reason. None of us can know the truth until we pass on ourselves."

"But I was dead," she corrected. "For six months."

"That was not dead." Her mother's face twisted into something like disappointment. "Do you not remember?"

Lore had no idea what her mother was talking about. Of course, she didn't remember. Nothing had happened. She had floated in that in-between place until she'd heard Abraxas calling for her, likely because her soul refused to leave his side.

As if she could hear Lore's thoughts, her mother's mouth twisted with sadness. "No, darling. If a soul could pause its inevitable decline, then I would have stayed for you. I would have been here for you, waiting all this time."

Her heart stuttered in her chest. Not another wave of pain this time, but a realization that her memories had been taken from her. She did not know what was happening to her body, her magic, or even now. More choices taken from her and a life that she couldn't quite live. Not yet, at least.

"Then what is happening to me?" she asked, her voice a hoarse whisper. "I know something changed. My power is out of control and I cannot seem to make it do what I want. There are other changes too. Compulsions, I'll call them, that want me to do things I'd never thought before."

"Your power is yours, and only amplified right now." Her mother's gaze turned sad, and she reached for Lore's hands. "Listen to me, daughter of mine. Your body is struggling in the realm of the living. It can only sustain so much pain. You can hide here from it all you want, but sooner rather than later, there will not be a body for you to go back to."

Lore swallowed hard. "Then how do I stop these incidents from happening?"

"You have to remember."

The whisper echoed throughout the great hall, but it didn't help.

"I can't remember," Lore hissed. "Nothing happened in that time while I was between realms. I was floating in nothing for six months and then I awakened because I heard him call out for me. That's all."

"It was so much more than that."

"Then why can't you tell me?" The shout erupted from her in a burst of frustration and she felt the great hall shake beneath her feet. Lore shook her head to clear it, an apology already on her lips.

But her mother released her hands and backed away. "You've already been here too long, Lore. You need to go back to your body."

"Just tell me what I need to know."

"I cannot tell you the secrets of the dead." Her mother took another few steps back, her expression twisting as though something hurt. "You need to go before you cannot wake up. I have kept you here too long."

"Wait, I just want to say goodbye—"

Lore froze as she smelled it first. Smoke. The fires that had set her mother ablaze had smelled like that. She remembered the coiling smoke that had come out of Abraxas's nose as he stared down at her mother with obvious pity. The smoke had reached her nose first, before the flames had burst out of his mouth.

The same flames that now licked at her mother's skirts. They started around her shin, a new way to watch the woman she loved most die.

"Mother," she whispered, reaching out her hands as though she could help. "Let me—"

"Go!" her mother screamed, and the word was so similar to the first time she'd died. She even wore the same expression she'd made when she realized that her daughter would watch her die. "Leave this place, Lore!"

But she didn't know how.

As the flames licked at her mother's skin and her eyes turned glassy and gray, Lore knew that she would be forced to see this moment many times in her dreams again.

Biting her lip hard, she squeezed her eyes shut and wished herself away from this place.

CHAPTER 23

They waited for almost a full day. Abraxas stood in the doorway with a fresh pile of cloth in his hands. The siren captain had proved useful in a situation like this, as she'd kept a lot of fabric aboard the ship.

Why? He didn't ask. Abraxas didn't care why she'd kept it. All he knew was that they needed to keep Lore cold and the wet fabric would help. The fevers had set in overnight. Rowan's poison could no longer stop her listless movements.

"She fights," the elderly elf had said, patting his shoulder in the middle of the night. "That is all we can ask of her."

She'd fought long enough. Abraxas had stood beside her for battle after battle, and they had both grown tired of it.

Sighing, he shifted the fabric in his arms and gave a little nod to the siren waiting outside the door. "I'll let you know if anything changes," he said. "She hasn't woken yet."

"She probably won't for a while if it has anything to do with her powers." Allura let out a little shudder. "I've never seen anything like it. She kept up a wind that made our ship move faster than a leviathan and then killed it herself. I didn't even know that was possible."

For all they knew, it wasn't. Or at least, it hadn't been possible before Lore.

"Thank you," he said again. He'd already thanked her four times on their walk back to the cabin, but Allura didn't seem bothered by it.

Instead, she tilted her head to the side and surveyed him as she had the last time. "I was expecting you to be cruel, you know. Everyone talks about the King's dragon like you're some demon who will hunt us all down. But you're not half bad."

He'd take the compliment even if it was a little back handed. He knew that there was something underneath all that. Perhaps a measure of forgiveness that he hadn't been aware he needed.

"I'll send someone to find you if she wakes."

Allura waved a hand in the air and turned to go. "No need! She'll find me when she's ready."

The sailors were already cutting down trees at the edge of the forest. He knew they would find wood strong enough to replace their masts. But their work was slow, and he had to wonder if that was partly because they wanted their gold, partly because the isle fascinated them... and because they were all waiting for Lore to wake.

It had only been a day, he reminded himself as he returned his attention to the darkness. Only one day felt like a lifetime.

He stepped through the fabric barrier that Rowan had hung as a door and walked inside. The elves were at the bed, and for a moment, he could pretend that Lore spoke with them. They put their heads together, murmuring in the darkness of the room.

Abraxas had wanted them to light candles. To open up the windows so that she wouldn't be shrouded in shadows. But Rowan had insisted that she needed to rest, and no one could achieve any healing when the sun was beaming in their face.

But he knew she'd want to see the sun. And the moon.

Draven looked up from where they were talking and paused. "Abraxas. You're back."

Was he not supposed to be? Immediately the hairs on his arms raised, as if they were his spines. He straightened his shoulders and glared at the other man. "Yes, I am."

"We were just talking about how to get her to eat. But it's only been a day. Food isn't as concerning as water." Draven sighed and took a big step back from her bedside. "Rowan was the one who brought it up. You can stop looking at me like that."

Like what? Like he wanted to devour the deep monger, so he didn't have to look at that concerned expression on his face any more?

He knew he had to let go of that old pain for a little while, though. Lore needed all of them to be at the ready. They were the only ones who could look over at her while she fought her way back to them. Again.

He dropped the blankets in his arm on the table nearby and braced himself on the edge of it. "I'll get the water down her throat."

"You can't drown her."

He growled at Draven, the sound coming from deep in his belly. "I'm aware."

What did the other man think he was going to do? Kill her? Abraxas might not have the most delicate hand of those in here, but he was the most concerned about losing her. He'd only just gotten her back, after all. Draven had been enjoying an entire romantic journey across the seas with her.

And just what had that deepmonger tried to do during it? No one else was here with Lore. None of their other friends had taken the risk of coming this far with her, and yet, here Draven was. Ready to do whatever it took to keep her alive.

Baring his teeth, he tried to wrestle that jealousy back underneath his skin. He needed to bury that deep inside himself so he didn't...

"Oh," Rowan breathed. "Welcome back."

The room was suddenly full of electricity. He could feel her stare on him as though she'd touched him.

Abraxas turned to find Lore's eyes wide open. Her back seized again, twisting her body into unnatural angles as though she reached for him. Rowan was the first to grab her shoulders, and then Draven hesitantly stepped forward when Abraxas didn't move.

He couldn't. Those mismatched eyes had pinned him in place as her hands finally, finally uncurled. The immense power inside her flexed. An invisible wall shoved the other two elves away from her as she rolled off the bed onto the floor. With a heave of breath, she crawled toward him. Hand over hand.

He blinked and the tension that had filled him released. Abraxas lunged for her, gathering her up against his chest and holding her head underneath his chin.

Lore's hands convulsed against him, clutching him closer to her while she mumbled against his chest.

"What?" he asked, smoothing his hands up and down her back. "I can't hear you, Lore."

"I just need to catch my breath," she wheezed. "I'm all right. I just need to... to catch my breath."

He glanced up at Rowan as though the other man might help. But even Rowan was looking down at her, shocked that she'd used her power right upon waking, but also that she was still not herself.

Helpless, he even looked at Draven, hoping that the deepmonger might have some kind of plan for him to follow. But the dark elf stood in the shadows with his eyes wide and his mouth slightly open. Apparently she'd yet to use her power against him, and even he had been surprised by the feel of it.

Rowan leaned down and patted her shoulder. Abraxas hated seeing someone else touch her when she didn't want to be touched. She even shrank into him, trying to get away from Rowan's gentle hand.

"We'll leave you two alone," Rowan said. "If she needs anything or has any more pain..."

He let the sentence trail off because Abraxas already knew what the other man would say. If there was more pain, then he had more medicine. Old medicine from the elves that even Abraxas wouldn't know how to give her.

But she might not want more medicine if it would make her sleep again. She might need to be awake to give herself some time to breathe. To be alive. He knew that feeling well.

Giving the other two elves a nod, he waited until they left the cabin before he stooped to see her face. "Lore?" he asked quietly. "Can you speak to me?"

"I don't want more medicine," she whispered against his neck. "I just want to stay here with you for a few seconds. If that's all right."

Of course, it was all right. She could stay in his arms for the rest of their lives if she wanted. He'd managed with the addition to his front. Like a backpack.

His heart swelled a bit in his chest. There was a primal pleasure in knowing that of everyone else. She sought comfort from him. She wanted to be in his arms, listening to his breath, even after she had awoken from such terrible torment.

Shifting, he leaned his back against the cot and held her tightly. He didn't know how long it took her to stir, only that it was a great long while before he felt her sigh against his neck and straighten.

"It's strange to be in a room with so many elves," she said, rubbing her eyes. "It's hard to get used to."

That was what she had to say after scaring years off all their lives? Abraxas rolled his gaze up to the ceiling and told himself to seek what little patience he could find there. "You've been in a room with lots of elves before."

"Only a few times. Even being in the room with Margaret and Draven together is rare." She finished scrubbing her eyes and met his gaze. She looked tired, even though she'd been resting for over a day. "I'm sorry for scaring you. Again."

"I have a feeling you'll do that for the rest of our lives."

"I didn't mean to. I don't know what happened, just that the power inside me seemed to swell a little more than I could handle." She shrugged. "Apparently, I should expect more of that soon. I have to remember what happened to me while I was... was..." She struggled with the words before she fell silent.

He knew this was a lot to ask of her so soon after such pain. Lore didn't have to tell him everything she'd experienced, or why she had experienced it.

He cupped the back of her neck and drew her head down until their foreheads touched. Breathing her in, he whispered, "You don't have to explain anything, Lore. I'm just glad you're back with me."

She grabbed onto his forearms and squeezed hard. As though she was trying to imprint his feeling into her memory. As though she wanted to feel him against her for a little while longer.

Didn't she know how much she meant to him? He'd gone to war for her. Forsaken every rule that he'd put in place for his own life. She was the reason he breathed, and if he had to endure worry over her well being for the rest of his time in this realm, then he would.

Every day was a blessing when she was in it. She had to know that.

"I saw my mother," she whispered, her breath fanning over his face. "She said she forgave you a long time ago."

He stiffened. She'd seen her mother? The woman he had burned alive while she screamed up at him without a single ounce of fear? He'd never forgotten the beautiful elf who had stood up to the King until the very end. She'd been fearless even when faced with death.

The guilt of her death was a burden he'd carried for a very long time. She had deserved more than a bitter end with her last moments in a dungeon and then staring down the maw of a dragon. If she had lived, he had no question that Lore's mother would have ridden at the forefront of their battle. A banshee's call upon her lips as she struck fear into the heart of every Umbral Knight on that battlefield.

Instead, she had died in pain. Tied up. Unable to defend herself or her daughter, who had watched from afar.

He would never forget that woman, regardless of her forgiveness.

"You saw your mother?" he asked. "In a dream or—"

"More than that," she affirmed his fear. "She said there was something I had to remember from my time away. She said if I didn't remember it, then I would die."

His spine stiffened at the mere implication. She would not die, not while he was here with her. The last time he'd left her to deal with any situation on her own was the only time that she'd gotten hurt. He would not fight a separate battle while she ran off on her own. Not again.

He took a deep breath, watching as she lifted a bit from her position braced against him. "Then we need to help you remember."

"I don't think anything happened, though. There was nothing but peace before I heard Beauty praying to me. Like I was some kind of goddess." Lore pressed her fingers against her throat, checking her own pulse before shaking her head. "I feel like I'm alive. Living and breathing and not a divine being who came back from the dead. But now I fear what I have forgotten."

So did he.

Abraxas knew she'd changed. He'd have to be a fool not to notice her eyes, the way her hands seem to disappear when she was angry, or how the power crackled around her. But now he'd experienced it. He'd felt the blast of her magic throwing Rowan and Draven away from her. The electric crackle of her sudden rage before she reined it in.

Perhaps what she feared was true. She was a divine being who had returned to them. Or perhaps a divine being had possessed her and now used her body to enact its will. They would all find out sooner or later. Unfortunately, he feared that would come at a cost of even more pain.

"We'll figure it out," he murmured as he drew her back closer to him. Placing his chin on the top of her head, he rocked her side to side as she shuddered.

"I don't want to be a divine being," she said against his pulse. "I want to be me again, but I don't know if that's ever going to be possible."

"I wish I could tell you not to be afraid." He really did. He'd shoulder the world for her if it would help. "So much of this is outside of our knowledge, Lore. We cannot fight against it."

"I want to."

"I know." He kissed her temple and stared into the shadows of the cabin. "If I could fight it for you, I would."

And so they stayed like that, curled up on the floor for hours on end. He held her. She held him.

They found what little solace they could while wrapped in each other.

CHAPTER 24

Everyone kept telling her to take it easy. There was no way she could help around the camp when she'd just been laid out and in pain. They wanted her to rest. To sleep. Here, eat this new food we've found that tastes delicious. Why don't you linger next to the fire while everyone pampers you?

If one more person told her to relax, she was going to scream.

Lore didn't know how to do what they asked of her. Sitting on her hands while everyone else worked felt wrong. Sure, she had been ill. And yes, she had scared everyone with that wild flailing and likely seizure that had knocked her out for at least a day. She understood they didn't want to do anything that would make it worse.

Or make her seize up again.

It was a terrible thing to feel her body completely outside of her own control. All she'd been able to do was endure while she slipped into that dreaming realm. She didn't want to experience that again, but she wanted to be herself, too. She wanted to be useful around camp and to encourage the people she'd traveled with to be more comfortable here and around dragons. There was much she could help with.

Instead, she sat on a log in front of a fire and made sure it didn't go out. That was the most difficult job the elderly elf would give her.

Poking at the fire with a stick, she sighed and plopped her head down onto her hands. If they'd wanted to kill her from boredom, then they were doing a fine job of it. Give her a few more days and she'd off herself.

"Psst." The whisper interrupted her melancholy musings.

She glanced around, still not quite sure what she was hearing. No one in the camp wanted her to get involved with anything, so it couldn't be someone from the camp... could it?

"Psst," the hiss came again. This time, Lore knew it came from her right. She didn't want Rowan to come out of the cabin and scold her for moving around, so she stood up and stretched. If she gave her body a few of those snaps and pops that it always needed, he would think little of her taking a short walk around the clearing afterwards. He'd allowed her that before.

But this time, she knew the sound came from the bushes behind his house and that meant she should wander over there and investigate. Surely no one would get mad at her for that.

Lore's body felt lighter the closer she got to the bushes. Already she saw the glint of green eyes waiting for her. Green as the forest leaves with the sun filtering through them. Green like the eyes of her son.

Trying her best to not look like she was getting into trouble, she crouched down beside the bush. "I didn't realize you two already had your human forms."

Hyperion moved a branch out of his way and grinned up at her. She was shocked at how handsome he looked, although she shouldn't have been surprised. Abraxas was handsome as well, but Hyperion? If she'd brought him to the courts, then every woman in Umbra would have fought and scratched to get to him. Thankfully, the boy would never have to endure that kind of attention. Not as long as she was alive.

"Few people know," he said, his voice the sound of thunder in the distance. "Father knows, and Rowan, of course, but the rest have no idea who we are."

"Careful with that. The sailors will take one look at an unfamiliar person and run you through."

"I'd like to see them try." He gave her a feral grin that changed into something softer. Something that saw right through her discomfort. "You want to get out of here, don't you?"

She absolutely did. If only so that she could meet up with his sister and see what her daughter looked like as well. It was so strange to think of them as her children when they so clearly were adults now. They could have been her siblings if they walked by someone who didn't know them.

And yet... A part of her softened every time she looked at them. She wanted to hold them, stroke their hair, tell them stories like she should have when they were younger. Although even back then, they wouldn't have had hair. Her children had always had scales, and that had never bothered her before.

She crouched beside the bush and cast a nervous glance toward the cabin. "They'll be awfully angry if I sneak away now. They think I should be resting."

"After what happened?"

She nodded, biting her lips. "They think I could make it happen again if I'm not careful enough."

"Then we'll be very careful." He stuck his hand out through the leaves and she stared down at his calloused palm.

Callouses, already. He hadn't been lying about and not helping anyone. Her son had been working hard, likely from sun up till sun down if those marks were any indicator.

Lore slid her hand into his and disappeared into the greenery with him. "Come on," she whispered. "We need to get as far away from here as possible before Rowan realizes I'm gone."

Hyperion let out a little laugh that floated up into the leaves above them. The trees seemed to bend out of their way as they raced away from the clearing. They stayed quiet, low, moving as though they were creatures of the forest. No one could track them, save his father, perhaps. Abraxas would catch her scent on the wind anywhere and find her.

But she didn't want anyone to interrupt, so Lore guided her son through the trees in the best way she could. Even elves would have a hard time finding her.

Silverfells knew the forest. And the trees knew her.

She felt free in this moment, running through the tangled brush with her son, who sprinted beside her. They were free. Together. They didn't have anyone hunting them, no King to fear, no world to change. Her mind captured this moment, carefully wrapping it up in a blanket in her mind to forever keep it safe.

Hyperion gave her a wild grin as he leapt over a fallen log. The look in his eyes was a challenge. He wanted to push her. He wanted her to run with him through the forest like they would have in the old days. Before humans had threatened either of their kind.

Or perhaps he thought he could beat her since she had been ill only a few days ago. Foolish boy.

He thought she had lost her touch, or that he could race her in the forest when that was what she was made to do. Lore's very spirit grew among trees like this. Sure, they moved for him because he was a dragon and therefore respected him. But they were part of her.

Speeding up, she sent him an answering grin of her own before launching forward. She ran with all the speed that only an elf had, the wind whipping in her hair as her heart thundered in her chest. It had been too long since she'd run like this. Since she'd been free to use every muscle in her body to propel herself forward.

Hyperion seemed to understand. As he ran, he threw things in her direction. Twigs, leaves, a fallen log, all of it that Lore leapt over with all the grace of a deer. Only once they were both slick with sweat and breathing hard did she grasp the trunk of a tree and spin herself around. She landed in a crouch in front of him, waiting for him to slide on his hip until he nearly ran into her.

"You've gotten quick," she said, her chest heaving with every inhalation. "But not quick enough."

"Apparently." He leveraged himself upright, sitting with his hands in the moss and dirt streaking his pants. "I just wanted to make sure you were still feeling like yourself. You know, after..."

His words trailed off, but she knew what he meant. Abraxas had filled them in on what was happening to her. Or maybe her children were just more observant than she'd thought. Lore wasn't the same person she had been, and that had gotten even worse after her attack.

The power inside her wanted to feed, she realized. And sometimes it had to feed on her to take the edge off of that hunger.

Rubbing her hands up and down her arms, she willed them to remain as they were. No one needed to see her disappearing, especially not her children. Not after they had waited for her so long. She would not scare them.

Lore needed a distraction. Something to keep her mind off the power welling inside her and screaming to be released.

She stood and looked around them, trying to peer through the golden light of the forest as though she could learn more about their surroundings. She had no idea where they had run off to, and she'd never seen a map of this area either. They were well and truly lost in her eyes.

"Where are we?" she asked, hoping Hyperion had at least been here before.

He shrugged before holding out his hand for her to help him stand. "Probably near the old settlement by now. Of a sort, I suppose. We were running toward the pools because Nyx wanted to see you."

Their hands clapped together with a solid thwack, and Lore heaved him upright. Her strength startled him, she thought. His eyes grew wide with shock before he cleared his throat and steadied himself.

He was taller than she'd thought he'd be. Apparently, all dragons were giants. He made even Abraxas look short.

Staring up at his long, lanky figure, she lifted a brow. "Well, you grew rather unexpectedly."

"I am a full grown dragon now." His chest puffed out with pride. "I'm not a small creature. I was never born to be one."

"Of course not." She patted his chest and then turned away from him, absentmindedly trying to find a way for them to hide in case they needed to. "Now, where is your sister?"

"Through here, mother." The words felt like an arrow flying through her chest.

As Hyperion walked ahead of her, Lore tried her best to wrangle her emotions back where they needed to be. She didn't want to scare her children with more tears, but she hadn't expected them to call her mother.

How long had it been since she'd come to terms with never hearing that word? Years. Perhaps a hundred. She'd fought with the knowledge that children would not be hers for such a long time, and now they were here. Right in front of her.

They were people now, not just scaley beasts that looked like little pets. They were a man and a woman with thoughts of their own and futures to plan out. So quickly, as well.

"How is it you two are adults in your human form?" she asked as she trailed along behind him.

"Dragons grow differently than the rest of you. We cannot be children for long, not without risking ourselves. Our mothers can only look after something so tiny for a short while." He looked over his shoulder and shrugged. "The crystals helped too. Both of us have taken the memories to preserve them for longer. Tanis said it was a good plan, since she's the only one who can protect them."

There was that name again.

Tanis.

She'd heard Abraxas say it before, with that soft smile on his face. The fondness in both her mate's and her son's eyes made her bristle. Who was this woman?

They walked out of the forest toward a field dotted with sapphire pools of water. There were so many little ponds here, all of them seemingly deep. Lore clasped her hands to her chest as she surveyed the beauty of it all, shocked that she'd never known this was here. Lily pads and bright pink flowers dotted each pool.

They were obviously well taken care of, she noted. Small stone walls were set up along the edges of each one, and no algae dared grow on those surfaces. She'd thought, at the very least, this place would have fallen into some kind of disrepair.

"Nyx has spent a lot of her days here," Hyperion said. "She's been fixing up each pool as though more sapphire dragons are going to join us at any time."

That explained it. Although sadness weighed in his words.

They all knew it would take a long time for more dragons to join them. And though neither Hyperion nor Nyx were actually related, they were brother and sister to their core. She couldn't imagine them doing what it would take to make eggs.

Lore shivered. The mere thought disgusted her.

A cold blast of wind tangled around her shoulders, tugging her away from Hyperion.

"She's just over there," he said, pointing into the distance. "That's her favorite pool. She said it's warmer than the others. Strange for a sapphire dragon to like something so heated."

Indeed. But her mind wandered over his words as she felt that cold breeze again. Where was that coming from? A whisper in her mind wanted her to go find it. To walk down into those shadows where the cold had preserved something important. Something for her eyes only.

She turned away from her son and noticed the ground had given way some distance from the pools. It had folded as though the land underneath it was hollow, and even from here she could see the faint outline of stairs. It was from those depths that the cold air whistled, and the ground seemed to shake underneath her. Tilting her forward, toward the stairwell and the darkness that beckoned.

"Mother?" Hyperion's voice broke through her strange thoughts. "Are you all right?"

"Yes," she replied, but Lore didn't think she was. Something was inside the earth here. And whatever it was, it wanted to speak with her, or see her, or show her something that shouldn't exist.

Right now, however, she had another plan. She needed to spend time with her children. Children who she had neglected and that she'd promised to be there for.

So instead of investigating the strange magic, she forced her attention back to Hyperion and grinned. "Perhaps we should introduce a little cold water to your sister's pool then, if it's so unusual that she enjoys the heat."

His brows furrowed. "She'd hate that."

"That is the point."

As though her meaning finally dawned on him, Hyperion's frown changed into a wide grin. "I like your plan, Mother."

CHAPTER 25

"What do you mean you lost her?" Abraxas snarled.

He tried to keep a good hold on his temper. Rowan had been given an impossible task, after all. Everyone expected the elf to keep Lore quiet and calm, and that simply wasn't something that his mate did well.

But losing her? By all the gods and goddesses, how had he lost her?

Lore was barely herself, although this morning he had to admit she was walking around a little better than she had been just a few days ago. She'd expressed her anger at being locked up again. Her words, not his. And then she'd said she wanted a task to help out around the campsite.

There just wasn't anything for her to do. Rowan already knew what his job was, and that was watching her. Draven had gone off to help with the ship, and the siren's people knew what they were doing in fixing that massive beast of a boat. Abraxas had to knock trees down for them because they'd proven to be quite slow at hand chopping them. He'd thought that many people might know how to do it all in a hurry, but they didn't.

What else did she want to do? There was no food needing to be hunted. No garden to till. The life that they all led here was rather regimented. It would take time for them to come up with a task for her, and besides, she needed to heal.

"I imagine you drove her to her breaking point," Rowan replied, sipping at his tea from his seat by the fire. "She was bored out of her mind sitting here throwing twigs. I watched her break one up into a hundred pieces just yesterday. Did you know that? The tiniest of twigs and somehow she managed to tear it into little individual pieces just to throw them into the fire one by one. She counted them all."

That didn't sound like Lore. She was hasty, his woman. She enjoyed throwing large logs onto the fire and watching them burn. He'd even seen her build a bonfire once just to stand in front of the flames, staring at them as though she dared them to burn her.

She was not, and never would be, the kind of person who had the patience to sit in front of a fire and do that. Maybe he had bored her past what she could reasonably endure.

Rustling from the bushes behind them announced another person walking into the clearing. He turned, hope already pushing his tongue to call out her name. Except he didn't smell her on the air and he knew that brim fire scent anywhere.

Draven walked out of the bushes, muttering about sirens and threats of locking him in a cabin again. He paused, frozen, when he saw the expression on Abraxas's face.

"What did I do this time?" he asked, holding up his hands. "I promise,

I have no idea where Lore is."

"Well, that's the problem, isn't it?" Abraxas snarled.

He turned away from the other elf, focusing his attention on the ground in front of him as though he could stare straight through it. Where would she go? This isle was big, and he supposed he could change into the dragon to search for her. The problem with that form was that he couldn't see through the trees. It was easier to hide from him even if he could cover more ground.

Draven slid by him, careful not to get within grabbing reach before sinking down on another log by the fire. "What's gotten into him today?" he asked Rowan.

"Lore's gone."

"Ah, took her long enough."

If his glare could have set the deepmonger on fire, then the elf would have already been roasted. Abraxas had to take a bit of time to calm the anger in his mind before he snarled, "What did you say?"

"She was so damned bored. Begging anyone who walked by for a chance to help. No one said yes, of course." Draven flicked a small chunk of bark into the fire. "Because of you. Everyone's scared of the crimson dragon, who doesn't want his mate to touch anything heavier than a feather. I'm surprised she didn't run away earlier."

"She doesn't know this island," he snarled. "There are all manner of creatures out in those woods, and she's injured."

"Not really all that injured," Rowan muttered, but then stilled when Abraxas turned that glare onto him. "What? She's not. She had an attack, but I've been keeping a close eye on her, and I consulted with Tanis. We don't think she's injured, per say. Just that another attack could be triggered at any point."

Abraxas lifted his hands to his hair. "Then wouldn't that be all the more reason to keep her safely in the camp where she can be seen if she has another attack?"

"I suppose so." Rowan set his teacup on the ground and sighed. "But I'm trying to take care of my own mate as well, Abraxas. I cannot look after them both all the time."

Draven looked between the two of them, a deep furrow between his eyes as he tried to keep up. "Are you saying there's another elf here?"

"No," Abraxas snarled before replying to Rowan. "Listen to me. If you want those sailors off our shores, then I have to help them. There is no one else that can bring down trees large enough to be suitable for their masts. Otherwise, I'd be watching out for her."

The elderly elf straightened his shoulders and stood up. Where was he going? About to leave?

But Rowan just shook himself and replied, "I can only do so much, dragon. I cannot be in two places at once, and everyone seems to need me these days."

That furrow hadn't left Draven's brow. He looked down, then looked back up and asked, "Then is there another dragon? That's not possible, is it?"

Rowan glanced over at him and grinned. "Did you think Abraxas and Lore were the first pairing of elf and dragon? Such a love match has been happening for centuries, dear boy. My dragon is fierce and beautiful. You'll like her."

He was going to crack both of their heads together if neither of them could focus on the conversation at hand. Lore was missing. He didn't care that Tanis was taking longer to hatch those eggs than she should, or that Rowan was busy. He didn't feel any obligation to explain any of this to Draven, who had wandered into this conversation without being invited, anyway.

Baring his teeth, he snarled, "Would the two of you shut up and listen to me?"

Both the elves looked at him, back at each other, and then at him again.

Draven cleared his throat. "Yes, yes. Very terrifying that Lore is out on her own. She'll come back, I'm sure."

"How can you be certain of that? She does not know this land. There are no maps of Dracomachia and she could have staggered out into the desert region by now. Any manner of creature might have attacked her, and she has no weapons."

With a grave nod, Draven replied, "Indeed. I have seen quite a few boar prints out there. I've heard they can gut the strongest of men with one swipe of their tusks. Quite alarming."

He felt all the blood drain from his face.

He had to go get her. Had to kill every boar on this damned island, so there was no more threat. He needed to—

Draven burst into laughter.

The fool should have known that would not help the situation. Abraxas played through all the ways he could snap the deep monger's neck before Draven got a hold of himself.

"She's a goddess, Abraxas! What are you worried about her for? I pity any creature who tries to attack her. I saw what she did to that leviathan close up. She's a monster when she wants to be." Draven shrugged. "It's impressive, but I don't worry about her at all."

Well, someone had to. She might have all these magical powers and all the abilities in the world, but that didn't make her invincible. She could still feel pain. They'd all seen that in close detail. She could still get hurt and have to heal. Why did that not disturb anyone else?

Growling under his breath, he glared at Draven and stayed silent. Otherwise, he might say something stupid and make the deepmonger attack him. Like how he thought the dark elf was weak for letting Lore fight her battles on her own, or perhaps the other man had lost his touch now that he'd found a comfortable place to rest his head.

Draven apparently knew the thoughts that were going through Abraxas's mind. He simply shrugged and flicked another bit of bark into the flames. "The way I figure, what's the likelihood of someone dying twice? At least so close together. She's already taken that risk, didn't like it, and came back. She won't make the same mistake twice."

But she wasn't immortal. She'd told him that whatever power brewed inside her could kill her, so why should he not fear losing her again?

No one understood the horrible feeling of loss that had taken over him after she'd been gone. No one could sense the pain that had ricocheted through his body at all times. Surely they should know that he couldn't lose her again. Wouldn't. The mere thought of it made his heart do strange things in his chest and his palms slick with sweat.

He was panicking, he realized. He needed to find her, or he feared the dragon would burst out of his skin. Maybe he should change anyway. He could... he could...

Their children burst out of the bushes, chattering loudly about their plans for tomorrow. Their plans with their mother.

Hyperion snickered at something Nyx said, and then exclaimed, "You know she doesn't care to see that! You just want to go because it's your favorite place to be."

"Well, if it's my favorite, then maybe mother will like it just as much."

"She's not a dragon."

"And you're just a child." Nyx sniffed and tilted her nose into the air. "You wouldn't understand why I find that place so beautiful or why Mother would want to see it."

"I know exactly why you want her to see it," he corrected with a snort. "And I think she'd be more interested in climbing the mountains with me tomorrow. She enjoyed running through the forest, and I think she needs to use her body more. It'll root her spirit into her physical form."

The two of them stepped in front of Abraxas. They had nowhere else to go unless they wanted to run into his chest, and he didn't intend to let them get very far, anyway. Reaching out, he grabbed the two of them by their shirts and hauled them close.

"Where is your mother?" he asked through gritted teeth.

Both of his children looked at each other, and then at him. "Um..." they said in unison.

If they were trying to hide Lore because she had asked for a little time alone, arguably, he'd be proud of them. They sided with their mother, who wanted adventure, and he could see how she had passed down her skills to them. Certainly. But to lie to him? They knew better than to try.

Sighing, he gave them both a little shake. "I'm waiting."

Hyperion was the first one to crack, as always. "She said she wanted to explore a little more on her own."

"By herself?" he ground out. "You realize this forest is dangerous."

Nyx shook her head. "Mother said she has plenty of skills in battle and survival."

"Did she have a weapon?"

His daughter bit her lip and then looked back at her brother.

"No weapon, then," Abraxas sighed. "And you thought after that attack she had that she would be fine out in the wilderness where no one would notice if she had another one?"

Hyperion hissed out a long breath, perhaps understanding what Abraxas was trying to say. But then his son frowned back at him. "She will not have another attack so soon. She said she was fine."

"Ah, and she's a healer now?" He released his hold on both of their shirts, setting them away from him before he tossed them onto their asses. "Where did you leave her?"

"By the pools," Nyx mumbled, straightening her shirt and running her hand down the now wrinkled fabric.

"And where did she say she was going?"

"There were caves nearby that she thought might be interesting to look in," Hyperion replied. "She said there was no dark magic coming out of them, but something about them made her want to see what was inside."

He felt the warmth of another person beside him and glanced over to see Rowan had nearly pressed himself against Abraxas's arm. "Caves?" the elf asked.

Hyperion nodded.

"But there are no caves there. I've been through the old ruins and the pools many times. There are no caves other than the ones I slipped through to get into the crystal mine." Rowan frowned. "Is that where she was going?"

"No, not the crystal mine." Hyperion shrugged, though his eyes already moved around them as though he searched for an escape. "It showed up when we first got there. Mother was looking at it with an odd expression, but she said nothing else until we were ready to leave."

That was all the information he needed to hear. Abraxas knew that any hidden cave that sprang to the surface after Lore's arrival meant something evil. Something bad. He had to get her out of that cave and he was furious that his children hadn't seen the danger.

He made eye contact with Rowan and saw the other elf had come to a similar conclusion.

"Find her," Rowan said. "I'm sure it's nothing, but there are many secrets on this isle that none of us know about."

"I won't be long." He clasped the other man's hand in his and shook it hard. "Keep an eye on the children, at least, will you?"

"I can't watch everyone."

"You need the practice."

Abraxas headed toward the trees, but paused when he saw the rather stunned expression on Nyx's face. She stared back at the fire, her eyes wide and her mouth slightly open. When he followed her gaze, all he saw was Draven staring back at her. The dark elf had also seemed to still, a strange expression on his own face.

"Absolutely not," Abraxas snarled, pointing at the deep monger and forcing the man's attention to him. "You keep your hands off my daughter. Every finger that touches her is one I will cut off and wear as a necklace, you hear me?"

Draven gave him a dumbfounded nod, but his eyes kept straying back to Nyx.

"I don't have time for this right now," Abraxas growled before turning back to the trees.

Everyone seemed to have gone insane today. Even him.

CHAPTER 26

Lore stood at the edge of the pools, watching the sun play over the tiny ripples. Nyx had done all this herself, Hyperion had claimed. It was hard to imagine her daughter deep in the wells of these ponds, ensuring that the springs weren't clogged and that the surrounding stones hadn't shifted.

But everything had changed since she'd last seen them. Everything.

Lore tilted her head back to the breeze and let it play over her features. She loved the feeling of the wind here. No smoke tinged it with an acidic bite, and there was no horrid smell that drifted along with it. Instead, the air was crisp and clean.

The whole island was like that, though, she supposed. Everywhere here was clean and well growing. Like a place untouched by people, even though there were still some of them who remained.

Her children had left her a little while ago, and she knew she should hurry. As much as she liked to think her companions would leave her to her own devices for the afternoon, she knew Abraxas. He'd want to hover over her as he had for the past week.

Lore was not hurt. She was not injured. She was perhaps in a little danger from herself, but how were they going to prevent that? The power inside her wasn't going anywhere—it was likely to get worse—and she might as well lean into that knowledge.

No one could stop the pain or the danger that came from within her. So why should they waste their time trying to control it when it was uncontrollable?

Finally, she pulled herself away from the pools and back toward the hole in the ground that had called out to her. She wasn't sure what kind of magic lay within that darkness. Perhaps something that would try to attack her. But it felt familiar to her. Or that she was familiar to it.

Strangely, there was no fear in her heart as she wandered toward the outline of the stairs. The grass had laid on top of it like someone had placed a blanket over furniture. She gave a tentative stomp to the area where the stairs should continue downward and felt it give underneath her boot. She didn't sink right through the space, so the roots of this grass had grown tangled and deep.

"Strange," she muttered, but continued on.

Lore stomped a few more times and then a small gap opened in the earth. Not much of one, but enough for her to lean down and start digging with her hands.

Dirt clung to her fingers and wiggled underneath her nails. It wasn't a pleasant feeling, but one that she was very familiar with. The grass wasn't too hard to pull up by the clod, handful after handful, until there was a big enough opening for her to squeeze through.

She had the thought that maybe she should make the opening bigger. Just in case she was in a rush or something lived inside this new cavern. But there were no other markings that anything existed down there, and what were the chances that she'd get chased out?

The memory of spiders living without death inside a warlock's tower sent a shiver down her spine. She'd make the hole bigger. Just in case.

That took up more time than she'd wanted to waste, however. The dirt had wriggled into the fine wrinkles of her hands, so even when she wiped them off on her borrowed trousers, she still couldn't get the color off. She'd need a bath after this. Eyeing the pools just outside of the tunnel she'd found, she tried to remember which one was warm.

"Ah, it doesn't matter," she said to herself. "You'll get clean on the way out."

And with that, she slid through the ground into the hole.

Lore conjured a small ball of light. Her power surged to the forefront, excited to be used, and she blinded herself before she got control of it again.

"Stop that," she hissed. "You'll take my eyes out if you keep that up."

As if the magic cared. It would give her new eyes. She had the sudden thought, as though someone else had whispered in her mind. She did not need this mortal flesh or this weak body. The power could give her a new one and she would never know the difference.

Lore forced the power to dim until the ball of light wasn't giving her a splintering headache. Blinking away the spots of light in her vision, she peered through the darkness and followed the stairs down... down... down beyond the reach of her light and even deeper into the heart of the earth.

"What is this place?" she muttered, only to have her voice echo back at her.

She swallowed at the eerie sound, but continued on. The stairs were strangely dry when she had expected them to be slick with condensation. The air was dry too, she realized. Even with the pools so close.

Bracing herself on the wall, she hesitated when she felt the grooves underneath her fingers. She held the light closer and peered at the markings.

Elvish runes.

She'd recognize them anywhere, although she was shocked to see them here.

"So that's why it's dry," she murmured, tracing her fingers over a particular rune that she'd seen in her mother's cabinet. "What are you doing down here, though?"

Even more curious now, she moved down the stairs with a little more confidence and purpose. If the elves had built this place, and surely they had, then she was welcome. Whatever spells they'd used to make it difficult for others to find would ignore Lore. She hoped, at least.

The stairs evened out to a polished floor at the bottom. The darkness was heavy here, fighting back against the light she'd brought with her. That wouldn't do.

Lore lifted her hand a little higher, twisting her fingers delicately in the air as though plucking apart the light. At her beckoning, it shredded itself into ten separate orbs. She tossed each one into the air and let it wander where it wished. Light flooded the room as her power flexed a little more.

She'd thought perhaps this was a hidden chamber for the elves who'd lived here to hide. There might be spells thrown about, boxes of food, beds for those who might be wounded. Instead, what she found was something like a library.

There were a few bookshelves that had long ago crumbled. Their wood brittle with the drying spells and the scrolls that were left there had shattered underneath the weight. But there were holes in the walls. Hundreds of them. Carved by talented hands with markings on top of each one. Some of them were prophecies, others were spells, some she suspected might be family recipes.

This wasn't quite a library, she realized. It was the desperate attempt of elves who had lived here to preserve something of their people. They hadn't wanted their lives to be swallowed up by the dragons. They had hoped, in leaving something here, that their own people would someday find it.

Running her fingers over the dust on the walls and the thick cobwebs—made by normal spiders—she cleared what she could off the nearest hole. The scroll inside covered up a rune etched into the very stone. A preserving spell, she thought, although she'd never seen one before.

The power inside her recognized more than just hidden stairwells, she realized.

"Well," she muttered as she pulled out a scroll. "What history lingers here?"

She felt an unnatural magic, like static along her spine. Slowly putting the scroll back in its place, she turned around. Lore half expected to see another elf standing there. Or perhaps the skeleton of one who had been locked up in here for centuries to protect this place.

Instead, all she saw was the gossamer visage of a woman with pale white hair and violet eyes. Her form shimmered in between two of the fallen bookshelves, warping as though her spell wasn't quite strong enough to keep her here for a long time.

"I wondered if you'd find this place," the unknown woman said.

"Was I supposed to?"

"Your people made it for you a very long time ago, so yes. You were." The woman glanced around as if she were surprised by the state of the room as well. "I've only seen this in memories, you see. The elves who lingered with the dragons always wanted to be sure that the elf in the prophecy would find some part of herself here. That you would be provided with knowledge of your people, as the prophet always knew you would have little."

Lore bristled at the suggestion. She knew about her people and the elves. Her mother had been one, and Lore was half elf! By the gods, did the old elves really think she had lost so much?

"I know about my own history," she hissed.

"They did not believe you would know all of it." The specter gestured behind her. "Please. Read the scroll, and see what it is they thought was so important for you to know."

Did the other woman want her to reveal the elves' secrets? Lore wasn't all that certain. But she still turned around and pulled the scroll out again, letting her gaze pour over it.

Even as she read the history of the elven clans, a story she did not know, she wondered more about the woman behind her. Was she a spirit? That would explain why Lore could see through her. Or maybe the woman was a mirage from a spell. She'd heard of spells that could do that, after all. But why would the elves leave someone who wasn't real to guard their most precious history and secrets? Their message for someone they believed would change the world?

"Well?" the woman said in her ear. "Is it anything you've heard before?"

Lore flinched away from the specter and dropped the scroll onto the ground. "By the gods, don't do that!"

"Sorry." The woman didn't seem all that apologetic. She even tilted her head to look at the lettering on the scroll that she could see. "I wish I could read elvish. I'm so curious to know what they thought was important."

Lore pressed a hand against her thundering heart. "It's just about the history of the clans."

"Is that so?"

"There are many clans, each from a different part, all nonsense. The clans have disbanded, though maybe the old elves thought that would never happen." She pinched the bridge of her nose, wondering why she was giving up so much information to this woman in the first place. "Who are you?"

The woman blinked owlishly at her. "Why do you want to know that?"

"Because you're standing in front of me when I think you might be dead."

Again, the woman blinked at her before a little snort echoed from her mouth. "I do forget sometimes that I look like this when projecting. It's been a long time since I've had to try, you know. I'm not dead."

"Are you sure?"

"I can still feel my physical body, so yes. I'm sure."

Lore arched an eyebrow and crossed her arms over her chest. "I've seen everyone on this island so far, I think. None of them look like you."

"Ah, that's because we haven't met yet. I've been rather preoccupied." The woman pointed to another scroll. "Can you take this one out? I'm particularly interested in their notations about farming. I remember their skills being rather advanced."

Why not? Talk to the not-ghost, show her all the secrets of the elves. What could go wrong?

Lore stomped over to the hole and thrust her hand into it. The scroll inside came away easily, although she could see there was more beyond it. Secrets, secrets, what was it with the ancient elves and secrets?

Unrolling it, she didn't even look at the contents before holding it up to the creature, who claimed it was not a ghost. "This?"

"Yes." The woman floated closer to her, one arm hugging her own waist, and the other lifted to trace where she was. "Oh, I wish I knew more of this. I can pick out a few words here and there, but none of it will make sense. Could you read it out loud?"

Lore rolled her eyes before turning the paper to face herself. "Irrigation of lands required only by magical properties to produce enough food to feed a village. The first spell is a simple one and ends with the forty ninth spell of the hardest difficulty... Why am I reading this to you?"

The woman appeared shocked again, clearly surprised that Lore had taken a tone with her. "I thought you'd be interested as well."

"In farming?" Lore asked.

"Well, you are going to stay here for a while longer, aren't you? Abraxas seemed to think that you would want to remain here with him and the children."

Abraxas?

She knew Abraxas?

Lore looked this other woman over, noting the beauty of her face and the way her white blonde hair swept back from her aggressive features. This was a woman who could fight if she needed to, or become a scholar with the best of them.

"Tanis?" she asked, her words a little hesitant. "Are you the one everyone has spoken of?"

"Oh good, they told you about me. A woman has to fear that she'd been forgotten while she's not present." Tanis smiled at her, the expression soft. "And you're the elf of legends, I suspect. Otherwise you wouldn't be here."

"Lore," she replied, frowning. "Have you been here the whole time?"

"Not quite. I'm elsewhere, and I'm certain that Abraxas will bring you to see me sooner now that we've unofficially met." Tanis gestured up and down her body. "There are better ways to meet, of course. Now, Rowan told me that you've been struggling. Not quite an illness, per say, but an overgrowth of something. What exactly did he call it?"

"Power," Lore said. "I don't know what he called it, but that's what it is. I have more magic than I ever have before, and I cannot control it."

"Oh, I think it's more than that. The power inside you is swelling up, reaching into the farthest parts of your body and unfortunately, your body is not quite large enough to contain it. We need to work on that. Or figure out how to get rid of all the excess." Tanis tapped her lip, then wandered down the room. "I had hoped there would be something here for you."

Lore watched the spirit of the woman wander before asking, "Did you send this room for me to find?"

"Goodness, no. I don't have that much magic in me. That was all your ancestors who prepared for your arrival."

That made little sense, though. "Rowan said he was the prophet who saw me."

"He saw the details. Though there were many of them who saw the same end. The elves have always known there would be a time when their influence ended. They assumed only one of them would be able to find this place." Although Tanis looked at her then, a troubled expression appeared on her face. She hesitantly added, "Although that is odd, now that you point it out."

Lore lifted her arms from her sides and shrugged. "Everything that has happened to me has been odd."

"Hm." Tanis tapped her lip again before nodding. "That settles it, then. I need to see you in person. Not like this."

"I thought you were—"

"Abraxas is outside waiting for you. Tell him to bring you to me. Now." Tanis's expression hardened. "I fear all of our lives are at stake."

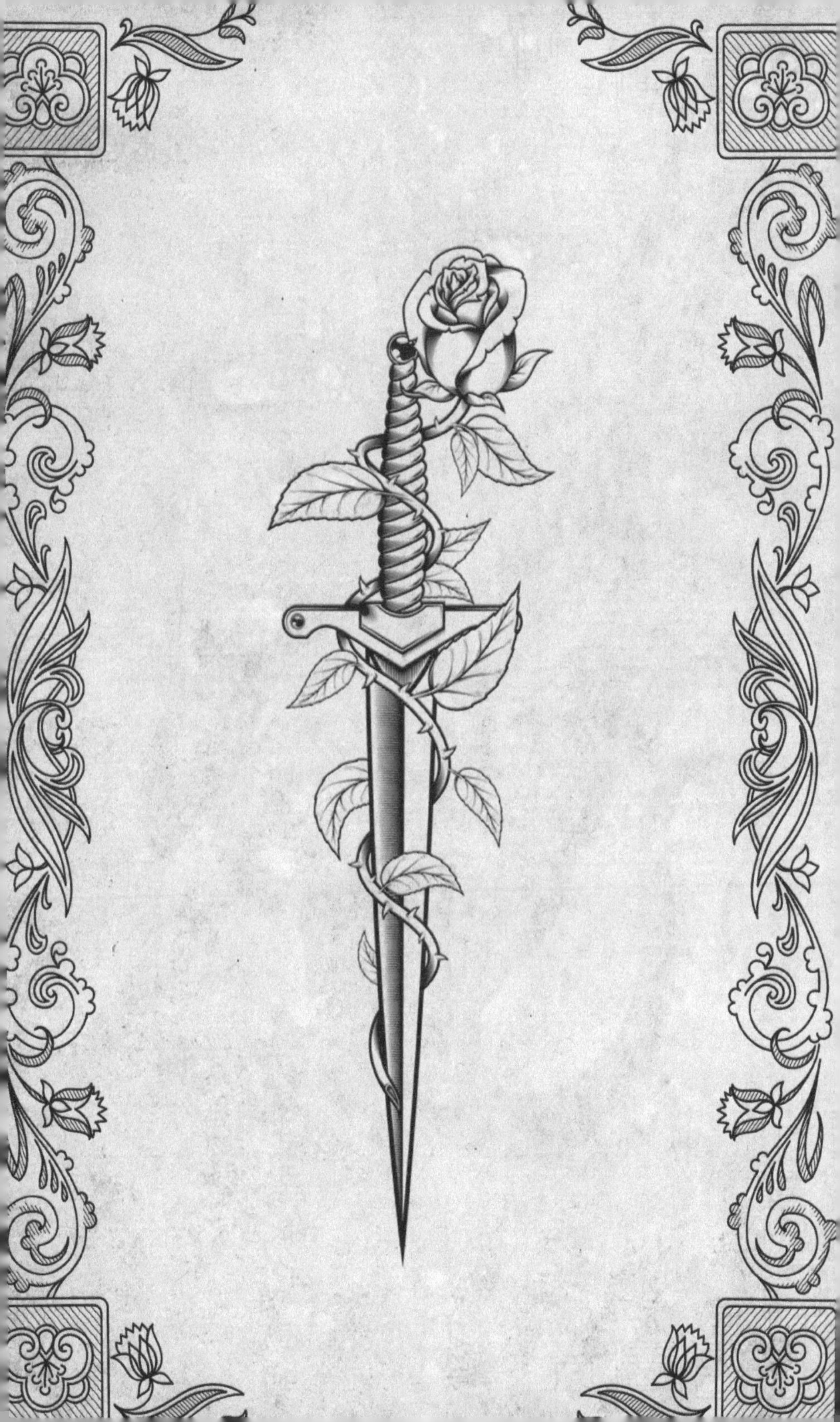

CHAPTER 27

Abraxas had told himself to be gentle once he found her. She'd only done what she thought needed to be done. Lore had sent their children back to relative safety while she investigated something she'd found in the earth.

Once he had started off from his family, however, he knew that his anger would get the better of him. He held himself in check for their children. Those younglings didn't deserve to see the genuine anger of a dragon male who had been betrayed by his mate. They might not even understand the reasoning behind his anger.

He certainly didn't.

Stomping through the forest, he tried to piece through his thoughts before he got to her. Was it because she risked her life again? Of course. He hated how she thought everything had to be done on her own, and by risking herself, she was saving others.

"Stubborn woman," he muttered as he stomped hard on a twig that snapped underneath his weight. "Stubborn, foolish, selfish woman."

He couldn't live without her. She knew that. She knew all the struggles he'd been through without her. And still, at the very first chance, she put herself in harm's way. Again. Without him.

Did she think he couldn't protect her? Was that what all of this was about?

He reached up to grab a branch in his way and ripped it off the tree. The trunk groaned at the force of his pull, but he didn't care if he took the whole tree down. He couldn't even fly over the forest because the damn leaves would hide her from him. And he couldn't look for her in that crimson form, which meant he was weaker than he usually was as well.

Maybe this form was the problem. She didn't like him when he was human.

Just the passing thought made him snort. She liked him just fine when he was in his mortal form. That wasn't the problem. Most likely Lore didn't want to let anyone get harmed because of her, and that selfish thought meant she charged head first into idiotic situations.

With a sigh, he stood at the pools with his hands on his hips. He needed to tell her how this affected all of them. Everyone back at camp was worried sick because she was gone, and she should feel guilty for that.

Of course, no one at camp worried about her but him. Even Rowan, who had been at her bedside for so long, making sure that she was well fed and rested, hadn't seemed all that bothered by her disappearance.

How? How were they not all scrambling to their feet, grabbing their weapons, and charging into the woods with her name on their lips? They had to know she was in trouble. He could feel it in his gut. She was terrified and alone and he wasn't there....

"Abraxas." The whispered word made him turn away from the pool and glance toward the treeline. Tanis stood there, her arms crossed over her chest as she looked at him. "Go easy on her."

He had no idea she could project herself like this. Somehow, it made him even more afraid of the beautiful dragoness. She had more power than he realized. "This magic is forbidden for our kind."

"I thought we were breaking all the old rules?" She arched a brow and then tilted her head back to laugh. "I'm helping, Abraxas. It's not like I can help in any other way."

"Hatch your eggs."

"They have decided to be slow coming into our world. More people have need of me than just these eggs. At least this way I can be of some service."

She could keep her opinions out of his relationship, is what she could do. He winced at the thought.

A small part of him knew he should listen to her. She'd been a dragon in a relationship with an elf for hundreds of years now. She and Rowan had centuries of happiness to pull from if they were to give him advice. But a much larger part of him wanted to scream at her for trying to interfere.

He and Lore would figure this out on their own. He would convince her to stay in the cabin and not go outside unless necessary. He'd lock her in there if he had to. He'd drag a mountain in front of the door and no one would be able to get into her room other than him then. How would she like taking risks at that point?

Tanis gave him a look. "You cannot keep her locked away from adventure, Abraxas. It's who she is. You would have nothing more than a husk of the woman you love if you deny her this."

He knew that. He did. She wouldn't want to be a kept woman any more than he'd want to be a pet.

Abraxas raked his fingers through his hair, more frustrated than he'd ever been in his life. "She's going to drive me mad again, Tanis. I cannot see her wandering off on her own knowing that there is danger in these woods."

"There is less danger here than if she stayed in the cabin by herself."

"How can you say that?" he thundered, his shout carrying through the forest and sending a wave of birds fleeing their nests. "We have lived here for so long that we are blind to the dangers this place brings. There are animals here who could feast on her flesh. She could get lost in these woods and not know how to return. She could starve or die of thirst before I ever found her."

"She is an elf. She's built to deal with all these so-called dangers. You do not have to fear her getting lost or hungry."

"She was born in a city, Tanis. I know you think all elves have a natural talent for the wilds, but that doesn't mean she's ever had a chance to put it in practice. I refuse to let her continue on like this without someone looking over her." His chest rose and fell with his anger, his words heated and his eyes warm. He could feel his eyes had turned back into that of a dragon.

Tanis's form had become crisp with this vision, no longer wavering in front of him. And that meant he could easily see the look of disappointment on her face, the frustration that creased her mouth. "Fine, then. Go down into that ancient place and yell at her. See how far it gets you. But bring her to me, Abraxas. I might be able to help with that problem of hers."

The visage of the dragon disappeared, and he was glad of it. Let her disappear back to her cavern with her children. She had bigger things to focus on than him and his relationship.

He turned toward Lore's scent and knew she'd gone underground before he saw the opening beside the stairs. She'd destroyed the grass over it, but it still wasn't a big enough opening for him to slip through.

And now she made him do work to save her. He knew this was petty anger. Lore didn't even think of him when she was digging through the earth to find wherever these stairs went, but that made him even more angry. She should have known that he would come for her. She should have known that he wouldn't let her go on her own when any manner of creature could be waiting.

A memory of giant, hairy spider legs played before him. He'd always known that the damned warlock's tower would haunt him for the rest of his life. Gritting his teeth, he resolved to tear those spiders limb from limb if they dared touch his Lore.

He marched down the stairs like a man going to war. His hands lingered on his sides, where he had placed a few knives. Although he doubted that he'd need them. In this state, Abraxas could tear the head of a man straight off his shoulders and he wouldn't struggle.

His eyes adjusted to the darkness, seeing better than any mortal could, but he didn't have to wait that long. Lore had lit up the bottom of the stairs with tiny glowing globes. Like little moons.

They made it seem like daylight in the cavern. He lifted an arm to cover his face for a moment before lowering it slowly.

All the anger in him drained out at the sight before him. Lore stood in the back of the room, her arms laden with scrolls. There was dust in her hair and a cobweb stuck to her shoulder, but she didn't seem to notice any of that. Instead, she focused on the words of the scroll. Her lips moved as she read, as though she couldn't stop herself from trying out the sounds of whatever spell was written there.

She looked so beautiful standing there. So alive.

It made his heart hurt knowing that she was well and here and still with him. He couldn't be angry at her when he loved her so much that the feeling overflowed in his chest and nearly burst out of him.

She glanced up at him and arched a delicate brow. Those mismatched eyes glowed in the light of her orbs. Or just the pale one, he realized. Just that pale eye that saw far too much. Right through him, even.

"She said you were outside," Lore said quietly. "I thought I had more time to pick and choose what I would like to read."

You should have come to me before you did this. You put yourself in unnecessary danger, he thought.

"What are they?" They weren't the words he'd meant to say, not when he wanted to chide her for taking risks. Instead, he stepped forward into the room and avoided crunching through any pieces of fallen parchment.

"Messages from the elves that lived here. Apparently, they always knew that someone like me would come, even before Rowan saw my face in that prophecy." She held up the scroll she had unraveled. "It's ancient elvish, but I can still read most of it. I think Rowan will be able to read the rest."

He should spank her for making him worried. He should tie her to a tree and tell her that he'd be back after he finished her job.

Instead, he stood behind her, leaned over her shoulder, and peered down at the words. "These are all spells to make trees grow."

Lore leaned back into him and stared in shock. "You can read ancient elvish?"

"Among many other languages, yes."

Her lips curved into a delicate grin. "You are very surprising, Abraxas."

"Is it all that surprising that I know so much? I am ancient, Lore." Though not as old as they'd thought. He hadn't shared with her what the crystals did. Perhaps a part of him worried that she would see it as a flaw in Nyx.

Like Abraxas, their daughter had seen and known too much. Far more than anyone her age should know.

Lore's smile faded a little, but then she shook her head. "There is so much here for us to know. Too much, really, but I'm so surprised that all of it has been left here for me. Tanis seemed surprised as well. She said that she wasn't aware any of this was here, or why they knew about me before the prophecy had been written. It's all so confusing."

"You met Tanis?" he asked, shocked that she'd gotten that far in her discoveries. "When did you meet her?"

"Well, I didn't really meet her. I saw her." Lore shrugged and then peered down at the scroll in her hand again. "I need to bring these back to camp after we meet with her. These will keep me busy translating them into a language all of us can read."

A job, he realized. That was what she'd been seeking. Lore didn't want to put herself in danger and she didn't care about adventure all that much anymore. She just wanted to be useful, and he'd told her she couldn't be.

Whatever lingering anger remained drained out at the realization. He moved away from the heat of her body to seek out something in this room that would be useful. In the beginning, all he saw were more cobwebs as Lore pulled out a few more scrolls to bring with them.

"We can return," he said with a slight chuckle. "You don't have to bring the entire room."

"It's open now, though. Whatever water gets in here is bound to destroy some of these scrolls. I just want to keep them safe."

He watched as she ran a delicate finger over the edge of one. As though she could thank the ancestors just by touching their edges. As if she could touch the family members who were long gone.

If he'd found more of those crystals, he supposed he might have done the same thing. Even if the crystals couldn't give him memories from the older dragons, they still were something that others like him had touched.

His fingers finally grabbed onto something that resembled a sling. It wasn't much fabric, most of it moth eaten or falling apart, but it would last.

"Here," he breathed, bringing it over to her. "This should work."

"It absolutely will." Her eyes lit up with happiness and she stuffed as many scrolls into the bag as she could into the bag. "Thank you. Do you know where Tanis is, then? She seemed to think you would."

"I do."

He didn't want to bring her there, but what was the harm? She'd find out that there were more dragon eggs. He just hadn't wanted to add to her stress.

Maybe Tanis was right. He had to give her more things to do or she would lose her mind. She needed to be involved with everything here, and thus, that meant she had to at least see what they were up against.

Besides, if Tanis could help her control the power, then everything would be worth it.

Sighing, he watched as she started up the stairs without him. "There's something I should tell you about Tanis."

"Yes, I know!" she shouted back, already disappearing out of his sight. "She's not dead! She told me."

That... wasn't at all what he was going to say. Why did Lore think Tanis was dead?

Ah, right. The spectral visage that she'd used to speak with them. Lore should have known that was a spell. Hadn't Goliath done the same thing to speak with them all those months ago?

His chest hurt at the thought of the little man who had been such a bright light in their lives. He should be here. The dwarf would have loved to see how the dragons lived, and how many tunnels and caverns there were. He could already imagine Goliath marching through the caves of crystals, certain he'd find gemstones among them.

The weight of loss was heavy, Abraxas admitted to himself as he walked after Lore. Perhaps too heavy for either of them to carry alone. And as such, he should be more delicate with her. She'd lost everyone as well, after all.

He reached the sunlight to see her standing beside the pools, her face turned toward the sun. The wind played with the tendrils of her hair. Her expression was peaceful, and he hadn't seen that expression in a very long time.

Abraxas quietly approached her and held out his arm for her to take. "Let's go visit Tanis, shall we?"

The brilliant smile on her face was one that he never wanted to forget.

CHAPTER 28

Lore had promised herself that she wouldn't wander off and scare anyone. But then she'd seen the cavern and heard the call from her ancestors, and what had she done? Wandered. When she had heard Abraxas was waiting for her, she had been certain that he would be angry.

He'd every right to be. The last time she'd wandered off on her own, he'd had to watch her die. He'd seen nothing left but the remains of her magic and... Well. He could shout and yell at her with no arguments on her end. She deserved it.

Instead, he'd merely stood behind her. Close enough to feel so tempting in the way he leaned over her. And he hadn't yelled.

Lore found herself surprised. He was supposed to yell at her. To get angry. To be the controlling man who wanted her to never touch a sharp thing again. Instead, he'd proven that he had some self-control left.

Strange.

She didn't know how to feel about it, but she also didn't want to bring it up as they trudged through the forest. All she wanted right now was to enjoy the moments they had together. Because every single one of them felt important these days.

Swinging the bag over her back so it wouldn't get tangled in the bushes, she called out, "Where are we going?"

"You said you wanted to see Tanis."

"I do." Lore wrestled with a particularly angry branch before she burst out of the bushes onto the small plain that he'd brought her to. There was another path around the bushes, she realized as she glanced behind them. He'd made her fight through them and battle every limb on purpose.

A snarl was already on her face. She spun around to tell him exactly what she thought of that.

Only to see a wide grin on his own as he watched her. He'd known. Of course he had. And this was her punishment for wandering off.

Lore sighed and planted her hands on her hips. "That's just petty, you know."

"It's better than yelling." He walked over to her and wiped a stinging welt on her face. A thin line of blood coated his finger, and he brought it to his mouth to lick clean. "You deserve a punishment for scaring me like that."

"I don't mean to scare you when I disappear." She said the words as an apology for more than just wandering through the woods. But they both knew that. "I can't control it all the time."

"I know." He bent down to press their foreheads together, breathing her in for a moment before he straightened. "To ask you not to wander is like asking a horse not to run. Or a bird not to fly. You want to see the world in all its glory. Caging you will get us nowhere."

Why would he say all that when he knew how sensitive she was already feeling about it? Lore still felt guilty that she had made him worry, and she didn't want to make him feel bad either.

Sighing, she tucked herself under his arm and wrapped her own around his waist. "Come on, then. Let's go see Tanis. I assume my punishment is over, or are you going to make me walk through more bushes?"

He dropped a kiss to the top of her head. "Only a few stinging nettles along the way, love."

They both laughed, and she felt more at home than she had in a very long time. Here, with Abraxas, walking through the forest.... It was everything she'd ever wanted.

How long had it been since she'd assumed they would both die on a battlefield? That they would never stop running their entire lives? Now she was here, with him, walking through the forest as she'd always dreamt they would. The trees moved in the wind and the smile on his face warmed her heart.

This was what she'd been waiting for. A knot in her soul that she hadn't realized was still there eased. It finally released, untangled, freed her from the torment of its existence, and she could breathe again.

Lore squeezed her arm around his waist one more time, laughing at the look he gave her. She didn't care where they were going, as long as he was there with her.

Abraxas led her to a system of caverns. The wind whistled out of it, sounding like a woman shrieking as it blasted past them.

"Tanis is in here?" she shouted over the noise.

He nodded and plunged to the darkness. She thought maybe she should conjure another light, but the moment he led them down a separate cavern, away from the wind, she realized she didn't have to. Someone had lit torches all along the walls and cleared their path, so there was nothing to trip on.

Shocking, really. She'd never thought Dracomaquia would have so many hidden places underground. Dragons didn't seem to be cave dwelling creatures, in her experience.

"Tanis lives in the caves?" she asked, her voice echoing a bit.

"Not really. She's just here for a small amount of time, and then she'll be back." The odd smile on his face was slightly wistful. "Everything will be different once she's back at camp."

Lore expected that was because Tanis ran the place. She couldn't get a read on whether Abraxas liked her, or if he just respected the hell out of the woman. Both were good, she supposed. He should respect the woman that led the camp and who wanted to help them. Although she didn't want to know if he liked her. That ugly jealousy flared a bit in her chest before she shoved it back into the shadows of her mind.

She would not be jealous here. There was no reason for her to be jealous. Abraxas had never given her any reason to even question he might have looked at another...

They rounded a corner and her vision was filled with the glistening body of a violet dragon. Her scales were almost see though they were such a crystal clear amethyst. Lore watched as the dragon breathed, its hide moving up and down with an immense amount of power.

The dragon's eyes were on them as they moved toward them. Violet and all seeing, just as the woman's form had been.

So this was Tanis. Another dragon.

Lore sucked in a breath. "There was another dragon here?"

Abraxas nodded, bowing his head to Tanis and then glancing over at her with a smile. "Yes. There was. Tanis has been here since the time of the dragons ended. She hid when we were attacked and the others were destroyed with balls of acid. Like your rebellion had tried to attack me with."

She wouldn't wonder where they'd gotten the information to kill a dragon. Surely this was all connected, wasn't it?

"But why—" She wanted to ask why Tanis had hidden herself away down here. She wanted to know why a dragon would stay in the caverns rather than come out and meet all of them. After all, their children had made themselves known to the sailors. Surely another dragon might as well have come out of hiding, too.

But then Tanis shifted and Lore saw three dragon eggs pressed up against her belly. They were larger than the eggs she'd seen before, much larger, in fact.

Fresher?

Something dark twisted in her chest, like someone had shoved a knife in between her ribs. The ache spread through her, a cold numbness that she couldn't stop no matter how hard she tried. Lore could barely breathe as her eyes locked on the crimson egg that was pressed against this dragon's heart.

A crimson egg that shouldn't be able to be birthed. None of them should. Unless...

She glanced over at Abraxas and noted the pride in his features. He looked at those eggs as though they were his. And for all she knew... they were.

They had to be.

It all made sense now. The reason Abraxas had hung on for as long as he had. He'd come to this island, ready to end all of it once his children were safely here. And then he'd met another female dragon, one who had begged him to help bring about the next age of dragons and to give their line a chance.

Lore might have done the same if there were no more elves. She might have looked at Rowan and decided to give it a chance, no matter how small of a chance it was. And there had been a time when she would have done anything to see the line of dragons continue. She wanted people across Umbra to look at the sky and not feel so much fear when they saw the silhouette of a long neck and leathery wings.

But that twisted feeling in her grew. That horrible cold sensation that grabbed her around the throat until she couldn't breathe.

Abraxas was supposed to be loyal to her. He was supposed to keep her in his heart, no matter what happened to the rest of the world. Instead, they stood before the proof that he could not do that.

Dragon eggs. This beautiful dragon with soft eyes who looked at him as though he had given her the world. And maybe he had.

"Lore," he breathed, his eyes still on Tanis. "This is the last of the amethyst dragons. These eggs are our future, and soon she will hatch them and bring them into the world. Our goal of seeing a realm full of dragons may yet come to pass."

Her heart caught in her throat and the power pressed against her tongue. She already knew what it wanted. Kill. Destroy the person who was to be her competition and let them see who was more powerful. He wanted a female dragon? She was nothing compared to Lore, and Lore's power could turn her into dust.

But that wasn't right. She wasn't this person. She wasn't...

She needed air.

Lore nodded at Tanis and gasped. "I don't know if this is the right time to meet. I'll return once the scrolls are safely hidden again. They could get ruined here."

The dragon's expression twisted in confusion, but Lore had no intent to stick around to hear what she had to say. Instead, she turned on her heel and left.

"Lore?" Abraxas's voice called after her.

The other dragon murmured something, and Lore couldn't stand to hear what it was. She didn't care what quiet moments the two of them had together. She just needed to get away before she tore the entire cavern down around their heads.

Already her hands had disappeared. She glanced down at the glass-like features, flexing her fingers and watching the world warp underneath them. The power whispered if she would not kill the dragon, then she could change the fabric of time. Already, through her warped palms, she saw golden threads. Just one tug, the power claimed, and time would warp. Abraxas would never meet Tanis, because Tanis would never exist.

This was why the ancients feared her, she realized. One tug, and Tanis disappeared. Another pull, and Abraxas would never have left Umbra. They could all go home. She could rip and tear at the fabric of time, altering it to her whims, and no one would ever know.

Except her.

Lore would know and that guilt would eat her alive from the inside out. At that thought, the power inside her grew angry. It tore at her heart and lungs, making her feel as though everything inside her ached. That power would eventually rot, she worried, and she had no idea what rotten magic like that would do to her.

"Lore!" Abraxas called out again, snapping her out of her reverie the moment her feet hit the ground outside of the caves. “Where are you going?”

“Back to the caverns,” she croaked, her voice hoarse.

She staggered forward, only to stop when Abraxas stood in front of her, blocking her way. She didn’t have time for this. What if all the power inside her exploded out, and he was caught in the crossfire? What if she couldn’t control herself and that power lashed out at him?

His fingers caught her chin and forced her to look up into his worried eyes. “What is going on?”

No. He wouldn’t break her this time. She had every right to be angry at him and how he had moved on, even when they’d promised they’d never to do that. He was her mate, or so he claimed, and he shouldn’t have been able to do this to her.

Lore glared up at him, pouring all her anger into her gaze and hoping he felt the sear of it. “Nothing is wrong.”

“Why does it feel like you’re mad at me?”

She shook his hand off her face and stalked around him, tension and anger riding on her shoulders. “I’m not angry at you.”

“I know you well enough to know that’s a lie.”

Of course it was a lie. And he did know her well enough! Even if he’d thought she was dead, wouldn’t he realize she’d haunt him if he chose another? He was hers and she was his. That was what they had said to each other.

Coming back to find him here was hard enough. But to know that he had moved on? And so quickly?

Blowing out an angry breath, she shook her head and walked away from him. “Go back to Tanis, Abraxas. If she thinks she knows how to fix the powers inside me, then you can get all the details. Right now, I cannot be in that cavern."

"I thought you'd want to see the eggs." He sounded so lost. And maybe a little hurt. "Did I do something wrong?"

"No," she said and then kept walking until she reached the tree line.

That, at least, was the truth. He'd done nothing wrong at all. She was the person in the wrong here. She was the broken one who couldn't stand to see him make a choice that must have been difficult. He had to choose between his love for her and the future of his species.

Of course, he'd chosen the latter. She would have been angry with him if he hadn't.

But, as she turned to look over her shoulder before making her way back to the camp, she couldn't help feeling that cold ache again as he returned to the caves. He wanted a family. A wife. Someone who could give him a future that was more than just longing for what they couldn't have.

She'd pressed a hand to her aching heart without even realizing it. The moment she did, Lore flexed her hands against the thudding there and willed it to slow.

Her powers didn't work on herself, apparently. The thundering heart ache never went away. Never died down.

Instead, it walked with her through the forest. Knowing that her disappointment would never go away.

CHAPTER 29

Something had changed, and he had no idea what he'd done.

Abraxas watched Lore from across the fire, as he had done many times after leaving those caves. She refused to allow anyone into the cabin with her to sleep, not even him. Lore claimed that her dreams had turned dark and the powers inside her were begging to get out. She didn't want to hurt anyone when she wasn't in control.

But he'd stayed up a few of those nights and watched the cabin in case she needed him. Nothing had happened. No blast of magic, no crackle of energy, nothing but an aching quiet that had spread out onto the grounds around the building.

Rowan claimed the cabin was unnaturally cold when he went inside, but Lore seemed quite comfortable. Her hands had not yet returned to normal, however, and that concerned Rowan.

Abraxas waited for the other man to join him. Neither wanted Lore to realize that Rowan was giving him information about her wellbeing. Lore was already secretive enough about the changes happening to her. The last thing they needed was to make her even more angry when she realized the two of them were conspiring.

The sailors had joined them for dinner tonight, however, and that should give them plenty of time to talk. Allura grabbed Lore the moment she stepped foot near the cabin. The captain liked to talk, although not to men. Strange for a creature like that.

Abraxas lifted his mug of ale to his lips and took another sip. The sailors had brought it up from the boats, and though he didn't think it was strong enough to get a dragon drunk, it had warmed his belly.

The log creaked as another body sat beside him. He glanced over to see glistening dark skin and rolled his eyes. "Draven."

"Abraxas."

"Why are you sitting next to me?"

"Because I would also like to know how Lore is doing." Draven lifted his own tankard to his lips. "You aren't the only one worried about her."

Of course he knew that, but he still didn't want Draven sitting in on this time. He liked to think that he and Rowan were saving Lore with their quiet mumblings and planning on how to get her out of the cabin more and how to get her to eat more food. If Draven wanted to know about her wellbeing, then he could wait with the rest of them to hear from Lore herself.

Abraxas opened his mouth to tell the young man just that, but Rowan was already walking toward them. The older elf had a strange look in his eyes as he approached. A look that made Abraxas worried.

"What is it?" he asked even before Rowan had stopped in front of them.

"Hush." Rowan placed a finger against his lips and glared at Abraxas.

"You make too much noise when you're nervous."

"Well, then you shouldn't give me a reason to be nervous. Why do you look so strange?"

Rowan sat down on the other side of the small fire. There were many dotted around the area. They couldn't make a fire big enough for everyone to sit around these days, and the sailors were quite happy to stay to themselves.

He flashed a look toward Lore where she stood with the siren, but the two women were still deep in conversation. Every now and then they would look over in his direction, but he had a feeling that was Allura surveying their surroundings. The siren never looked comfortable, even when she was standing beside her own ship.

Grinding his teeth, he felt his jaw pop and his teeth creak together as he watched them. All he wanted was for Lore to get better. He wanted her to feel more like herself and maybe, just maybe, they would make their own cabin together. She wouldn't stay in this dusty elf's home while they all waited for Tanis to return.

Sighing, he lifted his drink to his lips and returned his attention to Rowan. "How is she?"

He'd deal with Draven later, since the young man had barged into this meeting without permission.

Rowan gave him a quick nod. "She's doing better. As you can see, her arms are all but returned to normal. They still flare sometimes. I've noticed particularly when she is alone and not distracted, they will suddenly turn back into whatever substance the magic turns them into. But for the most part, she has gotten that back under control."

"And the cold?"

Draven glanced at him sharply, then back to Rowan. His brows were furrowed in concentration, as though he were listening with every ounce of his being. The elf didn't have to look so invested, Abraxas wanted to grumble.

"Yes," Rowan said, coughing into his hand. "That has gotten a little better, although I cannot say it is comfortable yet in the cabin."

"I cannot understand why she's so insistent on remaining in that cabin. It's like she's angry with me and I cannot understand why." As soon as Abraxas said the words, he knew that was the truth. She was angry with him. And for a reason he still couldn't figure it out.

He held his mug poised in the air, ready to sip, but he stared into the fire instead. Having forgotten about the alcohol that might make this easier.

"She's angry at you?" Draven asked. "What were you doing before all this happened?"

A flare of pride made his skin sizzle. "We were visiting the tomb where all the elves had left her notes, something she was quite happy about. I helped her carry many of those articles here."

"They've been quite helpful, actually," Rowan added. "I didn't know half of what was written there, but the ancient elves were far more advanced than us. It's a shame that culture was lost as other creatures took over."

Draven rolled his eyes. "Your culture might have been lost. The Ashen Deep have been living in the same way for thousands of years. I could have told you much of what is in those scrolls. Anyway, she isn't angry about that. Then what did you do?"

"Tanis had projected her image into that tomb, so we then went to meet her. Lore saw the eggs, Tanis, and then she decided she wanted to leave. I thought maybe her power had swelled, and perhaps that is why she's angry at me. I brought her into a situation where she could have caved an entire mountain down upon Tanis and the eggs."

Was that it? Had Lore thought he was irresponsible for bringing her there when she couldn't control his power? He mused on the thought, letting it simmer in his mind. It sounded right. It sounded like something she would do, taking on the entire world's struggles.

What a shame. He'd thought she'd at least want to touch one of the eggs, as she had with their own children. It should have been a moment she could savor, looking those eggs over, knowing that they'd done something right after all their losses.

The dragons were not gone yet. Wasn't that what they had fought for? They had spent all this time to ensure that the dragons continued forward. This would make it all so much easier than that responsibility remaining entirely on Nyx and Hyperion.

"She met Tanis?" Draven asked.

"Yes. Tanis asked to see her, and Lore wanted to go." Why did the back of his neck bristle at the other man's tone?

Draven snorted into his cup, obviously enjoying this moment. "So you... brought her to see Tanis and a nest of eggs after you haven't seen Lore for months on end?"

Again, what was this fool getting towards? "Yes, of course. Why would I not bring her there? She is angry that I've risked the lives of the little ones. I already know the problem, Draven."

"You don't." Draven arched an eyebrow. "And I can see that I'll need to spell this out for you. All right. Put yourself in her shoes, Abraxas. She's been gone for almost a year now. You've made yourself a comfortable home here with friends and another dragon, which has probably always been in the back of Lore's mind. And then you bring her into a cave where there are more dragon eggs, something you yourself have told her is impossible because there were no more eggs left. So she sees you. Tanis. And eggs that shouldn't exist. Are you getting it now?"

No, he wasn't.

What did any of that have to do with the risk he'd taken in bringing her to that cavern? She didn't like to take risks with other people's lives, although she was quite good at putting herself at risk. And if she'd seen the eggs...

The eggs.

The impossible eggs that he himself had claimed they'd never find. She must have thought—

Abraxas groaned and palmed his head. "She thinks they're my eggs."

He didn't have to look to see Draven's nod. "She thinks they're yours and Tanis's eggs, my friend. Unfortunately, that puts her in quite the predicament when she feels like you've carted her through the entire forest, through a slippery cave, to meet the woman you've been mating with to keep the dragon race going."

Rowan's slight huff of breath caught his attention. Abraxas glanced over at the elderly elf to see his wide smile.

"What?" Abraxas asked.

"The thought of Tanis and you is quite amusing, I'll admit. But I can imagine that Lore has been angry for exactly that reason. I know I wouldn't be able to handle it. She wants the dragons to flourish as much as you do. So she cannot tell you not to talk with Tanis or even continue what the two of you must have done. But it will eat her up inside."

Abraxas sighed and drained the rest of his drink. "Well, then. This is going to be a little more difficult to fix than I initially thought."

But a part of his soul stretched. He was pleased to know she could even get jealous. Lore had never had the opportunity to feel so about him, and yes. It was quite pleasant to know that she cared enough to not want him with another woman.

Chest puffing, he stood up and stretched his arms over his head. "I suppose I should go fix this, gentlemen."

Draven rolled his eyes. "You should have fixed it in the moment, but you're a dolt who doesn't understand women."

If he could have burned the man alive right then and there, Abraxas would have. Glaring again, he snarled, "At least I have a woman."

The answering flash in Draven's eyes suggested the man had a comeback. And Abraxas didn't miss how the elf's eyes trailed slightly behind him, where he knew his daughter stood.

To Abraxas, Nyx was still a child. To any other species, she also still would have been nothing more than a babe. But dragons aged differently. They experienced the world in different ways, and she had the body and mind of a woman. Unfortunately. He so wished she hadn't consumed those damned crystals and stayed a child for a little longer.

Still, he narrowed his eyes at Draven and hissed, "A necklace made of your fingers. Remember that."

He didn't look to see if Draven felt even an ounce of fear at the threat. Knowing that elf? He didn't care.

Meandering past the fires, he took his time to congratulate the sailors on making good work on their boat. A few of them thanked him for felling the trees that would remake their mast. They still weren't certain if they could fix the sails, but they were making good headway.

He could feel Lore's eyes on him the closer he got. And a part of him wondered if she was getting nervous just having him closer. She still loved him, clearly if she was feeling that awful jealousy. She just didn't know how to reconcile herself to this new fact.

Finally he stood in front of her and Allura, an amused smile on his face as Lore ignored him.

The siren, on the other hand, looked him up and down with disdain. "What do you want?"

Wonderful. Lore had filled the siren in on everything, and apparently Allura was not interested in hearing his side of the story. He couldn't blame her. If any of his friends had said their mate had procreated with another to keep their own species alive, then he would have had a hard time enjoying their company as well.

Arching a brow, he ignored the siren and instead focused his attention on Lore. "Can we talk?"

"I planned on talking with you soon, just not yet." Her hands flashed in and out of existence. "I need to get my mind wrapped around a few more things, Abraxas. We both know we need to talk. Tonight, can that be enough?"

He pretended to think about it. He even went so far as to tap his lip, as though he was really mulling over her words. Then, without hesitation, he bent down and tossed Lore over his shoulder.

Sure, it was a risk. She could have exploded with power and tossed him to the opposite end of the clearing. But she didn't. The only thing he felt was the faintest electrical charge when her hands slammed down on his back.

"What are you doing?" she shouted, although she must have ignored the laughter that erupted behind him.

He shrugged, jostling her on his shoulder while he steadied her with a hand on her bottom. "We need to talk."

"Abraxas, put me down."

"Not likely for a bit. I don't want anyone listening to us."

She kept arguing with him as he stomped through the undergrowth, but Abraxas didn't mind. He'd missed hearing her voice, and if the only option he got was her scolding him, then he'd take it. She still had a lyrical quality to her words that made his heart squeeze in his chest. He adored her, even when she was mad.

He winded through the path of the woods, bringing them to a clearing much smaller than the one Rowan and Tanis had settled in. Only then did he set her down.

Immediately, Lore stumbled away from him. Her hair was in her face and her breathing was ragged, even though he was the one who had carried her here.

"Of all the stupid, foolhardy, ridiculous, idiotic—"

Abraxas grabbed onto her, smoothing the hair out of her face so she could see him. "They're not my eggs."

Her jaw dropped open. "Excuse me?"

"They're not mine," he repeated, gently tucking strands of her hair behind her ears. "Tanis had those eggs before the fall of the dragons, before I was even born. She hid them in the mountain in the hopes that someone like me would eventually come here. She's been waiting to hatch them until it was safe to bring the dragons back. They aren't mine, Lore. They never were."

The stunned silence that came from her made him quite proud of himself. He might not have handled her fear the moment she'd felt it, but he'd handled it well, eventually.

Abraxas smoothed his thumb over the peak of her cheekbone. "There has only ever been you, Lore. I almost died without you, and the thought of even living a single day without you in my life puts me back in the same place."

She tilted her chin up, that stubborn jaw already clenched. "You may have found another reason to stay alive."

"Ah, but there has never been another reason. There has only been you." He leaned down and pressed a kiss to her forehead. "Only you."

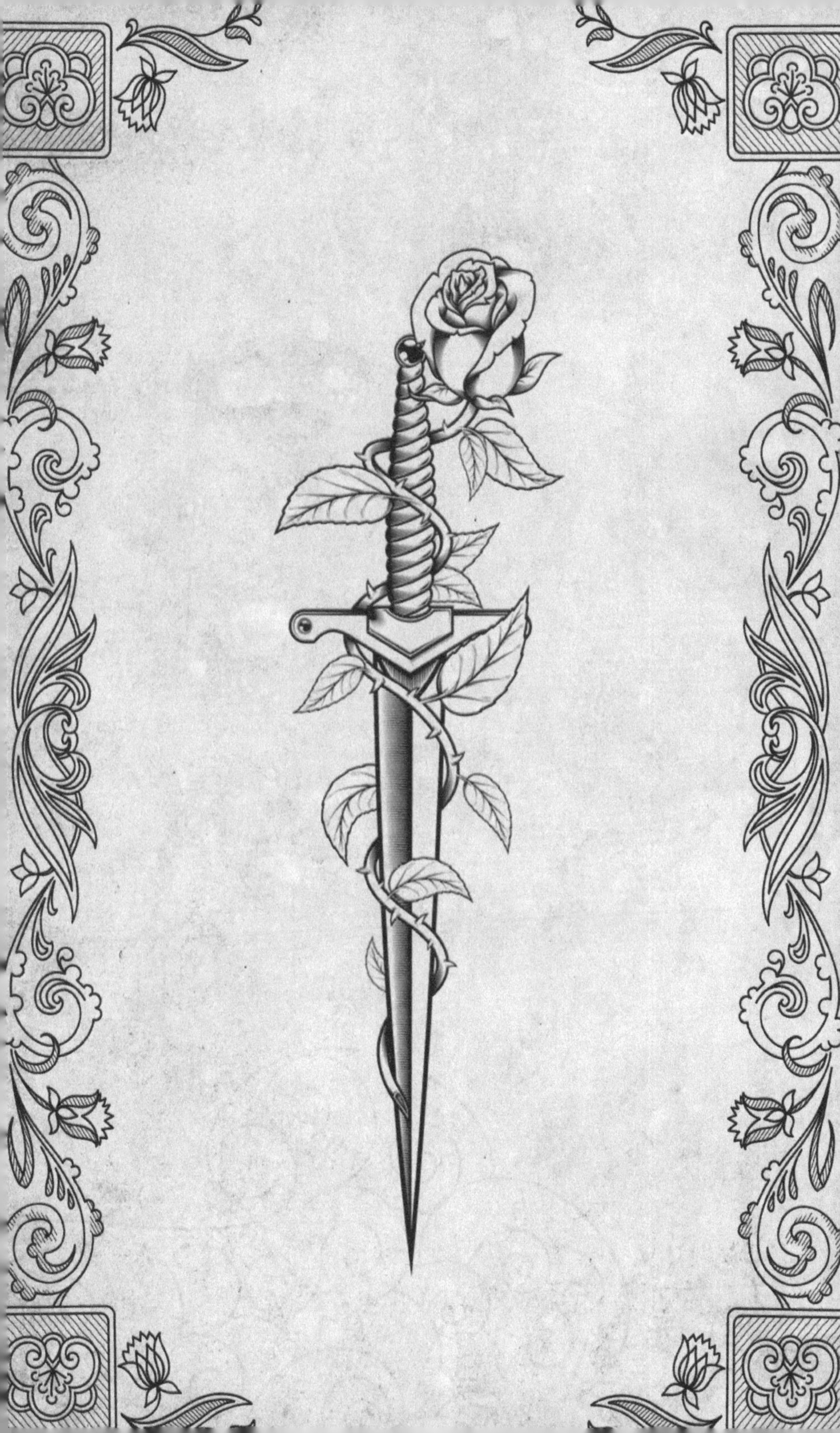

CHAPTER 30

Lore felt like an idiot.

She'd seen Tanis and those eggs, and suddenly everything had rushed forward until she couldn't control it. Herself. Any of what she had felt. It was all wrong, and she had been here suffering because, of course, Abraxas would do anything he could to continue the line of dragons.

She hadn't thought to ask if those eggs had been around since he got here. She hadn't even tried to understand what was going on. Instead, she'd jumped to her own conclusions and now she was the fool who had caused so much trouble.

All this time with him, wasted. They could have explored the entire island by now and she'd spent an entire week letting her new powers take control over everything. She'd had to argue with herself so many times not to leave the cabin and turn him into dust. Now, all she wanted was to curl up in his arms and apologize for wasting a week of good days. A week when she wasn't in pain.

Sighing, she shifted forward and let her forehead thud against his collarbone. "I'm sorry."

"There's no need to apologize." Abraxas wrapped his arms around her tightly. "I would have thought the same thing if I was in your situation, and I should have explained it better."

"I just thought... Well. Eggs, Abraxas. You said there weren't any others, and if there were eggs out there, then it would be nearly impossible to hatch them."

"I didn't know Tanis existed. Or what she had done to protect her own children." His breath lifted his chest, and she rode the wave of his body like a ship out to sea. "I didn't know what a dragon mother would do to keep her children safe. Mine certainly did little."

She sighed and looped her arms around his waist. "I don't have an excuse for the way I acted, and I don't think you should try to give me one."

"It is already forgotten, Lore." She felt his lips press against the top of her head. "I'm just glad to get you back."

She wanted to rage at the words. He shouldn't let her off the hook so easily. He shouldn't let her get away with bad behavior like that and then tell her it was all right for her to act that way. She should have at least gotten some of his anger directed at her.

But then she remembered that Abraxas rarely got angry. And when he did, it was only to protect her. They'd been apart for a while now, and she didn't have to make them stay apart even longer if she didn't want to.

Or she could keep this over their heads and dance around him as though he'd surrounded himself with broken glass.

Pulling back, she stared up into his eyes and nodded. "Then it is done."

"It is."

"Can I leave the cabin, then? Rowan is an interesting companion, but all he wants to talk about are the scrolls. I've already brought him hundreds of them and he pours over them in great detail. I understand he's one of the few who can still read them, but I'm so bored."

Abraxas tilted his head back and laughed. She watched the strong muscles of his neck flex in the moonlight, and an overwhelming sensation of love took over her. She wanted to kiss him. She wanted to dance with him in front of the fires, like the sailors had been doing every night. But mostly, she just wanted to snuggle into him and hear more about what he'd been doing in her absence.

When he stopped laughing, Abraxas looked down at her with a soft expression on his face. "You know I'm more than happy to have you with me."

"I don't even know where you sleep."

"Outside, mostly." He pointed back toward the camp, though slightly up. "I've taken to sleeping on the cliffs up there. I can see more from where I rest, and the views are better."

"Better?" She couldn't imagine there were any better views than the ones they'd already seen. This place was beautiful. More so than Umbra, which had centuries of people tearing apart the land. Dracomaquia didn't suffer from any of that. The landscape was wild and untamed, and it called to her very soul.

"So much better." He held out his hand for her to take, his eyes glittering in the darkness. "Come, Lore. Let me show you."

How was she going to ever say no to that? Lore placed her hand in his and together, they strode out of the woods. Thankfully, Abraxas did not make her walk through the crowd of people who were certainly waiting for them after the scene he'd made.

They walked through the forest nearby, though. Lore caught a glimpse of the fires, so far in the distance that no one was likely to see them. Except two elves, of course, who were at their own fire talking with each other.

As though they could sense her, both Draven and Rowan looked up. They must have seen the two of them walking along the ridge of the mountain before they began to climb.

She liked to think both men smiled. Though Draven and she had a rather complicated relationship, she had a feeling it wasn't as complicated as before. He'd eased in his adoration. Perhaps because of the spell Allura had put him under while they were on the ship.

Or for another reason.

Lore paused in her climbing to glance back and noticed that Nyx had sat down with Draven and Rowan. The three of them talked, though Draven was gesturing wildly as he did when he was telling one of his outlandish stories.

There was something there. She'd noticed it a few times this week and hadn't wanted to bring it up to Abraxas. The mother in her hesitated at the thought of Nyx already being old enough for this. but the other part of her, the side that knew magical creatures well, understood that Nyx wasn't a child at all. And Draven certainly wasn't either.

"You all right?" Abraxas called back.

"Fine," she replied, and turned toward him to keep his attention on her. "Where are we going?"

"Up."

Well, she could have guessed that herself. They'd been moving in that direction for a while now. But how far "up" were they going?

Though she didn't mind using her body. Pouring over ancient elven texts was interesting and all, but she'd grown so tired of sitting still. Lore wanted to move. Her soul needed to see what Dracomachia could offer them.

Although, she supposed there was always a part of her that would miss Umbra. A part of her that feared what might happen in her absence. It was a silly worry. She'd given them everything she had, including her life. If they couldn't figure it out without her, then the kingdom deserved to fall.

Abraxas stopped on an outcropping just above her and reached out his hand. "It's a big leap from where you are."

Not too large, but enough that she would have to jump into the air and hope she caught the edge of the cliff. Or his hand. Giving him a wild grin, she launched herself off the cliff edge and toward him. There was never any hesitation in her movements. Not with him. She knew that Abraxas would catch her. Even if she fell, he'd catch her long before she hit the ground.

Abraxas caught her by the wrist and drew her up onto the cliff beside him. She dangled from his grip, never once worrying about the height or if he'd let her go. He wouldn't. She never questioned that at all.

The last second, just as her feet touched the stone, her hands disappeared. Abraxas wrapped an arm around her waist, drawing her against his chest so quickly that she let out a little "oof".

"Are you all right?" he asked, shaken that he'd almost dropped her.

But she wasn't all that worried. He hadn't. And if Lore had discovered anything in this strange time in her life, it was that she couldn't worry about the what ifs. She survived. No one had tumbled off the cliff, nor had anything bad happened. Letting go of those worries was the best way to stay in the moment.

She pushed him away from the edge, following him with every step as he hadn't let go of her waist. "I'm fine. We're both fine."

"I thought you were getting control of that?" He peered down at her, then frowned. "Unless you're still angry at me and you aren't telling me."

Lore rolled her eyes and released him. "I'm not angry with you. It is legitimately that I cannot control it. I don't know what I do to make my hands disappear, let alone what other emotions cause it. Sometimes I swear it's just random."

Or that the power was trying to sabotage her. She glanced behind her down the long depths of what would have been her tumble toward death and shivered. It didn't feel right that she could have ended up down there, and yet... No. She refused to think about it. Abraxas would have caught her in his dragon from before she'd had to use her powers to save herself.

He watched her with a gaze that saw far too much. "You think it wants you to use the magic?"

"Yes." She looked him in the eyes. "It wants to be used, and it whispers that to me every single moment of every single day. There is a beast that lives inside me. One that hungers for more power and to prove just how far we can go. But I also know the consequences of listening to it."

Or at least she thought she did. Even after waking up, she hadn't felt all that wrong. Her body had been sore and she could tell that there had been pain moments before she'd woken, but... She didn't remember it.

The power liked to whisper that the price of her magic wasn't something she ever really had to pay. Her body would endure it, not Lore herself.

Thoughts like that were dangerous, though.

Abraxas seemed to understand that she needed a distraction. He drew her closer to him, tucking her underneath his arm once again and turning her around. "This is what I wanted you to see."

And before them, the sky opened up. She watched as streaks of bright green, blue, and yellow warped across the sky. They gently moved like waves, but so far above them. As though they were underneath the sea.

"What are they?" she asked, her breath catching in her throat.

"A message from the gods. My mother used to claim that the sky was never dark in Dracomachia, and I never knew what she meant until I came here." He shifted her in front of him, wrapping his arms around her so she could lean against his back. "This is why I come up here every night. Just to be a little closer to those lights. And to the gods themselves."

She stared up in wonder at the lights and couldn't help but think they weren't the gods. She'd died. No gods waited for her on the other side, just a blank darkness and the need to return. Along with the wish that she could be here with all her people. Even if that meant giving up that everlasting sense of peace.

But she didn't have to taint the moment with those thoughts. Instead, she looked up and watched the beauty of the world unfurl before them. Perhaps, if she squinted hard enough, she would see her mother again. Her ancestors. All the elves who had come before and would come after, all combined in the bright soul of that light.

That she could stand by. She could believe that those lights were all the people in her family who had loved her and never stopped. Even in death.

She didn't know how long they stood there, watching the sky return from bright green to the darkness of the night. Only then did Abraxas draw her away from the stars.

"There's not much up here for comfort," he said quietly. "But—"

When he hesitated, she smiled up at him. "We've both slept in worse. I just want to be close to you tonight."

He curled his fingers with hers and drew her toward what might have once been a cave. Rocks covered the entrance now, but it provided covering over their head in case it rained.

Abraxas had piled up blankets in one corner, a thick coating of them with multiple deer hides for warmth. A small stone circle marked where he would put his fire if he needed one, and there was even a small contraption that she wondered if he used it to cook with.

"I didn't know you had a place outside of the clearing," she murmured as she looked around.

"No one else does either. I'd appreciate it if we could keep that between us." He sat down on the edge of the furs, and she could see he wanted her to join him. He just didn't know how to ask her to.

Lore didn't wait for him to ask. She joined him with a soft sigh, relaxing on the furs that were so plush, she wondered what kind of deer could have made them. "This is lovely," she mumbled as she looked out at the stars. "It's like we're floating above the world."

"I just like being away from the others," he said with a soft grunt. "But the view isn't half bad."

"Half bad? This is a place where poets would come to write. Where lesser men realize their faults and come to mend such things. This is a place for quiet contemplation."

He nudged her with his shoulder. "Quiet contemplation? And yet you haven't stopped talking since we arrived."

His teasing words soothed her fear that she'd ruined something between them. "Oh hush," Lore replied, though she allowed him to draw her into his arms.

They both laid down on the furs and remained in the silence. She traced her fingers over his forearms, her back against his chest. She took more comfort than she'd thought possible in feeling his breath against her spine.

"You know, I can feel your magic when you touch me like that." His breath teased the back of her neck. "It's like little sparks of lightning along my skin."

She hated that. She didn't want him to feel her power when she didn't intend on it. "It doesn't seem to be going away."

"Are you feeling worse?"

She shrugged. "Sometimes the same. Sometimes I don't feel like myself at all. Like someone else has crawled underneath my skin."

"Hmm." His hum rumbled through her entire body. "At least here you can find some peace."

"That's what it was like being dead," she whispered. "No pain. No fear. Just peace and quiet."

"How could you let that go?"

She flattened her palm on his arm, feeling him jump with the electric surge that moved through her fingers. "For you, Abraxas. Because I couldn't leave you."

CHAPTER 31

Their camp settled into something that almost seemed like peace. Abraxas enjoyed the week after he and Lore had settled the matter which had split them apart.

He hadn't been lying when he told her to forget everything. There was no room for anger between them, not when they were both reminded of how little time they had. Even centuries would not be enough with her, and they knew how finite time was.

They'd taken to sleeping up in the mountains together, regardless of the looks the sailors gave them. Even Draven seemed to make faces when they passed him. Although Draven didn't make a face of disgust like the others. Instead, his expression was something of pride. As if he'd had something to do with their reconciliation.

Of course he had. But Abraxas would be the very last person to ever admit it.

The sailors had nearly finished the masts in the past week's time. The sail, however, continued to be a problem. No one knew how to patch any fabric together so it was sturdy enough to withstand the winds home to Umbra.

Allura didn't seem all that bothered by it, though. Rowan had given her permission to send her men out into the wilds to find whatever treasure they could. It took a few days for them to return with anything worthwhile, but the first sight of gold had turned the siren into a different creature altogether.

Abraxas stood at the edge of the forest and watched a group of those sailors return with yet another few handfuls of gold. There wasn't much on the isle. No one had brought gold with them to work with the dragons, and most of the people who had been here were kidnapped out of their villages.

Whatever remained was the lingering memories of a people long lost. They had no idea that their wealth would eventually fall into the hands of people he could only call pirates.

Perhaps that should upset him more than it did. Abraxas was just happy that the gold wouldn't melt into the land and someone would find a use for it.

"I'm surprised they've found so much," Rowan muttered beside him. "Can you imagine? Coming all this way just for a few handfuls of gold."

"People have gone farther for less."

"In the old days." The expression on Rowan's face said he didn't approve. "I'd prefer they waste their time on that ship instead of wandering. I don't want any of them to stumble upon Tanis and her cave."

"That's why we told them the area near the pools is off limits." Although, even Abraxas knew that was a weak explanation. Tanis was in a cave that connected to many parts of their world. For all they knew, that part of Dracomachia could have another entrance elsewhere. The sailors might still find her, even for all that they'd done to prevent such a thing from happening.

Rowan shook his head. "It's barely enough to satisfy. I'm not sure if you noticed, but they're doing less and less work on the ship and more work sending people out into our lands. It feels wrong."

Nothing was wrong. Allura just knew there was very little time. The sails weren't getting fixed. She had to solve that problem and had no idea how to do so. Instead, she was bolstering her mens' morale by showing them how they hadn't made a mistake in coming here.

But she only had so much time before they realized maybe they weren't getting back home. The sailors would not like that conversation.

Abraxas looked back at the ship. He never knew why his gaze directed in a certain way until he saw Lore crest a hill. Or in this case, she walked up to the edge of the ship while talking with Allura. The two of them were always trying to figure out the problem. Unfortunately, this seemed like a problem that couldn't be figured out so easily.

"Is there anything in those elven documents that might help us weave?" Abraxas asked, although he'd asked the same thing yesterday.

"Not yet."

"Ask Lore to bring a few more up, then."

"I'm still upset I can't just get them myself," Rowan grumbled.

They'd found out the hard way that the magic of that place would only let Lore in. Rowan still had a few scorch marks on his back that refused to heal.

"Thankfully, Lore doesn't mind retrieving scrolls on whatever topic you see fit to ask for." Although, he had heard her grumbling a few times about old elves who couldn't stop reading.

Glancing around them, he felt something shift in his chest. He had been content here before Lore had found him. His family had settled into a life that suited them, and while it wasn't the best kind of life, it was better than most. Until the sailors came, and suddenly he saw people smiling. Regularly. The land even seemed happier as the trees turned bright emerald and the grass spread like a carpet of green below their feet.

Or maybe it was just him, he mused. Maybe he was happier knowing that he could turn around at any point and that Lore would be there. Waiting for him. Ready to continue this wild and crazy journey that they had both dreamt of for such a long time.

This is what they had fought for. And now? They finally had it.

Sighing a little, he rubbed at the ache where his heart was. It felt right. All of this felt so right.

"Stop it," Rowan grumbled. "You look like me when I'm staring at Tanis, and I thought I was the only one who felt like that. You'll bruise my pride."

"Ah, but isn't that the way all men look at women who have shattered their worlds?" He didn't mind admitting it, especially to the elf who knew how he felt. Rowan had endured the same life changing love that he had, and there was no one else in this world who could understand it as well.

They both knew what it felt like to love a storm, and how that storm could bring healing rains or thunderous quakes.

The bushes rustled behind them, and Abraxas steeled himself for one of his children to come barreling out. They had both been incessantly needy lately, and he didn't know how to tell them he had better things to do than listen to their complaints about each other.

They needed time apart. Unfortunately, the island wasn't big enough to give them both the space they desperately needed.

But it wasn't Nyx or Hyperion who staggered through the bushes. It was Draven. His eyes were wild and his hair tangled around his face. He gasped, "It's Tanis! She said to come get you. The eggs are ready."

Both he and Rowan froze. They stared at each other, and Abraxas recognized the look of pure fear in Rowan's expression. He'd felt the same when his own eggs had shown signs of hatching. Would he be a good father? Would he be able to keep them safe?

"We have to go," Abraxas told him, gently pushing him toward the caves. "You first."

"The eggs," Rowan repeated, his face devoid of all color. "They're hatching? Now?"

"Yes!" Draven replied with a laugh, then clapped his hand to the other man's shoulder. "You're about to be a father at the ripe age of... what? Two thousand?"

"Five hundred, you little brat."

"Ah, well. You should be a grandfather twice over by now, instead you had to start your life late. Go get your children, otherwise your wife will burn the entire island to the ground in her anger." The deep monger stepped away from them and gave Abraxas a little nod. "Do I need to get anyone else?"

None of the sailors, that was for certain. He didn't want them knowing about this momentous occasion until it was all said and done. But he glanced over his shoulder and said, "Get Lore. Just don't tell her what's happening in front of that siren. I like the woman well enough, but I don't trust her."

"Neither do I. I'm glad you're thinking straight at least." Draven gave him another nod, then stepped out of his way. "Tanis specifically asked for you. I think she was worried one of the eggs wouldn't hatch."

"Then we need Lore." She was the only one of them who knew how to break a dragon out of its egg.

And Abraxas feared Tanis wouldn't allow them to. She still adhered to the old ways and... and...

He couldn't let his mind go down into that dark path. The old ways no longer served anyone, and both Tanis and he believed that. If Lore could help the egg that wasn't doing well, then she would. Lore was good at that.

They rushed away from the shore and through the forest. Rowan was markedly quicker than Abraxas, a new discovery that surprised him to the core. The elf had always made it appear that his age had slowed him down. But now? He flew through the forest to get to Tanis's side.

There wasn't the underlying terror for his wife that many mortal men would feel. Tanis would survive even if none of her eggs hatched. But they all felt the bone deep worry that this wouldn't work. That their hopes and dreams would be dashed upon the ground. And how would any of them come out the other side of that battle?

Reaching the cave, Abraxas watched Rowan slip into the darkness without even casting a spell. Apparently, the elf knew the way by heart at this point.

Abraxas blew out a small breath of fire, giving life to a fire sprite that would join the others in the fire pits. It happily guided him through the caves, making little mewling noises as water droplets from the ceiling came too close. It wasn't a safe place to bring a little one like that, but he'd make sure it stayed alive.

The caves seemed quieter today. As if even the earth itself knew something momentous was occurring. The birth of three dragons on these lands after centuries without them.

These caves had seen countless dragons walk through them. So many mothers who dreamt of having children beside them. And dragons who were hiding their clutch, hoping the future would be kinder to them. Perhaps they would discover more eggs in these tunnels. More souls that had been dormant for so long that no one could hear them anymore.

Rounding the corner, he poked his head into the cavern where Tanis had been waiting with the eggs. Her great serpentine body was spread out throughout the entire space, no longer curled up around the eggs, wedged underneath the rock as she had been for weeks now.

Her sides heaved with breath as she stared at the eggs that rocked on the stone that had been their nest. The eggs were so many vibrant colors, and it seemed now that they were even more colorful than before. Especially the violet egg. That one pulsed with power that he hadn't seen in a very long time.

But, even though that egg commanded attention, his eyes strayed to the crimson egg. The one he should have had already. The dragon who had haunted his nightmares for months. In a way, it felt as though he was getting that egg back in this moment.

The crimson egg was the only one that did not move. The other two, the violet and gold, had no problem. Already he could see cracks forming underneath their gemstone shells.

"The crimson?" he asked.

"I haven't felt movement from that one in a while." She took a deep breath and let it out through her nose. "It was fine just yesterday. I know it was fine."

The stress had made her not see the situation correctly. He could tell. Tanis was so nervous that her children would never awaken that she didn't know how to help it. Couldn't, in that form.

"Would you like me to try?" he asked.

Her head swiveled to look at him. Her eyes filled with tears, even in this form. "I'm not sure I would let you. Something in me wants no one near those eggs while they're hatching. I can't move a muscle."

Ah, well, that would complicate things. Especially if she would attack him for coming near her eggs. It made sense, he supposed. Dragon mothers were incredibly protective of their young.

"And Lore?" he asked. "Will you let her near them?"

"She is also a mother." Her hide twitched, flicking with annoyance, before settling. "I believe I will let her."

"You know I will protect her. If you..." Abraxas hesitated to even say what he was thinking. He'd bring this entire cave system down and claw his way out with Lore in his mouth if he had to. She would not die because of Tanis's brood madness.

"I know," Tanis replied. "I'm trying to keep it under control."

"See that you do," he warned, although he knew he didn't have to. Tanis had yet to even truly meet Lore, but he knew the dragon wouldn't harm her willingly. Tanis wanted them all to continue forward together. She wouldn't risk that without a good reason.

At least, he hoped she wouldn't.

It took a very short amount of time for them all to hear the pitter patter of feet rushing toward them. Lore burst into the room, her hair wild and her eyes wide.

"The eggs?" she asked. "Draven said there was one that—"

He knew the moment Lore paused that Tanis had turned on her. Hissing, Abraxas already felt the change coming over him a little too quickly to stop. But he couldn't change in this room without threatening the roof of the cave.

Lore didn't move. She just let Tanis growl and then stepped around him. She moved like a wild horse stood in front of her, rather than a snarling dragon who would kill her for threatening her eggs.

"We didn't meet in the best way," she said, toeing closer and closer to Tanis. "I know you don't trust me to be near those eggs, but I need to try. Tanis. You're in there. The logic that I remember from when we spoke, it's still there. I can save your baby. Please. Let me try."

Though she still hissed and the frills along her neck were raised, Tanis at least moved her head out of the way.

Lore looked at him and he felt rage shaking his hands. He knew what that look meant, though.

He nodded toward the eggs. "Try. I'll keep you all safe."

"Are you sure?"

"No," he snarled. "But we have to try."

Lore squared her shoulders and moved forward with the bravery he'd always admired.

CHAPTER 32

The dragon's side heaved before her, and Lore eyed the massive creature with no small amount of distrust. She knew a dragon mother would do anything for her eggs. Gods above, Lore would do anything for her own children and she wasn't even a dragon.

Tanis was a new mother as well. And her eggs weren't hatching the way they were supposed to. Two of them wriggled with the creatures within, having no issues whatsoever. But the crimson egg didn't rock. Just like Nyx had been when she hatched.

The little one needed coaxing. It needed to wake up from that comfortable slumber, and she had a feeling this one knew more comfortable in that slumber than Nyx.

They all were dormant for hundreds of years in that sleeping realm before they were born. Lore wasn't sure how she was so certain of that. But some part of her knew she had been in the same realm as these children before they were born. She knew they were all together in that comforting quiet.

Who wanted to leave that place? No one. She'd only left because she knew there was someone waiting for her. Someone whose soul would not let her own rest until she had rejoined him.

These little ones had nothing like that. Of course, they had their mother, who they likely wanted to meet. And a big wide world that would welcome them with open arms. But that wasn't enough for some of them. Some wanted to stay in that quiet place and never have to fear for their lives.

Sighing, she took one more step toward the eggs and froze when Tanis growled. The low noise vibrated through her leathery throat and her eyes turned wild. There were more whites in her gaze than there was a pupil.

Lore held her hands up as though she could relax the dragon just by doing so. "I'm going to shift the two eggs that are moving toward you, Tanis. We all want you to be the first one they see."

She wasn't sure if her gut instinct about imprinting was right, but her children had seemed to know which parent they were more likely to reach out to, and that came from who they had seen first.

Tanis seemed to nod, although the movement was jerky and not well controlled.

Each step felt as though she were drawing herself toward her doom. But Lore grabbed onto the violet and gold eggs, and lifted them without the dragon trying to eat her. Not that she'd get close enough. Lore trusted that he would keep her safe.

Gently, she set the eggs down close to Tanis and watched a giant wing fold over them and drag them close to the amethyst dragon's still glowing belly. The eggs rocked faster near that heat, already quaking to get closer to the realm they knew was close.

They'd be fine, she thought with a soft smile on her face. They would attack the world with so much vigor.

Turning her attention to the crimson egg, she tried to think about how to coax this one into existence. It wasn't going to be easy. If the tiny dragon was anything like Abraxas, then it was effortlessly stubborn and thought it could do whatever it wanted. An elf telling it to come into the world wouldn't be enough to convince.

So she would need to try what she'd done with Nyx. She had to tell it that the world wanted to see its face.

All she had to see was if Tanis would let her anywhere near the egg at all. Lore glanced over at the mother dragon and waited until the first egg cracked open and then a glimpse of her first child was revealed.

Now was her chance. Lore took the remaining three steps toward the crimson egg and plopped down behind it. Wrapping her arms and legs around it gave the baby the warmth it needed to hatch, but also would prevent Tanis from biting her. If she bit Lore, then she would inevitably harm the egg as well.

Another low growl filled the room. Tanis had seen what she'd done, and the dragon did not appreciate the trickery.

"Lore," Abraxas said quietly. "Be careful."

"I'm working on the plan right now," she hissed in reply. Although there was no plan. She had no idea what she was going to do right now other than convince the child to fight.

Tanis couldn't bite her. At least she knew she was safe from the dragon's wrath. For now. But she only had so much time left before Tanis would give up on the child and take out the person who she would now blame.

She was in a precarious position, Lore thought, but the adrenaline running through her veins made her feel more alive than she had in weeks. This was what she had been born to do. Adventure. Living.

Tilting her head, she pressed her cheek to the warm scales that surrounded the egg. "Hello, little one."

There was no answering movement or sound from within the egg. But she could almost feel the life within it.

As though...

The power inside her surged. She let it filter through her skin, the glittering magic slowly turning her into a glowing light that surrounded the egg. Her arms disappeared again, and through her palms, she could see the dragon.

It rested with its head curled into its belly, eyes closed, sides barely moving. This wasn't what she wanted to see. It couldn't hear her if it was enjoying quiet this much.

A pulse of angry magic pressed against her skin, ready to force the child to awaken. But that wasn't right. She couldn't shake the babe awake and then force it to pay attention to her.

It was a baby. They were more delicate and needed a softer touch.

So she eased the magic into something else. She forced it to warp into a quiet touch of a loving presence. Not a mother, but something similar. An aunt, perhaps.

The magic sank through the outside scales of the egg and then deeper. Wrapping around the soul of the little beast who was so needed in this realm.

"You have to wake up," she whispered, knowing that her word would filter through that other realm. "We need you, little one. And I know it isn't what you want to hear. You want to stay wrapped up in that warm darkness and rest. But you cannot. It is not the time for resting."

Through her palm, she could see the dragon's tail lash with anger. It was disturbed, she realized. Like a babe twitching at the sound of a dog barking.

A soft smile crossed her face. So she annoyed the little monster. Good. It needed to be annoyed so it could fight its way out of that world.

"Rest is not for you," she said. "You were not born to sleep in that realm while the world fought around you. You were born to fight. To feel the rage burning inside you and to test the very foundation of the realm. You will battle your way out of that darkness. And then you will enter this world screaming with frustration because you know it would be easier to rest. But you were not born for easy."

Another twitch, this time with an answering blink, as though the babe wanted to open its eyes for the first time, but couldn't within the egg.

Lore looked up and met Abraxas's worried expression. Though it wasn't his child, he wanted this crimson dragon to hatch. Yes, there were other dragons now. But this was an opportunity to see another who looked like him. Who understood the strange desires that were deep inside him and only him?

This child would be the answer to so many questions that he'd been afraid to ask for years now. Centuries even.

Dipping low, she pressed her lips to the egg. "There is another who is like you. Another crimson dragon whose body flares with anger before anything else. He knows how that heat burns inside you. White hot and ready to tear into the fabric of the world. He knows you, even before you have hatched. And he waits for you, little one. He's been waiting for such a long time."

Then she felt it.

A press back against her magic. So powerful it almost rivaled the stolen power that threatened to rip through her body at all times.

The power of this child was so immense and different from anything she'd ever felt before. But wasn't that the gift of the dragons? They were all powerful, and that was why they were feared. Eventually, that fear of them had destroyed any opportunity that they might have had to flourish.

Power was terrifying. It made people fear. And fear would drive many into making mad choices that couldn't be changed.

All of those thoughts and more came at the brush of the crimson dragon's mind. It was afraid to come into this world because it didn't know what it would mean for it to be here. For so many to be afraid of it.

"No," she whispered. "Little one, you cannot control others, but you can encourage them to change. You can be the proof that they need not fear you or what you might do. You will be the change the world needs and you will help guide it into a new age. A new realm."

It didn't want to.

The little boy inside that egg didn't want that weight of responsibility that no one else needed to have when they were born.

"Neither did I," she whispered. "But I still took the chance, willing or not. I leapt into the world and I bent it to my will. Now, I am here. Though I am still afraid, I now have so much love in my life that I came back from the dead to feel that love once more."

Lore let her memories filter through the connection they shared. She let the little dragon peek through her mind and memories until it opened its eyes inside the egg. As though it could see her through the shell, they made eye contact.

Though she feared for a moment that bond, she knew that this little one didn't mistake her as its mother. They'd shared another bond in those moments between their minds. Something else entirely.

They were two creatures who knew what it meant to be dead, and two creatures who had survived the realm of darkness to come out into the light.

Lore smiled down at it and smoothed her hand over the shell. "Can you fight your way out of this on your own? Or shall I help you?"

The eye roll of a response was all the answer she needed. The crimson dragon needed no more help to get out of its shell than it ever would when it hatched.

It knew how powerful it would be. It also knew that there was no reason for it to fear anything here. Soon, it would take the world underneath its massive wing.

Just as the dragons were meant to do. Just as they were supposed to do all those years ago.

Lore slid her legs out from underneath the egg and stood with it in her arms. She'd forgotten how large the dragon eggs were. Time had smoothed that memory away, because she wanted to think of them all as little babies. But the egg filled her arms as she carried it over to its mother.

Tanis eyed her with suspicion, but then snuffled out a short breath as Lore settled the egg against her belly.

"He'll fight now," Lore said. "He just needed a little coaxing."

"Coaxing?" Tanis asked, her mouth warping around the words.

"He was afraid." Lore shrugged. "I don't blame him for that fear. There is much unknown in the world, and coming into it now of all times was a hard choice."

"He should have trusted that I wouldn't bring him into this realm if I did not believe there was a chance for him to add good to it," Tanis grumbled.

"And yet, he does not know you. Mothers are not always kind." She touched Tanis's wing with a soft glide. "I believe you will be an excellent mother, though. Just as you were to my children while I was gone."

The anger faded out of the dragon's eyes, and Tanis gave her a curt nod. "It was my pleasure to watch over them until their own mother could join us."

"I might never have," she whispered.

"But you did. And that counts for something."

With that, Tanis curled her tail around her children and then coiled her body around them. Rowan appeared over her shoulder, clambering up the mountain of dragon before sliding down her scales into the center where their children battled into the damp cave air.

Lore backed away from them until her spine hit a warm chest.

Abraxas wrapped his arm around her waist, pulling her against him with a soft sound. "You did well."

"I did very little other than to convince the boy to join us."

"Boy?" he asked, his voice little more than a guttural sound in her ear. "He'll protect many from the moment he hatches."

"He will." The hairs on her arms raised at the thought of his power. "He's nearly as strong as me. I touched his magic, Abraxas. It is... unending."

"Dragons always are."

She smiled at Tanis and Rowan as they cooed over their children, each baby dragon dragging itself out of its egg and then chattering up at their parents. The look on Rowan's face was one of terror and utter happiness. She knew that look, even though the expression had been on Abraxas's dragon face.

He feared the future for nothing. They would love him just as he loved them.

Tanis seemed a natural with the little ones, surprisingly. She lifted one up in her mouth and deposited it on the other side of her tail when the golden one wanted to pick a fight. They were all just... a family. Instantly.

Tears pricked her eyes. Silly, that. She knew what a family looked like. But she'd forgotten how emotional it made her to see children who got to have one.

Abraxas caught a tear that slid down her cheek. "What's this?"

"Happiness," she whispered. "Just happiness."

He hugged her tighter, and it felt as though a bubble grew in her chest. A bubble of happiness and light and air that filled her so much she was near to bursting. This was what contentment felt like, she thought.

Until the bubble popped.

Her body sagged in Abraxas's arms, and she couldn't stop herself. It was like the darkness had a mind of its own now. She couldn't fight it. There was nothing she could do to stop it.

"Lore?" she heard Abraxas ask before he swore loudly. "Rowan! Tanis!"

No, she didn't want to interrupt the moment their family met. She didn't have any right to do that. She didn't want anyone to worry about her when there were little babies right there who wanted to meet their parents.

As the darkness stole her vision, she felt her hands curl into her chest. She tried to stop them, but nothing she could do would pull her fingers away from that horrible... awful... terrible feeling of... of...

"When did she use magic?" Rowan hissed, grabbing into her wrists and holding them tightly.

"She didn't," Abraxas replied. "She must have used it to speak with the crimson egg. But, I thought... What is happening?"

"We have less time than I thought," the ancient elf replied, and Lore felt her body lift off the ground before the darkness whispered in her mind for her. The last thing she remembered hearing was, "Tanis will help us."

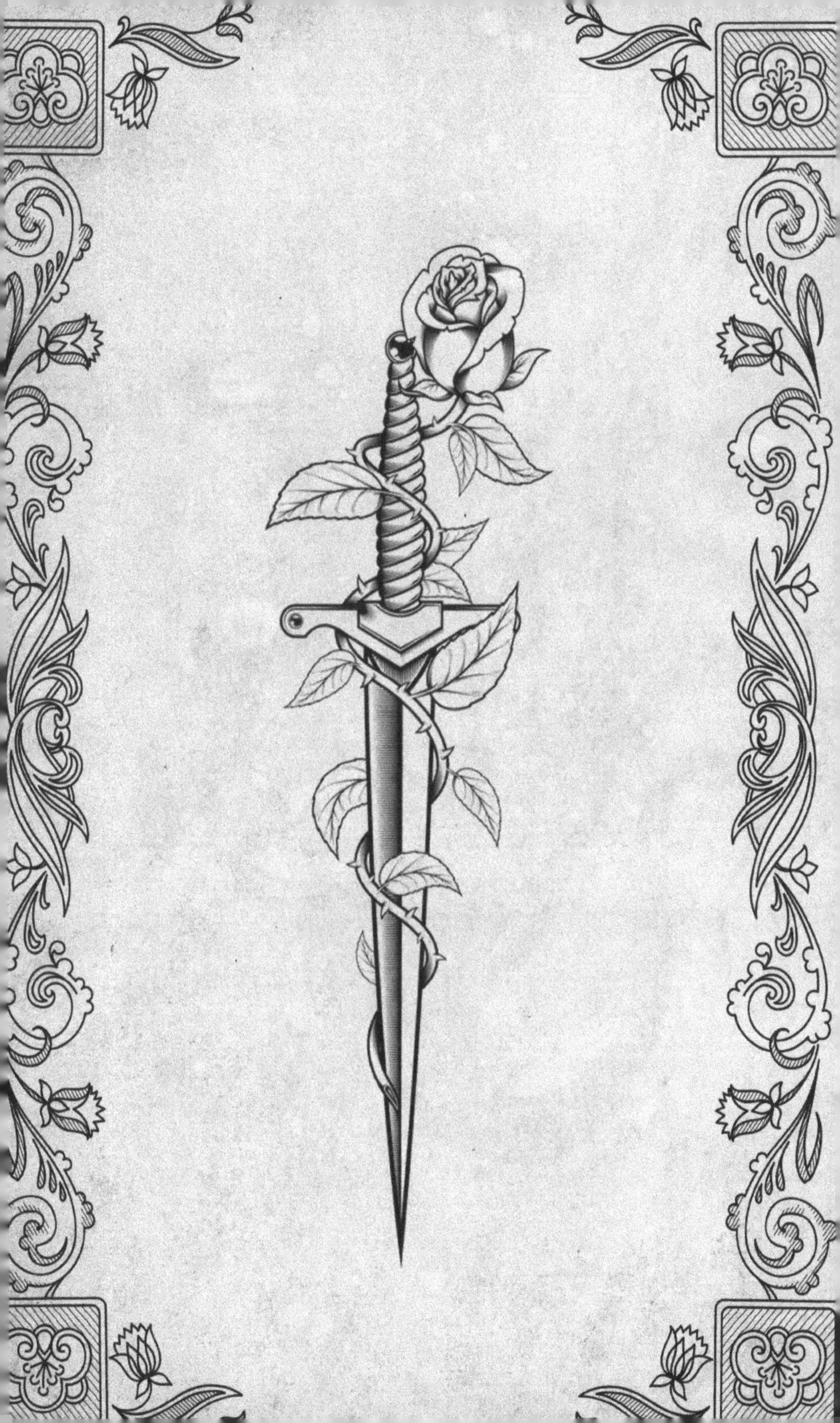

CHAPTER 33

Abraxas carried her back to the clearing with his heart thundering in his chest. He'd thought... No, he'd hoped that this was over. That she'd only suffer like this the one time and then the power would settle underneath her skin. But he'd been wrong. So very wrong.

She trembled in his arms, seizing every few minutes until she eased again. The magic was too powerful for her form to contain, and it tortured her body.

And he could do nothing for her.

He wanted to fight an enemy. To turn into a dragon and tear at the magic until it released her. He wanted to put his fist through stone until there was nothing left but a bloody stump, if that would help her.

This was not an enemy a dragon could defeat, however. There was nothing he could battle to make this easier for her. All he could do was hold her and run through the forest while hoping someone, somewhere, would know how to fix this problem.

Or perhaps she would die. Perhaps he would look at her one day and that would be the last time he saw her. Again.

"Quickly," Rowan said, his eyes wide and his breath coming out of his lungs in thunderous, ragged sounds. He pointed to the bed and then attacked his jars of herbs as though they were the only thing that would save her.

Though Abraxas appreciated the speed, he knew there was nothing in this earthly realm that could slow this process. Even Lore knew that.

She would endure, as she always had. She would fight her way back to him, but this time, he feared she might not make it back. Every time, he feared it.

Lore seized again as he settled her onto the bed. "What do I do?"

"The same as last time. Grab onto her hands so she doesn't break those wrists. We'll have to risk it in a moment, because I'll need you to hold her head back for me. Draven's keeping an eye on the dragonlings, so we won't have any more help until Tanis gets here."

Abraxas grabbed onto her wrists, gently keeping them in place as frustration set in. "Why is Tanis coming and not Draven?"

"She had an idea for how to help, but I'm not sure if it's going to be the safest choice." Rowan's arms were filled with herbs that he dumped on top of Lore again. This time, at least, he knew which jars to yank open and which herbs to gather up into his fist. "It'll be dangerous for both of them, but it's the only option we have."

"Why?"

Rowan tilted her head back and pried her jaw open. "All right, let go of her wrists quickly and then we'll jam this into her mouth."

"What is this even doing?" Abraxas quickly grabbed onto her jaw and forced it open for the other elf.

"Mainly keeping her from biting off her own tongue, but it'll settle her body again. More this time than last time." Rowan packed the greenery into her mouth and then slammed her jaw shut. "It would kill someone who wasn't like her. I didn't know if I could use this much, but the elven documents she procured stated otherwise. We'll see."

Anger flooded through his veins. Abraxas would have pinned the elf to the wall if he wasn't holding onto Lore's hands. "Did you just kill her?"

Rowan took a deep breath and held it as he stared down at Lore. She didn't convulse though. Slowly, her body settled like it had the last time. Her hands even lost their awkward angle.

"No," Rowan replied, although there was a healthy amount of surprise in the word. "I did not."

"Did you think you might?" Abraxas snarled.

"The documents said that whoever came back in her position would need the herbs. It specified nothing other than that, so I assumed it would be safe for me to give them to her. There's only so much I know, Abraxas, and much of that is limited by whatever the ancestors thought to write down." Rowan puffed up his chest as though that might even remotely intimidate Abraxas. "I'm doing my best to help her, just as you are."

Of course he was. But Abraxas still wanted to hit something, and this elf was the closest person within reach.

Her hands dropped out of his, limp. Too limp. He stared down at her prone body and wondered when their life had come to this. They were supposed to be living in blissful happiness. That was the point, wasn't it? All that fighting had to have some reason for them to... What? End up here?

Sighing, he pressed his fingers to his eyes and pushed hard. At least a little pain would make him ground himself. He could do something if he just thought about it hard enough.

But nothing came to mind. He could do nothing but stand here and wait for the world to turn on its axis again and give her back to him.

That anger surged again. Gruffly, he snarled, "Where is Tanis?"

"With our newborn children. I would imagine it will take her a bit to get here."

"Where is the dragon who thinks she knows how to save my mate?" Abraxas shouted, standing up over Lore's body.

He could protect her. That's all he could think about right now. If anyone tried to even touch her, then he would rip their head from their shoulders and throw it across the room. If only to do something. Anything in this moment when she laid there as if she was already gone. He had to do something.

"Abraxas," Rowan said, lifting his hands and backing away from the cot. "You know, I don't mean to harm her. I never would. We have to help her and if that means that I have to force some medicine down her throat, then so be it."

"I will not stand by and watch her die."

"No one would expect you to do that. Tanis thinks there's another way. She thought there was a note on the margins of a document that suggested a Memory Keeper could help all this."

"Then where is she?" Abraxas flexed his hands at his sides, nearly losing his mind with grief.

"Here." Tanis ducked her head into the cabin and strode through.

She looked as she always did. White hair perfectly in place, a violet gown clothing her body and floating around her like she was underwater.

Her arms were bare, fingers free of jewelry. She was a vision in this room of darkness, and it was all Abraxas could do to hold himself together.

Relief at her presence flooded through him at the same moment that grief threatened to overwhelm him.

"Can you?" he asked, the words shaking through the very core of his body. "Can you help her?"

"I will try." Tanis paused in the doorway, watching Lore for any movement before she approached the bed. "She's losing the battle, Abraxas. I thought I made it clear that she needed to figure out what happened in her time beyond."

"She remembers nothing."

"Then she should have forced herself to remember," Tanis snapped. "Bring me a chair, Rowan. I think we'll all be here for a while this time."

What was she doing? Abraxas knew better than to interrupt a Memory Keeper who was setting herself up, but this was not a wounded dragon that needed treatment. Lore wasn't one of their kind. Tanis couldn't reach into an elf's memory and rip out thoughts she needed to put into a crystal.

It shouldn't even be possible for someone to do that to a dragon, and yet, it was. Tanis had told him stories about all the memories she'd seen in her life. Even the memories she'd had to steal for the betterment of dragon kind.

Lore wasn't like them, though. She wouldn't survive a dragon ripping at her mind like that. She needed more protection... More...

He lunged forward as Tanis sat down behind Lore and seemed to ready herself. "You know you cannot do that."

"I can."

"I will not let you."

Tanis met his gaze, her violet eyes soft with compassion. "I stood by while you let your elf touch my eggs. I fought against every instinct that told me to kill her. Right now, I need you to do the same for me."

"She is my mate," he said, his words breaking around the fear of losing her again.

"I have lived through the loss of her with you before, Abraxas. I have seen the end of you and I know you fought against it for many months in hopes that she might return to you. Somehow. And she did. So what I need from you at this moment is to hang onto that hope that has helped you through so much." Tanis gave him a little nod. "I believe you can do that. Hold your hope close and stay out of my way."

If only that were something tangible he could cling to. If only it was something he could actually grip so that he had something to do other than stand here with his arms awkwardly at his sides.

"At least tell me what you plan to do to her. Please."

Tanis sighed and looked down at Lore. She took her time arranging the strands of hair around Lore's head, gently twisting them into spirals and coils. "The books that she found claimed someone could help the elf if she could not access her memories. That it isn't breaking the rules for another to dip into her mind and guide her. The plan was for that to be another elf who would then escort her through the realm of darkness that she's spoken of. They'd bring her to her memories."

Abraxas only barely followed what she was saying. "So you're going into her mind to help her? Is that what you're saying?"

"I'm going to try." Tanis looked back at Rowan, and the nerves in her expression were enough to set Abraxas on edge again. "I think Rowan must have told you that this is rather dangerous?"

"He did."

"Her mind is unknown territory. To all of us. There is no way for me to be sure where she is or how to find her. I have experience in this. For many years. So I should be able to find her and help walk her through her memories."

The pause at the end made him even more nervous. "And if you can't?"

"Then both of us are lost." She shook her head as though freeing herself from the nerves. "But that will not happen. I will not allow either of us to be swallowed by that darkness. Trust me, Abraxas."

"I trust you," he whispered. "But I do not want to lose either of you."

"Few want to lose anyone they love."

A pang of pain had him rubbing his chest to get rid of it. He wouldn't lose anyone today. He'd make sure of it.

Although, Abraxas also knew there was no way he could be sure of that. He couldn't stop losing either of them if this was the choice Tanis made. They would both disappear into that darkness that Lore had spoken of and then he would have to wait until one of them returned. That was how this all worked. He waited, and they fought.

"It is not natural for a crimson dragon to stand by and allow another to fight," he mumbled, hoping she understood what he said.

"It is not," Tanis agreed. "But you have more to fight for than ever before. Keep yourself safe, Abraxas, and be ready the moment she wakes. We have no idea what will happen once she collects all these memories again. If we are lucky, she will be well. If we are not lucky..."

Tanis didn't need to tell him of the risks. He'd seen some of the power that Lore had in her. He'd watched her kill a leviathan out to sea. By the gods, his mate was more powerful than anyone one person had a right to be.

If anyone could survive this, it was Lore. She would fight and she would drag Tanis along with her if she had to.

Sighing, he nodded. "Then go into her mind. But quietly, Tanis. I can't see her in any more pain."

Tanis placed her hands on either side of Lore's head and then met his gaze. "I cannot promise it will be without pain. You know that."

Having another person invading her mind was bound to be painful. He knew. Lore could seize again, but the herbs that Rowan had given her might help prevent it. Maybe just a little.

Swallowing hard, he nodded again. No words came to mind. He couldn't reply to her without betraying just how terrified he was in his moment. His Lore. His beautiful, powerful elf who had always captivated him was on her own with this one. He was so tired of her being alone.

Tanis's hands flexed. She tilted her own head down until all he could see was the crown of white hair.

He wondered if he would know the moment that she'd connected with Lore's mind. When a dragon Memory Keeper ripped open the delicate film that protected each person's mind from another's.

Then, he realized he couldn't miss that moment.

Lore jerked in Tanis's hands, even through the medication that should have been powerful enough to kill her. Her body moved, twisting away from Tanis's hands as her face warped into something horrible and aching.

Abraxas stepped forward, only to pause when Rowan's hand clapped against his chest.

"You cannot rip them apart," the elf said. "If you tear either of them from this moment, then neither will survive. We are both stuck here. We have to watch what happens and we trust that neither of them took this risk without understanding the consequences."

Tanis had taken the risk with full knowledge of what she was about to do. But Lore hadn't agreed to any of this. And Rowan knew that. The other elf had been there when they'd talked, and he'd seen how broken Lore had looked when she'd awoken the first time this had happened.

Rowan patted his chest one more time. "We've both got our women on the line," Rowan said quietly. "Let us not fight while they already battle."

He supposed he could do that. He could manage while... while...

Abraxas settled heavily on the ground beside the bed and waited for either of them to wake up. Rowan sat beside him.

Both men set up a vigil as they watched the women they loved.

CHAPTER 34

Lore stood up in the mist that swirled around her. She'd been here before, she was quite certain of that. But she didn't remember exactly where it was. The air was cold; she knew that. Goosebumps rose on her arms, but that wasn't quite right either. They weren't goosebumps. She could feel them, but when she lifted her arm in front of her eyes, all she saw was smooth skin.

Of course, she remembered. She'd gotten sick after helping the baby dragon hatch.

Or perhaps not sick. Her body had merely remembered that the power inside her was a little too great for her to wield on her own. But she hadn't used a great deal of magic to make contact with the crimson dragon! Lore had used more power to help Allura and her crew than she did in slipping into the darkness with that baby.

Maybe it was the darkness itself. Maybe she wasn't supposed to touch it because it drew her too close to the power.

At the thought, the mist swirled more aggressively around

her legs. As though it agreed with the thought. She was too close, and therefore, she had ended up back here.

Humming low under her breath, she wanted to shout that she didn't appreciate being yanked here. Not when there was so much to do and her body could little afford such abuse.

Again, that voice whispered that it didn't care about her body. She could make herself a new one. A better one. A body that didn't feel the harshness of the world. She could weather any storm, any abuse, in a body like that.

"I enjoy being flesh and blood," she muttered while turning around to see where she was. "Shouldn't we be in a memory of mine?"

Apparently not.

There was nothing around her. No structure, no stairs, not even a plant to guide her. Instead, all she could see was the mist and a strange darkness that turned almost blue with a light that had no beginning. Impossible place, but then again, that was all she could see.

Lore picked a direction and started walking. And the entire time she moved, she berated the power for dragging her here again.

"I cannot keep coming here to argue with you," she snarled. "You know there is only so much I can survive, and if you want to stay in this body, then you need to give me a chance to find the explanation for this."

The voice never replied, but she had the distinct feeling that it was quite pleased with itself. As though it knew there was no chance that she'd find any explanation in a realm outside of this one.

The real world held no answers for her. Her body could suffer for ages and this power would find no pity for her. It didn't care that she was in pain or that she might die. Death was not the end for a creature or power like this.

Sighing, she shook her head and continued putting one foot in front of the other. "You must have something to show me. Why else would you drag me here?"

Again, no response.

"Did my mother figure something out, and she wanted to tell me more?"

The magic inside her was determined to remain silent about every question that she might have.

Lore would have continued forward forever. Stubbornness made her set her jaw and keep walking until everything in her burned. Until she felt the strange connection with her body become so tentative that she feared it might snap. But this was about proving a point to this dastardly magic that thought it ran her life.

"Lore." The sound of her name filtered through the darkness and the mist. "Lore, where are you?"

No one else should be here, at least not without her knowing. Her mother had appeared last time, but her mother hadn't called her to this place this time. Why would someone be calling her name?

Who would be calling her name?

The power tried to capture her attention again. The mist churned, nearly pointing in a direction that it wanted her to go. As though there was something there for her to find.

She knew a lie when she saw it. Lore knew that the power was trying to catch her and to hold her in this place. Of course, her heart yearned to continue seeking an answer. Why wouldn't she?

That lingering darkness clung to her shoulders and to her waist, as though someone had physically put hands on her. It took a while to turn away from it. Instead, she turned toward the voice and started trudging in that direction.

"Here!" she shouted. "I'm here!"

The warped voice continued calling out to her, long enough that she wondered if this was another trick by the magic. Maybe it would keep her in this dreaming realm for so long that she would wander until her body died. That was its plan, wasn't it? It wanted to be her body, so she had nothing left in the real world.

She couldn't let it. And her heart said to find the voice because they might help her. By the gods, she had to go with her gut. It had never led her wrong yet.

It took her far too long to find the voice, but eventually she recognized the sound of it.

"Tanis?" she called out, the mist stuffing into her mouth and trying to muffle her words. "Tanis, is that you?"

A blast of fire flared in the distance and Lore saw her. The tall dragon woman wielded fire in her palms and beat back the mist with every attack. A white gown swirled around her, nearly melding with the power as she turned and blasted balls of flames at every tendril that tried to touch her. The dim light flared in anger around her, but Tanis never once faltered. She was a stunning sight to behold.

Lore stumbled toward her, not sure what she should do to help. The power had dragged her under, after all, and that meant the power knew how to manipulate Lore's magic.

Sighing, Lore pulled her hair with her fingers and tried her best to figure out a plan. How could she help Tanis? She had to do something.

Tanis shouted, flames pouring through her body as she flared brightly with more fire that continued to blare around her fingers and an anger that would have made even the dragon gods jealous. There was so much power in her, and she never once seemed afraid of the mist.

Then Lore realized it was because Tanis wasn't afraid. No part of her feared the magic that attempted to overwhelm her. Because she didn't believe the magic here could defeat her.

And that was where Lore had gone wrong.

All she had to do was realize that this realm existed in her mind. They weren't in the darkness. They couldn't be. Her mother wasn't here. No one was here but Lore and Tanis.

"Stop," Lore whispered. The word burned through her. She wasn't alone. Tanis was here with her, and together, they would fight back whatever they had to.

The power pushed back against her. It wanted Lore to see what it wanted her to see. It wanted to control her mind and to force her to believe there was nothing here for her. That she was alone. That the power would be the only thing capable of saving her.

But it wasn't.

She could save herself.

"Enough!" Lore shouted, and a blast of familiar magic shuddered through her entire body. The mist rose in one last gasp of denial and anger, rising into the air in tendrils that froze all around them. The tendrils hovered there, waiting for her to say more. To order it to do something other than what it had been doing.

She didn't want to hurt it, though. The power had saved her many times.

This power would mold her into someone more than an elf who had been forgotten by her family and all others. This power would change the very realms. But it would not hurt her unless she allowed it to.

"Greedy thing," she muttered as she strode toward Tanis. "My apologies, Memory Keeper. It does not know what it does."

Tanis frowned, looking over Lore as though she'd never seen her before. "You seem different."

"Do I?"

"Older." Tanis shook her head. "No, that isn't quite right. You look like the leader of an elven clan. Knowledgeable in a way that you are not. At least, not in this lifetime."

"Perhaps this place reminds me of who I am." But Lore knew that wasn't exactly it. She had been here before. She knew that. Her soul remembered the hidden details of this place.

Not that it was an in between, or even the recesses of her mind. She remembered what it was like to walk here with others. Elves that had been here countless times before and who had wanted her to see... something.

Those memories weren't her own, though. They couldn't be.

Lore had never been here before. She'd never stood in these mists and looked around herself to find... find...

"Lore?" Tanis's voice broke through her thoughts. "Where did you go?"

"I'm right here." But she wasn't. Was she?

Lore looked down at her body and realized she'd disappeared again. Not just her hands. In this place, she disappeared entirely. All of her, gone as though she were part of the wisps themselves.

Sighing, she focused her attention on becoming more solid one more time. Her body fought against her. It didn't want to be seen. It wanted to disappear back into those memories that had some meaning. Memories that she should be able to recall, but was terribly afraid to remember.

Tanis's expression twisted into sadness. "You didn't remember yet."

"How am I supposed to remember something that I did not live?" Lore shrugged.

"That is entirely why you are here."

"I'm afraid." The words ripped out of her before she could catch them. And once those floodgates opened, Lore couldn't stop them from spilling out of her lips. "I fear what will happen if I do not grasp these memories. But I fear what will happen once I do. Why do I know this place, Tanis? Why do I remember being here but not what happened while I was here?"

"I cannot answer that." Tanis shook her head and reached out a hand for Lore to take. "You are the only person who knows what happened when you were here last."

"I do not want to remember."

"Then you will die. Your physical body cannot take more of this abuse, Lore. Even now, there may be..." Tanis hesitated and then finished. "Permanent damage."

Of course, there was always the threat of that. Lore knew what Rowan had told her, and that her body had seized many times before they had to pack herbs onto her tongue so that she didn't kill herself. She knew the dangers of it. She knew that there were only so many times she could arrive here before her body would give up.

She didn't want to give up.

She didn't want to die again.

Sighing, she nodded firmly. "I will disappear if I try to remember."

"I will hold your hand, then. You will not get far." Tanis continued to hold her hand outstretched. "Trust me, Lore."

Even though she was afraid, she put her hand in Tanis's. "Don't let go."

"I won't. I would never."

No one else had ever done that for her but Abraxas. Lore knew how difficult an ask it truly was.

She let her mind wander. Back onto that path of thought that had felt so dangerous. She'd been here before. She knew this place. Elves had once walked this misty plain, and she should know why it felt so familiar to stand here. Even if it was impossible to have felt it.

There. A small singular thought in her mind. A thread of knowing, even though she did not know. She followed it, trailing along the path that suddenly appeared in front of her feet.

She wasn't alone when she'd first arrived, she realized. Elves of old had guided her with strong hands and compassion.

"We know your pain," they had whispered. "It will only get worse. But you must walk this path and you must take this power to where you are needed most."

Where?

Where was she needed most?

It certainly wasn't Dracomaquia, where all the people were thriving and living in happiness. She wasn't needed in this place full of love and life.

But when she tried to follow that train of thought, it disappeared. Threaded through her fingers as though someone had tugged from the other end. Gone.

Lost.

Gasping, she opened her eyes and realized she stood in front of a wall. An actual stone wall that forced both her and Tanis to stop walking. It extended to her left as far as she could see, disappearing into the darkness. And when she looked to the right, it did the same.

"What is this?" Lore asked.

"A barrier of your own making," Tanis replied. She let their hands slip out of each other's grasp. "You have built a wall that only you can get over, Lore."

"How do I do that?"

Tanis stepped forward and placed her hand on the wall. Instantly, elven runes burst into life. The faintly blue tinged magic glowed on her features, casting the sharp contrast of her jaw and cheekbones into shadow. "I do not know."

Lore did.

She'd read those runes before. They were old elven runes meant only for a holy place. She thought... perhaps there was a chance that the ancients could help her get over this.

But that would mean returning to this realm once she found the holy place.

"Tanis?" she asked. "How many more times can I come back here?"

"From now on, it may be impossible to get you back." Tanis met her gaze. "This is the only time I can help you return, and if you cannot return on your own..."

Lore nodded. "I don't need you to continue. I know."

Again, Tanis held out her hand for Lore. But her brows were furrowed with worry, even as Lore slipped her fingers into the other woman's grasp. "We should return to our men."

"Then let's go." Lore glanced back at the wall one more time, reading the runes even though she'd never been able to read them before.

Find us. We can help.

CHAPTER 35

Abraxas didn't let her out of his sight for a long time after that. How could he? She'd had another attack, as Rowan liked to call them, and he'd sat by her side for three days. Three days watching her lie there.

Tanis had never moved. Not once. Her hands never strayed from the sides of Lore's head. Neither of them even twitched.

And though he knew that was a good thing that Tanis had somehow contained Lore's convulsions, it also made him fear they died. How many times he had held his finger under Lore's nose, just to make sure there was breath? Or laid his head on her belly to listen to the faint sound of her heart?

He couldn't keep doing this. He wouldn't survive it.

But he had no choice, just like Lore had no choice either. Together, they had to suffer through this storm so that they could come out on the other side. Alive.

Groaning, he let his head drop into his hands. He'd come up to the hidden cave where they had spent many of their nights. He wasn't sure why. There were many people who needed answers to questions, but he wanted to be alone. A few moments to get his head back on his shoulders.

He could do this. He could be here for Lore when she needed him to be and not being there for her would be the one thing he regretted for the rest of his life.

But he still saw the way she woke back up. He still saw the terror in her eyes until she found him.

She'd stroked her fingers through the strands of his oily hair and hoarsely whispered, "You haven't been taking care of yourself again."

He shouldn't be angry with her for stating the obvious. Of course, he hadn't been taking care of himself, though. She was dying, and he had been the weakling who stayed by her while he waited for her to wake back up. He didn't want her to die or to be in pain. And he couldn't save her. It made him feel useless.

Rocks shifted under someone's foot as they clambered up the mountain after him. He knew only one person would be so foolish to climb up after him, but he didn't want to see her right now. Lore couldn't see how upset he was. She didn't need his added stress to the ones she was already feeling. It was foolish to feel like this. He knew that. But... But...

Lore's head poked over the edge of the cliff where he sat and she stared up at him. "Want to give me a hand?"

Of course. The last time she'd had to launch herself at him to even get up here. The last thing he needed was for her to fall and then all of this to be over with before he could even scold her.

He sighed and stood. Abraxas helped her up the mountain and onto the cliff in front of him. He'd thought she would sit down beside him. Perhaps they both needed a few quiet moments where they could stare off into the sun and wait for the clouds to turn into recognizable shapes.

Instead, she glared. Clearly upset at him.

"What?" he asked.

"You're avoiding me."

"Yes." Abraxas would not hide it. "I am."

"Why is that?"

"Because every time I look at you, I remember what you looked like when you almost died and it makes me angry." He shouldn't have said it with so much bite. Softening his words, he added, "And because the thought of losing you is difficult for me. I don't want to see you in pain, Lore. I know there is nothing I can do to help."

"No, there is not." Lore planted her hands on her hips. "But I think there's a way to get through the barrier in my mind. I've been talking with Rowan. I know the runes that I read on the wall in my mind were ancient elvish. And I needed to talk with him about that."

"You can't read much ancient elvish," he reminded her. "That's why we had to bring the documents to Rowan in the first place."

"I know." She tapped a finger on her head. "But apparently when I am in my mind, I can read ancient elvish. Which got me thinking, perhaps I cannot read it only because of that barrier in my mind. It said for me to find them, and where better to connect with the gods than an ancient place where we used to worship them?"

Abraxas followed, but he still thought it was a silly idea. "You don't believe in the gods."

"I don't. But that doesn't mean there isn't something that wants to talk with me." She huffed out a breath. "Maybe that's the problem.

Maybe it's been the problem all along. The gods want to talk with me and I've been avoiding them, so of course they're angry with me."

"Lore." He shook his head. "There's nothing wrong with you or the gods. You are merely trying to settle into the power that you now have."

At least, that's what he hoped. Maybe if she used it more...

He almost said that she should try to use it more to get used to it, but then he saw her expression.

"What happened?" he asked.

"I tried to use a little magic. Just to warm up the tea that Rowan had brought me and I forgot about. I'd been reading some of the inscriptions on the documents that I shouldn't be able to read, and yet now I can. The tea had gone cold and..." She paused.

"And?"

"I had a small seizure. Nothing that sent me back into the darkness, and Rowan caught me before I fell and hit my head on anything. I was lucky he was there to catch me, and I know that. But I didn't think even something that small would harm me."

So she couldn't use any magic at all. The power inside her wanted something, and if she didn't figure out what it wanted, then it would continue to hurt her.

He bared his teeth in frustration. "Then what do you propose we do?"

"Pray."

Abraxas gave her a startled look, and one that clearly said he didn't think that would do much. Praying had never gotten him anywhere. But perhaps the dragon gods were more vicious than those of the elves.

"I know," she said with a slight chuckle. "I've gotten so desperate that I'm willing to pray to gods I don't believe in. I must sound insane."

"You sound desperate."

Lore giggled again, but the sound was not right. Nerves had bubbled up inside of her, and the only way to get them out was the odd sound that had erupted. "Maybe. Maybe I am. I don't want to die again, Abraxas. And I think the best way to survive is by finding one of those old ruins and trying to connect with whatever wants to connect with me."

"Understood. But are there even ruins here? The elves were only on this isle for a short time, Lore. It would make sense to return to Umbra, where there are ancient holy places." Like the crystalline palace they stayed at long ago.

He almost wished they were there. They could find safe harbor in the room that had made them invisible to all others' eyes. The room would have summoned them a comfortable bed, food, even music for them to listen to if they wished.

The two of them could hide from the world there for a very long time.

But of course, that would not be the way of it. Neither of them could hide for very long, and they knew that boredom would find them. A crimson dragon was no more suited for a life of ease than an elf who had saved an entire kingdom from themselves.

Sighing, Lore reached for his hand and linked their fingers together. "We have to try with the ruins we have here. I don't think I'll make the journey back to Umbra, even on your back."

He hated those words. He wanted her to be with him for centuries. And right now, even a journey to their home would kill her. Or him. Or both of them, because he wasn't long for this world if he watched her die again.

"Then we will try this one." He gave her hand a little squeeze back.

"Where is it?"

She pointed to a mountain range not too far off from them. "Over there, I think. Rowan said it was one of the peaks, but he wasn't sure which one. He wasn't with the other elves long enough to know where they'd set it up."

"Good to know," Abraxas grumbled. "That'll take us a few days to scout out, but we can find it."

"I was thinking..." She tucked a strand of hair behind her ear, and he knew whatever she was about to ask, he would give her. A thousand times over. "I was thinking perhaps we could fly there?"

"You hate heights."

"But I haven't flown on your back in a long time, Abraxas. And I wish to feel the wind in my hair again and to feel you underneath me."

She'd felt him underneath her plenty of times since she'd returned, but he knew that wasn't what she meant. He'd prefer the safer way, but he also knew he would deny her nothing.

"Fine," he replied. "But you will have to jump onto my back."

Lore shrugged as though that didn't terrify her at all. "I'm not so afraid of dying now that I've done it once before."

He bared his teeth at her. "Stop reminding me."

"Or you'll bundle me back up in the cabin and find the ruins on your own?"

"Precisely."

She grinned at him, shaking her head at his antics as though he were the strange one in this situation.

He wasn't strange. He was overprotective. Those were two very different things.

Abraxas ran straight off the cliff, throwing his body as far out into the air as he could and then disappearing into the clouds. It took a little time for him to shift. He hadn't been in his dragon form very much since Lore had been here. He hadn't needed the scaly beast to make any appearance. Besides, he'd like being with Lore every night. Holding her tightly in his arms had been the highlight of each day.

The dragon burst forth and the surge of power that came with it made him tilt back his head and roar. He had forgotten just how powerful it was to be a being like this.

Circling underneath the cliff, he did a few passes before he saw Lore leap into the air above him. She plummeted toward him, her form moving effortlessly fast.

She better not use any magic to make sure he caught her. Abraxas hadn't even thought about that risk before he had assumed she'd leapt onto him.

But Lore didn't use any magic. He didn't feel the crackle against his skin or the sudden spark that magic always felt like. Instead, she free falled through the air and trusted him to catch her. No matter how long it took him to get her.

It didn't take long. Abraxas positioned himself underneath her and she grabbed onto his spines with practiced ease. Lore hauled herself up onto his back, her laughter echoing in his ears.

And though they had a place to go and a journey to start yet again, Abraxas took the long way to the mountains. He wanted her to see their home from this new vantage point. He knew she needed to see how beautiful Dracomaquia was, and why they had sought to be here for so long.

Lore said little on their journey. Instead, every time he looked back at her, she was taking in every detail of the world around them. Lore didn't hesitate a moment to put all of this vision into her memory. So that she'd never forget it.

He loved flying with her like this. He loved seeing her smile and the way her entire body drank in his world.

Abraxas just loved her. With every fiber of his being and sharing this moment with her meant the world.

Banking to the left, he trailed her underneath a cloud. Just as he expected, Lore reached up and brushed her hands through the white, fluffy mist. She chuckled, and the sound was music to his ears.

"Still cold!" she called out, the wind dashing her voice to the side. "Still wet!"

"Clouds never change," he rumbled.

"I thought maybe they would be magical clouds here. That I could feel their softness this time."

If he could have made the clouds soft for her, he would. He'd make them feel like the soft down of a rabbit so she could gather them up into her arms and rest her head upon them every night. If it would make her happy, he'd do it.

Finally, they reached the other mountain range, too quickly for his liking. Abraxas would have preferred to spend the entire day flying through the sky. He could forget everything up here, and a part of him whispered that Lore forgot as well.

But the mountains needed to be explored. And as he glided above them, he already knew where they were going.

An elven ruin rested on the top of one mountain peak. He'd seen nothing like it before. A flat platform made of stone and tiles that created a swirling pattern toward the very middle. Four arches rose around it, one arch having crumbled in the middle, a second broken, but two of them were perfectly preserved.

"Can you land there?" Lore asked.

"I can try."

It was surprisingly easy to land in the center of it all, and the tiles didn't crack underneath his feet. Almost as though there was magic inside them, protecting them from a dragon's weight.

But why would that be?

He settled and Lore slid off his back, her brow furrowed in confusion as well. She kept her hand on his side as she walked around all of it and then huffed out a breath. "It's all so strange. Isn't it?"

"It is."

"I don't know what to do now," she admitted. "How does one even begin to pray?"

He shrugged, or at least tried to, with massive wings attached to his shoulders. "You just... do?"

She looked up at him with those big, wide eyes, and he sensed how lost she was in his moment. No god had ever been kind to her. No god had ever given her a reason to trust them.

Abraxas lowered his nose and then gently nudged her. "You do what you must, Lore. And I will watch over you while you do so."

CHAPTER 36

Rowan seemed to think all it would take was meditation. He claimed that the old gods didn't mind Lore having no experience with them, nor praying before. She thought that was a bit of a stretch. The old gods had always preferred to be worshiped by many people and in as many ways as possible.

The stories she'd been told as a child were whispers of creatures who preferred blood sacrifice in their honor. How they loved to hear the screams of their enemies that their followers would kill, slitting their throats and watching the blood pour out.

Margaret had loved to tell those stories around a campfire. Her eyes had gleamed with an unnatural glee as she told the rest of the elves how their gods had once been bloodthirsty, and it was the elves' foolish softness which had led to a change in how they worshiped.

Lore shook herself free from those thoughts. There was no

room for that here. She was not amongst the old elves. They were all dead and gone.

All that remained was this ancient place of worship. The air crackled around her, as though lightning might strike at any minute. The hairs on her arms raised. And the air had the faintest scent of metal to it. Blood? Not quite, she realized. Just metal and iron and steel. The faint memory of battles won through hard earned lives and countless souls that still screamed from that darkened place.

Abraxas spread his wings out behind her, stretching them even after their short flight. "This is the place?"

"It is," she murmured, her brows furrowed in concentration. "Now I'm supposed to meditate, according to Rowan."

"What does Rowan know?" he asked. "The old man told me he didn't remember the old gods any more than you do. They were from a time before dragons."

"I think he knows more than he lets on," she replied.

Rowan had survived for many years. Too many for her mind to even fathom. He had seen the beginning and end of empires and the fall of the world itself. He knew what it took to create an entire world again. If only he could share that information with them.

Sighing, she walked to the center of the whirling mosaic. The blue tiles glittered under her feet, and she wondered how they'd gotten the color to be so like the sky. Except, then she saw herself in it and realized they hadn't even tried. For what artisan could ever truly mimic the sky? The pieces of mirror showed the sky in all its beauty, abutted against elven made white shards that shone like pearls.

Sitting in the very center of all that felt right. She eased down onto her rump, crossing her legs and placing the backs of her hands on her knees.

Lore tried to meditate like that for a while. She held her spine straight and felt the wind play in the strands of her hair. But try as she might, all she could think about was how uncomfortable it was. Her ass hurt. Her back spasmed. She was too old for this kind of meditation. And even if she wasn't, why would they sit like this?

A hot breath blasted in her face as Abraxas chuckled. "You look like you sucked on something sour."

"This is not easy," she chastised him. "Even harder when a dragon is staring at you with such weight in his gaze."

"I am not."

"You are!"

But a small smile crossed her face at their argument. He was right. She was struggling with figuring out the best way to deal with all this. She had sat, still looking like she'd sucked on a lemon, before realizing that this wouldn't work.

Pretending to meditate was not and could not be, meditation.

Sighing, she ran her fingers through her hair and opened her eyes. "I'm not sure how to meditate like this. How does one let go and allow... what? The realm to flow through her?"

"Is that what Rowan said?"

She nodded, still hating the words herself.

"It is my understanding that meditation is more about centering yourself, rather than centering the world around you." Abraxas chuckled and then let the form of his dragon melt away.

He was better at changing here, she noticed. He was more likely to change regularly and without issue. As though it didn't hurt for him to force his form into a much smaller one. As though it didn't bother him to do so.

Biting her lip, she watched as he sauntered toward her. He was the picture of confidence. A man who never hesitated in the slightest with his movements or choices.

She didn't complain when he settled down onto the cold tiles behind her and placed his legs on either side of hers. His hands snaked around her waist, drawing her snug to his chest. "Here," he said, his voice guttural in her ear. "Let me guide you."

How could he think she would focus on anything when he was touching her like this? Lore's entire body clenched at his touch. Her heart thundered in her chest and her palms were slick with sweat. She thought of nothing other than trailing his hands down her sides and pressed them to her skin. Obviously, there was more to this. Certainly, he knew she would want to touch him and be touched in return.

A warm chuckle vibrated in her ear. "Clear your mind, elf. We're here for a reason other than that."

Heat burned her cheeks, and a blush turned her skin a bright red. She could feel it spread down her chest, but she refused to feel embarrassed by her need for him. He was everything to her.

A mate, yes. A man who she hoped one day would be her husband, certainly.

But Abraxas had become part of her as well. An important part of her soul, no matter how far they were spread from each other through the world and the ages.

Sighing, she leaned her head back on his shoulder and nodded. "Fine then, dragon. Lead me."

He let out a low hum that rocked through her entire body. The sound spread from her chest to her fingertips, down to her toes. Through every inch of her form until she could focus on nothing other than the sound.

It was the gravel of a mountain shifting on its base. It was the burble of water long trapped beneath the ice. Thunder in the distance as a storm rolled across the land, but wasn't quite reaching her just yet.

The sound grounded her. It helped her think. Helped her be a little more than what she was.

More than just Lore.

She followed the sound through the dark parts of her mind. Letting her thoughts play through memories and sounds and dreams until she realized she could meditate like this. She could disappear when the sound was in her ear and then maybe, just maybe, the ancient elves would speak to her.

They would tell her what it meant to be powerful and how to channel this magic in a way that wouldn't kill her. Wasn't that what the power wanted, after all? It didn't want her to think for even an instance that she was in control, but it also didn't want her to use it without knowledge.

Perhaps that was the secret.

Her body seemed a bit distant from her now as she sagged against his chest. She could still feel the connection with it. She still knew she was touching Abraxas and that his warmth helped ground her.

But she wasn't in that body anymore. She was somewhere in the ether, looking back at herself and her dragon, who had wrapped himself around her.

She saw a golden thread tangled around them. Not just light or a tie that would convince them to be together. No. This golden thread was far more than that.

Biting her lip, she realized that I tied them through more than just love. They were soul bound. Born to be with each other through hardship and strife.

Oh, she couldn't wait to tell him.

Lore turned her attention outward. To the sun in the sky and the clouds that bounced in the distance. There was something there, she thought. A light or an essence or a being that called out to her.

Her heart stuttered. Was that who she was supposed to talk to? Was that her mother waiting to give her more direction?

Wind buffeted her face. She could feel the great gust even through her soul, so far out of her body now it surprised her that she could feel anything at all.

A slight growl in her ear made shivers dance down even her corporeal spine. The wind she felt came from the strength of dragon wings, and there were very few who would think to interrupt them.

The power inside her flex, spreading out her soul a little too thin as she searched for the person who would join them. Which one was it? Tanis? Surely not.

Before she could feel the person, she saw the dragon lift over the edge of the holy ground.

Nyx blended in with the sky. Her scales reflected the blue all around her until she was a creature made of clouds and blue light. Her eyes glimmered with a bright happiness at the first feeling of wind under her wings.

"Mother!" Nyx called out, landing on the edge of the pad and scrabbling for purchase. "Look what Tanis taught us! It took me a bit but, look! I'm flying!"

Lore almost snapped back into her body, but she felt as though something prevented her from doing that. A wall appeared between herself and her body and no matter how hard she tried to break through, she couldn't.

"What?" she whispered, slamming herself against that barrier that prevented her from getting to her family. "I'm doing exactly as you asked. Let me go back to my family! This is not magic. This is meditation. It's—"

"Magic," a deep voice whispered in her ear.

Nyx changed back from her form, turning into that lovely girl with dark hair who could have taken an entire castle with her beauty alone. The elation on her face would soon break, Lore thought. The moment they realized that Lore couldn't get back to her body, all of that happiness would disappear. Again.

"What is mother doing?" Nyx asked as she struggled to find her footing.

"Meditating," Abraxas said. His voice came from so close to her ear, she could almost imagine that she was still in her body. "Rowan also told her to do this."

"Oh. So she didn't see me fly?" Nyx replied quickly. "I'll have to try again when she wakes. It's so tiring! And changing back and forth, it takes such a long time."

And then it happened.

Nyx's foot slipped off the back of the stone ledge. She was a dragon. Even if she fell, she could change and right herself. But Lore's heart still leapt into her chest and without thought she stretched out her hand.

Her body did the same.

Magic blasted out of her as she thought of what might happen if she didn't save her daughter. Nyx tumbling through the air, not able to change back into her dragon form because she was so startled that she couldn't bring herself to do it. That beautiful body dashed upon the rocks below after tumbling and screaming for her parents to save her.

Abraxas wouldn't be able to catch her. Not with the precious moments he'd have to waste ensuring that Lore didn't hit her head.

He must have felt the same fear. She knew his biceps flexed underneath her head, jolting as though lightning had struck him.

Lore didn't regret what she did. Her magic crowed with pleasure at being used and it launched out of her body through the air. It flew with all the speed that even a dragon could never match.

Though she feared it might strike her daughter too hard, it merely curled Nyx up into its arms. Golden and warm, the magic cushioned her mid air and then placed her back on the ledge.

The chuckle she heard this time was not from Abraxas. Nor was it from anyone that stood on that ancient elven ground with them. The sound was feminine and wily, something that she'd never heard before.

But in this strange between space, outside of her body and watching as all this happened, she could see the golden light that tied Lore to her daughter as well. This tie did not string back to her physical form and wrap around her heart like the thread with Abraxas did.

No. The glimmering thread tied right back to Lore's soul, where she floated outside of her body. It collected deep in the very roots of who she was, and who her daughter was. The tie of two women who would learn and grow from each other no matter their age or what life threw at them.

The ties between a mother and daughter. Ties that never dimmed, even though Lore hadn't been with her child for such a long time.

Tears burned in her physical eyes, and her soul seemed to glow ever brighter at the realization.

"That's what you wanted me to see, isn't it?" she asked the spirit who had laughed. "You wanted me to realize that none of this has been on my own."

"More than that," the unknown voice said.

Now she almost recognized it from another time. The rough voice that came from years standing in front of a fire. Years of smoke inhalation as the woman conjured images out of mist and fortunes out of thin air.

"Grandmother," Lore whispered.

The low hum of a response was one she shouldn't remember, but did.

Lore had never met her grandmother. The woman had long been dead before Lore's own mother had gotten pregnant, a detail that her mother had never elaborated on. Lore didn't know if her grandmother had died at the hands of humans, old age, or war. But now that she heard the voice, she knew exactly who waited for her.

She wrapped the glimmering thread around her fist, the one that connected her to Nyx even though she wasn't her blood child. "There is a connection between all of us, isn't there?"

"Yes."

"And that is what I have to remember?"

"Even more than that, child. Come with me and remember."

But she couldn't leave. Not again.

Nyx ran toward Lore the moment Abraxas realized something was wrong. A horrible, keening cry erupted from his mouth as he rocked her back and forth.

Lore wasn't sure if her body was having another seizure. Nyx obscured her view, and suddenly she didn't care if her physical form suffered. She cared only that her daughter would see it.

"We all will do anything for our daughters," her grandmother said. "Even brave death itself, if it means their future will brighten."

A knot unraveled in her chest. She was frightened, yes. She feared leaving them again, of course.

But a future that was easier for Nyx, Hyperion, Abraxas, and the rest. That was worth the risk. Perhaps she could figure out a way to fix all this.

There was no solution without her mother, grandmother, and all the mothers before that, though. She knew that now.

With the glimmering rope wrapped tightly around her fist, Lore turned toward the sound of her grandmother's voice and strode away from her body. Away from her family. Into a darkness that suddenly seemed a little less murky.

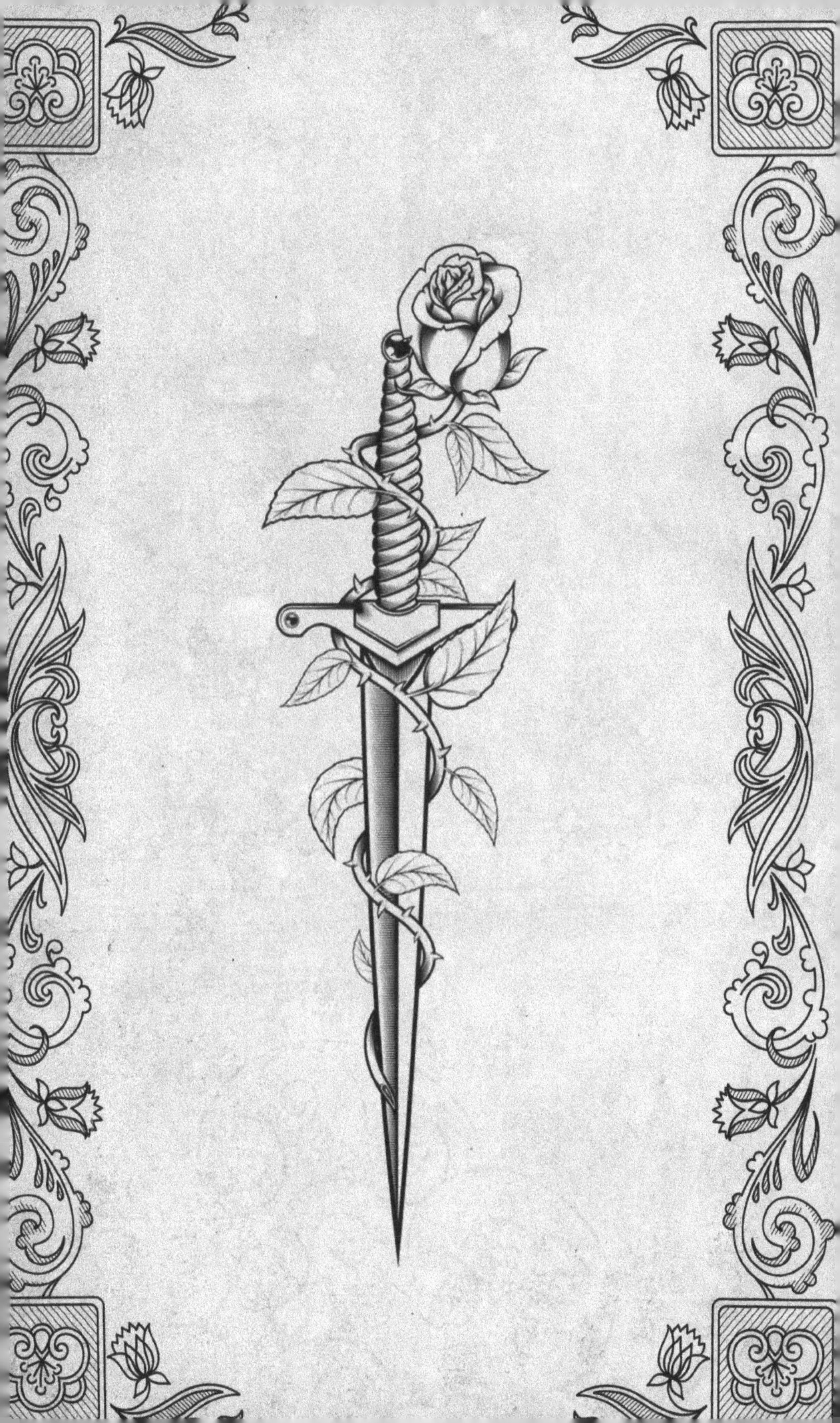

CHAPTER 37

The air here was thin.

Thinner than Lore had ever experienced, and it took a while for her to breathe. Or perhaps that was her physical body affecting the way she experienced this other realm.

The darkness did not hide the secrets of the dead. She knew that now. This was not the place where souls came to be born anew. She was not so lucky to know that place.

This was a realm of knowing. Of being. Of discovering the past, the present, and the future. It was more than just an unknown realm, but a place that would soon unravel the world before her.

The darkness pushed back against her feet as she walked through the murk and into the mire. Lore noticed more details this time as she strode through the shadows. The ground was wet, not just shiny. The air smelled musty and stale, as though she were in a cave rather than a wide open space. But mostly her eyes caught upon the wall where a few pieces of it had fallen through.

The wall that had been so stalwart and sturdy the last time she'd seen it, had fallen in on itself.

Words appeared. Elven runes that glowed with a golden power that seemed so familiar to her own.

Break the wall.

They didn't have to tell her twice.

Lore reached for the stone she could see was the most loose and then she pulled. Tugged. Ripped at every stone until her fingers were bleeding and her hands ached. This was the way through the wall, she realized. Time and energy and effort that proved she desired to know what was beyond it.

Lore could stare at it all she wanted. She could reason with the magic for years, but that did not mean she would ever get through. The only way to pass beyond the wall, was to tear it down bit by bit.

She had no way of knowing how long it took her to do so. Lore only knew that she fought her way until she felt the pain in her physical body. As though her actions here made her hands bleed there. The stones crumbled beneath her hands, some of them turning to dust that covered her palms with a fine powder. Others were more difficult, their sharp edges fighting back.

Eventually, however, she had made a person sized hole in the wall of her mind. Memories flooded through. Golden light, a healing tone, hands on her back and her shoulders after she'd died.

After she'd survived.

Frowning, Lore tried to peer through the gap to see beyond it, but she couldn't see much there. Just that it wasn't dark on the other side of the wall. There was only light.

She glanced behind her at the shadows and the darkness. What would happen when she walked through? Would she ever be able to return to this place? To the realm of her family?

She had to take the risk. Had to take the chance because no one else would. If she could figure out how to control her powers by meeting with whomever waited for her beyond, then she had to do so. Lore knew she would die either way.

Lore stepped through the gap and into the light.

Even in this spirit form, she had to throw her arm up over her eyes. The bright light burned through her retinas and it blurred everything before her. Until she could lower her arm, and then she felt her jaw drop in shock at what waited for her to see.

The realm beyond the darkness was a forest. Or a glade, she supposed, considering the trees outlining the area. There was a small pool with twinkling wisps dancing over the surface. A tiny waterfall flowed into it, the water burbling like laughter. The ground wasn't covered with grass, but a thick, cushiony moss that made her steps springy.

What was this place?

She didn't remember it; she didn't think. But then a memory did flutter to life.

She'd sat in this glade before. But she hadn't been alone, then.

The memories all burst forth, suddenly. She clutched her head as they all rolled through her, a headache blooming behind her eyes.

She'd died, but they hadn't allowed her to really die. They'd clutched at her hands in a place much worse or much better than the darkness. She'd felt the world pressing down on her, threatening to take her from the arms of those she loved and to put her somewhere that felt all at once like everything and nothing. Instead, she'd felt hands grasping at her arms, clutching her shoulders and holding her against them.

Hands that were lined with wrinkles.

Hands that were smooth and unblemished.

They had pulled her out and deposited her here. She'd seen her mother, her grandmother, and all the people before them. But even more, Lore had seen those who would come soon. She'd seen Nyx, she realized. She'd seen her daughter as the dark haired beauty and she'd seen her with a crown atop her head. There had been more. Children who didn't look like Lore but were still tied to her soul.

She'd seen the future here, and she'd known to fix it. She knew what to do, and then she'd let it all go.

When she'd cried about Goliath, they had held her. When she'd sobbed as she realized she needed to learn more about her magic, they assured her that time would pass sooner than she thought. And when she'd spoken of Abraxas, they had all sighed in pleasure at the love he'd shown her without question.

They were part of her. They were more than that. Each spirit who had guided her in this place came from a line of strong women spread out amongst the centuries.

Here, she was powerful. Not just because of her magic, but because of those who had come before.

All her family knew everything about her. They seemed to know what she wanted and how she liked to eat. What she wanted to do with herself in the future and the embarrassing stories of her past.

Lore took a step forward, reaching her hand out as though she could feel her mother again. Just by reaching.

Her mother had been with her all of those six months. The smiles and the laughter they had shared were like nothing she'd ever experienced.

Her memories of her mother were of quiet moments, sad evenings, and peace only when they could find it.

Now, her memories were filled with laughter and light.

"Mother," she whispered. "Can you come to me now? Or am I to forget everything that happened again?"

The quiet burble of the water continued, but there was no other sound in the glade.

A wrenching sob escaped from her mouth before Lore gathered herself up again. "I still don't know what to do. You called me here, and I know that there is goodness in it. I remember I have been here before, and that I have seen this place. That I have seen all of you. But that does not mean I remember why I was here or what guidance you provided me for the future. This power is eating me alive, and I need you all to... Be here."

Her heart broke at the silence. She remembered this place as full of feminine magic. The ground had fairly gleamed with it.

"Mothers," she whispered, her voice carrying over the sound of the trickling water. "Grandmothers. Daughters. Come to me, please. Teach me your secrets one last time so that I might return to our world with a heart full of light and a body that can survive the powers you gave me."

She thought, for a moment, that no one would come. Perhaps the spirits had given her all that they could, and this remembrance was only to tell her she'd missed something. She hadn't learned enough while she was here and now she would pay the punishment for it.

But then...

"Daughter."

Her mother's voice again. Lore squeezed her eyes shut with the sound that she'd been so certain she would never be blessed to hear again.

Turning around, she saw that her mother stood at the edge of the forest with her arms open wide.

Lore didn't hesitant. She sprinted across the glade, leaping over the stream and onto the moss beyond them. She flung herself into her mother's arms and held her tightly to her chest.

She could feel her mother's heart beating. Even in death.

"You're here," Lore whispered against her mother's neck. "I was so afraid you wouldn't come."

"I can deny my daughter nothing."

"I'm dying. Again." Lore released her hold to lean back and peer at her mother's eyes. "You know how to stop that."

"I already saved you from death once, my daughter. I'm not sure if I can do it multiple times." Her mother leaned back a little, looked her over with critical eyes as well. "You don't remember what you learned here. Do you?"

She'd thought that she did. There were countless hours of older, more powerful elves teaching her all they knew about the magic that had been given to her. Some of them were not so lucky as to be gifted with it, thus they had only heard the old legends. Others had wielded this magic themselves.

"I remember," she said firmly. "I remember all that you taught me, but I do not think it will be enough. Something is different with me. My body is not accepting the magic, and it's being eaten alive."

"I don't know how to help."

"Neither do I." Lore bit the inside of her lip, chewing through it with an aggression that burst blood upon her tongue. The metallic taste startled her.

Had she bitten her lip in the real world as well? Or did her mind only remember what blood tasted like?

Her mother reached out and touched a finger underneath Lore's nose. Her finger came away coated with blood, the red smear warning them both how little time was left.

"I will call the others," her mother said. "We will figure this out, daughter of mine."

Lore feared they might not be able to. Stomach twisting with fear, she watched as her mother walked into the forest.

That was right. She'd never been able to leave the glade while she was here. Beings waited for her in the shadows of those trees. They knew she was alive, and they wanted to take that power away from her.

Not her magic. But the essence of life itself.

One of the shadows moved behind the tree, peeling off of it and stepping aggressively toward her. Lore didn't have to be warned twice. She moved away from the tree line and back toward the bubbling water and the happiness that seeped out of it.

Was the pool magic?

That she couldn't quite remember. But being around it did make her feel as though bubbles were rising in her own chest. Happiness. Mirth. Love. They all sizzled and popped around her heart until she wasn't all that worried anymore. She'd been here before. They'd helped her before.

They would again.

The women emerged from the trees, one by one. A young girl that skipped into view, her bright pink skirts swirling around her. An elderly woman with soft, kind eyes. A hardened warrior still wearing her armor with blood splattered along the edges.

Her grandmother walked out last, hand in hand with her mother. They knew she was waiting for them.

The only person who wasn't here was Nyx, though Lore had a feeling that was because her daughter was still alive. Her soul couldn't be commanded here, even though she'd seen her before.

"My daughter?" she asked her mother.

"Still with her father in the waking realm. We could have called her forward, but..." Her mother eyed Lore's fist and a soft smile crossed her face. "For this, we only need what you've already brought with you."

"What I brought with me?"

Lore looked down at her own hand and realized for the first time that she still had her fingers curled around the golden thread that connected her to Nyx. The thread wasn't so much knotted now as it was woven through her fingers. Even though she must be very, very far from Nyx, the thread was still there. Still the same size and not stretched in the slightest.

"This?" she asked, lifting it up for the others to see. "This is what I needed to bring back?"

The question was silly to ask, though. Lore already knew the answer to her question. That was exactly what she needed to return with. Nyx was still alive and therefore they could not summon her as easily. They needed Lore to return with that thread so that she could... what?

The memory was still there. She just had to stop trying to force it.

Lore blinked and all the threads came to light. The one connecting her to her mother, to her grandmother, and to the future children that Nyx would have. All of them. All threads that were tangled and woven in between each other but each one connecting to each individual. Thousands of years of threads, all laid out before her.

Her mother stepped forward and gestured toward the threads in between them. "To control your power, my daughter, your task is to unravel the threads that bind us all together. You cannot cut them, for they will not be cut. You cannot sever the ties, for they are as binding as they are strong. The tapestry must be unwoven for you to weave it in your own way again."

Holding onto Nyx's thread a little tighter, Lore gave her mother a nod. "Then I shall begin."

CHAPTER 38

She was gone this time. Abraxas wasn't sure how he knew, but his gut said this was the last time he'd carry her down a mountain. The last time he'd feel her deep inhalations against his chest.

If she didn't fight her way back to him after this, then they wouldn't see her again.

He thought this moment would come with a horrible sense of shattering. That his heart would suddenly explode in his chest and he wouldn't be able to survive it.

It did not.

The ache in his chest had never really left, it seemed. He knew this pain well. They'd been old friends, he and the feeling in his chest. They had met long ago, and he supposed he'd never let it go.

So, as he walked down the mountain with his daughter at his side, he did not flinch. He did not cry. He was a cold and expressionless shield carrying the woman loved to her final resting place.

"I didn't know she was sick," Nyx said quietly, her voice cutting through his reverie. "I knew that she'd been quiet lately, and that you were all worried about her, but I didn't know."

"She's been sick since she died," he replied. "She broke through the very fabric of the world. Broke through our reality to come back to us."

"But then it should remain broken, should it not?" Nyx shook her head. "I refuse to believe she's being punished for returning to us. It's wrong, father. She should be able to stay here with us. Why else would she have been allowed to come back?"

To soothe old hurts.

To make promises she couldn't keep.

He looked down at her serene expression, and he couldn't help but wonder why she looked like that. So quiet. So at peace. When her entire family was falling down around her, breaking apart, she was the only one who got to rest.

He supposed she'd earned that, even if it made him angry.

"Father?" Nyx asked, as though she'd been asking him a question before that he didn't hear.

Sighing, he shook his head and returned his attention to his daughter. "There is something inside her that is burning through her. The power that she was given is too immense for her form to hold on its own."

"But I thought—"

His daughter didn't finish the sentence, but his heart stuttered in his chest at her words. "You thought?"

"I just..." She swallowed hard. "I had a dream about her, that's all. Before we got here. I was in a forest with her and a lot of other women. They told me she was going to be fine, so I always thought... Well, I knew she was going to come back. And I knew it wouldn't be easy but that they well prepared her for this moment. I guess I always thought that dream would come true."

If only it were that easy. If only their daughter's dream could pierce through the veil of time and break through to reality.

"I'm sorry your dream didn't come true," he replied quietly.

They didn't speak for the rest of the journey to the cabin. They didn't even talk when they paused in front of Rowan's house and waited for the elf to realize they were there.

Abraxas thought he was ready for this, but he wasn't. He thought he knew what their expressions would be when they walked out of the cabin. He could never anticipate the truth.

Tanis stepped out of the cabin first, her voice already light with pleasure. Certain that she'd sent them in the right direction. Her words stuck in her throat as she saw Lore limp in his arms.

Rowan came next, the smile on his face turning to one of pure and utter sadness. They couldn't have known that any of them would return like this. They must have thought that Abraxas would return with glorious news. That they had found their answers in that strange place where the elves used to worship.

Instead, he stood there with a body that was as good as dead in his arms.

"Abraxas!" a voice called out from the depths of the cabin. "Just get in here. We all have something rather interesting to show you. I think both you and Lore will want to know."

"Draven," he replied, his voice little more than a croak. "Come out here."

The hesitancy before he heard anything move beyond the shadows was enough of a response for him to know what had happened. Draven understood why he had to come outside. They all did.

The dark elf walked through the door with heavy footsteps and a heart that already showed in his eyes. He didn't want to see Lore like this.

But then again, none of them did.

"Again?" Draven asked, his voice quiet and reverent.

"For the last time," Tanis added.

Abraxas met the Memory Keeper's eyes, and he knew what she meant. Tanis surely had explained it to Lore. That another attack like this would be the last attack she survived.

They all knew it.

They'd all understood that their time with Lore could be limited far more than they'd ever thought. But none of them had thought it would happen so soon.

Draven was the first to move. He'd been with them since nearly the beginning, hadn't he? Abraxas couldn't remember the first time he'd met the elf, other than knowing he didn't like him. But that was before. Before all of this happened and before they had joined together in knowing that Lore was the most important thing in their lives.

He could forgive the man for falling in love with Lore. Who wouldn't?

The elf touched his finger underneath Lore's nose and it came away slick with blood. "This is new."

"She's never bled from the nose while out, no."

"Did she fall?"

Abraxas shook his head. "Of course not."

"You'd never let her fall." Draven sighed and took a step back. "So it's farther along than we thought. She's suffering."

"I don't think she's feeling anything at all." He looked at Tanis to confirm his words, though. Abraxas would have felt it if Lore was in pain, wouldn't he? Wouldn't he have known?

Tanis gave him a curt nod. "I don't think she's aware of any pain her body is going through. Does this feel different from before?"

He looked down at the still body in his arms. Her face was serene, as though in death itself. "She hasn't moved since she passed out. She has had no seizures, nothing to show that she's in any sort of pain at all."

"That is good." But the words didn't match the sad expression on Tanis's face. "I'm glad she's not in any pain."

Another voice shouted behind them, although the words were unintelligible. Hyperion sprinted across the grass, his eyes wild and tears already turning his eyes red and glistening.

"What happened?" He was frantic, looking over Lore and hovering his hands over her still form. As though touching her might make it worse. "What did you do to her?"

"What did I do to her?" Abraxas didn't have it in him to be angry at the boy, but they would have words about it later. "What do you think I did?"

"I don't know!" Hyperion tossed his hands in the air and then gestured all over Lore. "She was fine when I saw her last. She wasn't like this. She wasn't..."

Dead.

Dying.

Lost to them for all eternity.

An echoing pang of pain rocked through his chest. Abraxas would have rubbed at it to see if that helped, but he couldn't put Lore down.

Perhaps he wasn't as numb as he thought he was. Abraxas refused to let her leave his arms, even in this state. He intended to bring her to the top of the mountain, and they would mourn the loss of the life they had planned. They'd watch the stars come out one last time. Together.

Swallowing the pain again, he knew that there were things he had to do. He needed to get her settled. Comfortable. He needed her to be warm on that mountain top or all of this was for nothing.

"I need..." His voice broke as he searched for someone more familiar than these people who were all recent additions to his life. He wanted someone to hold him, damn it. He couldn't be their father or their leader when the woman he loved was... was...

His gaze caught on Draven's, as much as he hated to ask the elf for anything.

But Draven's arm was wrapped around his daughter's shoulder, and then Abraxas couldn't take his eyes away from that connection. They hugged each other, leaning upon the other for support as though they'd done it before.

How dare he?

Abraxas felt the flare of anger bright in his chest. It was familiar and hot and dark and angry and yes, that was right. He was a crimson dragon. He protected what was his.

"Why are you touching my daughter?" he snarled.

Draven immediately dropped his arm from Nyx's shoulders and took a big step back. "Because we're all looking at Lore and wondering what happened to her. Why would I... Abraxas, this isn't the right question to be asking right now."

"It's the only question to ask! Why was your arm around my daughter?"

Rowan placed a hand on his chest as Abraxas lunged forward at the other elf. Even with Lore in his arms, he could still hurt the young man. The deep monger might be fast, but he would never expect Abraxas to slam their foreheads together.

He had a harder head than Draven, he was certain of that. He'd knock the young man out and watch him bleed at his feet!

"Abraxas," Rowan snapped. "You're holding Lore in your arms and that's what you're worried about right now? Bring her inside. Maybe we can help."

"What help could you offer her that you haven't already tried?" He knew the question would sting, but he was right. They all knew it.

Lore had been seeking the way to fix this for a long time, and nothing had helped thus far. Did Rowan really believe they would find the answer to this in herbs and potions when they all knew what was happening?

They'd failed her. They had all failed.

Tanis cleared her throat and tugged her husband away from the angry crimson dragon. "Perhaps I can dip into her mind again, Abraxas. I know it's not particularly safe to do, but if I can find her, then, maybe..."

He shook his head. "Then maybe you wouldn't return to us either and more dragons would lose their mother. You will remain where you are, Tanis. I will not lose so many of our people today because of a power that was never asked for."

"Then what is your plan?" she asked. "Are you running away with her? Bringing her somewhere none of us could follow or help?"

"I don't have a better solution than that. I want to spend the rest of her time together quietly. Even if she can't hear me."

Hyperion took another step forward and placed his hand on Lore's chest. Abraxas was so startled that all he could do was look down at his son's hand, gently rising and falling with every breath Lore took. "Then we will go with you."

He looked between the two beloved faces of his children. Nyx stared at him with determination and Hyperion had already made it very clear that they would all travel together.

He'd wanted her to himself. Abraxas wanted to see the stars come out with just him and his beloved. But now he realized there was more to their life than that.

They had children. A family. They'd built the future they had always wanted to build, and unfortunately, she wasn't here to see that.

But that didn't mean she had to miss it all.

That damn lump in his throat returned. He could hardly swallow around it, and the damned emotion warped his voice. "All right. We'll all go there."

"Where?" Hyperion asked.

"To see the stars."

They nodded, eyeing him with great sadness as he walked out into the center of the clearing. Gently, he placed Lore down onto the soft grass with a murmured promise that he'd return in just a moment.

Because if they were going to watch the stars with their children, he would bring her to the very top of that mountain. Why should they linger on a small cliff when he could build her a fire unlike any other? They would look down upon the cabins where all their friends and family were. She'd see them all in a different light, from above, just as she would for the rest of time.

Abraxas let the dragon rip through his form and welcomed the pain. This hurt worse than it ever had before, but it was right that it did. He wanted it to hurt.

And then, once he shook out his neck, he took her in one clawed hand and lifted into the air. The laborious movements of his wings hid the sound of his children turning back into their dragon forms. But he knew they were behind him.

All three of them soared up into the sunset. Their first flight together, and one that suffered from so much tragedy.

They glided through the clouds, just as Lore would have loved. If she opened her eyes now, he was certain that she'd scream in fear. The thought almost made him chuckle. She hated heights, his Lore.

It took him no time at all to land on the mountain peak. He shifted again, too soon, too painful, and then cradled her against his heart.

This time was different, he realized. It didn't hurt so much to know that he had to say goodbye.

Maybe Tanis was right. Maybe he could change that obsession over to another. And as he watched his children turn into their forms, he realized that he'd let it go. There were more people for him to be present for in this life. Perhaps he had to lose her, but he would never lose his daughter or son.

Both of them settled on either side of him. Nyx took Lore's right hand and Hyperion took her left. Together, they all stared at the setting sun and waited for the night to come.

"Tell us a story about her," Nyx requested. "Something we don't know."

The first stars on the horizon twinkled to life, and Abraxas cleared his throat. "The first time I saw your mother for who she really was, she stood in the middle of a storm. She glared up from the balcony, in the middle of lightning and the thunder, like she dared the storm to attack her."

And so he told them everything. Every little detail he remembered until all the stars had twinkled to life.

CHAPTER 39

Unraveling took a lot longer than she'd expected. Of course, Lore had known it wouldn't be easy. Nothing good ever was. But she had no way to tell how long it took her to move around the family, past and future.

The webs were tangled.

So tangled that sometimes the knots seemed to meld into each other. She had to sit down into the moss and work at them with her fingers. Gently plucking away at the strings as though they were part of a harp that just wouldn't sing.

Her mother spoke to her the entire time, encouraging her when Lore got frustrated.

"Unraveling these is the reason your body will handle the magic. The knots were the parts that you were hanging up on. Every time you used your magic, it would travel down one of these strands and then get caught. You had to bring Nyx's strand here yourself, your own daughter's strand, to add into the rest of ours."

It made sense. Powerful magic like this wasn't just Lore's. Of course it wasn't.

She'd had been selfish to think that she was calling upon some power that had been gifted to her and her alone. This was old magic, family magic that had run through her blood for years. All of it gathered up into one immense power for one reason and one reason alone.

She would be the person to fulfill what her mother had planned. She was the one who would change the way this world worked, no matter how difficult that was.

They all knew it was a heavy burden for one person to bear. Thus, they had created this place for her to meet with them. To seek their guidance so that she wasn't alone.

But something had gone wrong.

Lore stopped to catch her breath and her mother crouched in front of her. "The threads tangled. When we thought this would be easier, it got more difficult. The threads were something we weren't paying attention to. All we wanted was to gather up each of our individual powers so that we could give them all to you. But while we did that, the threads were becoming more and more intertwined. By the time we noticed, we could only hope that it wouldn't matter."

"You still should have told me." Lore pulled at a particularly large snarl that overtook her lap. The golden threads all looked the same. That was the problem. If only they were individual to the person who they connected to, this all would be easier.

"I know." Her mother tucked a loose lock of hair behind Lore's ear. "We should have told you a great many things, daughter of mine. But now you are here, and I will answer all the questions that I can."

Lore didn't know what questions she had. There were too many of them and, at the same time, none at all.

"What can I not do with this stolen power?" she asked, tugging at the strands again.

"Gifted," her mother corrected.

"The question is still the same."

"We would prefer it if you didn't use that power to harm our own people. The point of gifting it to you was to ensure that you were bringing about a new age for magical creatures." Her mother pointed to a particular thread for Lore to try. "You've done very well so far. In fact, I'd argue that you brought about the change that the world needed without any of us asking you to do so. Without this power at your fingertips."

"Then why give it to me now?" And wasn't that the question she wanted answered? Why give her this impossible power if she'd already done everything that she was meant to do?

At her mother's sudden silence, Lore looked up and felt her stomach sink into the pit of her chest.

There was more.

"No," she whispered, shaking her head. "I've given everything I could. I died for them, mother. You saw me die, and you brought me back, but it wasn't because I deserved to live again, was it?"

Someone moved through the crowd and stood behind her mother. The wrinkled, beloved face of her grandmother showed lines of worry and concern.

"Did you think it would be that easy?" Her grandmother asked. The gnarled joints of her hand settled down on her mother's shoulder, connecting them as they apparently had always been in life. "You would fight off a single king and then the world would change? You left them alone, Lore."

"I left them because they should be able to do all of this on their own!" she thundered. "The Kingdom of Umbra has been given every chance it doesn't deserve. They fought beside me and they took back their own kingdom. All I had to do was kill a man who deserved to die. And now what? What else could I possibly do?"

"Lead them," her mother replied. "They are lost in a storm you created."

Frustration made Lore wish she could tear out her hair in this spirit realm. She had created nothing.

"Umbra was falling apart before I was even born," she argued. "Umbra will continue to fall apart. It is written in the future of that kingdom. Long before me."

"Then you will rewrite it. We chose you so that your children would not experience what we did. What you yourself experienced! Lore. You have a greater purpose than just to win a battle and move on. I never meant for you to be a warrior your entire life."

"Then what did you want me to be, mother? A queen?" Lore finished unraveling the last thread in her lap and then set them all gently on the ground. Even in her anger, she was not willing to risk death again. "Did you want me to take a throne from a King and put that crown atop my own head? I have no interest in leading anyone."

At her tone, her mother drew up in anger as well. They both stood, squared up against each other as though they were about to come to blows. "I expected you to do something! I don't care how you fix it, Lore. If you want a crown, then take it. If you don't, then make sure someone else who is worthy has a crown on their head."

"As if I could do that. I'm just an elf from a crumbling ruin of a town!

You made me into nothing better than a street rat."

"Then look." Her mother drew her arm back and magic warped through the air. "If you will not listen to me, then see what you have wrought."

A portal shimmered to life, glistening with power that Lore hadn't thought her mother could conjure in this place. What it showed through that magic, however, couldn't be true.

Images flashed by. Elves in chains, looking as though they were being dragged to the castle. Dullahan reaching through the bars of jail cells, trying their best to get a finger on their lost head so they might escape. Dwarves who were forced to make more armor and weapons than any city at peace should need.

More poverty.

More sadness.

Children who weren't eating, with hollowed out cheeks and lost expressions. Faces that showed they'd seen far too much.

"It takes time to fix things," Lore whispered, but even she knew that was a foolish argument.

Her mother shook her head, and the image changed again. The Umbral castle stood before them, as powerful and strong as it ever was. But now, there was an army in front of it. An army of elves that wore armor from the old days and a woman who had holed up into the darkness as though she could fix all the pain with shadows.

"Margaret." Lore pointed out an image of the woman pouring over documents spread out on a table. "She was the elf who fought with you, and the one who conscripted me."

"And you trusted her to run the kingdom you left behind?"

No. No one really could trust Margaret because she'd given none of them a reason to trust her. The woman hid secrets, but she'd fought beside Lore as well. There was a certain bond that came from sharing a moment with such blood with another person.

"I don't trust her," Lore replied. "But she fought for what was best for the entire kingdom and our people. I trust she will always strive to do what is best for the elves."

"She is lost." Her mother looked at the woman through the portal, her lips twisting with sadness. "Something in her broke a long time ago. She cannot see through the anger and the hatred in her own heart. She sees the humans as a scourge to be wiped from this earth. I fear she will spend the rest of her life trying to destroy them."

"I did not see any humans in pain from what you showed me."

"Did you not?" With another wave of her hand, her mother revealed the starving children and the too thin people again. "A kingdom cannot run on greed alone. It cannot flourish through hatred and languish in hope that something will change. Margaret does not know how to run a kingdom so that it thrives, but she will never give up that control to another person."

Lore already knew what her mother was getting at, but she wouldn't do it. "I will not kill another elf. I cannot do it."

"I'm not asking you to kill her. I'm asking you to help her see reason. Or do something that will change the course of time. Otherwise, what you will find is that the future is bright for Dracomachia, but your home, your people, will slowly fade out of existence as they all starve to death."

Again, Lore looked at the images. "Can you show me whatever you want?"

"Yes."

"Where are Beauty and Zephyr?" Her friends should have been

shown in the images. They were important for so many of the plans that Margaret had, so why weren't they shown at all?

The images changed, and she saw the magic flexing around the sides. The images grew wispy at the edges, as though her mother was losing a grip on the magic.

All she wanted was to make sure they were okay.

First, she saw Beauty. The young woman had returned to her father's home, it appeared. And though she'd lost a little weight and seemed rather pale, she was alive. But obviously unhappy, and she didn't look like the Beauty Lore knew.

Frowning, she pushed again. "And Zephyr?"

"I'm struggling to show you," her mother grunted. "It's hard to use the power. I gave it all to you."

Lore looked at the threads and frantically tried to find where the other knots were. But it looked like... She stared down at Nyx's thread that she'd never let go, and then she gave it a hard tug.

The thread loosened. It pulled through the others and then suddenly, she felt it give. All the power, all that tension that she hadn't known she was carrying, let go.

Lore inhaled, and it felt like she hadn't been able to breathe for a very long time until this moment. Right now, she could breathe again and, oh, how wonderful it felt.

She reached for her mother's hand and grasped it. Together, they pushed at the spell that would let them see into the realm beyond this one. She could feel how her mother had been using the spell. It was a shove of her individual mind, a push at the fabric of the realm that would force it to bend to her whim.

But there was another way. Lore used her power, her mother's power, her grandmother's power, and nudged the world into showing her what she wanted. She didn't force, she didn't slap at it or try to grip the world by the throat. All it took was a question and the slightest request for the magic to follow her desires.

Zephyr was shown in front of her, although he was on his knees in a dungeon she didn't recognize. The young man hung his head, lolling against his shoulder. His arms were strung up at his sides, attached to the walls with shackles that were far too tight. He had his entire weight resting on his wrists, which were already bent at an awkward angle.

"No," Lore whispered, although it sounded more like a growl. "What did she do to him?"

"He was the rightful king," her mother replied. "The king that should have been. The king that could have been. The humans wanted to see him on the throne before they would ever follow an elf. And Margaret found a way to get rid of him without killing him. Should she need to prove the young human is alive, then the mortals would be able to see that."

"It's cruel," Lore snarled.

"It is. Sometimes the old ways are not for the best."

Her mother moved to close the portal, but Lore wasn't done. Now that there were no knots in the threads of her power, she could use it a little better. She could feel the power pulling from another of her ancestors, a woman who had walked through this realm and the other with ease. A powerful woman who already knew what Lore wanted, and she desired to help.

Lore stepped up to the portal and tapped it with her finger. The magic there rippled like she'd touched a finger to water.

Then Lore just... walked through it. The magic clung to her shoulders and she could see the golden glow of a thread forcing her to remain attached to that in between realm. It wasn't that she was here, not really, but she could manifest in front of him.

Zephyr didn't react, and that frightened her. She wanted him to react, to at least lift his head. Some movement to prove that he was still alive.

But as she crouched in front of him, she could see his chest was still rising. With a gentle touch, she lifted his head. He flinched, and she wondered how cold her hand must feel.

His eyes were nearly swollen shut, but he looked up at her and he smiled when he saw her. "Lore," he said. "I must be dreaming."

"You're not." She pressed a kiss to his forehead. "Stay alive, Zeph. I'm coming home, and I'm coming to get you."

"That would be unwise. We'll start another war."

"For you, I would tear down the world." She drew back and framed his face with her hands. "You're a good man, Zephyr, and you do not deserve this."

"I will do what is right for our home."

A fierce flame burned inside her chest. "I will do what is right for you, Zephyr. Fuck the kingdom. The only people I care about are my family. And you are family."

He swallowed hard, eyes glistening with unshed tears. "I've never had family like you."

"Well now you do." She stood and headed back to the portal. At the last second, she turned around and cast him a smile. "Watch the skies. Margaret's reckoning will come on the wings of a dragon."

And with that, she stepped back through the portal with a plan in mind.

It was time for her to wake up again.

CHAPTER 40

He sat on the edge of the mountaintop, his head tilted back to the rising sun. Abraxas had sat up here for three full days. His children had returned to the cabin as it became clear Lore would not die any time soon.

She wasn't in too much pain, it seemed. Her nose hadn't bled since the first day and none of them had seen her seize or even twitch. Her body was still as death, but the pain was no longer there. He had to admit, that was better than before.

Hope burned in his chest. Nyx had said they would make her a small coffin, something comfortable for her to rest in while they waited for her to wake up. He'd thought that was a little morbid, but apparently his daughter would not be deterred.

Something about an old fairytale, and how there had been a woman who slept for a thousand years inside a glass case, only to be woken with the kiss of a loved one.

His daughter had never been so fanciful. He feared part of this change was Draven's influence.

The sun warmed his cheeks and he felt the bright burn all the way into his torn heart. He had to stay here for his children, Abraxas had come to terms with that. And it wasn't so much of a struggle this time. There was no choice. He'd be here because he wanted to watch them grow. To see the other dragonlings become larger versions of themselves.

Once Tanis let them be around the others, that was. The amethyst dragon had proven to be overly protective of her children.

Staring down into the clearing below them, he let out a small sigh. Already he could see Nyx and Draven doing their regular walk around the clearing. It wasn't much, and it kept them within his eyesight. He thought, perhaps, they knew he was watching them.

They could spend time together while he could see them. And for some strange reason, they both enjoyed spending time with each other.

"Oh, Lore," he muttered. "I wish you were here to give me advice on this one. I don't want to let her talk to him, but I also know that might be because I just don't like the man."

Warm hands slid along his ribs, dragging his back close to a heart that thundered against him and a warmth that spread stronger than the sun ever could. "And why don't you like him?"

Part of his mind wondered if this was a mirage. If he imagined her waking up again, as a cruel joke upon himself.

Another part knew that he'd see her again. After three days of no seizures, he'd let that worry of being alone again go. He'd simply been waiting for her.

Abraxas placed his hand on top of hers and pointed with the other. "Draven wanted you. And now he wants my daughter. I think it's more likely he wants to make me angry."

"Is it so surprising to think that someone could love her?"

"She's too young."

Lore pressed a kiss to the side of his neck. "Were you young at her age? Especially after absorbing all the memories from those crystals?"

No, he wasn't. But he was a crimson dragon and they were held to a much higher standard than the others. At least, he thought they were.

Grumbling, he shifted her hand until her palm was over his heart. Right where she should always be. "What would you have me do? Let them talk to each other when I have no idea what his intent is?"

"Perhaps. Or you could ask him why he has become so interested in our daughter. Or maybe, just maybe, you could trust her to know her own heart and that she can make these decisions on her own." Lore kissed him again, lingering this time until he turned his head toward her.

The sun turned her hair to liquid gold and her eyes the same color as the sea on a calm day.

She stared into his eyes, all the love that he felt reflected in those orbs. "You aren't surprised to see me."

"I knew you'd come back." He tucked a strand of her hair behind her ear. "You were never very good at staying away from me."

Her chuff of a laugh made heat bloom in his chest. Ah, he'd forgotten how love could feel. How sometimes she replaced the fires in his throat and gave him more power than a dragon should ever have.

Life without Lore wasn't the same. He would have gone on, this time. He would have continued their journey because that was the right thing to do. He was a dragon who knew how to live now, even without her.

But it wouldn't have been the same.

"Where did you go?" he asked.

"I had to get some answers about the magic itself. I'll tell you where it comes from, someday, but it's not coming from me." She smiled softly. "I had to untangle myself, to get rid of some knots that had been hanging around for a while."

"And the pain? The episodes?"

"Done." She nodded. "They will not return this time."

He had thought she'd be happier about that. Abraxas frowned and looked her over. "Why do you have that expression, then?"

"We have to go back." Lore had never hidden things well from him, and he knew if she said they had to go back, then they did. But... "Why?"

They'd created a life here. The life they wanted. Neither of them owed anything to the citizens of Umbra or anyone they left behind. But he saw her look at him meaningfully and he knew there were people they had left behind. People who mattered.

"Beauty?" he asked.

"Safe with her father, but I can't guess how long."

He squeezed his eyes shut as though in pain. His heart twisted in his chest, shuddering and jerking as though it knew her answer before he even asked the question. "Zephyr?"

"Margaret's using him as a political tool. He's locked up in a dungeon. He's in bad shape, Abraxas."

He squeezed his eyes shut and hissed out a low breath. "Of course. We should have guessed she'd play that game."

He wouldn't let the young man rot in a prison any longer than Lore would. They owed too much to that boy and all the things he'd given up. Abraxas still remembered how brave Zeph had been to rip up his safe life in that graveyard and join them on a mad hunt for the world. He was the brother of the King, and still he came with them.

No one would hurt that young man again, if Abraxas had his say. Even though it meant giving up their lives here to save him.

"Damn it," he hissed as he stood. "I just want to have a quiet life with you, and yet that seems impossible."

"I don't know if either of us are really cut out for a quiet life, anyway," Lore replied with a chuckle. She stood with him and wrapped her arms around his waist. "Be honest, would you be all right staying here? I can go by myself. Or I can deny all the gods and this magic. I can send it to someone else. We don't have to do this."

Abraxas didn't hesitate in his reply. "Of course we have to do this. They're our family, Lore."

The smile on her face lit up the entire world as the sun burst into view. "I feel the same way."

"Do you really have to go?" Nyx asked, her eyes wide with worry.

Abraxas tugged her into his arms. He held her tight against his heart and gestured for Hyperion to join them. Though his son was much less likely to be quite so demonstrative, he still rolled his eyes and ended up in the tight hug with them all.

"We do have to go," he breathed to his children. The waves crashed behind them, hiding his words from the others. "But once you are large enough to make the journey on your own, you will join us. Tanis already knows the plan. Listen to her, all right?"

Nyx nodded against his throat and then wiggled out of their embrace. She moved over to Lore, throwing her arms around her mother as though they'd never see each other again.

Both of their children must fear that. Every time they said goodbye to Lore, it seemed something happened.

He could only imagine the anxiety they felt in saying goodbye.

Hyperion was quick to get out of Abraxas's embrace as well, but he clasped his son's shoulder and looked him in the eye. "You know what I'm going say."

"Yeah." Hyperion shrugged his father's touch off his shoulder. "Look after my sister, I get it."

"No. Look after yourself." He wanted to make sure his son heard this, and heard it well. "There will be others to help soon, but you have to look after yourself first. I learned the hard way that if you don't take care of yourself, you can't take care of others either."

His son took a deep breath and nodded. Hopefully Abraxas had gotten through to him.

"I'll see you soon, son," Abraxas said, then patted his shoulder. "Sooner than you think."

Then he looked up and met the gazes of Tanis, Rowan, and Draven. They all stood off to the side, letting the family say goodbye.

Shockingly, the deepmonger had decided to stay here. Abraxas had said he could return with Allura and her crew, who had already started off into the sea. Abraxas would pull the ship when it needed the help during the journey. Draven could go home.

But he'd elected to stay here. Saying that Rowan needed another elf to help him with all the dragons here. However, Abraxas knew damn well it was for another reason. Already the deep monger's eyes were on his daughter and Lore.

Lore said that Abraxas should trust Nyx and not say anything. But if this was still going on when they got back, he would. Gods forbid it had gotten even more complicated by the time they returned home. He'd never eaten an elf, but he would if Draven touched his daughter.

The amethyst dragonling rolled over his foot, a happy grin on the baby's face as her brother tackled her. The crimson dragon was already larger than the others and infinitely more aggressive.

Stooping, Abraxas scooped up the angry little fireball and carried him underneath his arm to his mother. He deposited the squirming dragon into Tanis's waiting arms. "Are you going to be all right without us?"

"We'll be fine. Just return when you can." The troubled expression on her face hadn't let up since they told her where they were going. "And be careful, Abraxas. The world still has need of you. Both of you."

He gave her a nod. "I'll be around for a while yet."

Rowan and he clasped hands, holding onto each other with words that didn't need to be said. Rowan would look after all of them. He had no other choice.

And then Abraxas walked over to Lore and Nyx. "It's time."

They pulled apart, both their faces wet with tears. Lore let out a little laugh and wiped Nyx's face dry. "I'll see you before you know it! I love you, dear one."

As Abraxas stepped back to let the change roll through him, he watched Draven walk up and place a hand on Nyx's back. That anger fueled the change into something nearly painless as he stretched up his neck and roared into the sky. The ground shook beneath him, and he knew it was the warning Draven needed to ensure he kept his hands off their daughter.

When he lowered his head, he saw Lore laughing up at him. "Dramatic," she called out before walking over to him.

Lore had already said she preferred to start on his back. Then they would figure out how to get the both of them onto the ship. One step at a time

She clambered up onto him, settling between his spines as she always had. Comfortable. Confident.

Powerful.

Lore waved one last time, and Draven called out, "Be safe!"

"Take care of my children!"

"As you wish, Goddess!"

And Abraxas wondered what she looked like at that moment. An avenging goddess astride a blood red dragon, setting out to take back her kingdom and set to right followers who did not listen to her the first time.

He turned his face toward the setting sun and resolved himself to a long journey. After all...

They had one last battle to win.

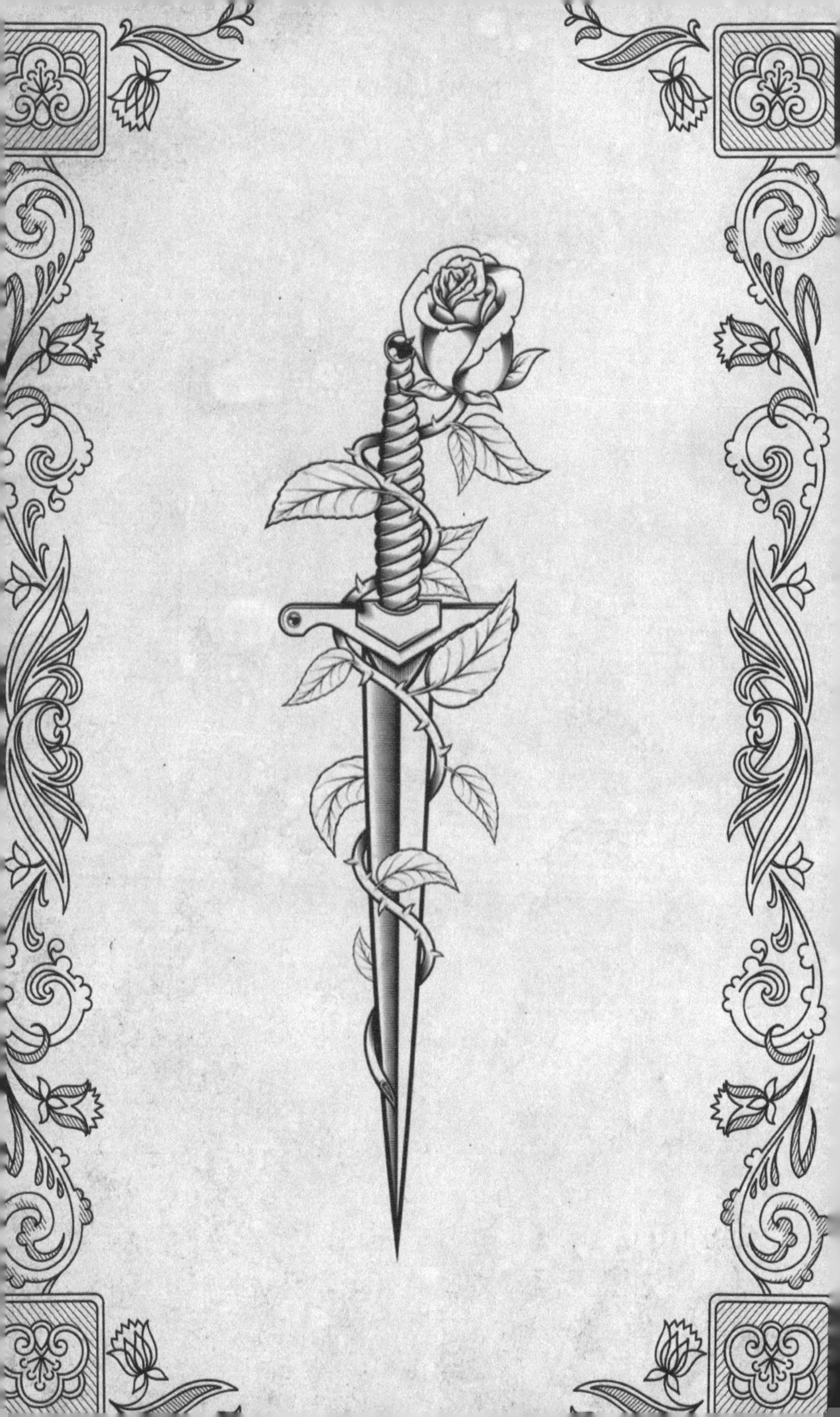

The story continues in Taloned Heart, preorder today!

ACKNOWLEDGEMENTS

Torn Heart is just one more book away from the end. If you liked this one, PLEASE go ahead and preorder the last book of this series.

I think you'll like it.

Formal thank yous to everyone who has read this series thus far, and I honestly cannot tell you how much you've changed my life. You are the reason for my happiness, my world, and all the good things that I have been so lucky to add tot his world.

I adore you. Really.

ABOUT THE AUTHOR

Emma Hamm is a small town girl on a blueberry field in Maine. She writes stories that remind her of home, of fairytales, and of myths and legends that make her mind wander.

She can be found by the fireplace with a cup of tea and her two Maine Coon cats dipping their paws into the water without her knowing.

For more updates, join my newsletter!

www.emmahamm.com

www.ingramcontent.com/pod-product-compliance
Lightning Source LLC
Chambersburg PA
CBHW010142030826
48979CB00032B/2833/J

* 9 7 9 8 9 8 6 5 6 4 4 5 6 *